A TEXT BOOK OF

MICROPROCESSOR

FOR
SEMESTER – II

SECOND YEAR DEGREE COURSE IN COMPUTER ENGINEERING

**Strictly According to New Revised Credit System Syllabus
of Savitribai Phule Pune University**
(w.e.f June 2016)

UDAY C. PATKAR
M.E. (IT)
Assistant Prof. & Head,
Comp. Engg. Deptt.
Bharati Vidyapeeth's Group of
Institutes Technical Campus,
College of Engineering,
Lavale, Pune – 43

ROMA A. KUDALE
ME (CN)
Assistant Prof.,
Comp. Engg. Deptt.
Sinhgad Tech. Edu. Society's
Smt. Kashibai Navale,
College of Engineering,
Vadgaon (Bk), Pune.

VINA M. LOMATE
ME (Comp. Engg.)
Assistant Prof. & Head,
Comp. Engg. Deptt.
R.M.D. Sinhgad School of Engg.
Warje, Pune.

PARTH SAGAR
ME (Comp. Engg.)
Assistant Prof.,
Comp. Engg. Deptt.
R.M.D. Sinhgad School of Engg.
Warje, Pune.

NIRALI PRAKASHAN
ADVANCEMENT OF KNOWLEDGE

N3579

MICROPROCESSOR (SE COMPUTER) ISBN 978-93-86353-18-4

First Edition : **January 2017**

© : **Authors**

Published By : Polyplate

NIRALI PRAKASHAN
Abhyudaya Pragati, 1312, Shivaji Nagar,
Off J.M. Road, Pune – 411005
Tel - (020) 25512336/37/39, Fax - (020) 25511379
Email : niralipune@pragationline.com

☞ **DISTRIBUTION CENTRES**

PUNE

Nirali Prakashan : 119, Budhwar Peth, Jogeshwari Mandir Lane, Pune 411002, Maharashtra
Tel : (020) 2445 2044, 66022708, Fax : (020) 2445 1538
Email : bookorder@pragationline.com, niralilocal@pragationline.com

Nirali Prakashan : S. No. 28/27, Dhyari, Near Pari Company, Pune 411041
Tel : (020) 24690204 Fax : (020) 24690316
Email : dhyari@pragationline.com, bookorder@pragationline.com

MUMBAI

Nirali Prakashan : 385, S.V.P. Road, Rasdhara Co-op. Hsg. Society Ltd.,
Girgaum, Mumbai 400004, Maharashtra
Tel : (022) 2385 6339 / 2386 9976, Fax : (022) 2386 9976
Email : niralimumbai@pragationline.com

☞ **DISTRIBUTION BRANCHES**

JALGAON

Nirali Prakashan : 34, V. V. Golani Market, Navi Peth, Jalgaon 425001,
Maharashtra, Tel : (0257) 222 0395, Mob : 94234 91860

KOLHAPUR

Nirali Prakashan : New Mahadvar Road, Kedar Plaza, 1st Floor Opp. IDBI Bank
Kolhapur 416 012, Maharashtra. Mob : 9850046155

NAGPUR

Pratibha Book Distributors: Above Maratha Mandir, Shop No. 3, First Floor,
Rani Jhanshi Square, Sitabuldi, Nagpur 440012, Maharashtra
Tel : (0712) 254 7129

DELHI

Nirali Prakashan : 4593/21, Basement, Aggarwal Lane 15, Ansari Road, Daryaganj
Near Times of India Building, New Delhi 110002
Mob : 08505972553

BENGALURU

Pragati Book House : House No. 1, Sanjeevappa Lane, Avenue Road Cross,
Opp. Rice Church, Bengaluru – 560002.
Tel : (080) 64513344, 64513355,Mob : 9880582331, 9845021552
Email:bharatsavla@yahoo.com

CHENNAI

Pragati Books : 9/1, Montieth Road, Behind Taas Mahal, Egmore,
Chennai 600008 Tamil Nadu, Tel : (044) 6518 3535,
Mob : 94440 01782 / 98450 21552 / 98805 82331,
Email : bharatsavla@yahoo.com

niralipune@pragationline.com | www.pragationline.com

Also find us on 🗗 www.facebook.com/niralibooks

Dedicated to...

Late Shri. Bhila Shankar Patkar &

Late Sau. Shakuntala Bhila Patkar

....Uday C. Patkar

Dedicated to My Beloved Parents

....Roma A. Kudale

....Vina M. Lomate

....Parth Sagar

PREFACE

It gives us great pleasure in publishing this text book on "**Microprocessor**" for the students of Second Year Degree Course in Computer Engineering. This book is strictly written according to **New Revised Credit System Syllabus** of Savitribai Phule Pune University (2015 Pattern).

As per the policy of the University, Engineering Syllabi is revised every five years. Last revision was in the year 2012. New revision is coming little earlier, as university has introduced **Online System of Examination** from year 2012.

As per the **New Credit System**, the **Online Examinations** Phase-I will be conducted based on First & Second Units and Phase II on Third & Fourth Units. The **Online** examinations will have objective types of questions with multiple choices. End Sem. Theory Examination will be based on all the six units and that will be conducted in traditional way and the Theory Course will have 4 credits.

It is our objective to keep the presentation systematic, consistent, intensive and clear presentation of concept through explanatory notes and figures. So we are sure that this book will cater for all your needs for this subject.

Main feature of this book is, **Complete Coverage** of the New Credit System Syllabus with large number of **Worked (Solved) Programs, Examples and Exercises.**

We have given Separate Book of Multiple Choice Questions (MCQ's) which will be very useful to the students especially for Online Examinations.

We take this opportunity to express our sincere thanks to Shri. Dineshbhai Furia, Shri. Jignesh Furia, Mrs. Nirali Verma and Shri. M. P. Munde and entire team of Nirali Prakashan namely Mrs. Deepali Lachake (Co-ordinator), who really have taken keen interest and untiring efforts in publishing this text.

The advice and suggestions of our esteemed readers to improve the text are most welcomed, and will be highly appreciated.

Pune   **Authors**

SYLLABUS

Unit I - 80386DX- Basic Programming Model and Applications Instruction Set   (09 Hrs)
Memory Organization and Segmentation - Global Descriptor Table, Local Descriptor Table, Interrupt Descriptor Table, Data Types, Registers, Instruction Format, Operand Selection, Interrupts and Exceptions

Applications Instruction Set - Data Movement Instructions, Binary Arithmetic Instructions, Decimal Arithmetic Instructions, Logical Instructions, Control Transfer Instructions, String and Character Transfer Instructions, Instructions for Block Structured Language, Flag Control Instructions, Coprocessor Interface Instructions, Segment Register Instructions, Miscellaneous Instructions.

Unit II – Systems Architecture and Memory Management   (09 Hrs)
Systems Architecture- Systems Registers, Systems Instructions.

Memory Management- Segment Translation, Page Translation, Combining Segment and Page Translation.

Unit III – Protection and Multitasking   (09 Hrs)
Protection- Need of Protection, Overview of 80386DX Protection Mechanisms, Segment Level Protection, Page Level Protection, Combining Segment and Page Level Protection.
Multitasking- Task State Segment, TSS Descriptor, Task Register, Task Gate Descriptor, Task Switching, Task Linking, Task Address Space.

Unit IV – Input-Output, Exceptions and Interrupts   (09 Hrs)
Input-Output- I/O Addressing, I/O Instructions, Protection and I/O

Exceptions and Interrupts- Identifying Interrupts, Enabling and Disabling Interrupts, Priority among Simultaneous Interrupts and Exceptions, Interrupt Descriptor Table (IDT), IDT Descriptors, Interrupt Tasks and Interrupt Procedures, Error Code, and Exception Conditions.

Unit V – Initialization of 80386DX, Debugging and Virtual 8086 Mode   (09 Hrs)
Initialization- Processor State after Reset, Software Initialization for Real Address Mode, Switching to Protected Mode, Software Initialization for Protected Mode, Initialization Example, TLB Testing
Debugging- Debugging Features of the Architecture, Debug Registers, Debug Exceptions, Breakpoint Exception

Virtual 8086 Mode- Executing 8086 Code, Structure of V86 Stack, Entering and Leaving Virtual 8086 Mode.

Unit VI – 80386DX Signals, Bus Cycles and 80387 Coprocessor   (09 Hrs)
80386DX Signals- Signal Diagram, Description of Signals 80386DX Bus Cycles- System Clock, Bus States, Pipelined and Non-pipelined Bus Cycles.

80387 NDP- Control Register bits for Coprocessor support, 80387 Register Stack, Data Types, Load and Store Instructions, Trigonometric and Transcendental Instructions, Interfacing signals of 80386DX with 80387.

CONTENTS

Unit III – Protection and Multitasking

Unit IV – Input-Output, Exceptions and Interrupts

Unit V – Initialization of 80386DX, Debugging and Virtual 8086 Mode

Unit VI – 80386DX Signals, Bus Cycles and 80387 Co-processor

CHAPTER 1

80386DX-BASIC PROGRAMMING MODEL AND APPLICATIONS INSTRUCTION SET

1.1 ARCHITECTURE

Introduction :

Features of Intel386 DX :

- Flexible 32-Bit Microprocessor

  8, 16, 32-Bit Data Types

  8 General Purpose 32-Bit Registers

- Very Large Address Space

  4 Gigabyte Physical

  64 Terabyte Virtual

  4 Gigabyte Maximum Segment Size

- Optimized for System Performance

  Pipelined Instruction Execution

  On-Chip Address Translation Caches

  20, 25 and 33 MHz Clock

  40, 50 and 66 Megabytes/Sec Bus Bandwidth

- Numeric Support via Intel387TM DX

  Math Coprocessor

- Complete System Development Support

  Software : C, PL/M, Assembler

  High Speed CHMOS IV Technology

  132 Pin Grid Array Package

  132 Pin Plastic Quad Flat Package

Block Diagram :

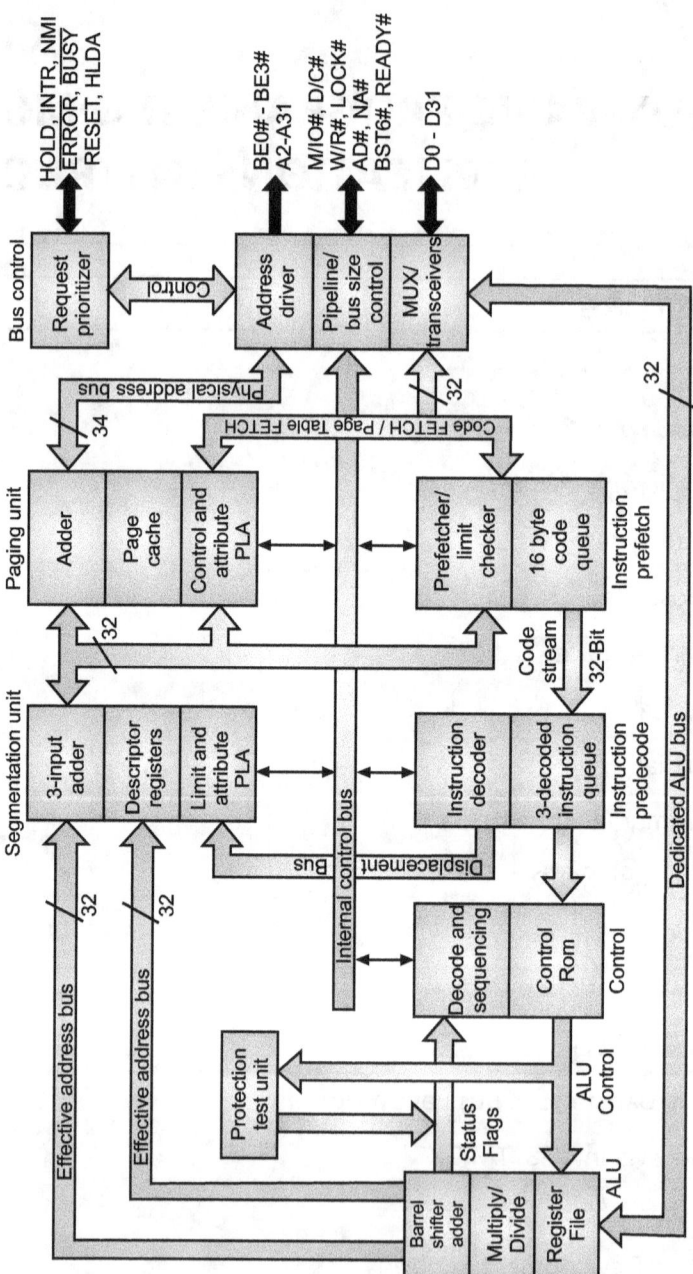

Fig. 1.1 : Block diagram of 80386DX processor

The Intel386 DX consists of a central processing unit (CPU), a memory management unit (MMU) and a bus interface (BI). The central processing unit consists of the execution unit (EU) and instruction unit (IU). The execution unit contains the eight 32-bit general purpose registers which are used for both address calculation, data operations and a 64-bit barrel shifter used to speed shift, rotate, multiply, and divide operations. The instruction unit decodes the instruction opcodes and stores them in the decoded instruction queue for immediate use by the execution unit. The memory management unit (MMU) consists of a segmentation unit and a paging unit. Segmentation allows the managing of the logical address space by providing an extra addressing component, one that allows easy code and data relocatability, and efficient sharing. The paging mechanism operates beneath and is transparent to the segmentation process, to allow management of the physical address space. Each segment is divided into one or more 4K byte pages. To implement a virtual memory system, the Intel386 DX supports full restart ability for all page and segment faults. The segmentation unit provides four-levels of protection for isolating and protecting applications and the operating system from each other.

The Intel386 DX has two modes of operation :

- Real Address Mode (Real Mode) and
- Protected Virtual Address Mode (Protected Mode).

In Real Mode, the Intel386 DX operates as a very fast 8086, but with 32-bit extensions if desired. Real Mode is required primarily to set up the processor for Protected Mode operation. Protected Mode provides access to the sophisticated memory management, paging and privilege capabilities of the processor. Within Protected Mode, software can perform a task switching to enter into tasks designated as Virtual 8086 Mode tasks. Finally, to facilitate high performance system hardware designs, the Intel386 DX bus interface offers address pipelining, dynamic data bus sizing.

The basic programming model consists of these parts :

- Memory organization
- Data types
- Registers
- Instruction format
- Operand selection
- Interrupts and exceptions

Register Overview

The Intel386 DX has 32 register resources in the following categories :

- General Purpose Registers
- Segment Registers
- Instruction Pointer and Flags
- Control Registers
- System Address Registers
- Debug Registers
- Test Registers

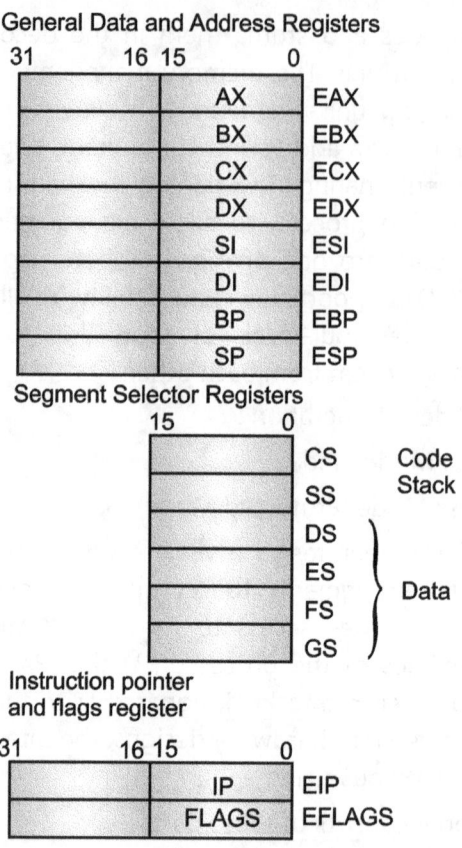

Fig. 1.2 : Register architecture

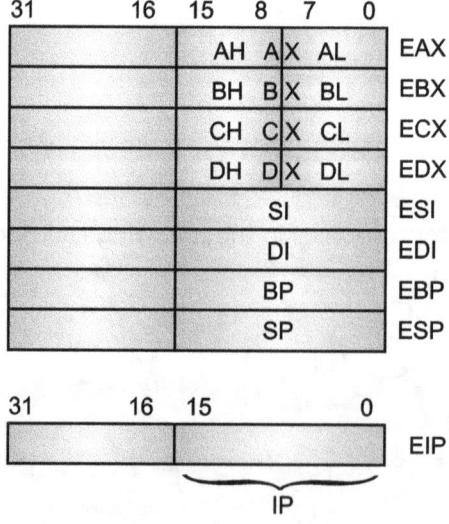

Fig. 1.3 : General purpose register and instruction pointer

General Purpose Registers :

There are eight general purpose registers of size 32 bits. They are used to hold data or address quantities. These registers support data operands of 1, 8, 16, 32 and 64 bits, and bit fields of 1 to 32 bits. They support address operands of 16 and 32 bits. The 32-bit registers are named EAX, EBX, ECX, EDX, ESI, EDI, EBP, and ESP. The least significant 16 bits of the registers can be accessed separately. This is done by using the 16- bit names of the registers AX, BX, CX, DX, SI, DI, BP, and SP. When accessed as a 16-bit operand, the upper 16 bits of the register are neither used nor changed. The lowest bytes are named AL, BL, CL and DL respectively. The higher bytes are named AH, BH, CH and DH respectively.

Instruction Pointer :

It is a 32-bit register named EIP. EIP holds the offset of the next instruction to be executed. The offset is always relative to the base of the code segment (CS). The lower 16 bits (bits 0±15) of EIP contain the 16-bit instruction pointer named IP, which is used by 16-bit addressing.

Flag Registers :

The Flags Register is a 32-bit register named EFLAGS. The defined bits and bit fields within EFLAGS, shown in Fig. 1.4. It control certain operations and indicate status of the Intel386 DX. The lower 16 bits (bit 0±15) of EFLAGS contain the 16-bit flag register named FLAGS, which is most useful when executing 8086.

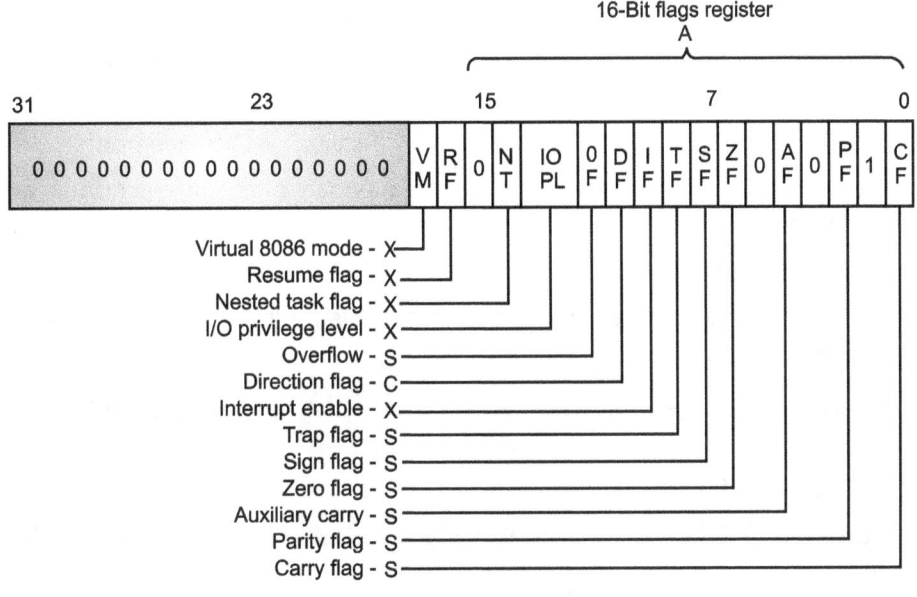

Fig. 1.4 : EFLAG register

Addressing Modes :

We can define addressing mode as the way by which we can find the operand. Similarly, where an operand is present whether at memory or register by specifying its location, 80386DX supports total 11 different ways to locate operands.

These are as follows :

- Register mode
- Immediate mode
- Direct Mode
- Register Indirect Mode
- Based mode
- Index mode
- Scaled Index Mode
- Based Index Mode
- Based Scaled Index Mode
- Based Index Mode with Displacement
- Based Scaled Index Mode with Displacement

- **Register Mode :** The operand is located in one of the 8, 16 or 32-bit general registers.
- **Immediate Mode :** The operand is included in the instruction as part of the opcode.

  The remaining 9 modes provide a mechanism for specifying the effective address of an operand. The linear address consists of two components : the segment base address and an effective address. The effective address (EA) of an operand is calculated according to the following formula.

$$EA = Base\ Register + (Index\ Register * Scaling) + Displacement$$

- **Direct Mode :** The operand's offset is contained as part of the instruction as an 8, 16 or 32-bit displacement.

  Example : INC Word PTR [800]

- **Register Indirect Mode :** A Base register contains the address of the operand.

  Example : MOV [ECX], EDX

- **Based Mode :** A BASE register's contents are added to a DISPLACEMENT to form the operands offset.

  Example : MOV ECX, [EAX + 32]

- **Index Mode :** An INDEX register's contents are added to a DISPLACEMENT to form the operands offset.

  Example : ADD EAX, TABLE [ESI]

- **Scaled Index Mode :** An INDEX register's contents are multiplied by a scaling factor which is added to a DISPLACEMENT to form the operands offset.

  Example : IMUL EBX, TABLE [ESI*4], 7

- **Based Index Mode :** The contents of a BASE register are added to the contents of an INDEX register to form the effective address of an operand.

  Example : MOV EAX, [ESI] [EBX]

- **Based Scaled Index Mode :** The contents of an INDEX register are multiplied by a SCALING factor and the result is added to the contents of a BASE register to obtain the operands offset.

  Example : MOV ECX, [EDX*8] [EAX]

- **Based Index Mode with Displacement :** The contents of an INDEX Register and a BASE register's contents and a DISPLACEMENT are all summed together to form the operand offset.

  Example : ADD EDX, [ESI] [EBP + 00FFFFF0H]

- **Based Scaled Index Mode with Displacement :** The contents of an INDEX register are multiplied by a SCALING factor, then the result is added to the contents of a BASE register and a DISPLACEMENT to form the operand's offset.

  Example : MOV EAX, LOCALTABLE[EDI*4] [EBP+80]

1.1.1 Data Types

The Intel386 DX supports all the data types commonly used in high level languages :

Bit : A single bit quantity.

Bit Field : A group of up to 32 contiguous bits, which spans a maximum of four bytes.

Bit String : A set of contiguous bits, on the Intel386 DX bit strings can be up to 4 gigabits long.

Byte : A signed 8-bit quantity.

Unsigned Byte : An unsigned 8-bit quantity.

Integer (Word) : A signed 16-bit quantity.

Long Integer (Double Word) : A signed 32-bit quantity. All operations assume a 2's complement representation.

Unsigned Integer (Word) : An unsigned 16-bit quantity.

Unsigned Long Integer (Double Word) : An unsigned 32-bit quantity.

Signed Quad Word : A signed 64-bit quantity.

Unsigned Quad Word : An unsigned 64-bit quantity.

Offset : A 16- or 32-bit offset only quantity which indirectly references another memory location.

Pointer : A full pointer which consists of a 16-bit segment selector and either a 16- or 32-bit offset.

Char : A byte representation of an ASCII Alphanumeric or control character.

String : A contiguous sequence of bytes, words or dwords. A string may contain between 1 byte and 4 Gbytes.

BCD : A byte (unpacked) representation of decimal digits 0 ± 9.

Packed BCD : A byte (packed) representation of two decimal digits 0 ± 9 storing one digit in each nibble.

1.2 INSTRUCTION SET

Instruction Format

Instructions consist of optional instruction prefixes, one or two primary opcode bytes, possibly an address specifier consisting of the ModR/M byte and the SIB (Scale Index Base) byte, a displacement, if required, and an immediate data field, if required.

Instruction prefix	Address prefix	Operand prefix	Segment override
0 or 1	0 or 1	0 or 1	0 or 1
Number of bytes			

Opcode	MODR/M	SIB	Displacement	Immediate
1 or 2	0 or 1	0 or 1	0,1,2 or 4	0,1,2 or 4
Number of bytes				

Fig. 1.5 : Instruction format

Smaller encoding fields can be defined within the primary opcode or opcodes. These fields define the direction of the operation, the size of the displacements, the register encoding, or sign extension; encoding fields vary depending on the class of operation. Most common instructions format that can refer to an operand in memory have an addressing mode byte following the primary opcode byte(s). This is called the ModR/M byte. It specifies the address form to be used. Certain encodings of the ModR/M byte indicate a second addressing byte, the SIB (Scale Index Base) byte, which follows the ModR/M byte and is required to fully specify the addressing form. Addressing forms may include a displacement immediately following either the ModR/M or SIB byte. If a displacement is present, it can be 8, 16 or 32-bits. If the instruction specifies an immediate operand, the immediate operand always follows any displacement bytes. The immediate operand, if specified, is always the last field of the instruction.

ModR/M and SIB Bytes

They contain the following information :

- The indexing type or register number to be used in the instruction.
- The register to be used or more information to select the instruction.
- The base, index, and scale information.

The ModR/M byte contains three fields of information :

The **mod** field, which occupies the two most significant bits of the byte, combines with the R/M field to form 32 possible values : eight registers and 24 indexing modes.

Format of ModR/M and SIB Bytes is shown in Fig. 1.6 and 1.7.

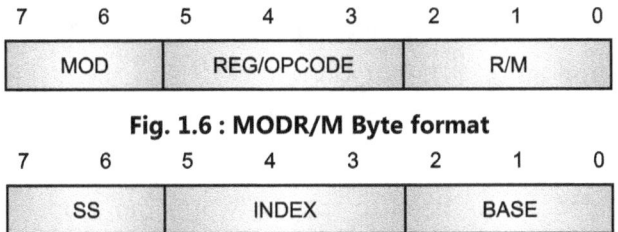

Fig. 1.6 : MODR/M Byte format

Fig. 1.7 : SIB (Scale, Index, Base) byte format

The REG field, occupies the next three bits following the MOD field, specifies either a register number or three more bits of opcode information. The meaning of REG field is determined by the first (opcode) byte of the instruction.

The R/M field, which occupies the three least significant bits of the byte, can specify a register as the location of an operand, or can form part of the addressing-mode encoding in combination with the MOD field as explained above.

The based indexed and scaled indexed forms of 32-bit addressing require the SIB byte. The presence of the SIB byte is indicated by certain encodings of the ModR/M byte. The SIB byte then includes the following fields :

- The SS field, which occupies the two most significant bits of the byte, specifies the scale factor.
- The INDEX field, which occupies the next three bits following the SS field and specifies the register number of the index register.
- The BASE field, which occupies the three least significant bits of the byte, specifies the register number of the base register.

Operand Selection :

An instruction may have zero or more operands. An example of a zero-operand instruction is the NOP instruction (no operation). An operand can be held in any of these places :

- In the instruction itself (an immediate operand).
- In a register.
- In memory.
- At an I/O port.

Immediate operands and operands in registers can be accessed fast as compare to operands in memory because memory operands require extra bus cycles. Register and immediate operands are available on-chip. Operands can be specified in implicitly or explicitly or in combination too.

Implicit Operand : AAM

By definition, AAM (ASCII adjust for multiplication) operates on the contents of the AX register.

Explicit Operand : XCHG EAX, EBX

The operands to be exchanged are encoded in the instruction with the opcode.

Implicit and Explicit Operands : PUSH COUNTER

The memory variable COUNTER (the explicit operand) is copied to the top of the stack (the implicit operand).

In explicit operands category, we need to specify two or more operands. Those operands may be overwritten with result or other value. This is the difference between source and destination operand. For most instructions, one of the two explicitly specified operands - either the source or the destination - can be either in a register or in memory. The other operand must be in a register or it must be an immediate source operand. This puts the explicit two-operand instructions into the following groups :

- Register to register
- Register to memory
- Memory to register
- Immediate to register
- Immediate to memory

Certain string instructions and stack manipulation instructions, however, transfer data from memory to memory. Both operands of some string instructions are in memory and are specified implicitly.

Immediate Operands :

Some instructions use data from the instruction itself as one (and sometimes two) of the operands. Such an operand is called an immediate operand. It may be a byte, word, or double-word. For example :

SHR STYLE, 2

One byte of the instruction holds the value 2, the number of bits by which to shift the variable STYLE.

Register Operands :

Operands may be specified by 32 bit or 16 bit or 8 bit general purpose registers. The 386 DX microprocessor has instructions for referencing the segment registers (CS, DS, ES, SS, FS, and GS). These instructions are used by application programs only if segmentation is being used.

Memory Operands :

Instructions with explicit operands in memory must refer the segment containing the operand and the offset from the beginning of the segment to the operand. Segments are specified using a segment-override prefix, which is a byte placed at the beginning of an instruction. If no segment is specified, simple rules assign the segment by default and an offset is specified in the various ways as follows :

- Most instructions which access memory contain a byte for specifying the addressing method of the operand. The byte, called the modR/M byte, which specify whether operand is present in register or memory. If operand is present in memory then address is calculated as segment register and any one value from SIB (Scale, Index, Base) and displacement. This way of calculation is very easy and flexible.

- A few instructions select segments by default :

A MOV instruction with the AL or EAX register as either source or destination can address memory with a doubleword encoded in the instruction.

String operations address memory in the DS segment using the ESI register. For example, MOVS, CMPS, OUTS, LODS, and SCAS instructions. And using the ES segment and EDI register. For example, MOVS, CMPS, INS, and STOS instructions.

Stack operations address memory in the SS segment using the ESP register. For example, PUSH, POP, PUSHA, PUSHAD, POPA, POPAD, PUSHF, PUSHFD, POPF, POPFD, CALL, RET

(A) Data Movement Instructions :

This category of instruction set provides convenient methods for moving bytes, words, or doublewords between memory and the processor registers. They come in three types :

1. General-purpose data movement instructions.
2. Stack manipulation instructions.
3. Type-conversion instructions.

1. General-Purpose Data Movement Instructions :

MOV (Move) transfers a byte, word, or doubleword from the source operand to the destination operand. The MOV instruction is useful for transferring data along any of these paths :

- To a register from memory
- To memory from a register
- Between general registers
- Immediate data to a register
- Immediate data to memory

The MOV instruction cannot move from memory to memory or from a segment register to a segment register.

MOV EAX, EBX which will transfer the contents from EBX register to EAX register.

XCHG (Exchange) : Swaps the contents of two operands. This instruction takes the place of three MOV instructions. It does not require a temporary location to save the contents of one operand while the other is being loaded. The XCHG instruction is especially useful for implementing semaphores or similar data structures for process synchronization.

There are three variants :

    XCHG reg, reg

    XCHG reg, mem

    XCHG mem, reg

You can exchange data between registers or between registers and memory, **but not from memory to memory** :

XCHG AX, BX; Put AX in BX and BX in AX

XCHG memory, AX; Put "memory" in AX and AX in "memory"

XCHG mem1, mem2; Illegal, can't exchange memory locations!

2. Stack Manipulation Instructions :

PUSH (Push) : Decrements the stack pointer (ESP register), then copies the source operand to the top of stack. The PUSH instruction often is used to place parameters on the stack before calling a procedure. The PUSH instruction operates on memory operands, immediate operands, and register operands.

PUSH BX ; Decrement SP by 2 and copy BX to stack

PUSH DS ; Decrement SP by 2 and copy DS to stack

PUSHA (Push All Registers) : Saves the contents of the eight general registers on the stack. This instruction simplifies procedure calls by reducing the number of instructions required to save the contents of the general registers. The processor pushes the general registers on the stack in the following order : EAX, ECX, EDX, EBX, the initial value of ESP before EAX was pushed, EBP, ESI, and EDI.

POP (Pop) : Transfers the word or doubleword at the current top of stack (indicated by the ESP register) to the destination operand, and then increments the ESP register to point to the new top of stack.

POP DX ; Copy a word from top of the stack to ; DX and increments SP by 2.

POP DS ; Copy a word from top of the stack to ; DS and increments SP by 2.

POPA (Pop All Registers) : Pops the data saved on the stack by PUSHA into the general registers, except for the ESP register. The ESP register is restored by the action of reading the stack (popping).

3. Type-Conversion Instructions :

The type conversion instructions convert bytes into words, words into doublewords, and doublewords into 64-bit quadwords. There are two kinds of type conversion instructions :

- Instructions which only operate on data in the EAX register.

  For example : CWD, CDQ, CBW, and CWDE

- Instructions, which permit one operand to be in a general register while letting the other operand be in memory or a register.

  For example : MOVSX and MOVZX

CWD (Convert Word to Doubleword) : This instruction copies the sign (bit 15) of the word in the AX register into every bit position in the DX register. It can be used to produce a doubleword dividend from a word before a word division.

Example :

```
.data
word_val SWORD -101 ; FF9Bh
  .code
MOV AX, word_val ; AX = FF9Bh
CWD              ; DX :AX = FFFFh :FF9Bh
```

CDQ (Convert Doubleword to Quad-Word) : This instruction copies the sign (bit 31) of the doubleword in the EAX register into every bit position in the EDX register. It can be used to produce a quadword dividend from a doubleword before doubleword division.

Example :

```
.data
dword_val SDWORD -101
  .code
MOV EAX, dword_val     ; EAX = FFFFFF9Bh
CDQ                ; EDX :EAX = FFFFFFFFh :FFFFFF9Bh
```

CBW (Convert Byte to Word): Copies the sign (bit 7) of the byte in the AL register into every bit position in the AX register.

Example :

```
.data
byte_val SBYTE -101
  .code
MOV AL, byte_val; AL = 9Bh
CBW               ; AX = FF9Bh
```

Note that both **9Bh** and **FF9Bh** both equal decimal **-101**, the only difference is the storage size.

CWDE (Convert Word to Doubleword Extended) : Copies the sign (bit 15) of the word in the AX register into every bit position in the EAX register.

MOVSX (Move with Sign Extension) : Extends an 8-bit value to a 16-bit value or an 8- or 16-bit value to 32-bit value by using the value of the sign to fill empty positions.

Syntax : MOVSX dest, source

MOVZX (Move with Zero Extension) : Extends an 8-bit value to a 16-bit value or an 8- or 16-bit value to 32-bit value by clearing the empty bit positions.

MOVZX dest, source

(B) Binary Arithmetic :

The arithmetic instructions of the 386 DX microprocessor operate on numeric data encoded in binary. Operations include the add, subtract, multiply, and divide as well as increment, decrement, compare, and change sign (negate). Both signed and unsigned binary integers are supported. Source operands can be immediate values, general registers, or memory. Destination operands can be general registers or memory. The arithmetic instructions update the ZF, CF, SF, and OF flags to report the kind of result which was produced. The kind of instruction used to test the flags depends on whether the data is being interpreted as signed or unsigned. The CF flag contains information relevant to unsigned integers; the SF and OF flags contain information relevant to signed integers. The ZF flag is relevant to both signed and unsigned integers; the ZF flag is set when all bits of the result are clear. Arithmetic instructions operate on 8-, 16-, or 32-bit data.

The **INC and DEC** instructions do not change the state of the CF flag. This instruction is used to update counters used for loop control without changing the arithmetic results. The ZF flag can be used to detect loop termination. The SF and OF flags support signed integer arithmetic. The SF flag has the value of the sign bit of the result. The OF flag is set in one of these cases :

- A carry was generated from the MSB into the sign bit but no carry was generated out of the sign bit

- A carry was generated from the sign bit into the MSB but no carry was generated into the sign bit

These instructions are divided into subcategories like

- Addition and Subtraction Instructions
- Comparison and Sign Change Instruction
- Multiplication Instructions
- Division Instructions

- **Addition and Subtraction Instructions :**

ADD (Add Integers) : Replaces the destination operand with the sum of the source and destination operands. The OF, SF, ZF, AF, PF, and CF flags are affected.

ADD AX,CX which will add contents of CX with contents of AX and store result in AX register.

ADC (Add Integers with Carry) : Replaces the destination operand with the sum of the source and destination operands, plus 1 if the CF flag is set. If the CF flag is clear, the ADC instruction performs the same operation as the ADD instruction.

ADD R1: R0 to R3 :R2

ADD R2, R0 ; Add low byte

ADC R3,R1 ; Add with carry high byte

INC (Increment) : Adds 1 to the destination operand. INC instructions to update counters in loops without disturbing the status flags resulting from an arithmetic operation used for loop control.

Example : AX = 7FFFh

INC AX ; After this instruction AX = 8000h

INC BL ; Add 1 to the contents of BL register

INC CL ; Add 1 to the contents of CX register.

SUB (Subtract Integers) : Subtracts the source operand from the destination operand and replaces the destination operand with the result. If a borrow is required, the CF flag is set. The operands may be signed or unsigned bytes, words, or doublewords. The OF, SF,ZF, AF, PF, and CF flags are affected.

SUB r13,r12 ; Subtract r12 from r13store result in r13 register.

SBB (Subtract Integers with Borrow) : Subtracts the source operand from the destination operand and replaces the destination operand with the result, minus 1 if the CF flag is set. If the CF flag is clear, the SBB instruction performs the same operation as the SUB instruction.

MOV EDX, 1 ; upper half

MOV EAX, 0 ; lower half

SUB EAX, 1 ; subtract 1 from the lower half, set CF.

SBB EDX, 0 ; subtract carry CF from the upper half.

DEC (Decrement) : Subtracts 1 from the destination operand. DEC instruction is used to update counters in loops without disturbing the status flags resulting from an arithmetic operation used for loop control.

- **Comparison and Sign Change Instruction :**

CMP (Compare) : Subtracts the source operand from the destination operand. It updates the OF, SF, ZF, AF, PF, and CF flags, but does not modify the source or destination operands. A subsequent Jcc or SETcc instruction can test the flags.

CMP AX, BX

This instruction performs the computation AX-BX and sets the flags depending upon the result of the computation.

NEG (Negate) : Subtracts a signed integer operand from zero. NEG instruction is used to change the sign of a two's complement operand while keeping its magnitude. The OF, SF, ZF, AF, PF, and CF flags are affected.

NEG destination

- **Multiplication Instructions :**

MUL (Unsigned Integer Multiply) : Performs an unsigned multiplication of the source operand and the AL, AX, or EAX register.

MUL BX which will perform multiplication of AX and BX and store result in AX register.

IMUL (Signed Integer Multiply) : Performs a signed multiplication operation. The IMUL instruction has three forms :

- A one-operand form. The operand may be a byte, word, or doubleword located in memory or in a general register. This instruction uses the EAX and EDX registers as implicit operands in the same way as the MUL instruction.

- A two-operand form. One of the source operands is in a general register while the other may be in a general register or memory. The result replaces the general register operand.

- A three-operand form; two are source operands and one is the destination. One of the source operands is an immediate value supplied by the instruction; the second may be in memory or in a general register. The result is stored in a general register. The immediate operand is a two's complement signed integer. If the immediate operand is a byte, the processor automatically sign-extends it to the size of the second operand before performing the multiplication.

    IMUL REG

- **Division Instructions :**

DIV (Unsigned Integer Divide) : Performs an unsigned division of the AL, AX, or EAX register by the source operand. The dividend (the accumulator) is twice the size of the divisor (the source operand); the quotient and remainder have the same size as the divisor. Table 1.1 gives overview of where quotient and remainder are saved after division.

Table 1.1 Various Operands Stored in GPR during Division

Operand Size/ Divisor	Dividend	Quotient	Remainder
Byte	AX register	AL register	AH register
Word	DX and AX	AX register	DX register
Doubleword	EDX and EAX	EAX register	EDX register

DIV BX which will divide contents of bx by contents of ax and result quotient get store at ax and remainder store at dx.

IDIV (Signed Integer Divide) : Performs a signed division of the accumulator by the source operand. The IDIV instruction uses the same registers as the DIV instruction.

For signed byte division, the maximum positive quotient is + 127, and the minimum negative quotient is - 128. For signed word division, the maximum positive quotient is +32,767, and the minimum negative quotient is -32,768. For signed doubleword division the maximum positive quotient is 2^{32} -1, the minimum negative quotient is -2^{31}.

Non integral results are truncated towards O. The remainder always has the same sign as the dividend and is less than the divisor in magnitude.

IDIV REG   For signed division

(C) Decimal Arithmetic :

Decimal arithmetic is performed by combining the binary arithmetic instructions (already discussed in the previous section) with the decimal arithmetic instructions. The decimal arithmetic instructions are used in one of the following ways :

- Packed BCD Adjustment Instructions
- Unpacked BCD Adjustment Instructions

- **Packed BCD Adjustment Instructions :**

DAA (Decimal Adjust after Addition) : Adjusts the result of adding two valid packed decimal operands in the AL, register.A DAA instruction must follow the addition of two pairs of packed decimal numbers tto obtain a pair of valid packed decimal digits as results. The CF flag is set if a carry occurs. The SF, ZF, AF, PF, and CF flags are affected. The state of the OF flag is undefined.

Example :

```
MOV BX, OFFSET PRICE ;Point BX at first element in array

MOV CX, 40 ;Load CX with number of ;elements in array

NEXT : MOV AL, [BX] ; Get elements from array

ADD AL, 07H ;Ad correction factor
```

DAA ; decimal adjust result

MOV [BX], AL ; Put result back in array

LOOP NEXT ; Repeat until all elements ;adjusted.

DAS (Decimal Adjust after Subtraction) : Adjusts the result of subtracting two valid packed decimal operands in the AL register. A DAS instruction must always follow the subtraction of one pair of packed decimal numbers from another to obtain a pair of valid packed decimal digits as results. The CF flag is set if a borrow is needed. The SF, ZF, AF, PF, and CF flags are affected. The state of the OF flag is undefined.

- **Unpacked BCD Adjustment Instructions :**

AAA (ASCII Adjust after Addition) : Changes the contents of the AL register to a valid unpacked decimal number, and clears the upper 4 bits. An AAA instruction must follow the addition of two unpacked decimal operands in the AL register. The CF flag is set and the contents of the AH register are incremented if a carry occurs. The AF and CF flags are affected. The state of the OF, SF, ZF, and PF flags is undefined.

Example : SUB AH,AH ; clear AH

```
    MOV AL,'6' ; AL := 36H
    ADD AL,'7' ; AL := 36H+37H = 6DH
    AAA        ; AX := 0103H
    OR AL,30H ; AL := 33H
```

AAS (ASCII Adjust after Subtraction) : Changes the contents of the AL register to a valid unpacked decimal number, and clears the upper 4 bits. An AAS instruction must follow the subtraction of one unpacked decimal operand from another in the AL register. The CF flag is set and the contents of the AH register are decremented if a borrow is needed. The AF and CF flags are affected. The state of the OF, SF, ZF, and PF flags is undefined.

Example 1 : Positive result

```
    SUB AH,AH ; clear AH
    MOV AL,'9' ; AL := 39H
    SUB AL,'3' ; AL := 39H-33H = 6H
    AAS ; AX := 0006H
    OR AL,30H ; AL := 36H
```

Example 2 : Negative result

```
    SUB AH,AH ; clear AH
    MOV AL,'3' ; AL := 33H
    SUB AL,'9' ; AL := 33H-39H = FAH
    AAS ; AX := FF04H
    OR AL,30H ; AL := 34H
```

AAM (ASCII Adjust after Multiplication) : Corrects the result of a multiplication of two valid unpacked decimal numbers. An AAM instruction must follow the multiplication of two decimal numbers to produce a valid decimal result. The upper digit is left in the AH register, the lower digit in the AL register. The SF, ZF, and PF flags are affected. The state of the AF, OF, and CF flags is undefined.

Example 1 :

```
MOV AL,3 ; multiplier in unpacked BCD form
MOV BL,9 ; multiplicand in unpacked BCD form
MUL BL ; result 001BH is in AX
AAM ; AX := 0207H
OR AX,3030H ; AX := 3237H
```

Example 2 :

```
MOV AL,'3' ; multiplier in ASCII
MOV BL,'9' ; multiplicand in ASCII
AND AL,0FH ; multiplier in unpacked BCD form
AND BL,0FH ; multiplicand in unpacked BCD form
MUL BL ; result 001BH is in AX
AAM ; AX := 0207H
OR AL,30H ; AL := 37H
```

AAD (ASCII Adjust before Division) : Modifies the numerator in the AH and AL registers to prepare for the division of two valid unpacked decimal operands, so that the quotient produced by the division will be a valid unpacked decimal number. The AH register should contain the upper digit and the AL register should contain the lower digit. This instruction adjusts the value and places the result in the AL register. The AH register will be clear. The SF, ZF, and PF flags are affected. The state of the AF, OF, and CF flags is undefined.

Example : Divide 27 by 5

```
MOV AX,0207H ; dividend in unpacked BCD form
MOV BL,05H ; divisor in unpacked BCD form
AAD ; AX := 001BH
DIV BL ; AX := 0205H
```

(D) Logical Operations :

The logical instructions have two operands. Source operands can be immediate values, general registers, or memory. Destination operands can be general registers or memory. The logical instructions modify the state of the flags.

The group of logical instructions includes :
- Boolean operation instructions
- Bit test and modify instructions
- Bit scan instructions
- Rotate and shift instructions
- Byte set on condition

- **Boolean Operation Instructions :**

The logical operations are performed by the AND, OR, XOR, and NOT instructions.

NOT (Not) : Inverts the bits in the specified operand to form a one's complement of the operand. The NOT instruction is a unary operation which uses a single operand in a register or memory. NOT has no effect on the flags.

NOT BX ; Complement contents of BX register. ; DX =F038h

NOT DX ; After the instruction DX = 0FC7h

The **AND, OR, and XOR** instructions perform the standard logical operations "and," "or," and "exclusive or." These instructions clear the OF and CF flags, leave the AF flag undefined, and update the SF, ZF, and PF flags.

OR AH, CL ;CL ORed with AH, result in AH. ;CX = 00111110 10100101

OR CX,FF00h ;OR CX with immediate FF00h ;result in CX = 11111111 10100101 ;Upper byte are all 1's lower bytes ;are unchanged.

- **Bit Test and Modify Instructions :**

This group of instructions operates on a single bit which can be in memory or in a general register. The location of the bit is specified as an offset from the low end of the operand. The value of the offset either may be given by an immediate byte or in a GPR.BT (Bit Test), BTS (Bit Test and Set), BTR (Bit Test and Reset), BTC (Bit Test and Complement) are few instructions which perform Bit Test and Modify.

- **Bit Scan Instructions :**

These instructions scan award or doubleword for a set bit and store the bit index (an integer representing the bit position) of the first set bit into a register.

BSF (Bit Scan Forward) scans low-to-high (from bit 0 toward the upper bit positions)

BSR (Bit Scan Reverse) scans high-to-low (from the uppermost bit toward bit 0)

- **Shift and Rotate Instructions :**

The shift and rotate instructions rearrange the bits within an operand.

These instructions fall into the following categories
- ➢ Shift instructions
- ➢ Double shift instructions
- ➢ Rotate instructions

➢ **Shift Instructions :**

SAL (Shift Arithmetic Left) : Shifts the destination byte, word, or doubleword operand left by one bit position or by the number of bits specified in the count operand or a value contained in the CL register.

SHL (Shift Logical Left) : It is another name for the SAL instruction. It is supported in the assembler.

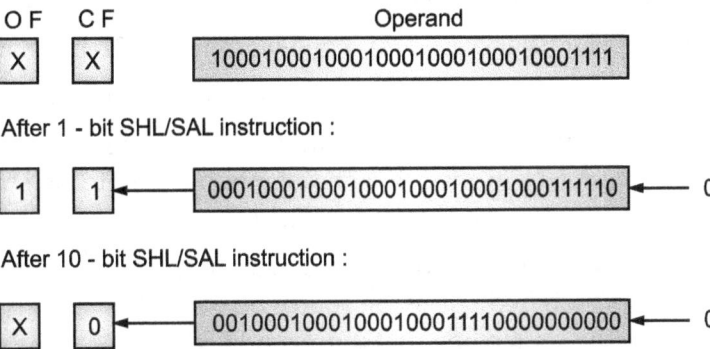

Fig. 1.8 : SHL/SAL instruction

SHR (Shift Logical Right) : Shifts the destination byte, word, or doubleword operand right by one bit position or by the number of bits specified in the count operand or a value contained in the CL register.

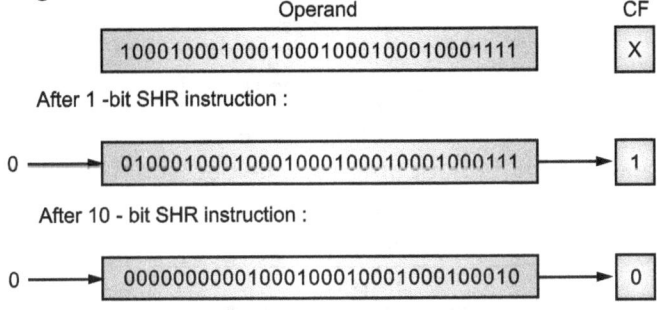

Fig. 1.9 : SHR instruction

SAR (Shift Arithmetic Right) : Shifts the destination byte, word, or doubleword operand to the right by one bit position or by the number of bits specified in the count operand or a value contained in the CL register.

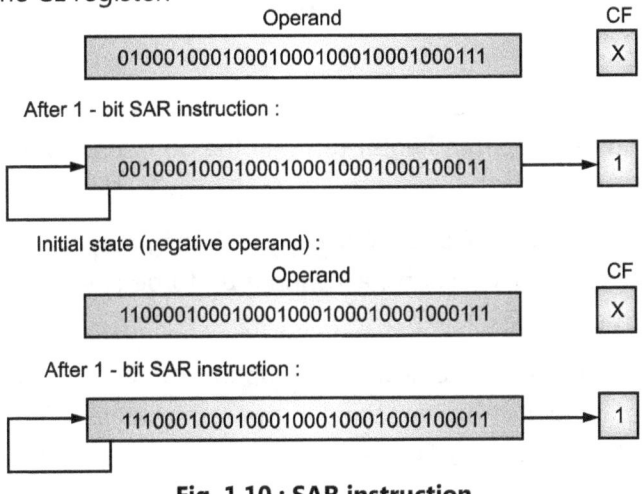

Fig. 1.10 : SAR instruction

➤ **Double-Shift Instructions :**

The double shifts operate either on word or doubleword operands, as follows :

- Take two word operands and produce a one-word result (32-bit shift).
- Take two doubleword operands and produce a doubleword result (64-bit shift).

Out of the two operands, the source operand must be in a register while the destination operand may be in a register or in memory. The number of bits to be shifted is specified either in the CL register or in an immediate byte in the instruction.

SHLD (Shift Left Double) : Shifts bits of the destination operand to the left, while filling empty bit positions with bits shifted out of the source operand. The result is stored back into the destination operand. The source operand is not modified.

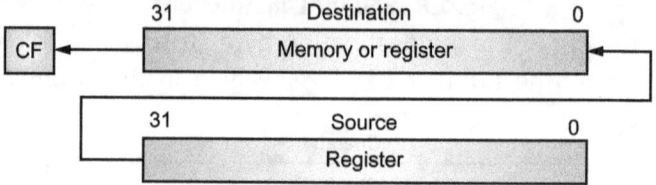

Fig. 1.11 : SHLD instruction

SHRD (Shift Right Double) : Shifts bits of the destination operand to the right, while filling empty bit positions with bits shifted out of the source operand. The result is stored back into the destination operand. The source operand is not modified.

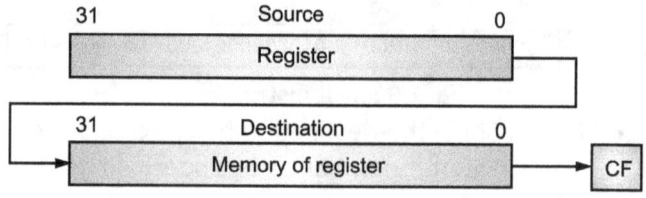

Fig. 1.12 : SHRD instruction

➤ **Rotate Instructions :**

Rotate instructions apply a circular permutation to bytes, words, and doublewords. Bits rotated out of one end of an operand enter through the other end. Unlike a shift, no bits are emptied during a rotation.

Rotate instructions use only the CF and OF flags. The CF flag may act as an extension of the operand in two of the rotate instructions, allowing a bit to be isolated and then tested by a conditional jump instruction (JC or JNC).

ROL (Rotate Left) : Rotates the byte, word, or doubleword destination operand left by one bit position or by the number of bits specified in the count operand (an immediate value or a value contained in the CL register). For each bit position of the rotation, the bit which exits from the left of the operand returns at the right.

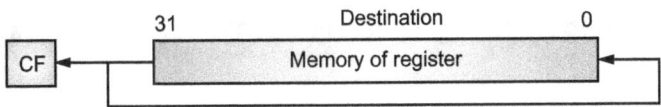

Fig. 1.13 : ROL instruction

BX = 01011100 11010011 ;CL = 8 bits to rotate

ROL BH, CL ; Rotate BX 8 bits towards left ;CF =0, BX =11010011 01011100

ROR (Rotate Right) : Rotates the byte, word, or doubleword destination operand right by one bit position or by the number of bits specified in the count operand (an immediate value or a value contained in the CL register). For each bit position of the rotation, the bit which exits from the right of the operand returns at the left.

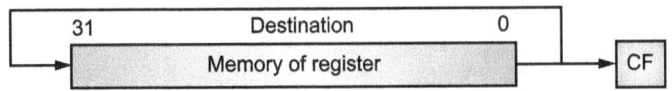

Fig. 1.14 : ROR instruction

ROR BL, 1 ; Rotate all bits in BL towards right by 1 bit position, LSB bit is moved to MSB ;and CF has last rotated bit. (2) ;CF =0, BX = 00111011

01110101

ROR BX, 1 ; Rotate all bits of BX of 1 bit position towards right and CF =1, BX =

10011101 10111010

RCL (Rotate Through Carry Left) : Rotates bits in the byte, word, or doubleword destination operand left by one bit position or by the number of bits specified in the count operand (an immediate value or a value contained in the CL register).

RCL DX, 1;   Word in DX of 1 bit is moved to left, and ; MSB of word is given to

CF and ;CF to LSB. ; CF=0, BH = 10110011

RCL BH, 1;   Result : BH =01100110 ;CF = 1, OF = 1 because MSB changed ;
CF =1,AX =00011111 10101001

MOV CL, 2; Load CL for rotating 2 bit position

RCL AX, CL; Result : CF =0, OF undefined ; AX = 01111110 10100110

- **Byte-Set-On-Condition Instructions :**

This group of instructions sets a byte to the value of zero or one, depending on any of the 16 conditions defined by the status flags.

SETcc (SetByte on Condition cc) loads the value 1 into a byte if condition cc is true; clears the byte otherwise

Test Instruction :

TEST (Test) : Performs the logical "and" of the two operands, clears the OF and CF flags, leaves the AF flag undefined, and updates the SF, ZF, and PF flags. The flags can be tested by conditional control transfer instructions or the byte-set-on-condition instructions.

The operands may be bytes, words, or doublewords.

The difference between the TEST and AND instructions is the TEST instruction does not alter the destination operand. The difference between the TEST and BT instructions is the TEST instruction can test the value of multiple bits in one operation, while the BT instruction tests a single bit.

TEST AL, BH ;AND BH with AL. no result is stored. Update PF, SF, ZF

TEST CX, 0001H ;AND CX with immediate ;number ;no result is stored, Update PF, ;SF

(E) Control Transfer :

The 386 DX microprocessor provides two types of control transfer.

- Conditional and
- Unconditional control transfer

Conditional Transfer Instructions :

The conditional transfer instructions are jumps which transfer execution if the states inthe EFLAGS register satisfies conditions specified in the instruction.

Conditional Jump Instruction :

A form of the conditional jump instructions is available which uses a displacement added to the contents of the EIP register if the specified condition is true. The displacement may be a byte or doubleword. The displacement is signed; it can be used to jump forward or backward.

Loop Instruction :

The loop instructions are conditional jumps which use a value placed in the ECX registers a count for the number of times to run a loop. All loop instructions decrement thecontents of the ECX register on each repetition and terminate when zero is reached.

LOOP (Loop While ECX Not Zero) : It is a conditional jump instruction which decrements the contents of the ECX register before testing for the loop-terminating condition. If contents of the ECX register are non-zero, the program jumps to the destination specifiedin the instruction.

Example :

```
MOV CX,9
MOV BX,05
toploop :ADD n, BX   ;n=n+bx
          LOOP toploop
```

LOOPE (Loop While Equal) and LOOPZ (Loop While Zero) : Are synonyms for the same instruction. These instructions are conditional jumps which decrement the contents ofthe ECX register before testing for the loop-terminating condition.

LOOPNE (Loop While Not Equal) and LOOPNZ (Loop While Not Zero) : Are synonyms for the same instruction. These instructions are conditional jumps which decrement the contents of the ECX register before testing for the loop-terminating condition.

Example :

```
MOV BX, OFFSET ARRAY1 ; point BX at start of the array
DEC BX
MOV CX, 100 ; put number of array elements in ;CX
NEXT :INC BX ; point to next elements in array
CMP [BX], OFFH ; Compare array elements ODH
LOOPNE NEXT
```

Executing a Loop or Repeat Zero Times :

JECXZ (Jump if ECX Zero) : Jumps to the destination specified in the instruction if the ECX register holds a value of zero. The JECXZ instruction is used in combination with the LOOP instruction and with the string scan and compare instructions.

Software Interrupts : The INT, INTO, and BOUND instructions allow the programmer to specify a transfer of execution to an exception or interrupt handler.

INTn (Software Interrupt) : Calls the handler specified by an interrupt vector encoded in the instruction. The INT instruction may specify any interrupt type. This instruction is used to support multiple types of software interrupts or to test the operation of interrupt service routines.

INTO (Interrupt on Overflow) : Calls the handler for the overflow exception, if the OFflag is set. If the flag is clear, execution continues without calling the handler.

BOUND (Detect Value Out of Range) : Compares the signed value held in a general register against an upper and lower limit. The BOUND instruction has two operands. The first operand specifies the general register being tested. The second operand is the base address of two words or doublewords at adjacent locations in memory.

Table 1.2 gives overall summary of conditional jump instructions

Table 1.2 : Summary of Conditional Jump Instructions

Unsigned Conditional Jumps		
Mnemonic	**Flag States**	**Description**
JA/JNBE	(CF or ZF) = 0	Above/not below nor equal
JAE/JNB	CF = 0	Above or equal/not below
JB/JNAE	CF = 1	Below/not above nor equal
JBE/JNA	(CF or ZF) = 1	Below or equal/not above
JC	CF = 1	Carry
JE/JZ	ZF = 1	Equal/zero
JNC	CF = 0	Not carry
JNE/JNZ	ZF = 0	Not equal/not zero
JNP/JPO	PF = 0	Not parity/parity odd
JP/JPE	PF = 1	Parity/parity even
Signed Conditional Jumps		
JG/JNLE	(SF xor OF) or ZF) = 0	Greater/not less nor equal
JGE/JNL	(SF xor OF) = 0	Greater or equal/not less
JL/JNGE	(SF xor OF) = 1	Less/not greater nor equal
JLE/JNG	((SF xor OF) or ZF) = 1	Less or equal/not greater
JNO	OF = 0	Not overflow
JNS	SF = 0	Not sign (non-negative)
JO	OF = 1	Overflow
JS	SF = 1	Sign (negative)

Unconditional Transfer Instructions :

The JMP, CALL, RET, INT and IRET instructions transfer execution to a destination in a code segment. The destination can be within the same code segment (near transfer) or in a different code segment (far transfer).

Jump Instruction :

JMP (Jump) : This instruction transfers execution from the current routine to a different routine. The address of the routine is specified in the instruction, in a register, or in memory. The location of the address determines whether it is interpreted as a relative address or an absolute address.

Call Instruction :

CALL (Call Procedure) : It transfers execution and saves the address of the instruction following the CALL instruction for later use by a RET (Return) instruction. CALL pushes the current contents of the EIP register on the stack. The RET instruction in the called procedure uses this address to transfer execution back to the calling program.

Return and Return from Interrupt Instruction :

RET (Return from Procedure) : It terminates a procedure and transfers execution to the instruction following the CALL instruction which originally invoked the procedure. The RET instruction restores the contents of the EIP register which were pushed on the stack when the procedure was called.

IRET (Return from Interrupt) : It returns control to an interrupted procedure. The IRET instruction differs from the RET instruction in that it also restores the EFLAGS register from the stack. The contents of the EFLAGS register are stored on the stack when an interrupt occurs.

(F) String and Character Transfer :

String operations manipulate large data structures in memory, such as alphanumeric character strings. The string operations are made by putting string instructions (which execute only one iteration of an operation) together with other features of the Intel386 architecture, such as repeat prefixes.

The string instructions are :

    MOVS - Move String
    CMPS - Compare String
    SCAS - Scan String
    LODS - Load String
    STOS - Store string

- After a string instruction executes, the string source and destination registers point to the next elements in their strings. These registers automatically increment or decrement their contents by the number of bytes occupied by each string element. A string element can be a byte, word, or doubleword. The string registers are :

ESI - Source Index Register
EDI - Destination Index Register

- String operations can begin at higher addresses and work toward lower ones, or they can begin at lower addresses and work toward higher ones. The direction is controlled by :

DF - Direction Flag

- If the DF flag is clear, the registers are incremented. If the flag is set, the registers are decremented. These instructions set and clear the flag :

STD - Set Direction Flag Instruction
CLD - Clear Direction Flag Instruction

- To operate on more than one element of a string, a repeat prefix must be used, such as :

  REP - Repeat while the ECX register not zero

  REPE/REPZ - Repeat while the ECX register not zero and the ZF flag is set

  REPNE/REPNZ - Repeat while the ECX register not zero and the ZF flag is clear

- **String Instructions**

MOVS (Move String) : It moves the string element addressed by the ESI register to the location addressed by the EDI register. The MOVSB instruction moves bytes, the MOVSW instruction moves words, and the MOVSD instruction moves doublewords. The MOVS instruction, when accompanied by the REP prefix, operates as a memory to- memory block transfer.

CMPS (Compare Strings) : It subtracts the destination string element from the source string element and updates the AF, SF, PF, CF and OF flags. Neither string element is written back to memory. If the string elements are equal, the ZF flag is set; otherwise, it is cleared. CMPSB compares bytes, CMPSW compares words, and CMPSD compares doublewords.

SCAS (Scan String) : It subtracts the destination string element from the EAX, AX, or AL register (depending on operand length) and updates the AF, SF, ZF, PF, CF and OF flags. The string and the register are not modified. If the values are equal, the ZF flag is set; otherwise, it is cleared. The SCASB instruction scans bytes; the SCASW instruction scans words; the SCASD instruction scans doublewords.

LODS (Load String) : It places the source string element addressed by the ESI register into the EAX register for doubleword strings, into the AX register for word strings, or into the AL register for byte strings.

STOS (Store String) : It places the source string element from the EAX, AX, or AL register into the string addressed by the EDI register.

(G) Instructions for Block Structured Language :

- These instructions provide machine-language support for implementing block-structured languages, such as C and Pascal. They include ENTER and LEAVE, which simplify procedure entry and exit in compiler generated code. They support a structure of pointers and local variables on the stack called a stack frame. ENTER (Enter Procedure) creates· a stack frame compatible with the scope rules of block-structured languages. In these languages, a procedure has access to its own variables and some number of other variables defined elsewhere in the program.

- The **ENTER** instruction has two operands. The first specifies the number of bytes to be reserved on the stack for dynamic storage in the procedure being entered. The second parameter is the lexical nesting level (from to 31) of the procedure. The nesting level is the depth of a procedure in the hierarchy of a block-structured program. The lexical level has no particular relationship to either the protection privilege level or to the I/O privilege level.

The ENTER instruction can be used in two ways : nested and non-nested. If the lexical level is 0, the non-nested form is used. The non-nested form pushes the contents of the EBP register on the stack, copies the contents of the ESP register into the EBP register, and subtracts the first operand from the contents of the ESP register to allocate dynamic storage. The nested form of the ENTER instruction occurs when the second parameter (lexical level) is not zero.

- **LEAVE (Leave Procedure) :** It reverses the action of the previous ENTER instruction. The LEAVE instruction does not have any operands. The LEAVE instruction copies the contents of the EBP register into the ESP register to release all stack space allocated to the procedure. Then the LEAVE instruction restores the old value of the EBP register from the stack. This simultaneously restores the ESP register to its original value. A subsequent RET instruction then can remove any arguments and the return address pushed on the stack by the calling program for use by the procedure.

(H) Flag Control

The flag control instructions change the state of bits in the EFLAGS register. They are subdivided as follows

- Carry and Direction Flag Control Instructions
- Flag Transfer Instructions

- **Carry and Direction Flag Control Instructions :**

The carry flag instructions are useful with instructions like RCL and RCR. They can initialize the carry flag, CF, to a known state before execution of an instruction which copies the flag into an operand.

The direction flag control instructions set or clear the direction flag, DF, which controls the direction of string processing. If the DF flag is clear, the processor increments the string index registers, ESI and EDI, after each iteration of a string instruction. If the DF flag is set, the processor decrements these index registers.

- **Flag Transfer Instructions :**

The flag transfer instructions allow a program to change the state of the other flag bits using the bit manipulation instructions once these flags have been moved to the stack or the AH register. There are different five instructions which deal with carry flag operations. Those are **STC (Set Carry Flag), CLC (Clear Carry Flag), CMC (Compliment Carry Flag), CLD (Clear Direction Flag), STD (Set Direction Flag).**

The LAHF and SAHF instructions deal with five of the status flags, which are used primarily by the arithmetic and logical instructions.

LAHF (Load AH from Flags) : Copies the SF, ZF, AF, PF, and CF flags to the AH register bits 7, 6, 4, 2, and 0 (Refer Fig. 1.15) respectively. The contents of the remaining bits 5, 3, and 1 are left undefined. The contents of the EFLAGS register remain unchanged.

SAHF (Store AH into Flags) : Copies bits 7,6,4,2, and from the AH register into the SF, ZF, AF, PF, and CF flags, respectively (Refer Fig. 1.15)

The **PUSHF** and **POPF** instructions are not only useful for storing the flags in memory where they can be examined and modified, but also are useful for preserving the state of the EFLAGS register while executing a subroutine.

7	6	5	4	3	2	1	0
SF	ZF	0	AF	0	PF	1	CF

Fig. 1.15 : Lower byte of EFLAG register

(I) Coprocessor Interface :

The 387 DX Numeric Coprocessor provides an extension to the instruction set of the base architecture. The coprocessor extends the instruction set of the 386 DX microprocessor to support high-precision integer and floating-point calculations. These extensions include arithmetic, comparison, transcendental, and data transfer instructions. The coprocessor also contains frequently-used constants, to enhance the speed of numeric calculations. The coprocessor instructions are embedded in the instructions for the 386 DX microprocessor, as though they were being executed by a single processor having both integer and floating-point capabilities. But the coprocessor actually works in parallel with the 386 microprocessor, so the performance is higher.

ESC (Escape) : It is a bit pattern which identifies floating-point arithmetic instructions. The ESC bit pattern tells the processor to send the opcode and operand addresses to the numeric coprocessor. The coprocessor uses instructions containing the ESC bit pattern to perform high-performance, high-precision floating point arithmetic. When the coprocessor is not present, these instructions generate coprocessor-not-available exceptions.

WAIT (Wait) : It is an instruction which suspends program execution while the BUSY# pin is active. The signal on this pin indicates that the coprocessor has not completed an operation. When the operation completes, the processor resumes execution and can read the result. The WAIT instruction is used to synchronize the processor with the coprocessor.

(J) Segment Register :

There are several distinct types of instructions which use segment registers. They are grouped together here because, if system designers choose flat model of memory organization, none of these instructions are used. The instructions which deal with segment registers are :

- Segment-register transfer instructions.
- Control transfers to another executable segment.
- Data pointer instructions.
- Interrupt-related instructions.

- **Segment-Register Transfer Instructions :**

Different forms of the MOV, POP, and PUSH instructions also are used to load and store segment registers. These forms operate like the general-register forms, except that one operand is a segment register. The MOV instruction cannot copy the contents of a segment register into another segment register. The POP and MOV instructions cannot place a value in the CS register (code segment). Only the far control-transfer instructions affect the CS register. When a segment register is loaded, the signal on the LOCK# pin of the processor is asserted. This prevents other bus masters from modifying a segment descriptor while it is being read.

- **Control Transfer Instructions :**

The far control-transfer instructions transfer execution to a destination in another segment by replacing the contents of the CS register. The destination is specified by a far pointer, which is a 16-bit segment selector and a 32-bit offset into the segment. The far pointer can be an immediate operand or an operand in memory.

Far CALL It is an inter segment CALL instruction places the values held in the EIP and CS registers on the stack.

Far RET it is an intersegment RET instruction restores the values of the CS and EIP registers from the stack.

- **Data Pointer Instructions :**

The data pointer instructions load a far pointer into the processor registers. A far pointer consists of a 16-bit segment selector, which is loaded into a segment register, and a 32-bit offset into the segment, which is loaded into a general register.

LDS (Load Pointer Using DS) : It copies a far pointer from the source operand into the DS register and a general register. The source operand must be a memory operand, and the destination operand must be a general register.

LDS ESI, STRING1

LES (Load Pointer Using ES) : It has the same effect as the LDS instruction, except the segment selector is loaded into the ES register rather than the DS register.

LES EDI, DESTINATION1

LFS (Load Pointer Using FS) : It has the same effect as the LDS instruction, except the FS register receives the segment selector rather than the DS register.

LGS (Load Pointer Using GS) : It has the same effect as the LDS instruction, except the GS register receives the segment selector rather than the DS register.

LSS (Load Pointer Using SS) : It has the same effect as the LDS instruction, except the SS register receives the segment selector rather than the DS register.

(K) Miscellaneous Instructions :

The following instructions are not included in above categories but are important as far as programming aspect is concerned.

Address Calculation Instruction :

LEA (Load Effective Address) : The source operand must be in memory, and the destination operand must be a general register. It puts the 32-bit offset to a source operand in memory into the destination operand. This instruction is especially useful for initializing the ESI or EDI registers before the execution of string instructions

LEA EBX, ARRAY

Processor places the address of the starting location of the variable labelled ARRAY into EBX.

No-Operation Instruction :

NOP (No Operation) : It occupies a byte of code space. When executed, it increments the EIP register to point at the next instruction, but affects nothing else.

Translate Instruction :

XLATB (Translate) : It replaces the contents of the AL register with a byte read from a translation table in memory. The contents of the AL register are interpreted as an unsigned index into this table, with the contents of the EBX register used as the base address.

1.3 MEMORY ORGANIZATION

Memory is divided into Byte, Word, Doubleword. Words are stored in two consecutive bytes in memory with the low-order byte at the lowest address, the high order byte at the high address. Dwords are stored in four consecutive bytes in memory with the low-order byte at the lowest address, the high-order byte at the highest address. In addition to these basic data types, the Intel386DX supports two larger units of memory : pages and segments. Memory can be divided up into one or more variable length segments, which can be swapped to disk or shared between programs. Memory can also be organized into one or more 4K byte pages. The Intel386 DX supports both pages and segments in order to provide maximum flexibility to the system designer. Segmentation and paging are complementary. Segmenrtation is useful for organizing memory in logical modules, and as such is a tool for the application programmer, while pages are useful for the system programmer for managing the physical memory of a system.

Address Spaces

The Intel386 DX has three distinct address spaces :

- Logical address
- Linear address and
- Physical.

A logical address consists of a selector and an offset. A selector is the contents of a segment register. An offset is formed by summing all the addressing components (BASE, INDEX, and DISPLACEMENT). Logical address is also known as Virtual address.

The segmentation unit translates the logical address into a 32-bit linear address. If the paging unit is not enabled, then the 32-bit linear address corresponds to the physical address. The paging unit translates the linear address into the physical address. The physical address is nothing but the address which appears on the address pins.

Segment Register Usage :

The main data structure used to organize memory is the segment. On the Intel386 DX, segments are variable sized blocks of linear addresses which have certain attributes associated with them. There are two main types of segments : code and data, the segments are of variable size and can be as small as 1 byte or as large as 4 gigabytes (232 bytes).

Segment Register Selection Rules :

To increase performance of processor, instructions do not need to explicitly specify which segment register is used. A default segment register is automatically chosen according to the rules which are listed in Table 1.3. In general, data references use the selector contained in the DS register; Stack references use the SS register and Instruction fetches use the CS register. The contents of the Instruction Pointer provide the offset. Special segment override prefixes allow the explicit use of a given segment register, and override the implicit rules. The override prefixes also allow the use of the ES, FS and GS segment registers.

Table 1.3 : Selection Rules

Kind of Memory Reference	Default Segment	Possible Segment Override Prefix
Code Fetch	CS	None
Destination of PUSH, PUSHF, INT, CALL, PUSHA instructions	SS	None
Source of POP, POPA, POPF, IRET, RET instructions	SS	None
Destination of STOS, MOVS, REP STOS and REP MOVS with DI as base register	ES	None
Other data references with EA using base register of		
[EAX]	DS	DS, CS, SS, ES, FS, GS
[EBX]	DS	DS, CS, SS, ES, FS, GS
[ECX]	DS	DS, CS, SS, ES, FS, GS
[EDX]	DS	DS, CS, SS, ES, FS, GS
[ESI]	DS	DS, CS, SS, ES, FS, GS
[EDI]	DS	DS, CS, SS, ES, FS, GS
[EBP]	SS	DS, CS, SS, ES, FS, GS
[ESP]	SS	DS, CS, SS, ES, FS, GS

1.4 SEGMENTATION

Segmentation provides the basis for protection. Segments are used to encapsulate regions of memory which have common attributes. All information about a segment is stored in an 8-byte data structure called a descriptor. All the descriptors in a system are contained in tables recognized by hardware.

Terminology :

There are few terms which we need to use for description regarding descriptors, privilege levels and protection. Those are as follows.

PL : Privilege Level- One of the four hierarchical privilege levels. Level 0 is the most privileged level and level 3 is the least privileged.

RPL : Requestor Privilege Level- The privilege level of the original supplier of the selector.

DPL : Descriptor Privilege Level- This is the least privileged level at which a task may access that descriptor

CPL : Current Privilege Level- The privilege level at which a task is currently executing, which equals the privilege level of the code segment being executed.

EPL : Effective Privilege Level- The effective privilege level is the least privileged of the RPL and DPL.

Task : One instance of the execution of a program. Tasks are also referred to as processes.

Descriptor Tables

The descriptor tables define all the segments which are used in an Intel386 DX system. There are three types of tables on the Intel386 DX which hold descriptors.

- Global Descriptor Table,
- Local Descriptor Table and
- Interrupt Descriptor Table.

1.4.1 Global Descriptor Table

The Global Descriptor Table (GDT) contains descriptors which are possibly available to all the tasks in a system. The GDT can contain any type of segment descriptor except interrupt and trap descriptors. Generally, the GDT contains code and data segments used by the operating systems and task state segments, and descriptors for the LDTs in a system. It is of size 6 Byte. (Refer Section 2.2.2.1).

1.4.2 Local Descriptor Table

LDTs contain descriptors which are associated with a given task. The LDT may contain only code, data, stack, task gate and call gate descriptors. LDTs provide a mechanism for isolating a given task's code and data segments from the rest of the operating system, while the GDT contains descriptors for segments which are common to all tasks. It is of size 16 bit. (Refer Section 2.2.2.2).

1.4.3 Interrupt Descriptor Table

The third table needed for Intel386 DX systems is the Interrupt Descriptor Table. The IDT contains the descriptors which point to the location of up to 256 interrupt service routines. The IDT may contain only task gates, interrupt gates, and trap gates. The IDT should be at least 256 bytes in size in order to hold the descriptors for the 32 Intel Reserved Interrupts. (Refer Section 2.2.2.3).

Differences between Intel386TM DX and 80286 Descriptors :

In order to provide operating system compatibility between the 80286 and Intel386 DX, the Intel386DX supports all of the 80286 segment descriptors. The first difference is the values of type field, base address field and limit field for 80286 these values are 24-bit base address and 16-bit limit, while the Intel386 DX system segment descriptors have a 32-bit base address, a 20-bit limit field, and a granularity bit.

Other difference is the interpretation of the word count field of call gates and the B bit. The word count field specifies the number of 16-bit quantities to copy for 80286 call gates and 32-bit quantities for Intel386 DX call gates. The B bit controls the size of PUSHes when using a call gate; if B=0 PUSHes are 16 bits, if B=1 PUSHes are 32 bits

1.5 INTERRUPTS AND EXCEPTIONS

The 386 DX microprocessor has two mechanisms for interrupting program execution :

- Exceptions are synchronous events which are responses of the processor to certain conditions detected during the execution of an instruction.
- Interrupts are asynchronous events typically triggered by external devices needing attention.

Interrupts and exceptions are alike in that both cause the processor to temporarily suspend the program being run in order to run a program of higher priority. The major distinction between these two kinds of interrupts is their origin. An exception is always reproducible by re-executing the program which caused the exception, while an interrupt can have a complex, timing-dependent relationship with programs. The operating system, monitor, or device driver handles exceptions and interrupts. Table 1.4 gives summary of Exceptions and Interrupts.

Table 1.4 Exceptions and Interrupts

Vector Number	Description
0	Divide error
1	Debugger call
2	NMI interrupt
3	Breakpoint
4	INTO-detected Overflow

Contd...

5	BOUND Range Exceeded
6	Invalid Opcode
7	Coprocessor Not Available
8	Double Fault
9	Coprocessor Segment Overrun
10	Invalid Task State Segment
11	Segment Not Present
12	Stack Exception
13	General Protection
15	Reserved by Intel
16	Coprocessor Error
17-31	Reserved by Intel
32-255	Maskable Interrupts

A divide-error exception; results when the DIV or IDIV instruction is executed with a zero denominator or when the quotient is too large for the destination operand.

- A debug exception may be sent back to an application program if it results from the TF (trap) flag.

- A breakpoint exception results when an INT3 instruction is executed. This instruction is used by some debuggers to stop program execution at specific points.

- An overflow exception results when the INTO instruction is executed and the OF (overflow) flag is set.

- A bounds-check exception results when the BOUND instruction is executed with an array index which falls outside the bounds of the array.

- The coprocessor-not-available exception occurs if the program contains instructions for a coprocessor, but no coprocessor is present in the system.

- A coprocessor-error exception is generated when a coprocessor detects an illegal operation.

Exceptions are classified as **faults, traps**, or **aborts** depending on the way they are reported and whether restart of the instruction which caused the exception is supported.

A **Fault** is an exception which is reported at the instruction boundary prior to the instruction in which the exception was detected. The fault is reported with the machine restored to a state which permits the instruction to be restarted. The return address for the fault handler points to the instruction which generated the fault, rather than the instruction following the faulting instruction.

A **Trap** is an exception which is reported at the instruction boundary immediately after the instruction in which the exception was detected.

An **Abort** is an exception which does not always report the location of the instruction causing the exception and does not allow restart of the program which caused the exception. Aborts are used to report severe errors, such as hardware errors and inconsistent or illegal values in system tables.

EXERCISE

1. Write a short note on features of Intel80386DX.

2. Draw and Explain block diagram of Intel80386DX.

3. What are the different components of programming model?

4. Explain Register overview of Intel80386DX along with suitable diagram.

5. Define addressing mode and explain any 2 addressing modes in detail.

6. Explain following addressing modes with example.

    (a) Based Index Mode

    (b) Based Scaled Index Mode

    (c) Based Index Mode with Displacement

    (d) Based Scaled Index Mode with Displacement

7. What are the different Data Types supported by Intel80386DX.

8. Write a short note on Instruction Format.

9. What is the significance of MOD R/M and SIB bit in instruction format.

10. Define following terms

    PL

    RPL

    DPL

    CPL

    EPL

    Fault

    Trap

    Abort

11. Draw and explain frame format of MOD R/M.

12. Draw and explain frame format of SIB.

13. List different categories of Instruction Set.

14. How is the Direction flag set or reset and what is its implication on index registers?

15. Write a short note on different block structured language instructions.

16. Explain following instructions

    PUSHA

    CWD

    SBB

    DAA

    AAA

    AAM

    SHL

    SHRD

    RCL

17. Write a short note on different descriptor tables.

18. Explain the difference between 80386DX and 80286 descriptors.

19. What is an instruction queue? Explain?

20. What is REP prefix? How it functions for string instructions?

21. Explain the instructions (i) LDS (ii) PUSHF (iii) TEST (iv) CLD

22. What is a stack? Explain the use and operation of stack and stack pointer?

CHAPTER 2

SYSTEMS ARCHITECTURE AND MEMORY MANAGEMENT

2.1 INTRODUCTION

Many of the architectural features of the 386DX microprocessor are used only by system programmers. The system-level architecture also supports powerful debugging features which can be used by application programmers during program development.

The system-level features of the Intel386 ™ architecture include :

- Memory Management
- Protection
- Multitasking
- Input/Output
- Exceptions and Interrupts
- Initialization
- Co-processing and Multiprocessing
- Debugging

2.2 SYSTEMS REGISTERS

These registers are used by system programmers. They are divided into five categories which are listed below.

- EFLAG Register
- Memory-Management Registers
- Control Registers
- Debug Registers
- Test Registers

2.2.1 EFLAG Registers

It is a 32-bit register. It defines various bits and indicates status of 386DX processor. Lower 16 bits (0 to 15) contain the 16-bit flag register called as FLAGS, which is most useful when executing 8086 and 80286 code. Fig. 2.1 shows structure of EFLAG Register.

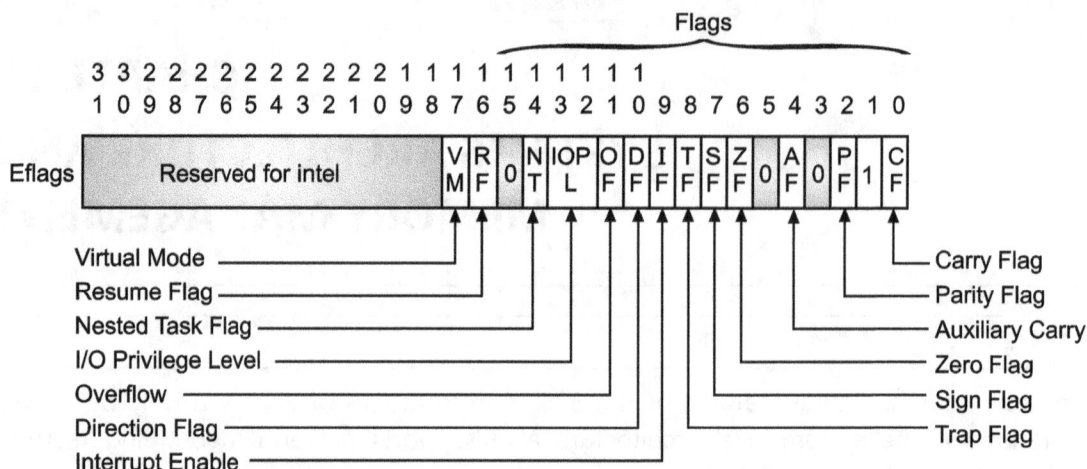

Fig. 2.1 : EFLAG register

VM (Virtual 8086 Mode, bit 17)

The VM bit provides Virtual 8086 Mode within Protected Mode. If it is set the Intel386 DX will switch to Virtual 8086 operation, handling segment loads as the 8086 does, but generating exception 13 faults on privileged opcodes. The VM bit can be set only in Protected Mode, by the IRET instruction (if current privilege level=0) and by task switches at any privilege level. The VM bit is unaffected by POPF.

RF (Resume Flag, bit 16)

The RF flag is used in association with the debug register breakpoints. When RF is set, it causes any debug fault to be ignored on the next instruction. RF is then automatically reset at the successful completion of every instruction except the IRET instruction and POPF instruction.

NT (Nested Task Flag, bit 14)

This flag applies to Protected Mode. NT is set to indicate that the execution of this task is nested within another task. If set, it indicates that the current nested task's Task State Segment (TSS) has a valid back link to the previous task's TSS. This bit is set or reset by control transfers to other tasks.

IOPL (Input/Output Privilege Level, bits 12-13)

This two-bit field applies to Protected Mode. IOPL indicates the numerically maximum CPL (current privilege level) value permitted to execute I/O instructions without generating an exception 13 fault or consulting the I/O Permission Bitmap. If the current privilege level is higher or more trusted than the IOPL, I/O executed without hindrance. If the IOPL is lower than the current privilege level, an interrupt occurs, causing execution to suspend. Note that an IPOL is 00 it is the highest or more trusted; if IOPL is 11, it's the lowest or least trusted.

OF (Overflow Flag, bit 11)

OF is set if the operation resulted in a signed overflow. Signed overflow occurs when the operation resulted in carry/borrow into the sign bit (high-order bit) of the result.

DF (Direction Flag, bit 10)

DF defines whether ESI and/or EDI registers post-decrement or post-increment during the string instructions. Post-increment occurs if DF is reset. Post-decrement occurs if DF is set.

IF (Interrupt Enable Flag, bit 9)

When IF flag is set, it puts the processor in a mode in which it responds to maskable interrupt requests (INTR interrupts). When IF flag is clear it disables these interrupts. IF flag has no effect on exceptions and Non Maskable Interrupt.

TF (Trap Flag, bit 8)

Setting the TF flag puts the processor into single-step mode for debugging. In this mode, the processor generates a debug exception after each instruction, which allows a program to be inspected as it executes each instruction.

2.2.2 Memory-Management Registers

There are four special registers which are defined to reference the tables or segments supported by the 80286 CPU and Intel386 DX protection model. These tables or segments are :

- GDT (Global Descriptor Table),
- IDT (Interrupt Descriptor Table),
- LDT (Local Descriptor Table),
- TR (Task Register).

The base addresses of these tables and segments are stored in special registers called as GDTR, IDTR, LDTR and TR, respectively.

2.2.2.1 GDTR (Global Descriptor Table Register)

This register holds the 32-bit base address and 16-bit segment limit for the global descriptor table (GDT). When data in memory is made any reference, a segment selector is used to find a segment descriptor in the GDT or LDT (Local Descriptor Table). A segment descriptor contains the base address of a segment.

2.2.2.2 LDTR (Local Descriptor Table Register)

This register holds the 32-bit base address, 16-bit segment limit, and 16-bit segment selector for the local descriptor table (LDT). The segment which contains the LDT has a segment descriptor in the GDT. There is no segment descriptor for the GDT. When a reference is made to data in memory, a segment selector is used to find a segment descriptor in the GDT or LDT. A segment descriptor contains the base address for a segment.

2.2.2.3 IDTR (Interrupt Descriptor Table Register)

This register holds the 32-bit base address and 16-bit segment limit for the interrupt descriptor table (IDT). When an interrupt occurs, the interrupt vector is used as an index to get a gate descriptor from this table. The gate descriptor contains a far pointer used to start up the interrupt handler.

2.2.2.4 TR (Task Register)

This register holds the 32-bit base address, 16-bit segment limit, and 16-bit segment selector for the task currently being executed. It references a task state segment (TSS) descriptor in the global descriptor table.

2.2.3 Control Registers

The Intel386 DX has four control registers of 32 bits, CR0, CR1, CR2 and CR3, to hold machine state of a global nature. Application programs can read this register to determine if a numeric coprocessor is present or not. Control register format is shown in Fig. 2.2.

CR0= Machine Control Register

CR1= Reserved

CR2= Page Fault Linear Address

CR3= Page Directory Base Address

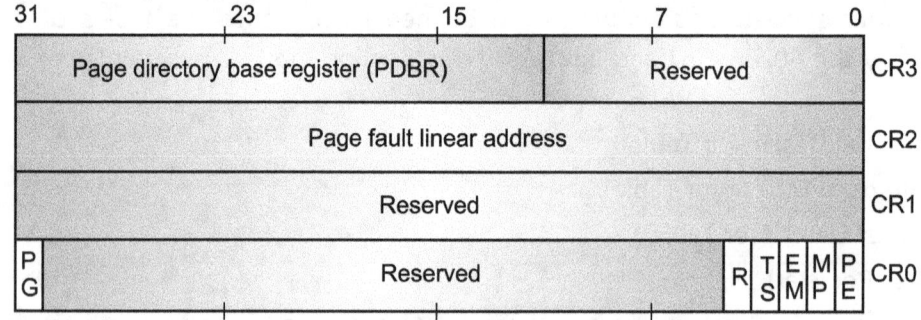

Fig. 2.2 : Control register format

CR0= Machine Control Register :

This register contains 6 defined bits for control and status purposes. The low-order 16 bits of CR0 are also known as the Machine Status Word, MSW. The defined bits are explained below.

PG (Paging Enable, bit 31) :

The PG bit is set to enable the on-chip paging unit. It is reset to disable the on-chip paging unit.

R (Reserved, bit 4) :

This bit is reserved by Intel. When loading CR0, care should be taken to not alter the value of this bit.

TS (Task Switched, bit 3) :

TS is automatically set whenever a task switch operation is performed. If TS is set, a coprocessor Escape opcode will cause a Coprocessor Not Available trap (exception 7).

EM (Emulate Coprocessor, bit 2) :

The Emulate coprocessor bit is set to cause all coprocessor opcodes to generate a Coprocessor Not Available fault (exception 7). It is reset to allow coprocessor opcodes to be executed on an actual Intel387 DX coprocessor which is the default case after reset.

MP (Monitor Coprocessor, bit 1) :

The MP bit is used in conjunction with the TS bit to determine if the WAIT opcode will generate a Coprocessor Not Available fault (exception7) when TS = 1. When both MP =1 and TS =1, the WAIT opcode generates a trap. Otherwise, the WAIT opcode does not generate a trap.

PE (Protection Enable, bit 0) :

The PE bit is set to enable the Protected Mode. If PE is reset, the processor operates again in Real Mode. PE may be set by loading MSW or CR0. PE can be reset only by a load into CR0. PE cannot be reset by the LMSW instruction.

CR1= Reserved :

CR1 is reserved by Intel processors for future use.

CR2= Page Fault Linear Register :

When an exception is generated during paging, the CR2 register has the 32-bit linear address which caused the exception.

CR3= Page Directory Base Register :

This register contains the physical base address of the page directory table. The Intel386 DX page directory table is always page aligned (4 Kbyte-aligned). The CR3 register is also known as the Page-Directory Base Register (PDBR).

2.2.4 Debug Registers

To provide advanced debugging abilities to the 386 DX microprocessor, Debug registers are used. It includes data breakpoints and the ability to set instruction breakpoints without modifying code segments. Debug Register Format is shown in Fig. 2.3.

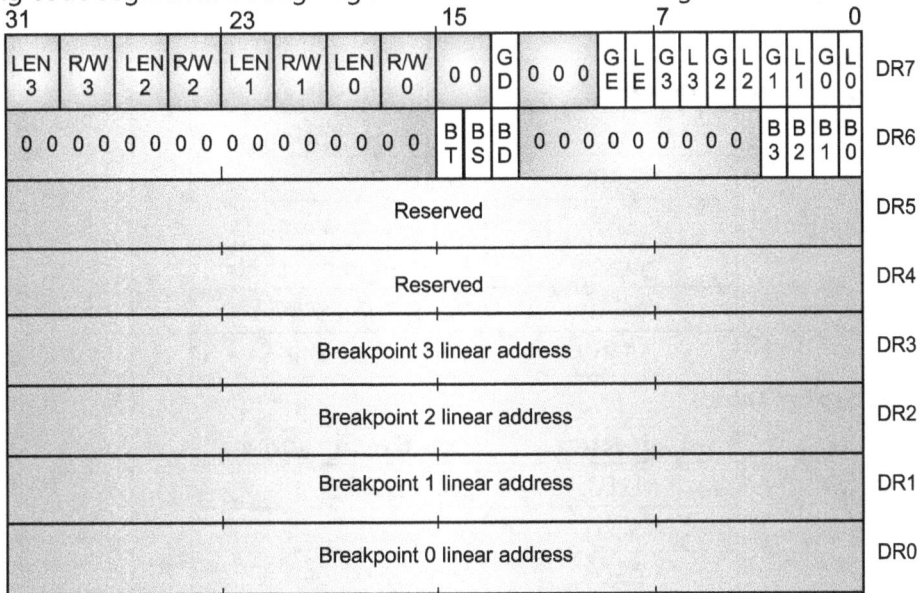

Note : 0 means intel reserved. Do not define

Fig. 2.3 : Debug register format

2.2.5 Test Registers

There are two registers which are used to control the testing of the RAM/CAM (Content Addressable Memories) in the Translation Look aside Buffer portion of the Intel386 DX. TR6 is the command test register, and TR7 is the data register which contains the data of the Translation Look aside buffer test. Test Register Format is shown in Fig. 2.4

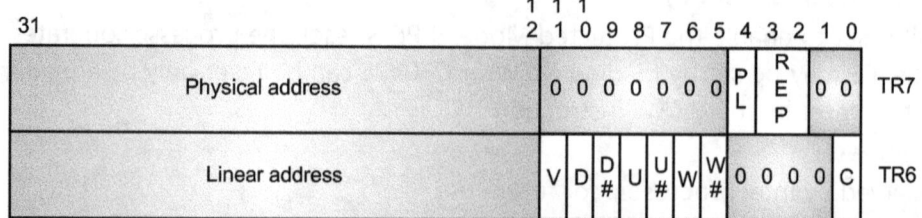

Fig. 2.4 : Test register format

2.3 SYSTEMS INSTRUCTIONS

System instructions deal with functions such as :

- Verification of pointer parameters
- Address descriptor tables
- Multitasking
- Co-processing and Multiprocessing
- Input and Output
- Interrupt Control
- Debugging
- System Control

Verification of Pointer Parameters :

Instructions	Description
ARPL	Adjust RPL
LAR	Load Access Rights
LSL	Load Segment Limit
VERR	Verify for Reading
VERW	Verify for Writing

Address Descriptor Tables :

Instructions	Description
LLDT	Load LDT
SLDT	Store LDT
LGDT	Load GDT
SGDT	Store GDT

Multitasking :

Instructions	Description
LTR	Load Task Register
STR	Store Task Register

Co-processing and Multiprocessing :

Instructions	Description
CLTS	Clear TS bit in CR0
ESC	Escape Instructions
WAIT	Wait Until Coprocessor Not Busy
LOCK	Assert Bus-Lock

Input and Output :

Instructions	Description
IN	Input
OUT	Output
INS	Input String
OUTS	Output String

Interrupt Control :

Instructions	Description
CLI	Clear IF flag
STI	Store IF flag
LIDT	Load IDT register
SIDT	Store IDT register

Debugging :

Instructions	Description
MOV	LOAD and store debug registers

System Control :

Instructions	Description
SMSW	Store MSW
LMSW	Load MSW
MOV	Load and Store CR0
HLT	Halt Processor

2.4 MEMORY MANAGEMENT

- Memory management consists of segmentation and paging. Segmentation is used to give each program several independent, protected address spaces. Paging is used to support an environment where large address spaces are simulated using a small amount of RAM and some disk storage.

- System designers may choose to use either or both these mechanisms. Segmentation allows memory to be completely unstructured and simple, like the memory model of an 8-bit processor.

- Access to segments is controlled by data which describes its size, the privilege level required to access it, the kinds of memory references which can be made to it (instruction fetch, stack push or pop, read operation, write operation, etc.), and whether it is present in memory.

- Segmentation hardware translates a segmented (logical) address into an address for a continuous, un-segmented address space, called a linear address.

- If paging is enabled, paging hardware translates a linear address into a physical address. If paging is not enabled, the linear address is used as the physical address. The physical address appears on the address bus coming out of the processor.

- Paging is a mechanism used to simulate a large, un-segmented address space using a small, fragmented address space and some disk storage. Paging provides access to data structures larger than the available memory space by keeping them partly in memory and partly on disk.

- A model for the segmentation of memory is chosen on the basis of reliability and performance. There are three types of model

  1. Flat Model
  2. Protected Flat Model
  3. Multi Segment Model

1. Flat Model :

- It is the simplest model. In this model, all segments are mapped to the entire physical address space.

- A segment is defined by a segment descriptor. At least two segment descriptors must be created for a flat model, one for code and one for data references.

- The segment selector for the stack segment may be mapped to the data-segment descriptor. For a flat model, each descriptor has a base address of 0 and a segment limit of 4 gigabytes. By setting the segment limit to 4 gigabytes, the segmentation mechanism is kept from generating exceptions for memory references.

It is shown in diagram

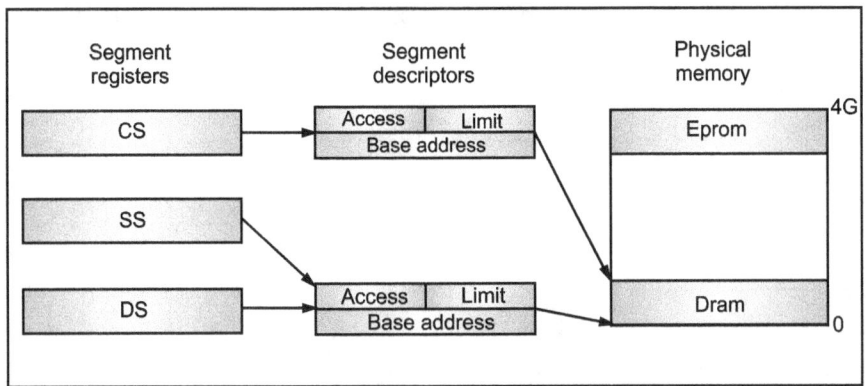

Fig. 2.5 : Flat Model

2. Protected Flat Model :

- The protected flat model is like the flat model, except the segment limits are set to include only the range of addresses for which memory actually exists.

- In this model, the segmentation hardware prevents programs from addressing non-existent memory locations. The consequences of being allowed access to these memory locations are hardware-dependent.

- A code and a data segment cover the EPROM and DRAM of physical memory. A second data segment has been created to cover EPROM. This allows EPROM to be referenced as data.

- It is shown in diagram

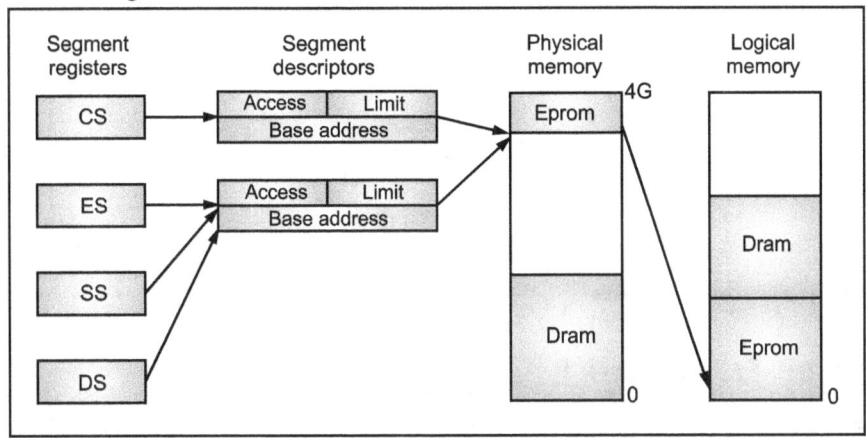

Fig. 2.6 : Protected Flat Model

3. Multi Segment Model :

- Here, the full capabilities of the segmentation mechanism are used. Each program is given its own table of segment descriptors, and its own segments.

- The segments can be completely private to the program, or they can be shared with specific other programs. Access between programs and particular segments can be individually controlled.
- Up to six segments can be ready for immediate use. These are the segments which have segment selectors loaded in the segment registers.

It is shown in diagram

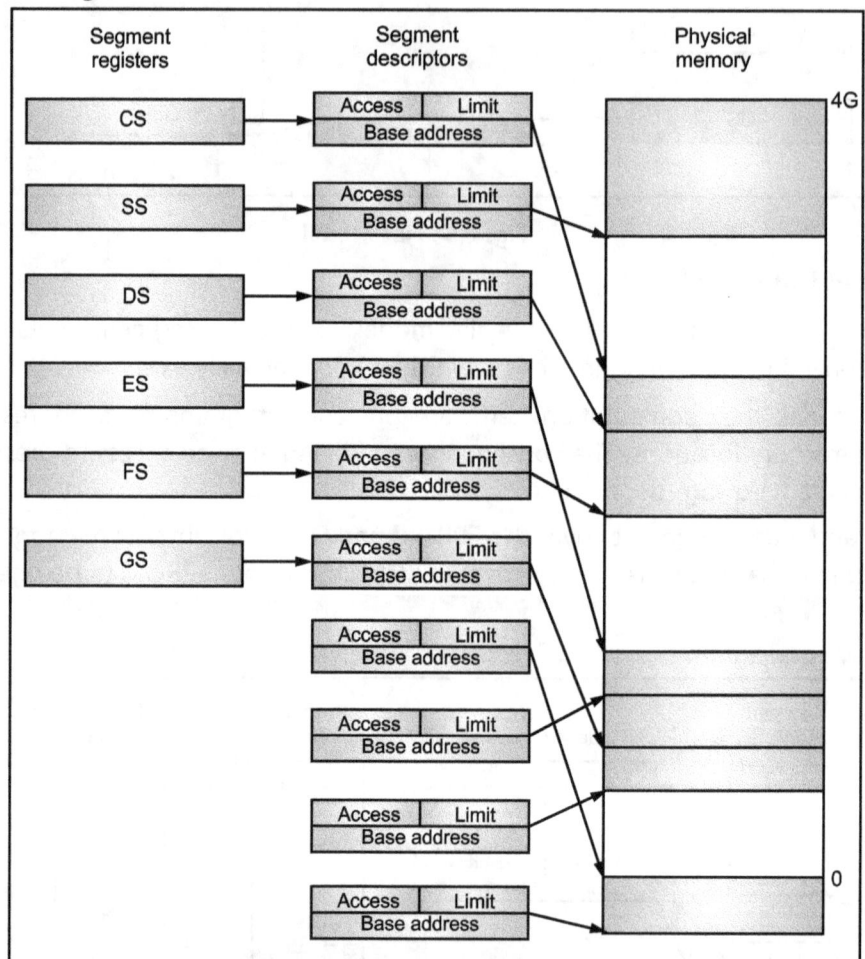

Fig. 2.7 : Multi segment Model

2.4.1 Segment Translation

- A logical address consists of the 16-bit segment selector for its segment and a 32-bit offset into the segment. A logical address is translated into a linear address by adding the offset to the base address of the segment.
- The base address comes from the segment descriptor, the segment descriptor comes from one of two tables, the Global Descriptor Table (GDT) or the Local Descriptor Table (LDT).

- There is one GDT for all programs in the system, and one LDT for each program which is being run. Every logical address is associated with a segment. There are the six segments whose segment selectors are loaded in the processor.

- The segment selector holds information used to translate the logical address into the corresponding linear address. Each logical address is associated with a segment. Only six segments are available for use. All these six segments have their segment selector loaded in the processor. These segment selectors hold information used to translate the logical address into the corresponding linear address. Segmentation is shown in figure

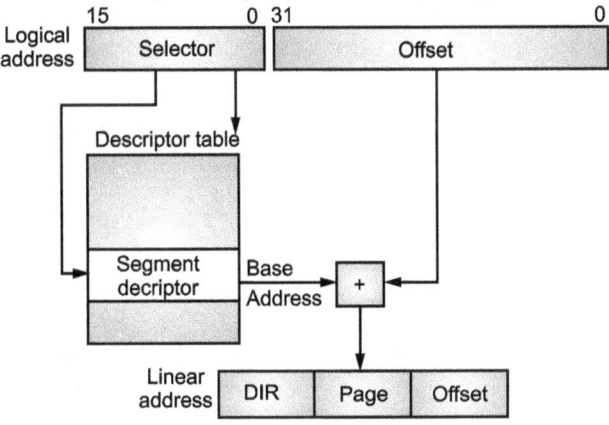

Fig. 2.8 : Segment Translation

- Segment registers holds segment selector for segments currently in use. When a segment selector is loaded, the base address, segment limit, and access control information also are loaded into the segment register. The segment selector contains a 13-bit index into one of the descriptor tables. The index is scaled by eight (the number of bytes in a segment descriptor) and added to the 32-bit base address of the descriptor table. It is shown in diagram

	16-Bit visible selector	Hidden Descriptor
CS		
SS		
DS		
ES		
FS		
GS		

Fig. 2.9 : Segment Registers

- The base address comes from either the Global Descriptor Table Register (GDTR) or the Local Descriptor Table Register (LDTR). These registers hold the linear address of the beginning of the descriptor tables. A bit in the segment selector specifies which table to use, if TI=0 select GDT and if TI=1 select LDT. Format of segment selector is as shown in Fig. 2.10.

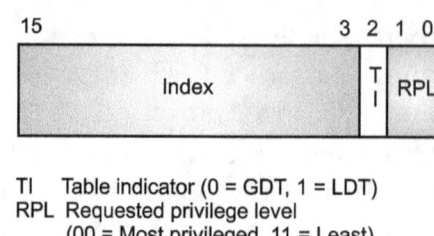

TI   Table indicator (0 = GDT, 1 = LDT)
RPL   Requested privilege level
      (00 = Most privileged, 11 = Least)

Fig. 2.10 : Format of segment selector

Index : Selects one of 8192 descriptors in a descriptor table. The processor multiplies the index value by 8 and adds the result to the base address of the descriptor table (from the GDTR or LDTR register).

Table-Indicator Bit : Specifies the descriptor table to use. A clear bit selects the GDT; a set bit selects the current LDT.

Requested Privilege Level : When this field contains a privilege level having a greater value (i.e., less privileged) than the program, it overrides the program's privilege level.

Segment Descriptors :

A segment descriptor is a data structure in memory which provides the processor with the size and location of a segment, as well as control and status information. Descriptors typically are created by compilers, linkers, loaders, or the operating system, but not application programs. Fig. 2.11 gives format of segment descriptor

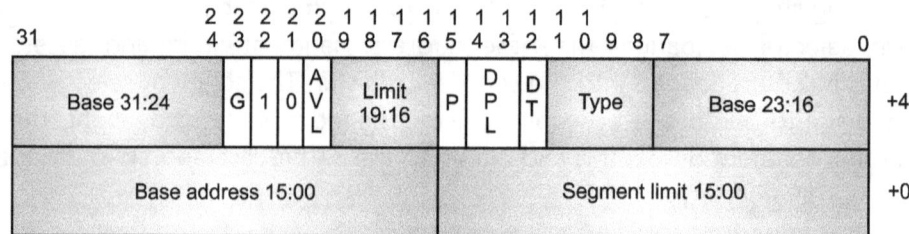

Fig. 2.11 : Format of segment descriptor

Descriptors are eight byte quantities which contain attributes about a given region of linear address space (i.e. a segment). These attributes include the 32-bit base linear address of the segment, the 20-bit length and granularity of the segment, the protection level, read, write or execute privileges, the default size of the operands (16-bit or 32-bit), and the type of segment. All the attribute information about a segment is contained in 12 bits in the segment descriptor.

Base : Defines the location of the segment within the 4 gigabyte physical address space. The processor puts together the three base address fields to form a single 32-bit value.

Granularity bit : Turns on scaling of the Limit field by a factor of 4096 (2^{12}). When the bit is clear, the segment limit is interpreted in units of one byte; when set, the segment limit is interpreted in units of 4K bytes (one page).

Limit : Defines the size of the segment. The processor puts together the two limit fields to form a 20-bit value. The processor interprets the limit in one of two ways, depending on the setting of the Granularity bit :

- If the Granularity bit is clear, the Limit has a value from 1 byte to 1 megabyte, in increments of 1 byte.
- If the Granularity bit is set, the Limit has a value from 4 kilobytes to 4 gigabytes, in increments of 4K bytes.

DT Field : The descriptors for application segments have this bit set. This bit is clear for system segments and gates.

Type : The interpretation of this field depends on whether the segment descriptor is for an application segment or a system segment.

Table 2.1 gives overview of type of segment along with its access rights like read only, write only or both.

Table 2.1 : Segment Type along with Access Rights

Number	E	W	A	Type	Description
0	0	0	0	Data	Read-Only
1	0	0	1	Data	Read-Only, accessed
2	0	1	0	Data	Read/Write
3	0	1	1	Data	Read/Write, accessed
4	1	0	0	Data	Read-Only, expand-down
5	1	0	1	Data	Read-Only, expand-down, accessed
6	1	1	0	Data	Read/Write, expand-down
7	1	1	1	Data	Read/Write, expand-down, accessed
Number	C	R	A	Type	Description
8	0	0	0	Code	Execute-Only
9	0	0	1	Code	Execute-Only, accessed
10	0	1	0	Code	Execute/Read
11	0	1	1	Code	Execute/Read, accessed
12	0	0	0	Code	Execute-Only, conforming
13	0	0	1	Code	Execute-Only, conforming, accessed
14	0	1	0	Code	Execute/Read-only, conforming
15	0	1	1	Code	Execute/Read-Only, conforming, accessed

DPL (Descriptor Privilege Level) : Defines the privilege level of the segment. This is used to control access to the segment, using the protection mechanism

Segment-Present Bit : If this bit is clear, the processor generates a segment-not-present exception when a selector for the descriptor is loaded into a segment register. When segment present or not present is managed with the help of some technique which is invisible to application programs, it is called virtual memory. A system may maintain a total amount of virtual memory far larger than physical memory by keeping only a few segments present in physical memory at any one time.

2.4.1.1 Segment Descriptor Tables

A segment descriptor table is an array of segment descriptors. There are two kinds of descriptor tables :

- The Global Descriptor Table (GDT)

- The Local Descriptor Tables (LDT)

There is one GDT for all tasks, and an LDT for each task being run. A descriptor table is an array of segment descriptors.

Descriptor Table Base Registers

The processor finds the Global Descriptor Table (GDT) and Interrupt Descriptor Table (IDT) using the GDTR and IDTR registers. These registers hold descriptors for tables in the physical address space. They also hold limit values for the size of these tables. The limit value is expressed in bytes. A limit value of 0 results in exactly one valid byte. Because segment descriptors are always eight bytes, the limit should always be one less than an integral multiple of eight (Le., 8N - 1). The LGDT and SGDT instructions read and write the GDTR register; the LIDT and SIDT instructions read and write the IDTR register. A third descriptor table is the Local Descriptor Table (LDT). The LLDT and SLDT instructions read and write the segment selector in the LDTR register. The LDTR register also holds the base address and limit for the LDT. It is shown in figure

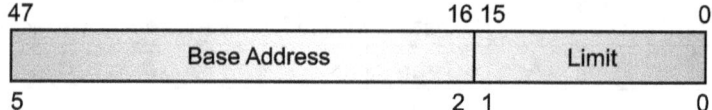

Fig. 2.12 : Format of descriptor table base register

2.4.2 Page Translation

The Intel386 DX uses two levels of tables to translate the linear address into a physical address. There are three parts of paging mechanism of the Intel386 DX.

- Page directory,

- Page tables, and

- Page frame

All memory-resident elements of paging mechanism are of same size, namely, 4K bytes. A uniform size for all the elements simplifies memory allocation and reallocation schemes due to which there will not be any problem with memory fragmentation. Paging mechanism is carried out as shown in Fig. 2.13.

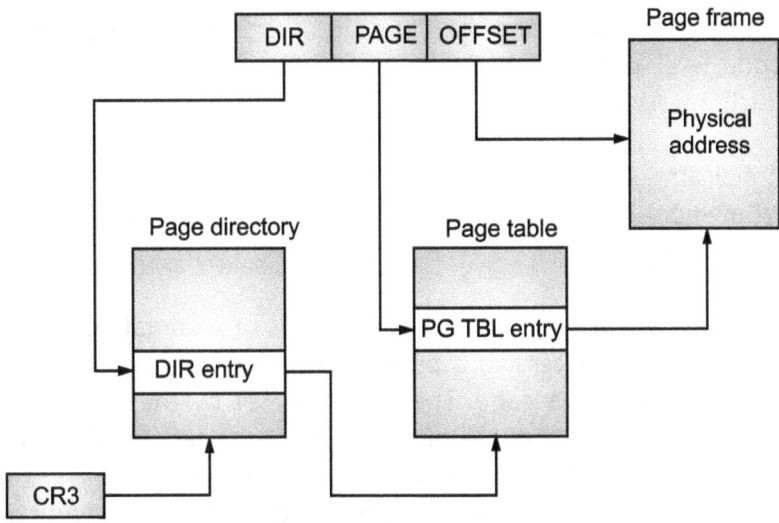

Fig. 2.13 : Paging mechanism

The addressing mechanism uses the **DIR** field as an index into a page directory, the PAGE field as an index into the page table determined by the page directory, and the OFFSET field to address an operand within the page specified by the page table.

Two levels of tables are used to address a page of memory. The top level is called the page directory. It addresses up to 1K page tables in the second level. A page table in the second level addresses up to 1K pages in physical memory. All the tables addressed by one page directory therefore, can address 1M or 220 pages. Because each page contains 4K or 2^{12} bytes, the tables of one page directory can span the entire linear address space of the 386 DX microprocessor ($2^{20} \times 2^{12} = 2^{32}$).

The physical address of the current page directory is stored in the CR3 register, also called the Page Directory Base Register (PDBR). Memory management software has the option of using one page directory for all tasks, one page directory for each task, or some combination of the two.

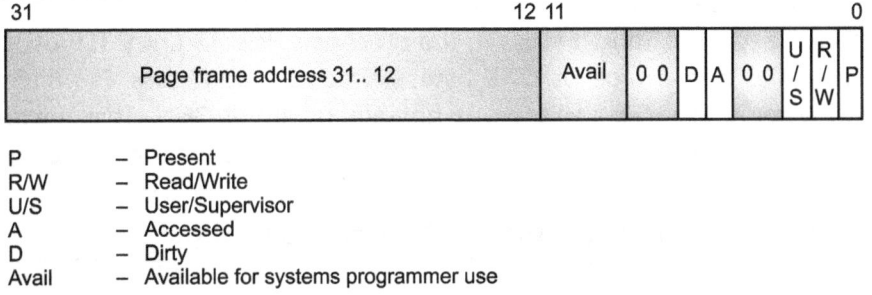

P	– Present
R/W	– Read/Write
U/S	– User/Supervisor
A	– Accessed
D	– Dirty
Avail	– Available for systems programmer use

Note : 0 indicates intel reserved. Do not define.

Fig. 2.14 : Page directory entry format

Page Frame Address

It is the base address of a page. Because pages are located on 4K-byte boundaries, the lowest 12 bits of the page frame address are always clear. In a page table entry, the upper 20 bits are used to specify a page frame address, and the lowest 12 bits specify control and status bits for the page. In a page directory, the page frame address is the address of a page table. In a second-level page table, the page frame address is the address of a page containing instructions or data.

Present Bit

The Present bit indicates whether the page frame address in a page table entry maps to a page in physical memory. When set, the page is in memory. When the Present bit is clear, the page is not in memory.

Accessed and Dirty Bits

These bits provide data about page usage in both levels of page tables. The Accessed bit is used to report read or write access to a page or second-level page table. The Dirty bit is used to report write access to a page. These bits are set by the hardware; however, the processor does not clear either of these bits. The processor sets the Accessed bits in both levels of page tables before a read or write operation to a page.

The processor sets the Dirty bit in the second-level page table before a write operation to an address mapped by that page table entry. The Dirty bit in directory entries is undefined.

Read/Write and User/Supervisor Bits

The U/S and R/W bits are used to provide User/Supervisor and Read/Write protection for individual pages or for all pages covered by a Page Table Directory Entry. The U/S and R/W bits in the first level Page Directory Table apply to all pages described by the page table pointed to by that directory entry. The U/S and R/W bits in the second level Page Table Entry apply only to the page described by that entry.

Translation Lookaside Buffer

The Intel386 DX paging hardware is designed to support demand paged virtual memory systems. However, performance would degrade substantially if the processor was required to access two levels of tables for every memory reference. To solve this problem, the Intel386 DX keeps a cache of the most recently accessed pages; this cache is called the Translation Lookaside Buffer (TLB).

The TLB is a four-way set associative 32-entry page table cache. It automatically keeps the most commonly used Page Table Entries in the processor. The 32-entry TLB coupled with a 4K page size, results in coverage of 128K bytes of memory addresses. For many common multi-tasking systems, the TLB will have a hit rate of about 98%. This means that the processor will only have to access the two-level page structure on 2% of all memory references.

2.4.3 Combined Segment and Page Translation

Flat Model

When the 386DX microprocessor is used to run software written without segments, it may be desirable to remove the segmentation features of the 386DX microprocessor. The 386DX microprocessor does not have a mode bit for disabling segmentation, but the same effect can be achieved by mapping the stack, code, and data spaces to the same range of linear addresses. Fig. 2.15 shows combined segmentation and paging.

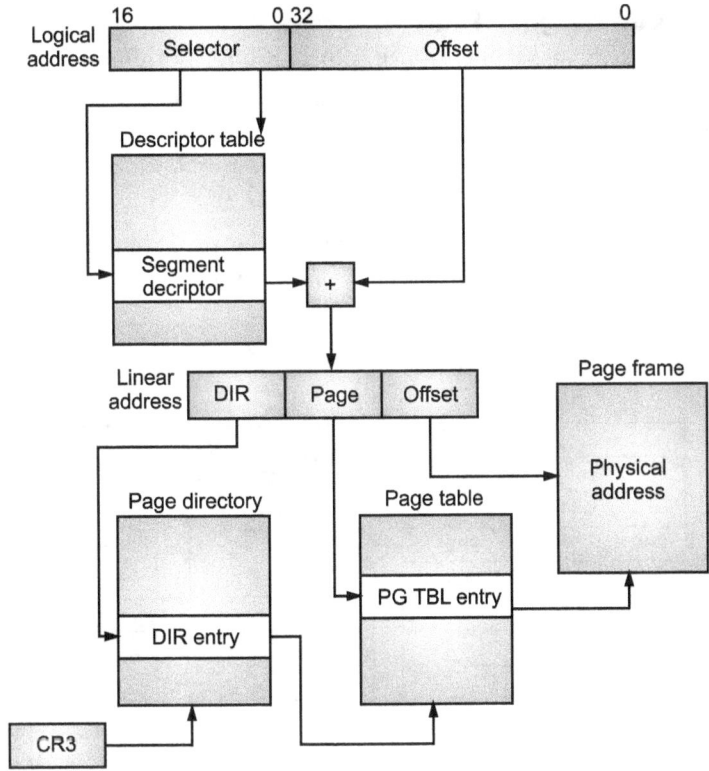

Fig. 2.15 : Combined segmentation and paging

If multiple programs are running at the same time, the paging mechanism can be used to give each program a separate address space.

Segments Splitted over Several Pages

Intel 80386DX supports an architecture in which segments are larger in size than page (4K bytes). For example, if any data structure which is present on thousands of pages and paging was not enable in such case access to any part of the data structure would require the entire data structure to be present in physical memory. With paging, only the page containing the part being accessed needs to be in memory.

Pages Spanning over Segments

In this architecture, it may be possible that size of segment is smaller than size of page. If one of these segments is placed in a page which is not shared with another segment, the extra memory is wasted. For example, a small data structure, such as a 1-byte semaphore, occupies 4K bytes if it is placed in a page by itself. If many semaphores are used, it is more efficient to pack them into a single page.

Segment Boundaries and Non-Aligned Page

The Intel386 architecture does not enforce any correspondence between the boundaries of pages and segments. A page may contain the end of one segment and the beginning of another. Likewise, a segment may contain the end of one page and the beginning of another.

Segment Boundaries and Aligned Page

Memory-management software may be simpler and more efficient if it enforces some alignment between page and segment boundaries. For example, if a segment which may fit in one page is placed in two pages, there may be twice as much paging overhead to support access to that segment.

Per Segment one Page Table

Memory management get simplify when there is an approach to combine Segmentation and Paging. In such approach, there will be one segment with its own Page table.

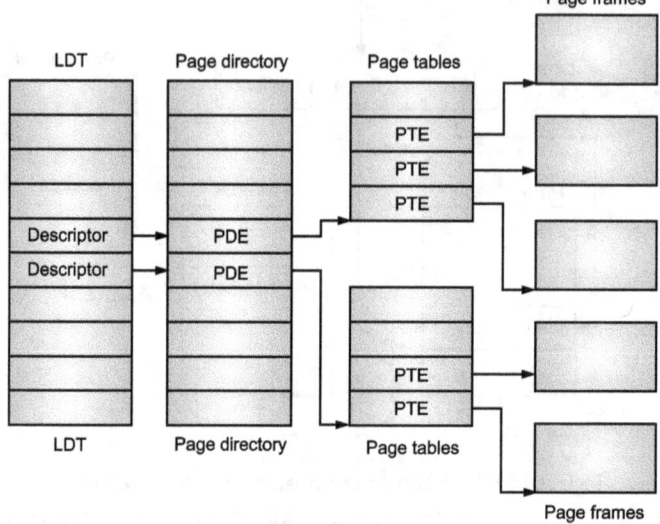

Fig. 2.16 : Segment with its own Page

EXERCISE

1. What are system-level features of the Intel386™ architecture? Explain any two of them.
2. What are system registers? Explain any three categories of them.
3. Write a short note on memory management registers.
4. Draw and explain control register structure.
5. Draw and explain debug register structure.
6. Explain functions handled by system instructions.
7. Write a note on different models used by segmentation.
8. Explain in detail how segment translation takes place with diagram.
9. Explain in detail how page translation takes place with diagram.
10. Draw the format of segment selector.
11. Draw and explain format of segment descriptor.
12. Draw and explain format of Page Directory Entry.
13. What is the role of Translation look aside buffer?
14. Draw diagram of combined segmentation and paging.
15. Explain segment type along with access right w.r.t. segment descriptor.

CHAPTER 3
PROTECTION AND MULTITASKING

3.1 NEED OF PROTECTION

The purpose of the protection features of the 80386DX is to help to detect and identify bugs. The 80386 supports sophisticated applications that may consist of hundreds or thousands of program modules. In such applications, the question is how bugs can be found and eliminated as quickly as possible and how their damage can be tightly confined. To help debug applications faster and make them more robust in production, the 80386 contains mechanisms to verify memory accesses and instruction execution for conformance to protection criteria. These mechanisms may be used or ignored, according to system design objectives.

3.2 OVERVIEW OF 80386DX PROTECTION MECHANISMS

Protection in the 80386DX has five aspects :

- Type checking

- Limit checking

- Restriction of addressable domain

- Restriction of procedure entry points

- Restriction of instruction set

The protection hardware of the 80386DX is an integral part of the memory management hardware. Protection applies both to segment translation and to page translation. Each reference to memory is checked by the hardware to verify that it satisfies the protection criteria. All these checks are made before the memory cycle is started; any violation prevents that cycle from starting and results in an exception. Since the checks are performed concurrently with address formation, there is no performance penalty. Invalid attempts to access memory result in an exception. The present chapter defines the protection violations that lead to exceptions. The concept of "privilege" is central to several aspects of protection.

Applied to procedures, privilege is the degree to which the procedure can be trusted not to make a mistake that might affect other procedures or data. Applied to data, privilege is the degree of protection that a data structure should have from less trusted procedures. The concept of privilege applies both to segment protection and to page protection.

3.3 SEGMENT-LEVEL PROTECTION

All five aspects of protection apply to segment translation :

- Type checking
- Limit checking
- Restriction of addressable domain
- Restriction of procedure entry points
- Restriction of instruction set

The segment is the unit of protection, and segment descriptors store protection parameters. Protection checks are performed automatically by the CPU when the selector of a segment descriptor is loaded into a segment register and with every segment access. Segment registers hold the protection parameters of the currently addressable segments.

3.3.1 Descriptors Store Protection Parameters

Fig. 3.1 highlights the protection-related fields of segment descriptors. The protection parameters are placed in the descriptor by systems software at the time a descriptor is created.

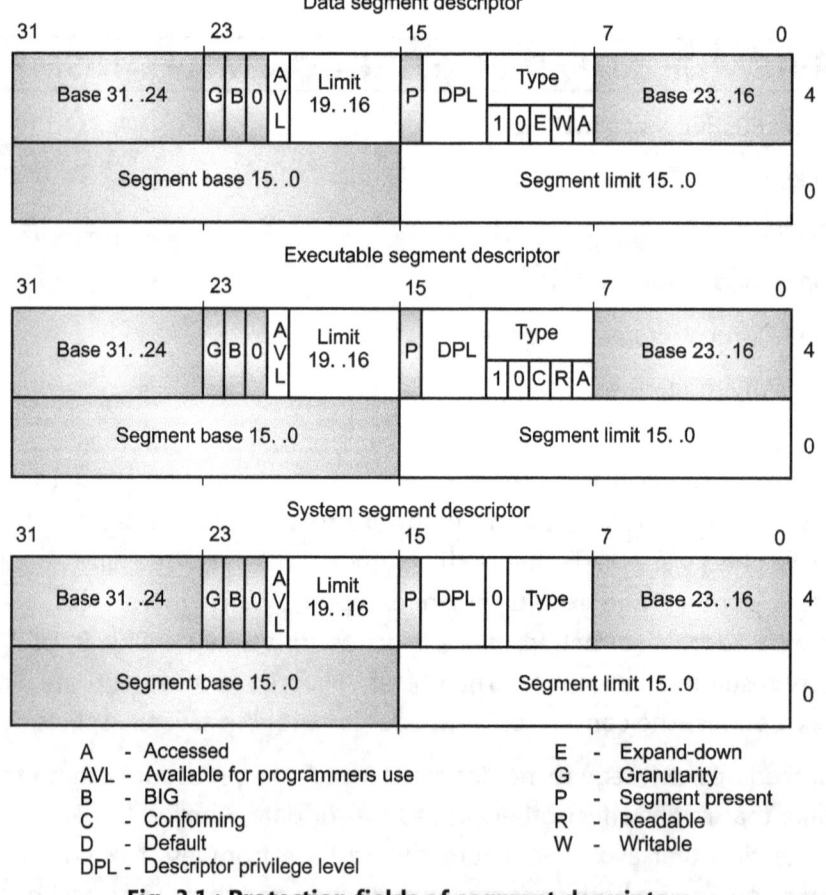

Fig. 3.1 : Protection fields of segment descriptors

In general, applications programmers do not need to be concerned about protection parameters. When a program loads a selector into a segment register, the processor loads not only the base address of the segment but also protection information. Each segment register has bits in the invisible portion for storing base, limit, type, and privilege level; therefore, subsequent protection checks on the same segment do not consume additional clock cycles.

3.3.1.1 Type Checking

The TYPE field of a descriptor has two functions :

- It distinguishes among different descriptor formats.
- It specifies the intended usage of a segment.

Besides the descriptors for data and executable segments commonly used by applications programs, the 80386DX has descriptors for special segments used by the operating system and for gates. Table 3.1 lists all the types defined for system segments and gates. Note that not all descriptors define segments; gate descriptors have a different purpose that is discussed later in this chapter.

The type fields of data and executable segment descriptors include bits which further define the purpose of the segment (refer to Fig. 3.1).

- The writable bit in a data-segment descriptor specifies whether instructions can write into the segment.
- The readable bit in an executable-segment descriptor specifies whether instructions are allowed to be read from the segment (for example, to access constants that are stored with instructions). A readable, executable segment may be read in two ways :
  - ➢ Via the CS register, by using a CS override prefix.
  - ➢ By loading a selector of the descriptor into a data-segment register (DS, ES, FS or GS).

Type checking can be used to detect programming errors that would attempt to use segments in ways not intended by the programmer. The processor examines type information on two kinds of occasions :

1. When a selector of a descriptor is loaded into a segment register. Certain segment registers can contain only certain descriptor types; for example :
   - The CS register can be loaded only with a selector of an executable segment.
   - Selectors of executable segments that are not readable cannot be loaded into data-segment registers.
   - Only selectors of writable data segments can be loaded into SS.
2. When an instruction refers (implicitly or explicitly) to a segment register. Certain segments can be used by instructions only in certain predefined ways; for example :
   - No instruction may write into an executable segment.
   - No instruction may write into a data segment if the writable bit is not set.
   - No instruction may read an executable segment unless the readable bit is set.

Table 3.1 : System and Gate Descriptor Types

Code	Type of Segment or Gate
0	reserved
1	Available 286 TSS
2	LDT
3	Busy 286 TSS
4	Call Gate
5	Task Gate
6	286 Interrupt Gate
7	286 Trap Gate
8	reserved
9	Available 386 TSS
A	reserved
B	Busy 386 TSS
C	386 Call Gate
D	reserved
E	386 Interrupt Gate
F	386 Trap Gate

3.3.1.2 Limit Checking

The limit field of a segment descriptor is used by the processor to prevent programs from addressing outside the segment. The processor's interpretation of the limit depends on the setting of the G (granularity) bit. For data segments, the processor's interpretation of the limit depends also on the E-bit (expansion-direction bit) and the B-bit (big bit). When G=0, the actual limit is the value of the 20-bit limit field as it appears in the descriptor. In this case, the limit may range from 0 to 0FFFFFH $(2^{20}-1$ or 1 megabyte). When G=1, the processor appends 12 low-order one-bits to the value in the limit field. In this case the actual limit may range from 0FFFH $(2^{12}-1$ or 4 kilobytes) to 0FFFFFFFFH $(2^{32}-1$ or 4 gigabytes).

For all types of segments except expand-down data segments, the value of the limit is one less than the size (expressed in bytes) of the segment. The processor causes a general protection exception in any of these cases :

- Attempt to access a memory byte at an address > limit.
- Attempt to access a memory word at an address ≥ limit.
- Attempt to access a memory doubleword at an address ≥ (limit-2).

For expand-down data segments, the limit has the same function but is interpreted differently. In these cases the range of valid addresses is from limit + 1 to either 64K or $2^{32}-1$ (4 Gbytes) depending on the B-bit. An expand-down segment has maximum size when the limit is zero. The expand-down feature makes it possible to expand the size of a stack by copying it to a larger segment without needing also to update intra stack pointers.

The limit field of descriptors for descriptor tables is used by the processor to prevent programs from selecting a table entry outside the descriptor table. The limit of a descriptor table identifies the last valid byte of the last descriptor in the table. Since each descriptor is eight bytes long, the limit value is N * 8 - 1 for a table that can contain up to N descriptors. Limit checking catches programming errors such as runaway subscripts and invalid pointer calculations. Such errors are detected when they occur, so that identification of the cause is easier. Without limit checking, such errors could corrupt other modules; the existence of such errors would not be discovered until later, when the corrupted module behaves incorrectly, and when identification of the cause is difficult.

3.3.1.3 Privilege Levels

The concept of privilege is implemented by assigning a value from zero to three to key objects recognized by the processor. This value is called the privilege level. The value zero represents the greatest privilege, the value three represents the least privilege. The following processor-recognized objects contain privilege levels :

- Descriptors contain a field called the descriptor privilege level (DPL).

- Selectors contain a field called the requestor's privilege level (RPL). The RPL is intended to represent the privilege level of the procedure that originates a selector.

- An internal processor register records the current privilege level (CPL). Normally the CPL is equal to the DPL of the segment that the processor is currently executing. CPL changes as control is transferred to segments with differing DPLs. The processor automatically evaluates the right of a procedure to access another segment by comparing the CPL to one or more other privilege levels. The evaluation is performed at the time the selector of a descriptor is loaded into a segment register. The criteria used for evaluating access to data differs from that for evaluating transfers of control to executable segments; therefore, the two types of access are considered separately in the following sections. Fig. 3.2 shows how these levels of privilege can be interpreted as rings of protection. The center is for the segments containing the most critical software, usually the kernel of the operating system. Outer rings are for the segments of less critical software. It is not necessary to use all four privilege levels. Existing software that was designed to use only one or two levels of privilege can simply ignore the other levels offered by the 80386. A one-level system should use privilege level zero; a two-level system should use privilege levels zero and three.

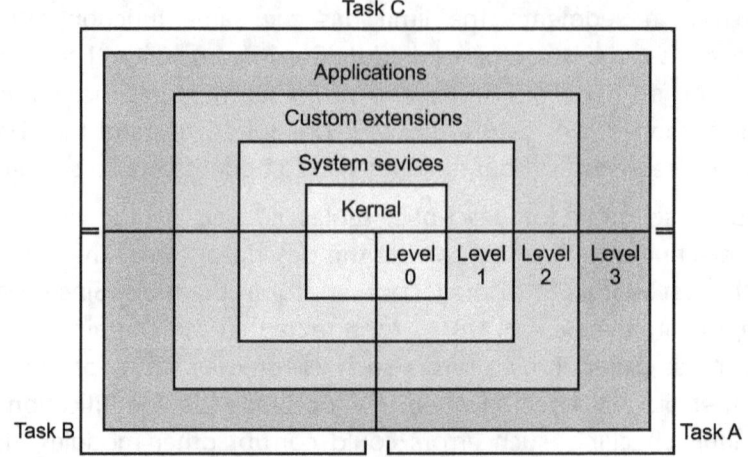

Fig. 3.2 : Levels of privilege

3.3.2 Restricting Access to Data

To address operands in memory, an 80386DX program must load the selector of a data segment into a data-segment register (DS, ES, FS, GS, SS). The processor automatically evaluates access to a data segment by comparing privilege levels. The evaluation is performed at the time a selector for the descriptor of the target segment is loaded into the data-segment register.

As Fig. 3.3 shows, three different privilege levels enter into this type of privilege check :

- The CPL (current privilege level).
- The RPL (requestor's privilege level) of the selector used to specify the target segment.
- The DPL of the descriptor of the target segment.

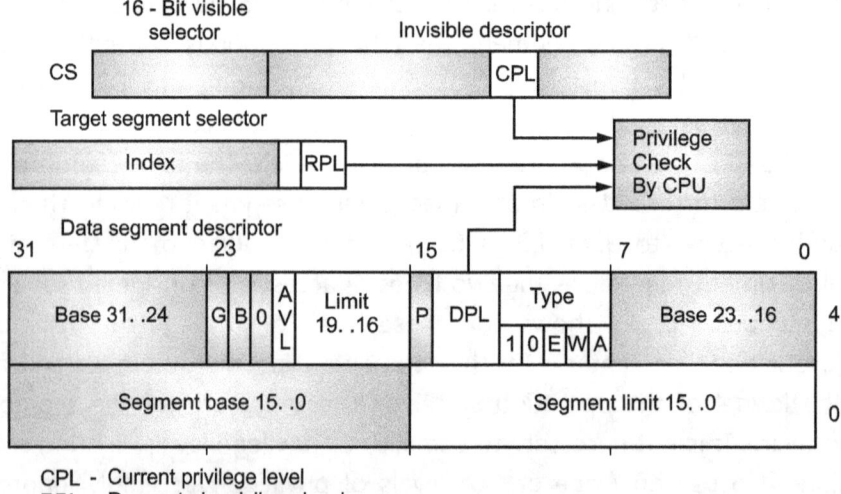

CPL - Current privilege level
RPL - Requestor's privilege level
DPL - Descriptor privilege level

Fig. 3.3 : Privilege check for data access

Instructions may load a data-segment register (and subsequently use the target segment) only if the DPL of the target segment is numerically greater than or equal to the maximum of the CPL and the selector's RPL. In other words, a procedure can only access data that is at the same or less privileged level.

The addressable domain of a task varies as CPL changes. When CPL is zero, data segments at all privilege levels are accessible; when CPL is one, only data segments at privilege levels one through three are accessible; when CPL is three, only data segments at privilege level three are accessible. This property of the 80386 can be used, for example, to prevent applications procedures from reading or changing tables of the operating system.

3.3.2.1 Accessing Data in Code Segments

Less common than the use of data segments is the use of code segments to store data. Code segments may legitimately hold constants; it is not possible to write to a segment described as a code segment. The following methods of accessing data in code segments are possible :

- Load a data-segment register with a selector of a nonconforming, readable, executable segment.
- Load a data-segment register with a selector of a conforming, readable, executable segment.
- Use a CS override prefix to read a readable, executable segment whose selector is already loaded in the CS register.

The same rules as for access to data segments apply to case 1. Case 2 is always valid because the privilege level of a segment whose conforming bit set is effectively the same as CPL regardless of its DPL. Case 3 always valid because the DPL of the code segment in CS is, by definition, equal to CPL.

3.3.3 Restricting Control Transfers

With the 80386DX , control transfers are accomplished by the instructions JMP, CALL, RET, INT, and IRET, as well as by the exception and interrupt mechanisms. Exceptions and interrupts are special cases that Chapter 9 covers. This chapter discusses only JMP, CALL, and RET instructions. The "near" forms of JMP, CALL, and RET transfer within the current code segment, and therefore are subject only to limit checking. The processor ensures that the destination of the JMP, CALL, or RET instruction does not exceed the limit of the current executable segment. This limit is cached in the CS register; therefore, protection checks for near transfers require no extra clock cycles.

The operands of the "far" forms of JMP and CALL refer to other segments; therefore, the processor performs privilege checking. There are two ways a JMP or CALL can refer to another segment :

- The operand selects the descriptor of another executable segment.
- The operand selects a call gate descriptor. This gated form of transfer is discussed in a later section on call gates.

As Fig. 3.4 shows, two different privilege levels enter into a privilege check for a control transfer that does not use a call gate :

- The CPL (current privilege level).
- The DPL of the descriptor of the target segment.

Normally the CPL is equal to the DPL of the segment that the processor is currently executing. CPL may, however, be greater than DPL if the conforming bit is set in the descriptor of the current executable segment. The processor keeps a record of the CPL cached in the CS register; this value can be different from the DPL in the descriptor of the code segment.

The processor permits a JMP or CALL directly to another segment only if one of the following privilege rules is satisfied :

- DPL of the target is equal to CPL.
- The conforming bit of the target code-segment descriptor is set, and the DPL of the target is less than or equal to CPL.

An executable segment whose descriptor has the conforming bit set is called a conforming segment. The conforming-segment mechanism permits sharing of procedures that may be called from various privilege levels but should execute at the privilege level of the calling procedure. Examples of such procedures include math libraries and some exception handlers. When control is transferred to a conforming segment, the CPL does not change. This is the only case when CPL may be unequal to the DPL of the current executable segment.

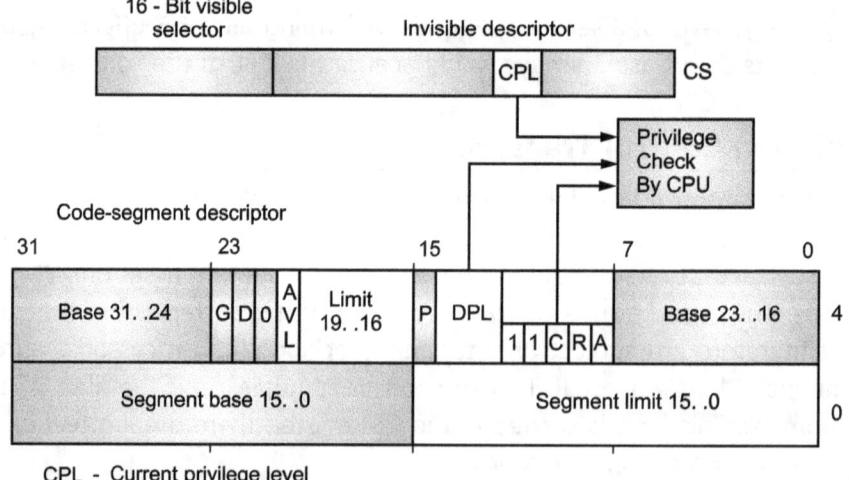

CPL - Current privilege level
DPL - Descriptor privilege level
C - Conforming bit

Fig. 3.4 : Privilege check for control transfer without gate

Most code segments are not conforming. The basic rules of privilege above mean that, for nonconforming segments, control can be transferred without a gate only to executable segments at the same level of privilege. There is a need, however, to transfer control to (numerically) smaller privilege levels; this need is met by the CALL instruction when used with call-gate descriptors, which are explained in the next section. The JMP instruction may never transfer control to a nonconforming segment whose DPL does not equal CPL.

3.3.4 Gate Descriptors Guard Procedure Entry Points

To provide protection for control transfers among executable segments at different privilege levels, the 80386DX uses gate descriptors.

There are four kinds of gate descriptors :

- Call gates
- Interrupt gates
- Trap gates
- Task gates

This chapter is concerned only with call gates. Task gates are used for task switching. Fig. 3.5 illustrates the format of a call gate. A call gate descriptor may reside in the GDT or in an LDT, but not in the IDT.

A call gate has two primary functions :

- To define an entry point of a procedure.
- To specify the privilege level of the entry point.

Call gate descriptors are used by call and jump instructions in the same manner as code segment descriptors. When the hardware recognizes that the destination selector refers to a gate descriptor, the operation of the instruction is expanded as determined by the contents of the call gate.

The selector and offset fields of a gate form a pointer to the entry point of a procedure. A call gate guarantees that all transitions to another segment go to a valid entry point, rather than possibly into the middle of a procedure (or worse, into the middle of an instruction). The far pointer operand of the control transfer instruction does not point to the segment and offset of the target instruction; rather, the selector part of the pointer selects a gate, and the offset is not used. Fig. 3.6 illustrates this style of addressing.

As Fig. 3.7 shows, four different privilege levels are used to check the validity of a control transfer via a call gate :

- The CPL (current privilege level).
- The RPL (requestor's privilege level) of the selector used to specify the call gate.
- The DPL of the gate descriptor.
- The DPL of the descriptor of the target executable segment.

The DPL field of the gate descriptor determines what privilege levels can use the gate. One code segment can have several procedures that are intended for use by different privilege levels. For example, an operating system may have some services that are intended to be used by applications, whereas others may be intended only for use by other systems software.

Gates can be used for control transfers to numerically smaller privilege levels or to the same privilege level (though they are not necessary for transfers to the same level). Only CALL instructions can use gates to transfer to smaller privilege levels. A gate may be used by a JMP instruction only to transfer to an executable segment with the same privilege level or to a conforming segment.

For a JMP instruction to a nonconforming segment, both the following privilege rules must be satisfied; otherwise, a general protection exception results.

$$MAX\ (CPL,\ RPL)\ \leq\ gate\ DPL$$

$$target\ segment\ DPL\ =\ CPL$$

For a CALL instruction (or for a JMP instruction to a conforming segment), both the following privilege rules must be satisfied; otherwise, a general protection exception results.

$$MAX\ (CPL,\ RPL)\ \leq\ gate\ DPL\ target\ segment\ DPL\ \leq\ CPL$$

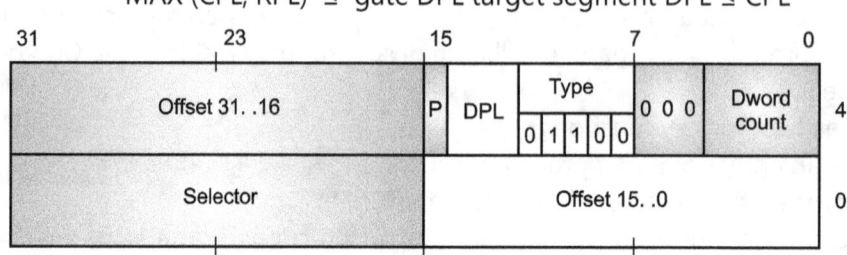

Fig. 3.5 : Format of 80386DX call gate

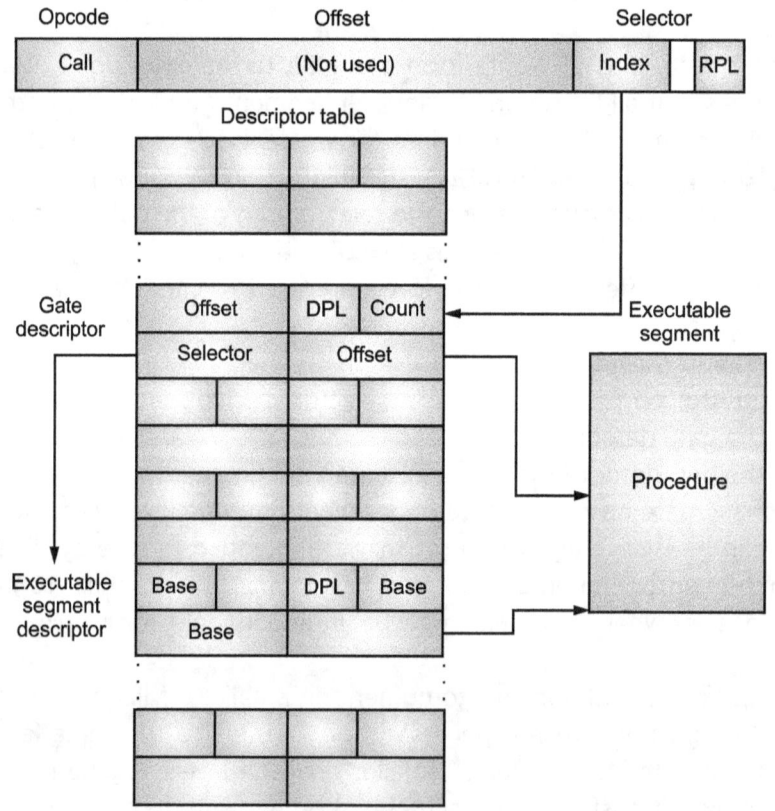

Fig. 3.6 : Indirect transfer via call gate

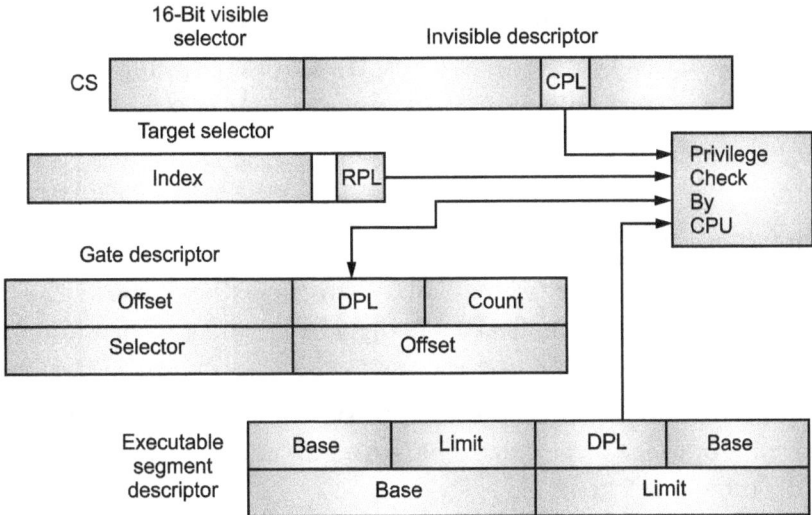

CPL - Current privilege level
RPL - Requestor's privilege level
DPL - Descriptor privilege level

Fig. 3.7 : Privilege check via call gate

3.3.4.1 Stack Switching

- If the destination code segment of the call gate is at a different privilege level than the CPL, an inter level transfer is being requested. To maintain system integrity, each privilege level has a separate stack. These stacks assure sufficient stack space to process calls from less privileged levels. Without them, a trusted procedure would not work correctly if the calling procedure did not provide sufficient space on the caller's stack.

- The processor locates these stacks via the task state segment (see Fig. 3.8). Each task has a separate TSS, thereby permitting tasks to have separate stacks. Systems software is responsible for creating TSSs and placing correct stack pointers in them. The initial stack pointers in the TSS are strictly read-only values. The processor never changes them during the course of execution.

- When a call gate is used to change privilege levels, a new stack is selected by loading a pointer value from the Task State Segment (TSS). The processor uses the DPL of the target code segment (the new CPL) to index the initial stack pointer for PL 0, PL 1, or PL 2. The DPL of the new stack data segment must equal the new CPL; if it does not, a stack exception occurs. It is the responsibility of systems software to create stacks and stack-segment descriptors for all privilege levels that are used. Each stack must contain enough space to hold the old SS :ESP, the return address, and all parameters and local variables that may be required to process a call. As with intra level calls, parameters for the subroutine are placed on the stack. To make privilege transitions transparent to the called procedure, the processor copies the parameters to the new stack. The count field of a call gate tells the processor how many doublewords (up to 31) to copy from the caller's stack to the new stack. If the count is zero, no parameters are copied.

The processor performs the following stack-related steps in executing an interlevel CALL.

- The new stack is checked to assure that it is large enough to hold the parameters and linkages; if it is not, a stack fault occurs with an error code of 0.

- The old value of the stack registers SS :ESP is pushed onto the new stack as two doublewords.

- The parameters are copied.

- A pointer to the instruction after the CALL instruction (the former value of CS :EIP) is pushed onto the new stack. The final value of SS:ESP points to this return pointer on the new stack.

Fig. 3.9 illustrates the stack contents after a successful interlevel call. The TSS does not have a stack pointer for a privilege level 3 stack, because privilege level 3 cannot be called by any procedure at any other privilege level.

Procedures that may be called from another privilege level and that require more than the 31 doublewords for parameters must use the saved SS:ESP link to access all parameters beyond the last doubleword copied.

A call via a call gate does not check the values of the words copied onto the new stack. The called procedure should check each parameter for validity. A later section discusses how the ARPL, VERR, VERW, LSL, and LAR instructions can be used to check pointer values.

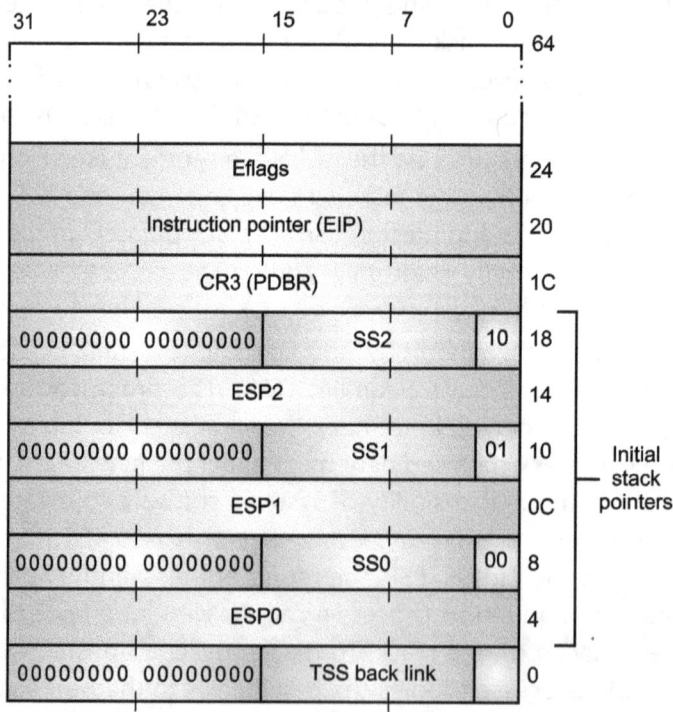

Fig. 3.8 : Initial stack pointers of TSS

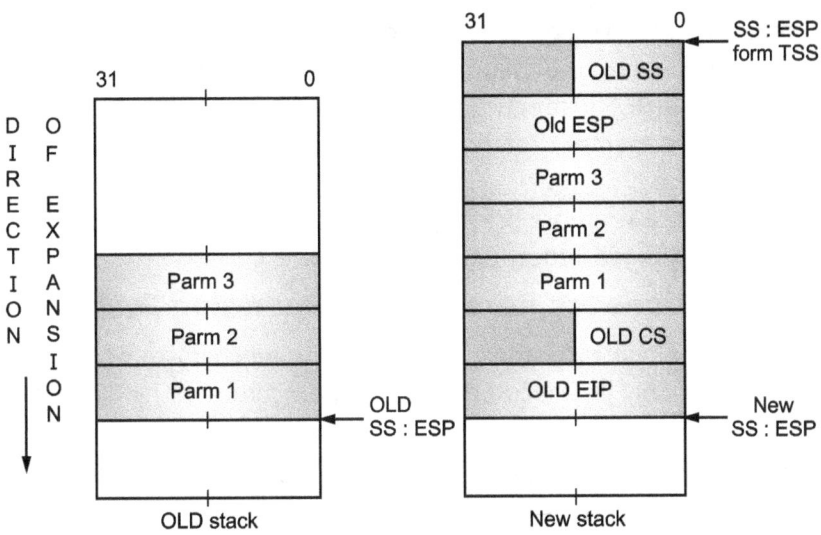

Fig. 3.9 : Stack contents after an interlevel call

3.3.4.2 Returning from a Procedure

The "near" forms of the RET instruction transfer control within the current code segment and therefore are subject only to limit checking. The offset of the instruction following the corresponding CALL, is popped from the stack.

The processor ensures that this offset does not exceed the limit of the current executable segment. The "far" form of the RET instruction pops the return pointer that was pushed onto the stack by a prior far CALL instruction. Under normal conditions, the return pointer is valid, because of its relation to the prior CALL or INT. Nevertheless, the processor performs privilege checking because of the possibility that the current procedure altered the pointer or failed to properly maintain the stack. The RPL of the CS selector popped off the stack by the return instruction identifies the privilege level of the calling procedure.

An intersegment return instruction can change privilege levels, but only toward procedures of lesser privilege. When the RET instruction encounters a saved CS value whose RPL is numerically greater than the CPL, an inter level return occurs. Such a return follows these steps :

- CS:EIP and SS:ESP are loaded with their former values that were saved on the stack.

- The old SS:ESP (from the top of the current stack) value is adjusted by the number of bytes indicated in the RET instruction. The resulting ESP value is not compared to the limit of the stack segment. If ESP is beyond the limit, that fact is not recognized until the next stack operation. (The SS:ESP value of the returning procedure is not preserved; normally, this value is the same as that contained in the TSS.)

- The contents of the DS, ES, FS, and GS segment registers are checked.

If any of these registers refer to segments whose DPL is greater than the new CPL (excluding conforming code segments), the segment register is loaded with the null selector (INDEX = 0, TI = 0). The RET instruction itself does not signal exceptions in these cases; however, any subsequent memory reference that attempts to use a segment register that contains the null selector will cause a general protection exception. This prevents less privileged code from accessing more privileged segments using selectors left in the segment registers by the more privileged procedure.

3.3.5 Some Instructions are Reserved for Operating System

Instructions that have the power to affect the protection mechanism or to influence general system performance can only be executed by trusted procedures. The 80386 has two classes of such instructions :

- Privileged instructions — those used for system control.
- Sensitive instructions — those used for I/O and I/O related activities.

3.3.5.1 Privileged Instructions

The instructions that affect system data structures can only be executed when CPL is zero. If the CPU encounters one of these instructions when CPL is greater than zero, it signals a general protection exception. These instructions include :

CLTS — Clear Task — Switched Flag

HLT — Halt Processor

LGDT — Load GDT Register

LIDT — Load IDT Register

LLDT — Load LDT Register

LMSW — Load Machine Status Word

LTR — Load Task Register

MOV to/from CRn — Move to Control Register n

MOV to /from DRn — Move to Debug Register n

MOV to/from TRn — Move to Test Register n

3.3.5.2 Sensitive Instructions

Instructions that deal with I/O need to be restricted but also need to be executed by procedures executing at privilege levels other than zero.

3.3.6 Instructions for Pointer Validation

Pointer validation is an important part of locating programming errors. Pointer validation is necessary for maintaining isolation between the privilege levels. Pointer validation consists of the following steps :

- Check if the supplier of the pointer is entitled to access the segment.
- Check if the segment type is appropriate to its intended use.
- Check if the pointer violates the segment limit.

Although the 80386 processor automatically performs checks 2 and 3 during instruction execution, software must assist in performing the first check.

The unprivileged instruction ARPL is provided for this purpose. Software can also explicitly perform steps 2 and 3 to check for potential violations (rather than waiting for an exception). The unprivileged instructions LAR, LSL, VERR, and VERW are provided for this purpose. LAR (Load Access Rights) is used to verify that a pointer refers to a segment of the proper privilege level and type. LAR has one operand a selector for a descriptor whose access rights are to be examined. The descriptor must be visible at the privilege level which is the maximum of the CPL and the selector's RPL. If the descriptor is visible, LAR obtains a masked form of the second doubleword of the descriptor, masks this value with 00FxFF00H, stores the result into the specified 32-bit destination register, and sets the zero flag. (The x indicates that the corresponding four bits of the stored value are undefined.) Once loaded, the access-rights bits can be tested. All valid descriptor types can be tested by the LAR instruction. If the RPL or CPL is greater than DPL, or if the selector is outside the table limit, no access-rights value is returned, and the zero flag is cleared. Conforming code segments may be accessed from any privilege level. LSL (Load Segment Limit) allows software to test the limit of a descriptor. If the descriptor denoted by the given selector (in memory or a register) is visible at the CPL, LSL loads the specified 32-bit register with a 32-bit, byte granular, unscrambled limit that is calculated from fragmented limit fields and the G-bit of that descriptor. This can only be done for segments (data, code, task state, and local descriptor tables); gate descriptors are inaccessible. (Table 3.2 lists in detail which types are valid and which are not.) Interpreting the limit is a function of the segment type. For example, downward expandable data segments treat the limit differently than code segments do. For both LAR and LSL, the zero flag (ZF) is set if the loading was performed; otherwise, the ZF is cleared.

Table 3.2 : Valid Descriptor Types for LSL

Type Code	Descriptor Type	Valid?
0	(invalid)	NO
1	Available 286 TSS	YES
2	LDT	YES
3	Busy 286 TSS	YES
4	286 Call Gate	NO
5	Task Gate	NO
6	286 Trap Gate	NO
7	286 Interrupt Gate	NO
8	(invalid)	NO
9	Available 386 TSS	YES
A	(invalid)	NO
B	Busy 386 TSS	YES
C	386 Call Gate	NO
D	(invalid)	NO
E	386 Trap Gate	NO
F	386 Interrupt Gate	NO

3.3.6.1 Descriptor Validation

The 80386 has two instructions, VERR and VERW, which determine whether a selector points to a segment that can be read or written at the current privilege level. Neither instruction causes a protection fault if the result is negative. VERR (Verify for Reading) verifies a segment for reading and loads ZF with 1 if that segment is readable from the current privilege level. VERR checks that :

- The selector points to a descriptor within the bounds of the GDT or LDT.
- It denotes a code or data segment descriptor.
- The segment is readable and of appropriate privilege level.

The privilege check for data segments and nonconforming code segments is that the DPL must be numerically greater than or equal to both the CPL and the selector's RPL. Conforming segments are not checked for privilege level. VERW (Verify for Writing) provides the same capability as VERR for verifying writability. Like the VERR instruction, VERW loads ZF if the result of the writability check is positive. The instruction checks that the descriptor is within bounds, is a segment descriptor, is writable, and that its DPL is numerically greater or equal to both the CPL and the selector's RPL. Code segments are never writable, conforming or not.

3.3.6.2 Pointer Integrity and RPL

The Requestor's Privilege Level (RPL) feature can prevent inappropriate use of pointers that could corrupt the operation of more privileged code or data from a less privileged level.

A common example is a file system procedure, FREAD (file_id, n_bytes, buffer_ptr). This hypothetical procedure reads data from a file into a buffer, overwriting whatever is there. Normally, FREAD would be available at the user level, supplying only pointers to the file system procedures and data located and operating at a privileged level. Normally, such a procedure prevents user-level procedures from directly changing the file tables.

However, in the absence of a standard protocol for checking pointer validity, a user-level procedure could supply a pointer into the file tables in place of its buffer pointer, causing the FREAD procedure to corrupt them unwittingly.

Use of RPL can avoid such problems. The RPL field allows a privilege attribute to be assigned to a selector. This privilege attribute would normally indicate the privilege level of the code which generated the selector. The 80386 processor automatically checks the RPL of any selector loaded into a segment register to determine whether the RPL allows access.

To take advantage of the processor's checking of RPL, the called procedure need only ensure that all selectors passed to it have an RPL at least as high (numerically) as the original caller's CPL. This action guarantees that selectors are not more trusted than their supplier. If one of the selectors is used to access a segment that the caller would not be able to access directly, i.e., the RPL is numerically greater than the DPL, then a protection fault will result when that selector is loaded into a segment register.

ARPL (Adjust Requestor's Privilege Level) adjusts the RPL field of a selector to become the larger of its original value and the value of the RPL field in a specified register. The latter is normally loaded from the image of the caller's CS register which is on the stack. If the adjustment changes the selector's RPL, ZF (the zero flag) is set; otherwise, ZF is cleared.

3.4 PAGE-LEVEL PROTECTION

Two kinds of protection are related to pages :

- Restriction of addressable domain.

- Type checking.

3.4.1 Page-Table Entries Hold Protection Parameters

Fig. 3.10 highlights the fields of PDEs and PTEs that control access to pages.

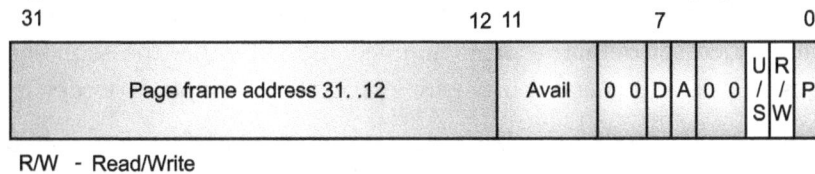

R/W - Read/Write
U/S   - User/Supervisor

Fig. 3.10 : Protection fields of page table entries

3.4.1.1 Restricting Addressable Domain

The concept of privilege for pages is implemented by assigning each page to one of two levels :

- Supervisor level (U/S=0) —— for the operating system and other systems software and related data.

- User level (U/S=1) —— for applications procedures and data.

The current level (U or S) is related to CPL. If CPL is 0, 1, or 2, the processor is executing at supervisor level. If CPL is 3, the processor is executing at user level. When the processor is executing at supervisor level, all pages are addressable, but, when the processor is executing at user level, only pages that belong to the user level are addressable.

3.4.1.2 Type Checking

At the level of page addressing, two types are defined :

- Read-only access (R/W=0)

- Read/write access (R/W=1)

When the processor is executing at supervisor level, all pages are both readable and writable. When the processor is executing at user level, only pages that belong to user level and are marked for read/write access are writable; pages that belong to supervisor level are neither readable nor writable from user level.

3.4.2 Combining Protection of Both Levels of Page Tables

For any one page, the protection attributes of its page directory entry may differ from those of its page table entry. The 80386 computes the effective protection attributes for a page by examining the protection attributes in both the directory and the page table.

3.4.3 Overrides to Page Protection

Certain accesses are checked as if they are privilege-level 0 references, even if CPL = 3 :

- LDT, GDT, TSS, IDT references.

- Access to inner stack during ring-crossing CALL/INT.

3.5 COMBINING PAGE AND SEGMENT PROTECTION

When paging is enabled, the 80386 first evaluates segment protection, then evaluates page protection. If the processor detects a protection violation at either the segment or the page level, the requested operation cannot proceed; a protection exception occurs instead.

For example, it is possible to define a large data segment which has some subunits that are read-only and other subunits that are read-write. In this case, the page directory (or page table) entries for the read-only subunits would have the U/S and R/W bits set to 0, indicating no write rights for all the pages described by that directory entry (or for individual pages).

This technique might be used, for example, in a UNIX-like system to define a large data segment, part of which is read only (for shared data or ROMmed constants). This enables UNIX-like systems to define a "flat" data space as one large segment, use "flat" pointers to address within this "flat" space, yet be able to protect shared data, shared files mapped into the virtual space, and supervisor areas.

3.6 MULTITASKING

To provide efficient, protected multitasking, the 80386 employs several special data structures. It does not, however, use special instructions to control multitasking; instead, it interprets ordinary control-transfer instructions differently when they refer to the special data structures. The registers and data structures that support multitasking are :

- Task state segment

- Task state segment descriptor

- Task register

- Task gate descriptor

With these structures the 80386 can rapidly switch execution from one task to another, saving the context of the original task so that the task can be restarted later. In addition to the simple task switch, the 80386 offers two other task-management features :

- Interrupts and exceptions can cause task switches (if needed in the system design). The processor not only switches automatically to the task that handles the interrupt or exception, but it automatically switches back to the interrupted task when the interrupt or exception has been serviced. Interrupt tasks may interrupt lower-priority interrupt tasks to any depth.
- With each switch to another task, the 80386 can also switch to another LDT and to another page directory. Thus, each task can have a different logical-to-linear mapping and a different linear-to-physical mapping. This is yet another protection feature, because tasks can be isolated and prevented from interfering with one another.

3.7 TASK STATE SEGMENT

All the information the processor needs in order to manage a task is stored in a special type of segment, a task state segment (TSS). Fig. 3.11 shows the format of a TSS for executing 80386 tasks. (Another format is used for executing 80286 tasks.)

The fields of a TSS belong to two classes :

1. A dynamic set that the processor updates with each switch from the task. This set includes the fields that store :
   - The general registers (EAX, ECX, EDX, EBX, ESP, EBP, ESI, EDI).
   - The segment registers (ES, CS, SS, DS, FS, GS).
   - The flags register (EFLAGS).
   - The instruction pointer (EIP).
   - The selector of the TSS of the previously executing task (updated only when a return is expected).

2. A static set that the processor reads but does not change. This set includes the fields that store :
   - The selector of the task's LDT.
   - The register (PDBR) that contains the base address of the task's page directory (read only when paging is enabled).
   - Pointers to the stacks for privilege levels 0-2.
   - The T-bit (debug trap bit) which causes the processor to raise a debug exception when a task switch occurs.
   - The I/O map base (refer to UNIT 4 for more information on the use of the I/O map).

Task state segments may reside anywhere in the linear space. The only case that requires caution is when the TSS spans a page boundary and the higher-addressed page is not present. In this case, the processor raises an exception if it encounters the not-present page while reading the TSS during a task switch. Such an exception can be avoided by either of two strategies :

- By allocating the TSS so that it does not cross a page boundary.
- By ensuring that both pages are either both present or both not-present at the time of a task switch. If both pages are not-present, then the page-fault handler must make both pages present before restarting the instruction that caused the task switch.

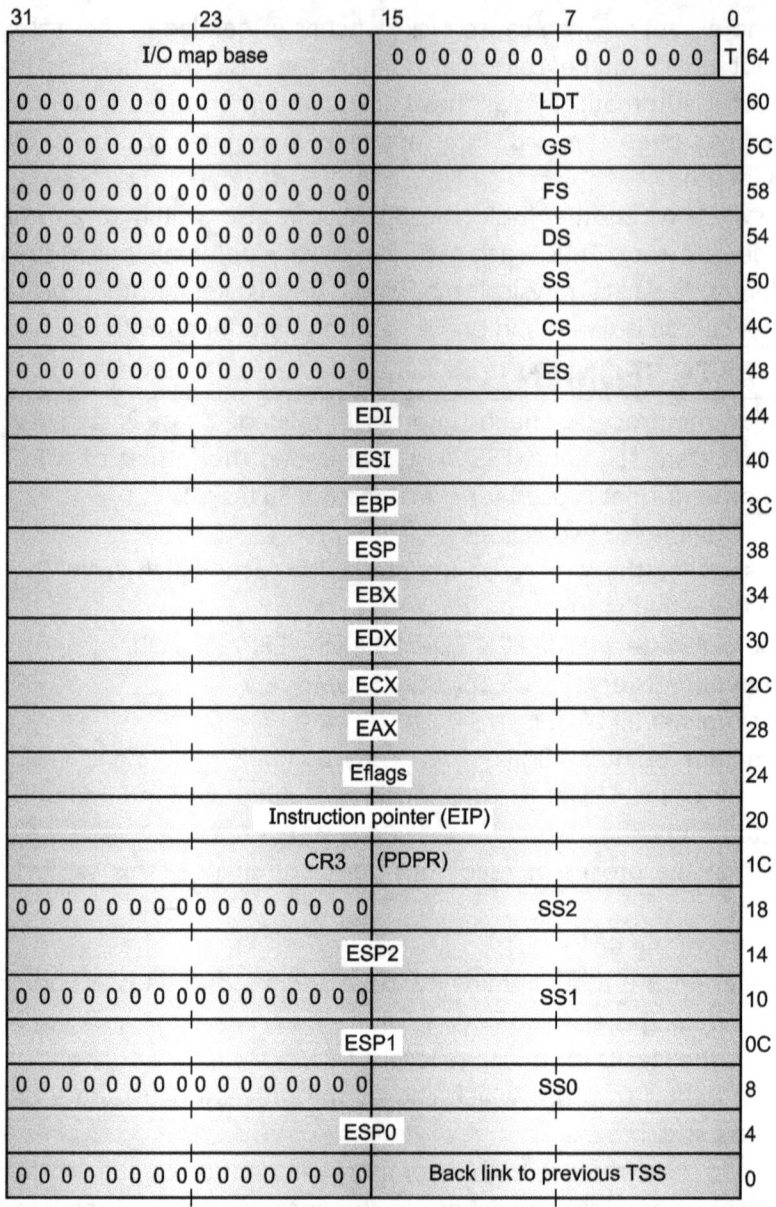

Fig. 3.11 : 80386 32-bit task state segment

3.8 TSS DESCRIPTOR

The task state segment, like all other segments, is defined by a descriptor. Fig. 3.12 shows the format of a TSS descriptor. The B-bit in the type field indicates whether the task is busy. A type code of 9 indicates a non-busy task; a type code of 11 indicates a busy task.

Tasks are not reentrant. The B-bit allows the processor to detect an attempt to switch to a task that is already busy. The BASE, LIMIT, and DPL fields and the G-bit and P-bit have functions similar to their counterparts in data-segment descriptors. The LIMIT field, however, must have a value equal to or greater than 103. An attempt to switch to a task whose TSS descriptor has a limit less that 103 causes an exception. A larger limit is permissible, and a larger limit is required if an I/O permission map is present. A larger limit may also be convenient for systems software if additional data is stored in the same segment as the TSS.

A procedure that has access to a TSS descriptor can cause a task switch. In most systems, the DPL fields of TSS descriptors should be set to zero, so that only trusted software has the right to perform task switching.

Having access to a TSS-descriptor does not give a procedure the right to read or modify a TSS. Reading and modification can be accomplished only with another descriptor that redefines the TSS as a data segment. An attempt to load a TSS descriptor into any of the segment registers (CS, SS, DS, ES, FS, GS) causes an exception.

TSS descriptors may reside only in the GDT. An attempt to identify a TSS with a selector that has TI=1 (indicating the current LDT) results in an exception.

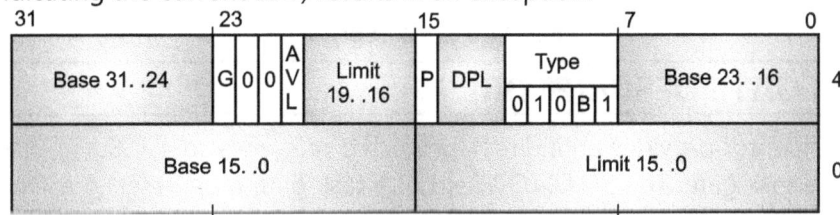

Fig. 3.12 : TSS descriptor for 32-bit TSS

3.9 TASK REGISTER

The task register (TR) identifies the currently executing task by pointing to the TSS. Fig. 3.13 shows the path by which the processor accesses the current TSS. The task register has both a "visible" portion (i.e., can be read and changed by instructions) and an "invisible" portion (maintained by the processor to correspond to the visible portion; cannot be read by any instruction). The selector in the visible portion selects a TSS descriptor in the GDT. The processor uses the invisible portion to cache the base and limit values from the TSS descriptor. Holding the base and limit in a register makes execution of the task more efficient, because the processor does not need to repeatedly fetch these values from memory when it references the TSS of the current task.

The instructions LTR and STR are used to modify and read the visible portion of the task register. Both instructions take one operand, a 16-bit selector located in memory or in a general register. LTR (Load Task Register) loads the visible portion of the task register with the selector operand, which must select a TSS descriptor in the GDT. LTR also loads the invisible portion with information from the TSS descriptor selected by the operand. LTR is a privileged instruction; it may be executed only when CPL is zero. LTR is generally used during system initialization to give an initial value to the task register; thereafter, the contents of TR are changed by task switch operations. STR (Store Task Register) stores the visible portion of the task register in a general register or memory word. STR is not privileged.

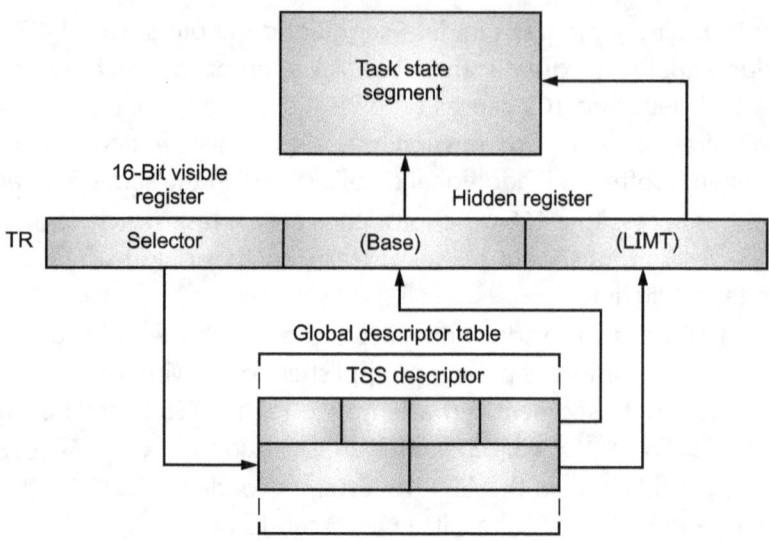

Fig. 3.13 : Task register

3.10 TASK GATE DESCRIPTOR

A task gate descriptor provides an indirect, protected reference to a TSS. Fig. 3.14 illustrates the format of a task gate. The SELECTOR field of a task gate must refer to a TSS descriptor. The value of the RPL in this selector is not used by the processor. The DPL field of a task gate controls the right to use the descriptor to cause a task switch. A procedure may not select a task gate descriptor unless the maximum of the selector's RPL and the CPL of the procedure is numerically less than or equal to the DPL of the descriptor. This constraint prevents untrusted procedures from causing a task switch. (Note that when a task gate is used, the DPL of the target TSS descriptor is not used for privilege checking.)

A procedure that has access to a task gate has the power to cause a task switch, just as a procedure that has access to a TSS descriptor. The 80386 has task gates in addition to TSS descriptors to satisfy three needs :

- The need for a task to have a single busy bit. Because the busy-bit is stored in the TSS descriptor, each task should have only one such descriptor. There may, however, be several task gates that select the single TSS descriptor.

- The need to provide selective access to tasks. Task gates fulfill this need, because they can reside in LDTs and can have a DPL that is different from the TSS descriptor's DPL. A procedure that does not have sufficient privilege to use the TSS descriptor in the GDT (which usually has a DPL of 0) can still switch to another task if it has access to a task gate for that task in its LDT. With task gates, systems software can limit the right to cause task switches to specific tasks.

- The need for an interrupt or exception to cause a task switch. Task gates may also reside in the IDT, making it possible for interrupts and exceptions to cause task switching.

When interrupt or exception vectors to an IDT entry that contains a task gate, the 80386 switches to the indicated task. Thus, all tasks in the system can benefit from the protection afforded by isolation from interrupt tasks. Fig. 3.15 illustrates how both a task gate in an LDT and a task gate in the IDT can identify the same task.

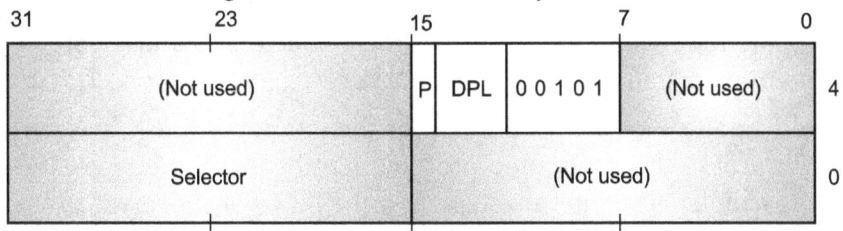

Fig. 3.14 : Task gate descriptor

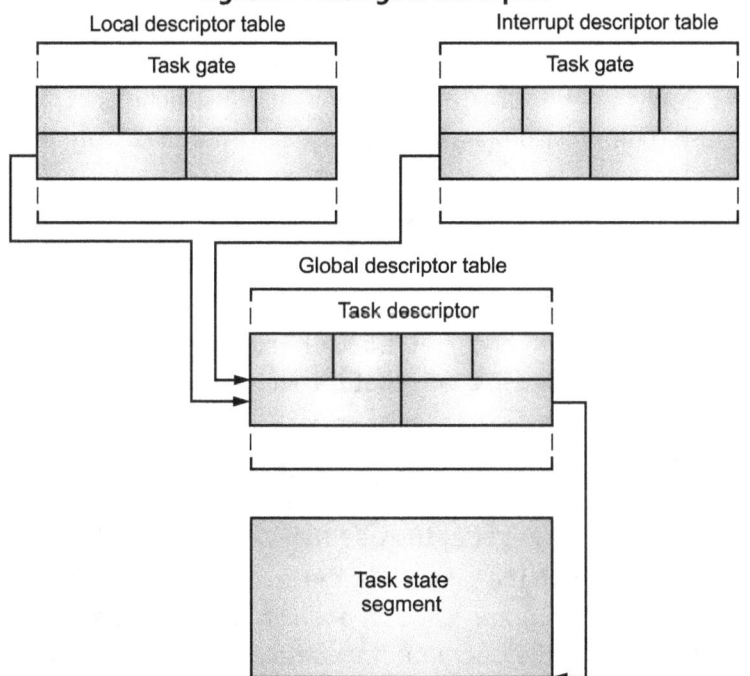

Fig. 3.15 : Task gate indirectly identifies task

3.11 TASK SWITCHING

The 80386 switches execution to another task in any of four cases :

- The current task executes a JMP or CALL that refers to a TSS descriptor.
- The current task executes a JMP or CALL that refers to a task gate.
- An interrupt or exception vectors to a task gate in the IDT.
- The current task executes an IRET when the NT flag is set.

JMP, CALL, IRET, interrupts, and exceptions are all ordinary mechanisms of the 80386 that can be used in circumstances that do not require a task switch. Either the type of descriptor referenced or the NT (nested task) bit in the flag word distinguishes between the standard mechanism and the variant that causes a task switch.

To cause a task switch, a JMP or CALL instruction can refer either to a TSS descriptor or to a task gate. The effect is the same in either case : the 80386 switches to the indicated task.

An exception or interrupt causes a task switch when it vectors to a task gate in the IDT. If it vectors to an interrupt or trap gate in the IDT, a task switch does not occur.

Whether invoked as a task or as a procedure of the interrupted task, an interrupt handler always returns control to the interrupted procedure in the interrupted task. If the NT flag is set, however, the handler is an interrupt task, and the IRET switches back to the interrupted task.

A task switching operation involves these steps :

- Checking that the current task is allowed to switch to the designated task. Data-access privilege rules apply in the case of JMP or CALL instructions. The DPL of the TSS descriptor or task gate must be less than or equal to the maximum of CPL and the RPL of the gate selector.

- Exceptions, interrupts, and IRETs are permitted to switch tasks regardless of the DPL of the target task gate or TSS descriptor.

- Checking that the TSS descriptor of the new task is marked present and has a valid limit. Any errors up to this point occur in the context of the outgoing task. Errors are restartable and can be handled in a way that is transparent to applications procedures.

- Saving the state of the current task. The processor finds the base address of the current TSS cached in the task register. It copies the registers into the current TSS (EAX, ECX, EDX, EBX, ESP, EBP, ESI, EDI, ES, CS, SS, DS, FS, GS, and the flag register). The EIP field of the TSS points to the instruction after the one that caused the task switch.

- Loading the task register with the selector of the incoming task's TSS descriptor, marking the incoming task's TSS descriptor as busy, and setting the TS (task switched) bit of the MSW. The selector is either the operand of a control transfer instruction or is taken from a task gate.

- Loading the incoming task's state from its TSS and resuming execution. The registers loaded are the LDT register; the flag register; the general registers EIP, EAX, ECX, EDX, EBX, ESP, EBP, ESI, EDI; the segment registers ES, CS, SS, DS, FS, and GS; and PDBR.

Any errors detected in this step occur in the context of the incoming task. To an exception handler, it appears that the first instruction of the new task has not yet executed.

Note that the state of the outgoing task is always saved when a task switch occurs. If execution of that task is resumed, it starts after the instruction that caused the task switch. The registers are restored to the values they held when the task stopped executing.

Every task switch sets the TS (task switched) bit in the MSW (machine status word). The TS flag is useful to systems software when a coprocessor (such as a numerics coprocessor) is present. The TS bit signals that the context of the coprocessor may not correspond to the current 80386 task.

Exception handlers that field task-switch exceptions in the incoming task should be cautious about taking any action that might load the selector that caused the exception. Such an action will probably cause another exception, unless the exception handler first examines the selector and fixes any potential problem.

The privilege level at which execution resumes in the incoming task is neither restricted nor affected by the privilege level at which the outgoing task was executing. Because the tasks are isolated by their separate address spaces and TSSs and because privilege rules can be used to prevent improper access to a TSS, no privilege rules are needed to constrain the relation between the CPLs of the tasks. The new task begins executing at the privilege level indicated by the RPL of the CS selector value that is loaded from the TSS.

3.12 TASK LINKING

The back-link field of the TSS and the NT (nested task) bit of the flag word together allow the 80386 to automatically return to a task that CALLed another task or was interrupted by another task. When a CALL instruction, an interrupt instruction, an external interrupt, or an exception causes a switch to a new task, the 80386 automatically fills the back-link of the new TSS with the selector of the outgoing task's TSS and, at the same time, sets the NT bit in the new task's flag register. The NT flag indicates whether the back-link field is valid. The new task releases control by executing an IRET instruction. When interpreting an IRET, the 80386 examines the NT flag. If NT is set, the 80386 switches back to the task selected by the back-link field.

3.12.1 Busy Bit Prevents Loops

The B-bit (busy bit) of the TSS descriptor ensures the integrity of the back-link. A chain of back-links may grow to any length as interrupt tasks interrupt other interrupt tasks or as called tasks call other tasks. The busy bit ensures that the CPU can detect any attempt to create a loop. A loop would indicate an attempt to reenter a task that is already busy; however, the TSS is not a reentrable resource.

The processor uses the busy bit as follows :

- When switching to a task, the processor automatically sets the busy bit of the new task.

- When switching from a task, the processor automatically clears the busy bit of the old task if that task is not to be placed on the back-link chain (i.e., the instruction causing the task switch is JMP or IRET). If the task is placed on the back-link chain, its busy bit remains set.

- When switching to a task, the processor signals an exception if the busy bit of the new task is already set. By these actions, the processor prevents a task from switching to itself or to any task that is on a back-link chain, thereby preventing invalid reentry into a task.

The busy bit is effective even in multiprocessor configurations, because the processor automatically asserts a bus lock when it sets or clears the busy bit. This action ensures that two processors do not invoke the same task at the same time.

3.12.2 Modifying Task Linkages

Any modification of the linkage order of tasks should be accomplished only by software that can be trusted to correctly update the back-link and the busy-bit. Such changes may be needed to resume an interrupted task before the task that interrupted it. Trusted software that removes a task from the back-link chain must follow one of the following policies :

- First change the back-link field in the TSS of the interrupting task, then clear the busy-bit in the TSS descriptor of the task removed from the list.

- Ensure that no interrupts occur between updating the back-link chain and the busy bit.

3.13 TASK ADDRESS SPACE

The LDT selector and PDBR fields of the TSS give software systems designers flexibility in utilization of segment and page mapping features of the 80386. By appropriate choice of the segment and page mappings for each task, tasks may share address spaces, may have address spaces that are largely distinct from one another, or may have any degree of sharing between these two extremes.

The ability for tasks to have distinct address spaces is an important aspect of 80386 protection. A module in one task cannot interfere with a module in another task if the modules do not have access to the same address spaces. The flexible memory management features of the 80386 allow systems designers to assign areas of shared address space to those modules of different tasks that are designed to cooperate with each other.

3.13.1 Task Linear-to-Physical Space Mapping

The choices for arranging the linear-to-physical mappings of tasks fall into two general classes :

- One linear-to-physical mapping shared among all tasks. When paging is not enabled, this is the only possibility. Without page tables, all linear addresses map to the same physical addresses.

  When paging is enabled, this style of linear-to-physical mapping results from using one page directory for all tasks. The linear space utilized may exceed the physical space available if the operating system also implements page-level virtual memory.

- Several partially overlapping linear-to-physical mappings. This style is implemented by using a different page directory for each task. Because the PDBR (page directory base register) is loaded from the TSS with each task switch, each task may have a different page directory.

In theory, the linear address spaces of different tasks may map to completely distinct physical addresses. If the entries of different page directories point to different page tables and the page tables point to different pages of physical memory, then the tasks do not share any physical addresses. In practice, some portion of the linear address spaces of all tasks must map to the same physical addresses. The task state segments must lie in a common space so that the mapping of TSS addresses does not change while the processor is reading and updating the TSSs during a task switch. The linear space mapped by the GDT should also be mapped to a common physical space; otherwise, the purpose of the GDT is defeated. Fig. 3.16 shows how the linear spaces of two tasks can overlap in the physical space by sharing page tables.

3.13.2 Task Logical Address Space

By itself, a common linear-to-physical space mapping does not enable sharing of data among tasks. To share data, tasks must also have a common logical-to-linear space mapping; i.e., they must also have access to descriptors that point into a shared linear address space. There are three ways to create common logical-to-physical address-space mappings :

- Via the GDT. All tasks have access to the descriptors in the GDT. If those descriptors point into a linear-address space that is mapped to a common physical-address space for all tasks, then the tasks can share data and instructions.

- By sharing LDTs. Two or more tasks can use the same LDT if the LDT selectors in their TSSs select the same LDT segment. Those LDT-resident descriptors that point into a linear space that is mapped to a common physical space permit the tasks to share physical memory.

  This method of sharing is more selective than sharing by the GDT; the sharing can be limited to specific tasks. Other tasks in the system may have different LDTs that do not give them access to the shared areas.

- By descriptor aliases in LDTs. It is possible for certain descriptors of different LDTs to point to the same linear address space. If that linear address space is mapped to the same physical space by the page mapping of the tasks involved, these descriptors permit the tasks to share the common space. Such descriptors are commonly called "aliases". This method of sharing is even more selective than the prior two; other descriptors in the LDTs may point to distinct linear addresses or to linear addresses that are not shared.

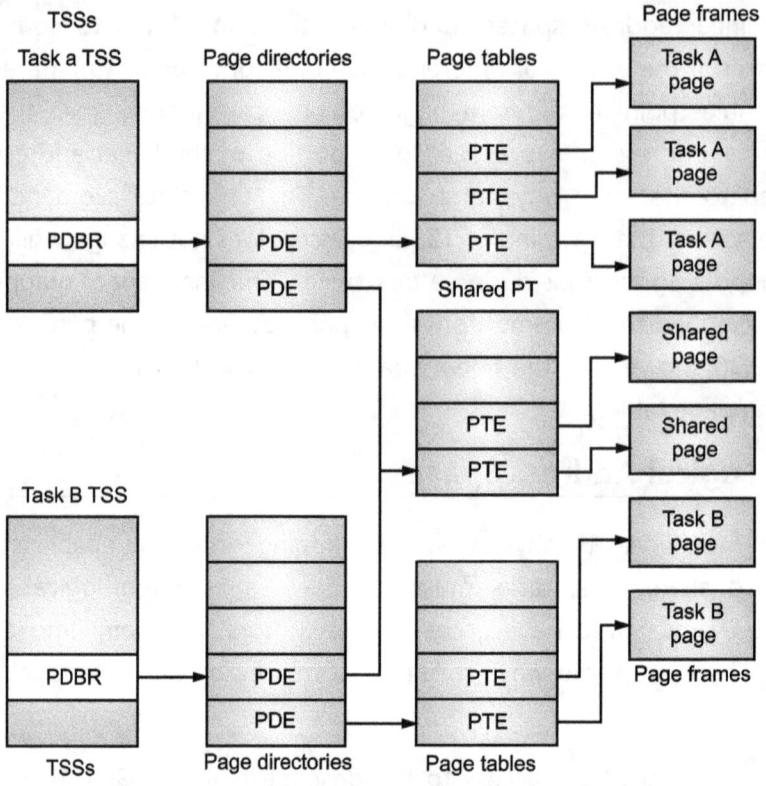

Fig. 3.16 : Partially-overlapping linear spaces

EXERCISE

1. What are the different aspects of protection mechanism in 80386?
2. Draw and explain protection fields of segment descriptor.
3. Write a short note on how privilege check for control transfer take place without call gate.
4. Write a short note on how privilege check for control transfer take place with call gate.
5. What is a gate descriptor? Explain any two types of them.
6. Draw and explain call gate format.
7. What is meant by sensitive instructions? Give example.
8. How does page level protection take place?
9. Enlist different registers and data structures that support multitasking.
10. Explain in detail Task State Segment.
11. Draw format of TSS Descriptor for 32-bit TSS.
12. What is the role of Task register?
13. Draw and explain the role of Task Gate Descriptor.
14. List out the situations where task switching takes place.
15. Write a short note on task linking.

CHAPTER 4
INPUT-OUTPUT, EXCEPTIONS AND INTERRUPTS

4.1 I/O ADDRESSING

The 80386 allows input/output to be performed in either of two ways :

- By means of a separate I/O address space (using specific I/O instructions).

- By means of memory-mapped I/O (using general-purpose operand Manipulation instructions).

4.1.1 I/O Address Space

The 80386 provides a separate I/O address space, distinct from physical memory, that can be used to address the input/output ports that are used for external 16 devices. The I/O address space consists of 2^{16} (64K) individually addressable 8-bit ports; any two consecutive 8-bit ports can be treated as a 16-bit port; and four consecutive 8-bit ports can be treated as a 32-bit port. Thus, the I/O address space can accommodate up to 64K 8-bit ports, up to 32K 16-bit ports, or up to 16K 32-bit ports. The program can specify the address of the port in two ways. Using an immediate byte constant, the program can specify :

- 256 8-bit ports numbered 0 through 255.

- 128 16-bit ports numbered 0, 2, 4, . . ., 252, 254.

- 64 32-bit ports numbered 0, 4, 8, . . . , 248, 252.

Using a value in DX, the program can specify :

- 8-bit ports numbered 0 through 65535

- 16-bit ports numbered 0, 2, 4, . . . , 65532, 65534

- 32-bit ports numbered 0, 4, 8, . . . , 65528, 65532

The 80386 can transfer 32, 16, or 8 bits at a time to a device located in the I/O space. Like doublewords in memory, 32-bit ports should be aligned at addresses evenly divisible by four so that the 32 bits can be transferred in a single bus access. Like words in memory, 16-bit ports should be aligned at even-numbered addresses so that the 16 bits can be transferred in a single bus access. An 8-bit port may be located at either an even or odd address. The instructions IN and OUT move data between a register and a port in the I/O address space. The instructions INS and OUTS move strings of data between the memory address space and ports in the I/O address space.

4.1.2 Memory-Mapped I/O

- I/O devices also may be placed in the 80386 memory address space. As long as the devices respond like memory components, they are indistinguishable to the processor. Memory-mapped I/O provides additional programming flexibility.

- Any instruction that references memory may be used to access an I/O port located in the memory space. For example, the MOV instruction can transfer data between any register and a port; and the AND, OR, and TEST instructions may be used to manipulate bits in the internal registers of a device (see Fig. 4.1).

- Memory-mapped I/O performed via the full instruction set maintains the full complement of addressing modes for selecting the desired I/O device (e.g., direct address, indirect address, base register, index register, scaling).

- Memory-mapped I/O, like any other memory reference, is subject to access protection and control when executing in protected mode.

4.2 I/O INSTRUCTIONS

The I/O instructions of the 80386 provide access to the processor's I/O ports for the transfer of data to and from peripheral devices. These instructions have as one operand the address of a port in the I/O address space. There are two classes of I/O instruction :

- Those that transfer a single item (byte, word, or doubleword) located in a register.

- Those that transfer strings of items (strings of bytes, words, or doublewords) located in memory. These are known as "string I/O instructions" or "block I/O instructions".

4.2.1 Register I/O Instructions

- The I/O instructions IN and OUT are provided to move data between I/O ports and the EAX (32-bit I/O), the AX (16-bit I/O), or AL (8-bit I/O) general registers.

- IN and OUT instructions address I/O ports either directly, with the address of one of up to 256 port addresses coded in the instruction, or indirectly via the DX register to one of up to 64K port addresses.

- IN (Input from Port) transfers a byte, word, or doubleword from an input port to AL, AX, or EAX. If a program specifies AL with the IN instruction, the processor transfers 8 bits from the selected port to AL. If a program specifies AX with the IN instruction, the processor transfers 16 bits from the port to AX. If a program specifies EAX with the IN instruction, the processor transfers 32 bits from the port to EAX.

- OUT (Output to Port) transfers a byte, word, or doubleword to an output port from AL, AX, or EAX. The program can specify the number of the port using the same methods as the IN instruction.

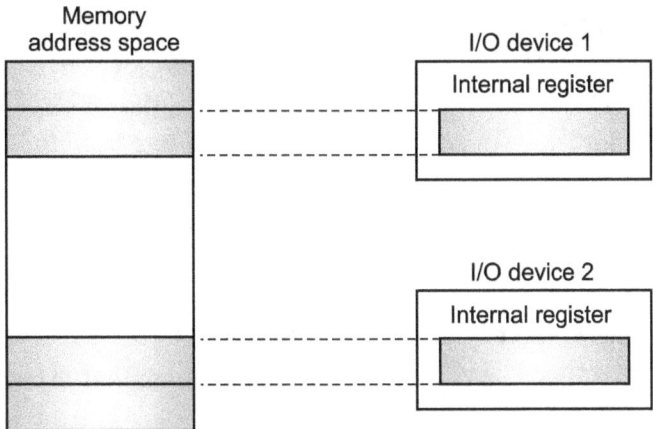

Fig. 4.1 : Memory-mapped I/O

4.2.2 Block I/O Instructions

The block (or string) I/O instructions INS and OUTS move blocks of data between I/O ports and memory space. Block I/O instructions use the DX register to specify the address of a port in the I/O address space. INS and OUTS use DX to specify :

- 8-bit ports numbered 0 through 65535

- 16-bit ports numbered 0, 2, 4, . . . , 65532, 65534

- 32-bit ports numbered 0, 4, 8, . . . , 65528, 65532

- Block I/O instructions use either SI or DI to designate the source or destination memory address. For each transfer, SI or DI are automatically either incremented or decremented as specified by the direction bit in the flags register.

- INS and OUTS, when used with repeat prefixes, cause block input or output operations. REP, the repeat prefix, modifies INS and OUTS to provide a means of transferring blocks of data between an I/O port and memory. These block I/O instructions are string primitives. They simplify programming and increase the speed of data transfer by eliminating the need to use a separate LOOP instruction or an intermediate register to hold the data.

- The string I/O primitives can operate on byte strings, word strings, or doubleword strings. After each transfer, the memory address in ESI or EDI is updated by 1 for byte operands, by 2 for word operands, or by 4 for doubleword operands.

- The value in the direction flag (DF) determines whether the processor automatically increments ESI or EDI (DF=0) or whether it automatically decrements these registers (DF=1).

- INS (Input String from Port) transfers a byte or a word string element from an input port to memory. The mnemonics INSB, INSW, and INSD are variants that explicitly specify the size of the operand.

- If a program specifies INSB, the processor transfers 8 bits from the selected port to the memory location indicated by ES :EDI. If a program specifies INSW, the processor transfers 16 bits from the port to the memory location indicated by ES :EDI.
- If a program specifies INSD, the processor transfers 32 bits from the port to the memory location indicated by ES :EDI. The destination segment register choice (ES) cannot be changed for the INS instruction.
- Combined with the REP prefix, INS moves a block of information from an input port to a series of consecutive memory locations. OUTS (Output String to Port) transfers a byte, word, or doubleword string element to an output port from memory.
- The mnemonics OUTSB, OUTSW, and OUTSD are variants that explicitly specify the size of the operand.
- If a program specifies OUTSB, the processor transfers 8 bits from the memory location indicated by ES :EDI to the selected port.
- If a program specifies OUTSW, the processor transfers 16 bits from the memory location indicated by ES :EDI to the selected port.
- If a program specifies OUTSD, the processor transfers 32 bits from the memory location indicated by ES :EDI to the selected port.
- Combined with the REP prefix, OUTS moves a block of information from a series of consecutive memory locations indicated by DS :ESI to an output port.

4.3 PROTECTION AND I/O

Two mechanisms provide protection for I/O functions :
- The IOPL field in the EFLAGS register defines the right to use I/O-related instructions.
- The I/O permission bit map of a 80386 TSS segment defines the right to use ports in the I/O address space.

These mechanisms operate only in protected mode, including virtual 8086 mode; they do not operate in real mode. In real mode, there is no protection of the I/O space; any procedure can execute I/O instructions, and any I/O port can be addressed by the I/O instructions.

4.3.1 I/O Privilege Level

Instructions that deal with I/O need to be restricted but also need to be executed by procedures executing at privilege levels other than zero. For this reason, the processor uses two bits of the flags register to store the I/O privilege level (IOPL). The IOPL defines the privilege level needed to execute I/O-related instructions.

The following instructions can be executed only if CPL ≤ IOPL :

　　IN — Input
　　INS — Input String
　　OUT — Output

OUTS — Output String

CLI — Clear Interrupt-Enable Flag

STI — Set Interrupt-Enable

- These instructions are called "sensitive" instructions, because they are sensitive to IOPL. To use sensitive instructions, a procedure must execute at a privilege level at least as privileged as that specified by the IOPL (CPL ≤ IOPL).

- Any attempt by a less privileged procedure to use a sensitive instruction results in a general protection exception. Because each task has its own unique copy of the flags register, each task can have a different IOPL.

- A task whose primary function is to perform I/O (a device driver) can benefit from having an IOPL of three, thereby permitting all procedures of the task to perform I/O.

- Other tasks typically have IOPL set to zero or one, reserving the right to perform I/O instructions for the most privileged procedures. A task can change IOPL only with the POPF instruction; however, such changes are privileged.

- No procedure may alter IOPL (the I/O privilege level in the flag register) unless the procedure is executing at privilege level 0.

- An attempt by a less privileged procedure to alter IOPL does not result in an exception; IOPL simply remains unaltered. The POPF instruction may be used in addition to CLI and STI to alter the interrupt-enable flag (IF); however, changes to IF by POPF are IOPL-sensitive.

- A procedure may alter IF with a POPF instruction only when executing at a level that is at least as privileged as IOPL. An attempt by a less privileged procedure to alter IF in this manner does not result in an exception; IF simply remains unaltered.

4.3.2 I/O Permission Bit Map

- The I/O instructions that directly refer to addresses in the processor's I/O space are IN, INS, OUT, OUTS. The 80386 has the ability to selectively trap references to specific I/O addresses. The structure that enables selective trapping is the I/O Permission Bit Map in the TSS segment (see Fig. 4.2).

- The I/O permission map is a bit vector. The size of the map and its location in the TSS segment are variable. The processor locates the I/O permission map by means of the I/O map base field in the fixed portion of the TSS.

- The I/O map base field is 16 bits wide and contains the offset of the beginning of the I/O permission map. The upper limit of the I/O permission map is the same as the limit of the TSS segment.

- In protected mode, when it encounters an I/O instruction (IN, INS, OUT, or OUTS), the processor first checks whether CPL ≤ IOPL. If this condition is true, the I/O operation may proceed. If not true, the processor checks the I/O permission map.

- Each bit in the map corresponds to an I/O port byte address; for example, the bit for port 41 is found at I/O map base + 5, bit offset 1.

- The processor tests all the bits that correspond to the I/O addresses spanned by an I/O operation; for example, a doubleword operation tests four bits corresponding to four adjacent byte addresses. If any tested bit is set, the processor signals a general protection exception. If all the tested bits are zero, the I/O operation may proceed.

- It is not necessary for the I/O permission map to represent all the I/O addresses. I/O addresses not spanned by the map are treated as if they had one bits in the map. For example, if TSS limit is equal to I/O map base + 31, the first 256 I/O ports are mapped; I/O operations on any port greater than 255 cause an exception.

- If I/O map base is greater than or equal to TSS limit, the TSS segment has no I/O permission map, and all I/O instructions in the 80386 program cause exceptions when CPL > IOPL. Because the I/O permission map is in the TSS segment, different tasks can have different maps.

- Thus, the operating system can allocate ports to a task by changing the I/O permission map in the task's TSS.

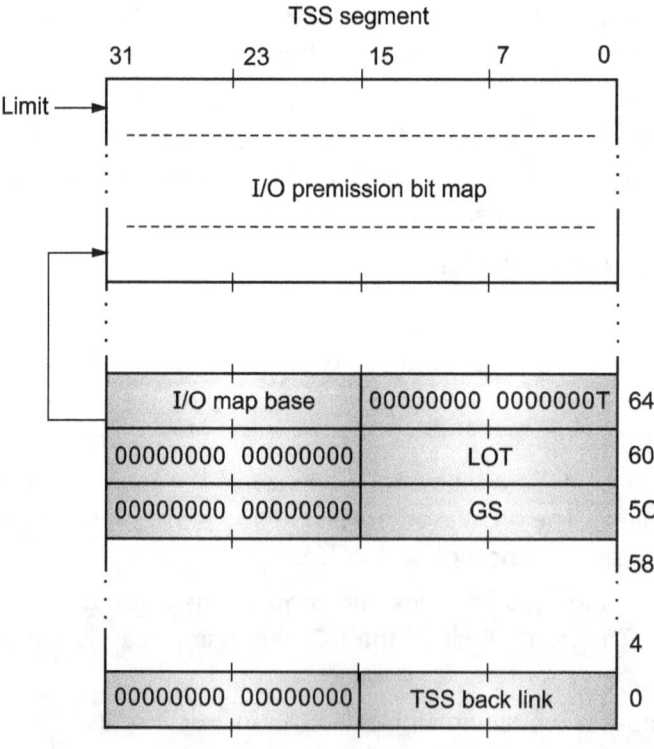

Fig. 4.2 : I/O Address bit map

4.4 EXCEPTIONS AND INTERRUPTS

Interrupts and Exceptions are special kinds of control transfer; they work somewhat like unprogrammed CALLs. They alter the normal program flow to handle external events or to report errors or exceptional conditions. The difference between interrupts and exceptions is that interrupts are used to handle asynchronous events external to the processor, but exceptions handle conditions detected by the processor itself in the course of executing instructions.

There are two sources for external interrupts and two sources for exceptions :

1. Interrupts
    *   Maskable interrupts, which are signaled via the INTR pin.
    *   Non-maskable interrupts, which are signaled via the NMI (Non-Maskable Interrupt) pin.

2. Exceptions
    *   Processor detected. These are further classified as faults, traps and aborts.
    *   Programmed. The instructions INT 0, INT 3, INT n, and BOUND can trigger exceptions. These instructions are often called "Software Interrupts", but the processor handles them as Exceptions.

This chapter explains the features that the 80386 offers for controlling and responding to interrupt when it is executing in protected mode.

4.5 IDENTIFYING INTERRUPTS

*   The processor associates an identifying number with each different type of interrupt or exception. The NMI and the exceptions recognized by the processor are assigned predetermined identifiers in the range 0 through 31. Not all these numbers are currently used by the 80386; unassigned identifiers in this range are reserved by Intel for possible future expansion.

*   The identifiers of the maskable interrupts are determined by external interrupt controllers (such as Intel's 8259A Programmable Interrupt Controller) and communicated to the processor during the processor's interrupt-acknowledge sequence.

*   The numbers assigned by an 8259A PIC can be specified by software. Any numbers in the range 32 through 255 can be used.

*   Exceptions are classified as faults, traps, or aborts depending on the way they are reported and whether restart of the instruction that caused the exception is supported.

Faults : Faults are exceptions that are reported "before" the instruction causing the exception. Faults are either detected before the instruction begins to execute, or during execution of the instruction. If detected during the instruction, the fault is reported with the machine restored to a state that permits the instruction to be restarted.

Traps : A trap is an exception that is reported at the instruction boundary immediately after the instruction in which the exception was detected.

Aborts : An abort is an exception that permits neither precise location of the instruction causing the exception nor restart of the program that caused the exception. Aborts are used to report severe errors, such as hardware errors and inconsistent or illegal values in system tables.

Table 4.1 : Interrupt and Exception ID Assignments

Identifier	Description
0	Divide error
1	Debug exceptions
2	Nonmaskable interrupt
3	Breakpoint (one-byte INT 3 instruction)
4	Overflow (INTO instruction)
5	Bounds check (BOUND instruction)
6	Invalid opcode
7	Coprocessor not available
8	Double fault
9	(reserved)
10	Invalid TSS
11	Segment not present
12	Stack exception
13	General protection
14	Page fault
15	(reserved)
16	Coprocessor error
17-31	(reserved)
32-255	Available for external interrupts via INTR pin

4.6 ENABLING AND DISABLING INTERRUPTS

The processor services interrupts and exceptions only between the end of one instruction and the beginning of the next. When the repeat prefix is used to repeat a string instruction, interrupts and exceptions may occur between repetitions. Thus, operations on long strings do not delay interrupt response. Certain conditions and flag settings cause the processor to inhibit certain interrupts and exceptions at instruction boundaries.

4.6.1 NMI Masks Further NMIs

While an NMI handler is executing, the processor ignores further interrupt signals at the NMI pin until the next IRET instruction is executed.

4.6.2 IF Masks INTR

The IF (interrupt-enable flag) controls the acceptance of external interrupts signaled via the INTR pin. When IF=0, INTR interrupts are inhibited; when IF=1, INTR interrupts are enabled. As with the other flag bits, the processor clears IF in response to a RESET signal. The instructions CLI and STI alter the setting of IF. CLI (Clear Interrupt-Enable Flag) and STI (Set Interrupt-Enable Flag) explicitly alter IF (bit 9 in the flag register). These instructions may be executed only if CPL ≤ IOPL. A protection exception occurs if they are executed when CPL > IOPL.

The IF is also affected implicitly by the following operations :

*   The instruction PUSHF stores all flags, including IF, in the stack where they can be examined.
*   Task switches and the instructions POPF and IRET load the flags register; therefore, they can be used to modify IF.
*   Interrupts through interrupt gates automatically reset IF, disabling interrupts. (Interrupt gates are explained later in this chapter.)

4.6.3 RF Masks Debug Faults

The RF bit in EFLAGS controls the recognition of debug faults. This permits debug faults to be raised for a given instruction at most once, no matter how many times the instruction is restarted.

4.6.4 MOV or POP to SS Masks Some Interrupts and Exceptions

*   Software that needs to change stack segments often uses a pair of instructions; for example : MOV SS, AX MOV ESP, StackTop If an interrupt or exception is processed after SS has been changed but before ESP has received the corresponding change, the two parts of the stack pointer SS :ESP are inconsistent for the duration of the interrupt handler or exception handler.
*   To prevent this situation, the 80386, after both a MOV to SS and a POP to SS instruction, inhibits NMI, INTR, debug exceptions, and single-step traps at the instruction boundary following the instruction that changes SS.
*   Some exceptions may still occur; namely, page fault and general protection fault. Always use the 80386 LSS instruction, and the problem will not occur.

4.7 PRIORITY AMONG SIMULTANEOUS INTERRUPTS AND EXCEPTIONS

If more than one interrupt or exception is pending at an instruction boundary, the processor services one of them at a time. The priority among classes of interrupt and exception sources is shown in Table 4.2. The processor first services a pending interrupt or exception from the class that has the highest priority, transferring control to the first instruction of the interrupt handler. Lower priority exceptions are discarded; lower priority interrupts are held pending. Discarded exceptions will be rediscovered when the interrupt handler returns control to the point of interruption.

4.8 INTERRUPT DESCRIPTOR TABLE

- The Interrupt Descriptor Table (IDT) associates each interrupt or exception identifier with a descriptor for the instructions that service the associated event.

- Like the GDT and LDTs, the IDT is an array of 8-byte descriptors. Unlike the GDT and LDTs, the first entry of the IDT may contain a descriptor.

- To form an index into the IDT, the processor multiplies the interrupt or exception identifier by eight.

- Because there are only 256 identifiers, the IDT need not contain more than 256 descriptors. It can contain fewer than 256 entries; entries are required only for interrupt identifiers that are actually used. The IDT may reside anywhere in physical memory.

- As Fig. 4.3 shows, the processor locates the IDT by means of the IDT register (IDTR). The instructions LIDT and SIDT operate on the IDTR. Both instructions have one explicit operand : the address in memory of a 6-byte area.

- Fig. 4.4 shows the format of this area. LIDT (Load IDT register) loads the IDT register with the linear base address and limit values contained in the memory operand.

- This instruction can be executed only when the CPL is zero. It is normally used by the initialization logic of an operating system when creating an IDT.

- An operating system may also use it to change from one IDT to another. SIDT (Store IDT register) copies the base and limit value stored in IDTR to a memory location. This instruction can be executed at any privilege level.

Table 4.2 : Priority among Simultaneous Interrupts and Exceptions

Priority	Class of Interrupt or Exception
HIGHEST	Faults except debug faults
	Trap instructions INTO, INT n, INT 3
	Debug traps for this instruction
	Debug faults for next instruction, NMI interrupt
LOWEST	INTR interrupt

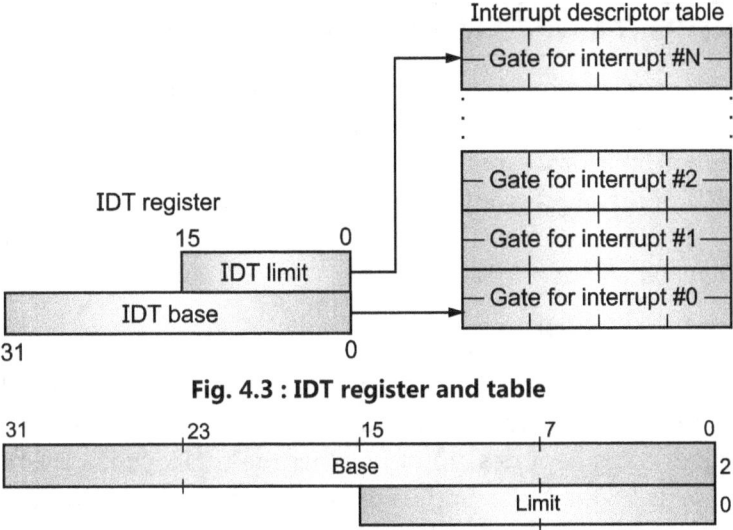

Fig. 4.3 : IDT register and table

31	23	15	7	0	
		Base			2
			Limit		0

Fig. 4.4 : Pseudo-descriptor format for LIDT and SIDT

4.9 IDT DESCRIPTORS

The IDT may contain any of three kinds of descriptor :

- Task gates

- Interrupt gates

- Trap gates

Fig. 4.5 illustrates the format of task gates and 80386 interrupt gates and trap gates.

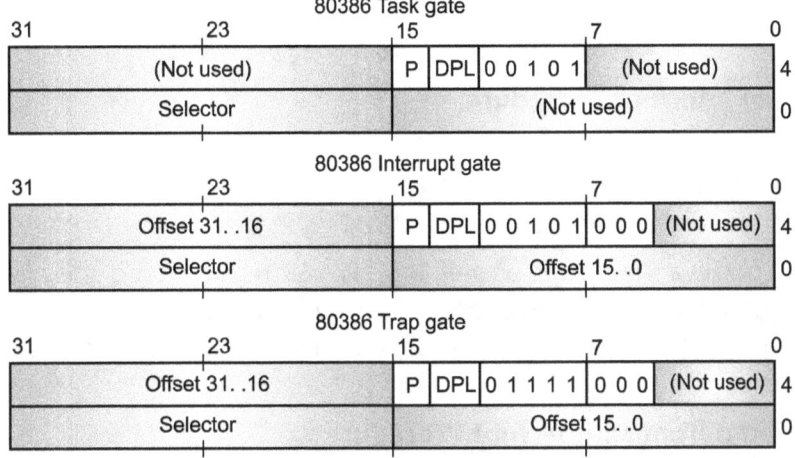

Fig. 4.5 : 80386 IDT gate descriptors

4.10 INTERRUPT TASKS AND INTERRUPT PROCEDURES

Just as a CALL instruction can call either a procedure or a task, so an interrupt or exception can "call" an interrupt handler that is either a procedure or a task. When responding to an interrupt or exception, the processor uses the interrupt or exception identifier to index a descriptor in the IDT. If the processor indexes to an interrupt gate or trap gate, it invokes the handler in a manner similar to a CALL to a call gate. If the processor finds a task gate, it causes a task switch in a manner similar to a CALL to a task gate.

4.10.1 Interrupt Procedures

An interrupt gate or trap gate points indirectly to a procedure which will execute in the context of the currently executing task as illustrated by Fig. 4.6. The selector of the gate points to an executable-segment descriptor in either the GDT or the current LDT. The offset field of the gate points to the beginning of the interrupt or exception handling procedure. The 80386 invokes an interrupt or exception handling procedure in much the same manner as it CALLs a procedure; the differences are explained in the following sections.

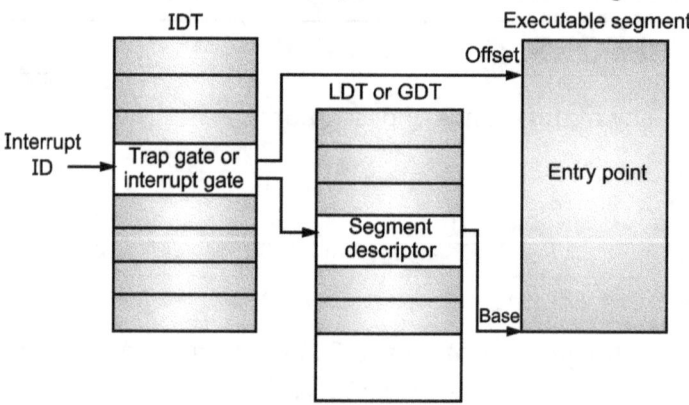

Fig. 4.6 : Interrupt vectoring for procedures

4.10.1.1 Stack of Interrupt Procedure

* Just as with a control transfer due to a CALL instruction, a control transfer to an interrupt or exception handling procedure uses the stack to store the information needed for returning to the original procedure.

* As Fig. 4.7 shows, an interrupt pushes the EFLAGS register onto the stack before the pointer to the interrupted instruction. Certain types of exceptions also cause an error code to be pushed on the stack. An exception handler can use the error code to help diagnose the exception.

4.10.1.2 Returning from an Interrupt Procedure

* An interrupt procedure also differs from a normal procedure in the method of leaving the procedure.

- The IRET instruction is used to exit from an interrupt procedure. IRET is similar to RET except that IRET increments EIP by an extra four bytes (because of the flags on the stack) and moves the saved flags into the EFLAGS register. The IOPL field of EFLAGS is changed only if the CPL is zero. The IF flag is changed only if CPL ≤ IOPL.

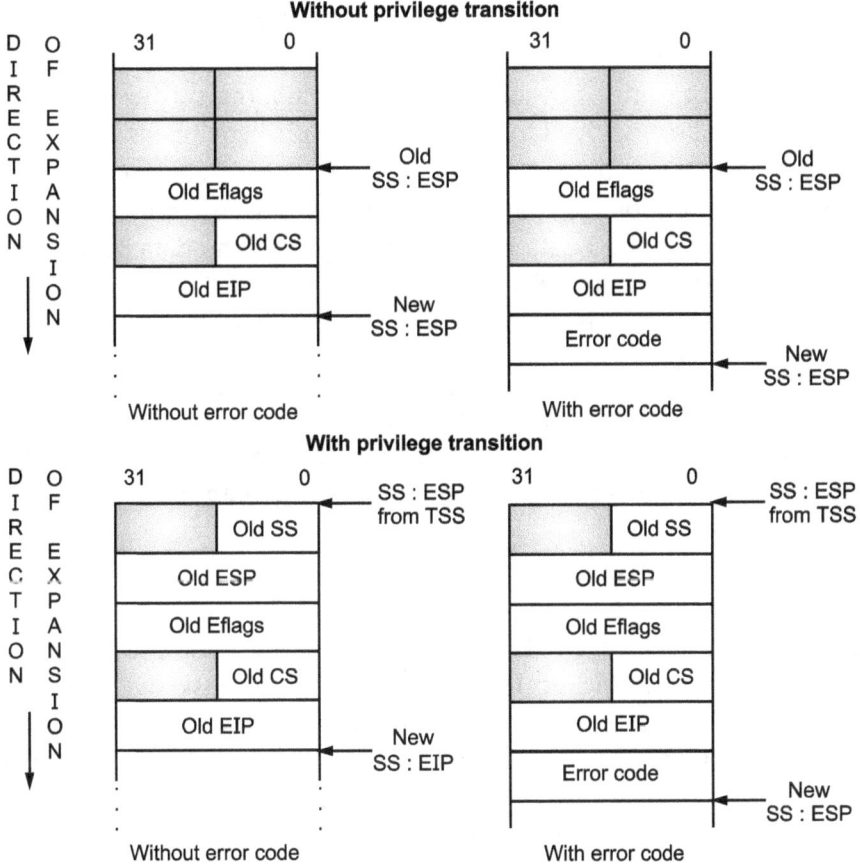

Fig. 4.7 : Stack layout after exception of interrupt

4.10.1.3 Flags Usage by Interrupt Procedure

- Interrupts that vector through either interrupt gates or trap gates cause TF (the trap flag) to be reset after the current value of TF is saved on the stack as part of EFLAGS. By this action the processor prevents debugging activity that uses single-stepping from affecting interrupt response.

- A subsequent IRET instruction restores TF to the value in the EFLAGS image on the stack. The difference between an interrupt gate and a trap gate is in the effect on IF (the interrupt-enable flag).

- An interrupt that vectors through an interrupt gate resets IF, thereby preventing other interrupts from interfering with the current interrupt handler. A subsequent IRET instruction restores IF to the value in the EFLAGS image on the stack. An interrupt through a trap gate does not change IF.

4.10.1.4 Protection in Interrupt Procedures

The privilege rule that governs interrupt procedures is similar to that for procedure calls : the CPU does not permit an interrupt to transfer control to a procedure in a segment of lesser privilege (numerically greater privilege level) than the current privilege level. An attempt to violate this rule results in a general protection exception. Because occurrence of interrupts is not generally predictable, this privilege rule effectively imposes restrictions on the privilege levels at which interrupt and exception handling procedures can execute. Either of the following strategies can be employed to ensure that the privilege rule is never violated.

- Place the handler in a conforming segment. This strategy suits the handlers for certain exceptions (divide error, for example). Such a handler must use only the data available to it from the stack. If it needed data from a data segment, the data segment would have to have privilege level three, thereby making it unprotected.
- Place the handler procedure in a privilege level zero segment.

4.10.2 Interrupt Tasks

A task gate in the IDT points indirectly to a task, as Fig. 4.8 illustrates. The selector of the gate points to a TSS descriptor in the GDT. When an interrupt or exception vectors to a task gate in the IDT, a task switch results. Handling an interrupt with a separate task offers two advantages :

- The entire context is saved automatically.
- The interrupt handler can be isolated from other tasks by giving it a separate address space, either via its LDT or via its page directory. The interrupt task returns to the interrupted task by executing an IRET instruction. If the task switch is caused by an exception that has an error code, the processor automatically pushes the error code onto the stack that corresponds to the privilege level of the first instruction to be executed in the interrupt task. When interrupt tasks are used in an operating system for the 80386, there are actually two schedulers : the software scheduler (part of the operating system) and the hardware scheduler (part of the processor's interrupt mechanism). The design of the software scheduler should account for the fact that the hardware scheduler may dispatch an interrupt task whenever interrupts are enabled.

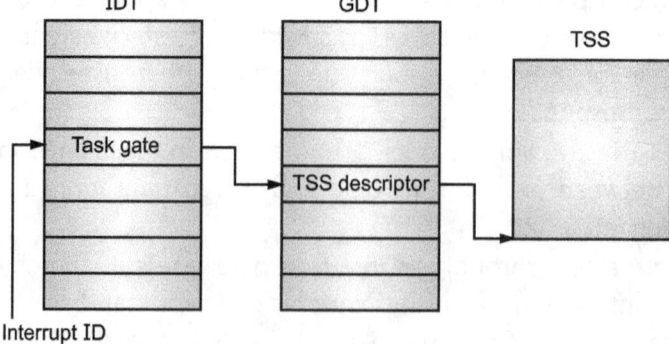

Fig. 4.8 : Interrupt vectoring for tasks

4.11 ERROR CODE

With exceptions that relate to a specific segment, the processor pushes an error code onto the stack of the exception handler (whether procedure or task). The error code has the format shown in Fig. 4.9. The format of the error code resembles that of a selector; however, instead of an RPL field, the error code contains two one-bit items :

- The processor sets the EXT bit if an event external to the program caused the exception.
- The processor sets the I-bit (IDT-bit) if the index portion of the error code refers to a gate descriptor in the IDT.

If the I-bit is not set, the TI bit indicates whether the error code refers to the GDT (value 0) or to the LDT (value 1). The remaining 14 bits are the upper 14 bits of the segment selector involved. In some cases, the error code on the stack is null, i.e., all bits in the low-order word are zero.

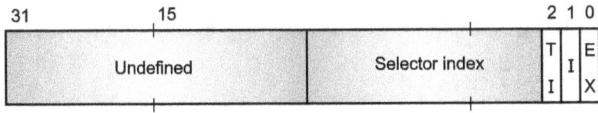

Fig. 4.9 : Error code format

4.12 EXCEPTION CONDITIONS

The following sections describe each of the possible exception conditions in detail. Each description classifies the exception as a fault, trap, or abort. This classification provides information needed by systems programmers for restarting the procedure in which the exception occurred :

Faults : The CS and EIP values saved when a fault is reported point to the instruction causing the fault.

Traps : The CS and EIP values stored when the trap is reported point to the instruction dynamically after the instruction causing the trap. If a trap is detected during an instruction that alters program flow, the reported values of CS and EIP reflect the alteration of program flow. For example, if a trap is detected in a JMP instruction, the CS and EIP values pushed onto the stack point to the target of the JMP, not to the instruction after the JMP.

Aborts : An abort is an exception that permits neither precise location of the instruction causing the exception nor restart of the program that caused the exception. Aborts are used to report severe errors, such as hardware errors and inconsistent or illegal values in system tables.

4.12.1 Interrupt 0 — Divide Error

The divide-error fault occurs during a DIV or an IDIV instruction when the divisor is zero.

4.12.2 Interrupt 1 — Debug Exceptions

The processor triggers this interrupt for a number of conditions; whether the exception is a fault or a trap depends on the condition :

- Instruction address breakpoint fault.
- Data address breakpoint trap.
- General detect fault.
- Single-step trap.
- Task-switch breakpoint trap.

The processor does not push an error code for this exception. An exception handler can examine the debug registers to determine which condition caused the exception. Refer to Chapter 12 for more detailed information about debugging and the debug registers.

4.12.3 Interrupt 3 —— Breakpoint

The INT 3 instruction causes this trap. The INT 3 instruction is one byte long, which makes it easy to replace an opcode in an executable segment with the breakpoint opcode. The operating system or a debugging subsystem can use a data-segment alias for an executable segment to place an INT 3 anywhere it is convenient to arrest normal execution so that some sort of special processing can be performed. Debuggers typically use breakpoints as a way of displaying registers, variables, etc., at crucial points in a task. The saved CS :EIP value points to the byte following the breakpoint. If a debugger replaces a planted breakpoint with a valid opcode, it must subtract one from the saved EIP value before returning.

4.12.4 Interrupt 4 —— Overflow

This trap occurs when the processor encounters an INTO instruction and the OF (overflow) flag is set. Since signed arithmetic and unsigned arithmetic both use the same arithmetic instructions, the processor cannot determine which is intended and therefore does not cause overflow exceptions automatically. Instead it merely sets OF when the results, if interpreted as signed numbers, would be out of range. When doing arithmetic on signed operands, careful programmers and compilers either test OF directly or use the INTO instruction.

4.12.5 Interrupt 5 —— Bounds Check

This fault occurs when the processor, while executing a BOUND instruction, finds that the operand exceeds the specified limits. A program can use the BOUND instruction to check a signed array index against signed limits defined in a block of memory.

4.12.6 Interrupt 6 —— Invalid Opcode

This fault occurs when an invalid opcode is detected by the execution unit. (The exception is not detected until an attempt is made to execute the invalid opcode; i.e., prefetching an invalid opcode does not cause this exception.) No error code is pushed on the stack. The exception can be handled within the same task. This exception also occurs when the type of operand is invalid for the given opcode. Examples include an intersegment JMP referencing a register operand, or an LES instruction with a register source operand.

4.12.7 Interrupt 7 —— Coprocessor Not Available

This exception occurs in either of two conditions :

- The processor encounters an ESC (escape) instruction, and the EM (emulate) bit ofCR0 (control register zero) is set.
- The processor encounters either the WAIT instruction or an ESC instruction, and both the MP (monitor coprocessor) and TS (task switched) bits of CR0 are set.

4.12.8 Interrupt 8 —— Double Fault

Normally, when the processor detects an exception while trying to invoke the handler for a prior exception, the two exceptions can be handled serially. If, however, the processor cannot handle them serially, it signals the double-fault exception instead. To determine when two faults are to be signalled as a double fault, the 80386 divides the exceptions into three classes : benign exceptions, contributory exceptions, and page faults. The processor always pushes an error code onto the stack of the double-fault handler; however, the error code is always zero. The faulting instruction may not be restarted. If any other exception occurs while attempting to invoke the double-fault handler, the processor shuts down.

4.12.9 Interrupt 9 —— Coprocessor Segment Overrun

This exception is raised in protected mode if the 80386 detects a page or segment violation while transferring the middle portion of a coprocessor operand to the NPX. This exception is avoidable.

4.12.10 Interrupt 10 —— Invalid TSS

Interrupt 10 occurs if during a task switch the new TSS is invalid. An error code is pushed onto the stack to help identify the cause of the fault. The EXT bit indicates whether the exception was caused by a condition outside the control of the program; e.g., an external interrupt via a task gate triggered a switch to an invalid TSS. This fault can occur either in the context of the original task or in the context of the new task. Until the processor has completely verified the presence of the new TSS, the exception occurs in the context of the original task. Once the existence of the new TSS is verified, the task switch is considered complete; i.e., TR is updated and, if the switch is due to a CALL or interrupt, the backlink of the new TSS is set to the old TSS. Any errors discovered by the processor after this point are handled in the context of the new task. To insure a proper TSS to process it, the handler for exception 10 must be a task invoked via a task gate.

4.12.11 Interrupt 11 —— Segment Not Present

Exception 11 occurs when the processor detects that the present bit of a descriptor is zero. The processor can trigger this fault in any of these cases :

- While attempting to load the CS, DS, ES, FS, or GS registers; loading the SS register, however, causes a stack fault.

- While attempting loading the LDT register with an LLDT instruction; loading the LDT register during a task switch operation, however, causes the "invalid TSS" exception.

- While attempting to use a gate descriptor that is marked not-present. This fault is restartable. If the exception handler makes the segment present and returns, the interrupted program will resume execution. If a not-present exception occurs during a task switch, not all the steps of the task switch are complete. During a task switch, the processor first loads all the segment registers, then checks their contents for validity. If a not-present exception is discovered, the remaining segment registers have not been checked and therefore may not be usable for referencing memory. The not-present handler should not rely on being able to use the values found in CS, SS, DS, ES, FS, and GS without causing another exception. The exception handler should check all segment registers before trying to resume the new task; otherwise, general protection faults may result later under conditions that make diagnosis more difficult. There are three ways to handle this case :

➢ Handle the not-present fault with a task. The task switch back to the interrupted task will cause the processor to check the registers as it loads them from the TSS.

➢ PUSH and POP all segment registers. Each POP causes the processor to check the new contents of the segment register.

➢ Scrutinize the contents of each segment-register image in the TSS, simulating the test that the processor makes when it loads a segment register.

This exception pushes an error code onto the stack. The EXT bit of the error code is set if an event external to the program caused an interrupt that subsequently referenced a not-present segment. The I-bit is set if the error code refers to an IDT entry, e.g., an INT instruction referencing a not-present gate. An operating system typically uses the "segment not present" exception to implement virtual memory at the segment level. A not-present indication in a gate descriptor, however, usually does not indicate that a segment is not present (because gates do not necessarily correspond to segments). Not-present gates may be used by an operating system to trigger exceptions of special significance to the operating system.

4.12.12 Interrupt 12 — Stack Exception

A stack fault occurs in either of two general conditions :

• As a result of a limit violation in any operation that refers to the SS register. This includes stack-oriented instructions such as POP, PUSH, ENTER and LEAVE, as well as other memory references that implicitly use SS (for example, MOV AX, [BP+6]). ENTER causes this exception when the stack is too small for the indicated local-variable space.

• When attempting to load the SS register with a descriptor that is marked not-present but is otherwise valid. This can occur in a task switch, an interlevel CALL, an interlevel return, an LSS instruction, or a MOV or POP instruction to SS. When the processor detects a stack exception, it pushes an error code onto the stack of the exception handler. If the exception is due to a not-present stack segment or to overflow of the new stack during an inter level CALL, the error code contains a selector to the segment in question (the exception handler can test the present bit in the descriptor to determine which exception occurred); otherwise the error code is zero. An instruction that causes this fault is restartable in all cases. The return pointer pushed onto the exception handler's stack points to the instruction that needs to be restarted. This instruction is usually the one that caused the exception; however, in the case of a stack exception due to loading of a not-present stack-segment descriptor during a task switch, the indicated instruction is the first instruction of the new task. When a stack fault occurs during a task switch, the segment registers may not be usable for referencing memory. During a task switch, the selector values are loaded before the descriptors are checked. If a stack fault is discovered, the remaining segment registers have not been checked and therefore may not be usable for referencing memory. The stack fault handler should not rely on being able to use the values found in CS, SS, DS, ES, FS, and GS without causing another exception. The exception handler should check all segment registers before trying to resume the new task; otherwise, general protection faults may result later under conditions that make diagnosis more difficult.

4.12.13 Interrupt 13 —— General Protection Exception

All protection violations that do not cause another exception cause a general protection exception. This includes (but is not limited to) :

- Exceeding segment limit when using CS, DS, ES, FS, or GS.
- Exceeding segment limit when referencing a descriptor table.
- Transferring control to a segment that is not executable.
- Writing into a read-only data segment or into a code segment.
- Reading from an execute-only segment.
- Loading the SS register with a read-only descriptor (unless the selector comes from the TSS during a task switch, in which case a TSS exception occurs.
- Loading SS, DS, ES, FS, or GS with the descriptor of a system segment.
- Loading DS, ES, FS, or GS with the descriptor of an executable segment that is not also readable.
- Loading SS with the descriptor of an executable segment.
- Accessing memory via DS, ES, FS, or GS when the segment register contains a null selector.
- Switching to a busy task.
- Violating privilege rules.
- Loading CR0 with PG=1 and PE=0.
- Interrupt or exception via trap or interrupt gate from V86 mode to privilege level other than zero.
- Exceeding the instruction length limit of 15 bytes (this can occur only if redundant prefixes are placed before an instruction).

The general protection exception is a fault. In response to a general protection exception, the processor pushes an error code onto the exception handler's stack. If loading a descriptor causes the exception, the error code contains a selector to the descriptor; otherwise, the error code is null. The source of the selector in an error code may be any of the following :

- An operand of the instruction.

- A selector from a gate that is the operand of the instruction.

- A selector from a TSS involved in a task switch.

4.12.14 Interrupt 14 — Page Fault

This exception occurs when paging is enabled (PG=1) and the processor detects one of the following conditions while translating a linear address to a physical address :

- The page-directory or page-table entry needed for the address translation has zero in its present bit.

- The current procedure does not have sufficient privilege to access the indicated page. The processor makes available to the page fault handler two items of information that aid in diagnosing the exception and recovering from it :

Field	Value	Description
U/S	0	The access causing the fault originated when the processor was executing in supervior mode.
	1	The access causing the fault originated when the processor was executing in user mode.
W/R	0	The access causing the fault was a read.
	1	The access causing the fault was a write.
P	0	The fault was caused by a not-present page.
	1	The fault was caused by a page-level protection violation.

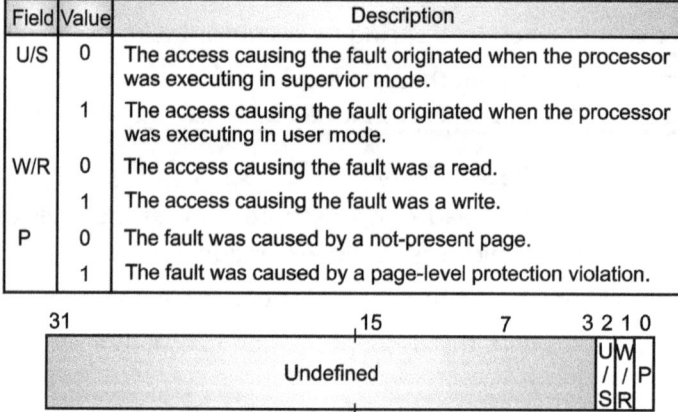

Fig. 4.10 : Page-fault error code format

- An error code on the stack. The error code for a page fault has a format different from that for other exceptions (see Fig. 4.10). The error code tells the exception handler three things :

    ➤ Whether the exception was due to a not present page or to an access rights violation.

    ➤ Whether the processor was executing at user or supervisor level at the time of the exception.

    ➤ Whether the memory access that caused the exception was a read or write.

- CR2 (control register two). The processor stores in CR2 the linear address used in the access that caused the exception (see Fig. 4.11). The exception handler can use this address to locate the corresponding page directory and page table entries. If another page fault can occur during execution of the page fault handler, the handler should push CR2 onto the stack.

4.12.14.1 Page Fault during Task Switch

The processor may access any of four segments during a task switch :

- Writes the state of the original task in the TSS of that task.

- Reads the GDT to locate the TSS descriptor of the new task.

- Reads the TSS of the new task to check the types of segment descriptors from the TSS.

- May read the LDT of the new task in order to verify the segment registers stored in the new TSS.

A page fault can result from accessing any of these segments. In the latter two cases the exception occurs in the context of the new task. The instruction pointer refers to the next instruction of the new task, not to the instruction that caused the task switch. If the design of the operating system permits page faults to occur during task-switches, the page-fault handler should be invoked via a task gate.

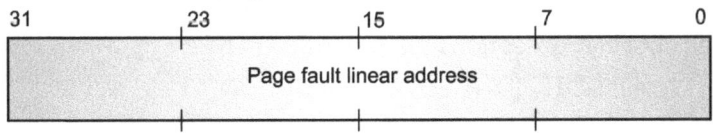

Fig. 4.11 : CR2 format

4.12.14.2 Page Fault with Inconsistent Stack Pointer

Special care should be taken to ensure that a page fault does not cause the processor to use an invalid stack pointer (SS :ESP). Software written for earlier processors in the 8086 family often uses a pair of instructions to change to a new stack; for example :

    MOV SS, AX

    MOV SP, StackTop

With the 80386, because the second instruction accesses memory, it is possible to get a page fault after SS has been changed but before SP has received the corresponding change. At this point, the two parts of the stack pointer SS :SP (or, for 32-bit programs, SS :ESP) are inconsistent. The processor does not use the inconsistent stack pointer if the handling of the page fault causes a stack switch to a well defined stack (i.e., the handler is a task or a more privileged procedure). However, if the page fault handler is invoked by a trap or interrupt gate and the page fault occurs at the same privilege level as the page fault handler, the processor will attempt to use the stack indicated by the current (invalid) stack pointer. In systems that implement paging and that handle page faults within the faulting task (with trap or interrupt gates), software that executes at the same privilege level as the page fault handler should initialize a new stack by using the new LSS instruction rather than an instruction pair shown above. When the page fault handler executes at privilege level zero (the normal case), the scope of the problem is limited to privilege-level zero code, typically the kernel of the operating system.

4.12.15 Interrupt 16 — Coprocessor Error

The 80386 reports this exception when it detects a signal from the 80287 or 80387 on the 80386's $\overline{\text{ERROR}}$ input pin. The 80386 tests this pin only at the beginning of certain ESC instructions and when it encounters a WAIT instruction while the EM bit of the MSW is zero (no emulation).

EXERCISE

1. Explain with the help of diagram Memory-Mapped I/O for 80386.
2. What are maskable and non maskable interrupts? Explain in detail.
3. What are string I/O instructions or block I/O instructions.
4. Write a note on Block I/O instructions.
5. Explain CPL & IOPL in detail.
6. With the help of diagram explain in detail I/O Address Bit Map.
7. How are Interrupts and exceptions identified?
8. What is IDT? Explain GDTR, IDTR, LDTR in detail.
9. Draw and explain IDT register in detail.
10. Explain Task gate descriptor in detail.
11. Explain Interrupt gate descriptor in detail.
12. Explain Trap gate descriptor in detail.
13. With the help of diagram explain Interrupt Vectoring for Procedures.
14. Write a note on Interrupt Vectoring for Tasks.
15. Draw and explain Error Code Format.
16. Classify the exception as a fault, trap, or abort in detail.
17. Explain in detail Page-Fault Error Code Format.
18. What is interrupt 0, interrupt 11, and interrupt 13?
19. Explain I/O instructions in details.
20. Explain Page Fault with Inconsistent Stack Pointer in detail.
21. Explain IDT descriptor in detail.
22. Write a note on exception task and exception conditions.

CHAPTER 5

INITIALIZATION, DEBUGGING, VIRTUAL 8086 MODE

5.1 PROCESSOR STATE AFTER RESET

A self-test may be requested at power-up. The self-test is requested by asserting the signal on the BUSY # pin during the falling edge of the RESET# signal. It is the responsibility of the hardware designer to provide the request for self-test, if desired. Reset initialization takes 350 to 450 CLK2 clock periods. If the self-test is selected, it takes about 2^{20} clock periods.

The EAX register is clear if the 386 DX microprocessor passed the test. A non-zero value in the EAX register after self-test indicates the processor is faulty. If the self-test is not requested, the contents of the EAX register after reset initialization are undefined. The DX register holds a component identifier and revision number after reset initialization, as shown in Fig. 5.1. The DH register contains the value 3, which indicates a 386 DX microprocessor. The DL register contains a unique identifier of the revision level.

The state of the CRO register following power-up is shown in Fig. 5.2. These states put the processor into real-address mode with paging disabled.

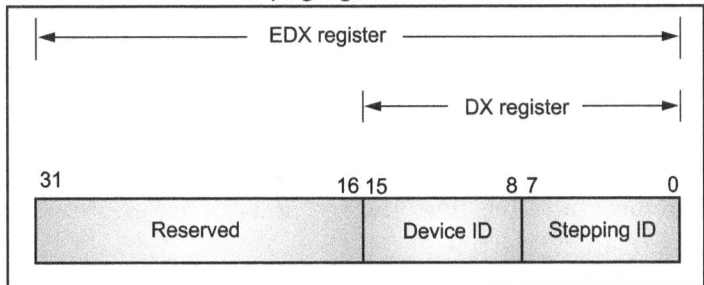

Fig. 5.1 : Contents of the EDX register after reset

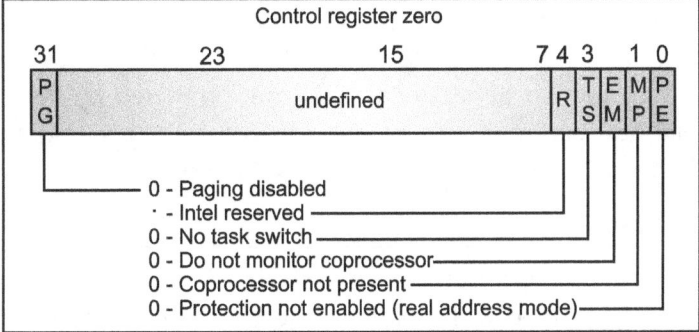

Fig. 5.2 : Contents of the CRO register after reset

The state of the EBX, ECX, ESI, EDI, EBP, ESP, GDTR, LDTR, TR, and debug registers is undefined following power-up. Software should not depend on any undefined states. The state of the flags and other registers following power-up is shown in Table 5.1.

Note that the invisible parts of the CS and DS segment registers are initialized to values which allow execution to begin, even though segments have not been defined. The base address for the code segment is set to 64K below the top of the physical address space, which allows room for a ROM to hold the initialization software. The base address for the data segments are set to the bottom of the physical address space.

Table 5.1 : Processor State Following Power-Up

Register	State (Hexadecimal)
EFLAGS	XXXX0002H[1]
EIP	0000FFF0H
CS	0F000H[2]
DS	0000H[3]
SS	0000H
ES	0000H[3]
PS	0000H
GS	0000H
IDTR (base)	00000000H
IDTR (limit)	03FFH
DR7	0000H

To preserve these addresses, no instruction which loads the segment registers should be executed until a descriptor table has been defined and its base address and limit have been loaded into the GDTR register.

5.2 SOFTWARE INITIALIZATION IN REAL-ADDRESS MODE

After reset initialization, software sets up data structures needed for the processor to perform basic system functions, such as handling interrupts. If the processor remains in real-address mode, software sets up data structures in the form used by the 8086 processor. If the processor is going to operate in protected mode, software sets up data structures in the form used by the 80286 and 386 DX microprocessors, then switches modes.

5.2.1 System Tables

In real-address mode, no descriptor tables are used. The interrupt vector table, which starts at address 0, needs to be loaded with pointers to exception and interrupt handlers before interrupts can be enabled. The NMI interrupt is always enabled. If the interrupt vector table and the NMI interrupt handler need to be loaded into RAM, there will be a period of time following reset initialization when an NMI interrupt cannot be handled.

5.2.2 NMI Interrupt

Hardware must provide a mechanism to prevent an NMI interrupt from being generated while software is unable to handle it. For example, the interrupt vector table and NMI interrupt handler can be provided in ROM. This allows an NMI interrupt to be handled immediately after reset initialization. Another solution would be to provide a mechanism which passes the NMI signal through an AND gate controlled by a bit in an I/O port.

Hardware can clear the bit when the processor is reset, and software can set the bit when it is ready to handle NMI interrupts.

5.2.3 First Instruction

When Execution begins with the instruction addressed by the initial contents of the CS and IP registers. To allow the initialization software to be placed in a ROM at the top of the address space, the high 12 bits of addresses issued for the code segment are set, until the first instruction which loads the CS register, such as a far jump or call. As a result, instruction fetching begins from address 0FFFFFFF0H. Because the size of the ROM is unknown, the first instruction is intended to be a jump to the beginning of the initialization software. Only near jumps may be performed within the ROM-based software. After a far jump is executed, addresses issued for the code segment are clear in their high 12 bits.

5.3 SWITCHING TO PROTECTED MODE

When switching to protected mode, a minimum set of system data structures must be created, and a minimum number of registers must be initialized.

5.3.1 System Tables

To allow protected mode software to access programs and data, at least one descriptor table, the GDT, and two descriptors must be created. Descriptors are needed for a code segment and a data segment. The stack can be placed in a normal read/write data segment, so no descriptor for the stack is required. Before the GDT can be used, the base address and limit for the GDT must be loaded into the GDTR register using an LGDT instruction.

5.3.2 NMI Interrupt

If hardware allows NMI interrupts to be generated, the IDT and a gate for the NMI interrupt handler need to be created. Before the IDT can be used, the base address and limit for the IDT must be loaded into the IDTR register using an LIDT instruction.

5.3.3 PE Bit

Protected mode is entered by setting the PE bit in the CR0 register. Either an LMSW or MOV CR0 instruction may be used to set this bit it is necessary to discard the instructions which already have been read into the processor. A JMP instruction immediately after the LMSW instruction changes the flow of execution, so it has the effect of emptying the processor of instructions which have been fetched or decoded.

After entering protected mode, the segment registers continue to hold the contents they had in real-address mode. Software should reload all the segment registers. Execution in protected mode begins with a CPL of 0.

5.4 SOFTWARE INITIALIZATION IN PROTECTED MODE

The data structures needed in protected mode are determined by the memory-management features which are used. The processor supports segmentation models which range from a single, uniform address space to a highly structured model with several independent, protected address spaces for each task. Paging can be enabled for allowing access to large data structures which are partly in memory and partly on disk.

5.4.1 Segmentation

A flat model without paging only requires a GDT with one code and one data segment descriptor. A flat model with paging requires code and data descriptors for supervisor mode and another set of code and data descriptors for user mode. In addition, it requires a page directory and at least one second-level page table.

A multi segmented model may require additional segments for the operating system, as well as segments and LDTs for each application program. LDTs require segment descriptors in the GDT. Most operating systems, such as OS/2, allocate new segments and LDTs as they are needed. This provides maximum flexibility for handling a dynamic programming environment.

5.4.2 Paging

Unlike segmentation, paging is controlled by a mode bit. If the PG bit in the CR0 register is clear, the paging mechanism is completely absent from the processor architecture. If the PG bit is set, paging is enabled. The bit may be set using a MOV CR0 instruction. Before setting the PG bit, the following conditions must be true :

- Software has created at least two page tables, the page directory and at least one second-level page table.
- The PDBR register (same as the CR3 register) is loaded with the base address of the page directory.
- The processor is in protected mode (paging is not available in real-address mode). If all other restrictions are met, the PG and PE bits can be set at the same time.

As with the PE bit, setting the PG bit must be followed immediately with a JMP instruction.

5.4.3 Tasks

If the multitasking mechanism is used, a TSS and a TSS descriptor for the initialization software must be created. TSS descriptors must not be marked as busy when they are created; TSS descriptors should be marked as busy only as a side-effect of performing a task switch. As with descriptors for LDTs, TSS descriptors reside in the GDT. The LTR instruction is used to load a selector for the TSS descriptor of the initialization software into the TR register. This instruction marks the TSS descriptor as busy, but does not perform a task switch. The selector must be loaded before performing the first task switch, because a task switch copies the current task state into the TSS. After the LTR instruction has been used, further operations on the TR register are performed by task switching. As with segments and LDTs, TSSs and TSS descriptors can be either pre-allocated or allocated as needed.

5.5 INITIALIZATION EXAMPLE

; ***

; This is an example of startup code to put either 80386/80376

; into flat mode. All of memory is treated as simple, linear RAM. There are no interrupt routines. The Builder creates the

GDT-alias and IDT-alias and places them, by default, in GDT[11 and GDT[21. Other entries in the GDT are specified in the Build file. After initialization, it jumps to a C startup routine. To use this template, change this jmp address to that of your code, or m~ke the label of your code "c_startup".

; ***

```
NAME FLAT                      ; name of object module
EXTRN   c_startup : near       ; this is the label jmped to after init
Pe_flag    que 1
data_sec   equ 20h             ; assume code is GDT[3], data GDT[4]
INILCODE SEGMENT ER PUBLIC USE32 ; Segment base at 0ffffff80h
PUBLIC    GDLDESC
Mov, edx, e3ffect gdt_desc xor ebx, ebx
gdLdesc    dq
mov bh, ah.mov bl, al db 67h
PUBLIC                         START
db 66h
start :
```

```
        cld                          ; clear direction flag
        Igdt cs : [ebx] smsw ax      ; check for processor (8037b) at reset
        test bl, 1                   ; use SMSW ratherthan MOV for speed
        jnz pestrat
realstart :                          ; is an 8038 b and in real mode
        db 66h                       ; force the next operand into 32-bit mode.
        mov eax, offset gdt_desc     ; move address of the GDT descriptor into eax
        xor ebx, ebx                 ; clear ebx
        mov bh, ah                   ; load 8 bits of address into bh
        mov bl, al                   ; load 8 bits of address into bl
        ab b7h
        ab bbh                       ; use the 32-bit form of LGDT to load
        lgdt cs : [ebx]              ; the 32-bits of address into the GDTR
        smsw ax                      ; go into protected mode (set PE bit)
        or al, pe_flag               ; only change the PE bit, leave other bits unchanged
        lmsw ax
        jmp next                     ; flush prefetch queue
pestart :
        mov edx,eax
        mov ebx,offset gdt_desc
        xor eax,eax
        mov ax,bx                    ; lowerportion of address only
        19dt cs :[eaxl
        xor ebx,ebx                  ; initialize data selectors
        mov bl,data_selc             ; GDT[3]
        mov ds,bx
        mov ss,bx
        mov es,bx
        mov fs,bx
        mov gs,bx
```

```
        jmp pejump
next :
        xor ebx,ebx                 ; initialize data selectors
        mov bl,data_selc            ; GDT[3]
        mov ds,bx
        mov ss,bx
        moves, bx
        mov fX,bx
        mov gs,bx
        db 66h                      ; forthe 80386, need to make a 32-bit jump
pejump :
        jmp far ptr c_startup       ; but the 80376 is already 32-bit.
        org 70h                     ; only if segment base is atOffffff80h
        jmp short start
INIT_CODE                 ENDS
END
```

This code should be linked with the application for boot loadable code. The following code illustrates a dummy application.

```
$title("Example Startup Code,Copyright 1989, Intel Corporation")
        name        dummy_application;
data      segment rw publich use32
dontworry     db      8 dup  (?)
be happy      db      4ah, 69h,6dh, 20h, 4bh, 26h, 52h
data    ends
code32        segment er public use32
        assume   ds :data, es :data
        public    int0,int1_3,int2,int4,int5,int6,int7,int8,int9
        public    int10,int11,int12,int13,int14,int16
        public    c_startup
data_vers     db       '5/3/89', ' Ver 1.00'
              db ' IntelCorporation '
```

c_startup :

        hIt

or aI, pe_flag Imsw, ax

imp next

smsw bx test

bl,l jnz

pestart

realstart :   db 66h

mov eax,offset gdt_desc xor ebx,ebx

mov bh,ah mov bl,al db 67h

db 66h

Igdt cs : [ebxl smsw ax

or aI, pe_flag Imsw ax

jmp   next

pe_flag equ 1

data_sec equ 20h ; assume code is GDT[31, data GDT[41

INILCODE SEGMENT ER PUBLIC USE32 ; Segment base at 0ffffff80h

PUBLIC   GDLDESC

Mov, edx, e3ffect gdt_desc xor ebx, ebx

gdLdesc   dq

mov bh, ah.mov bl, al db 67h

PUBLIC   START

db66h

start :

    cld

Igdt cs : [ebx1 smsw ax

or aI, pe_flag Imsw, ax

imp next

smsw bx test

bl,l jnz

```
pestart
realstart :                          db 66h
mov eax,offset gdt_desc xor ebx,ebx
mov bh,ah mov bl,al db 67h
db  66h
Igdt cs : [ebxl smsw ax
or aI, pe_flag Imsw ax
jmp     next
```

clear direction flag Check for processor (80376) at reset use SMSW ratherthan MOV for speed is an 80386 and in real mode. Force the next operand into 32-bit mode. move address of the GDT descriptor into eax clear ebx. Load 8 bits of address into bh load 8 bitsof address into bl. Use the 32-bit form of LGDT to load the 32-bits of address into the GDTR go into protected mode (set PE bit). Only change the PE bit, leave other bits unchanged flush prefetch queue

```
pestart :
    mov edx,eax
    mov ebx,offset gdt_desc
    xor eax,eax
    mov ax,bx                    ;  lowerportion of address only
19dt cs :[eaxl
xor ebx,ebx                      initialize data selectors
mov bl,data_selc                 GDT[31
mov ds,bx
mov ss,bx
mov es,bx
mov fs,bx
mov gs,bx
jmp pejump
                                 next :
xor ebx,ebx                      initialize data selectors
mov bl,data_selc                 GDT[31
mov ds,bx
```

```
mov ss,bx
moves, bx
mov fX,bx
mov gs,bx
db 66h forthe 80386, need to make a 32-bit jump
                                    pejump :
jmp far ptr c_startup               but the 80376 is already 32-bit.
org 70h                             only if segment base is at0ffffff80h
jmp short start
INIT_CODE                    ENDS
END
```

This code should be linked with the application for boot loadable code. The following code illustrates a dummy application.

```
$title("Example Startup Code,Copyright 1989, Intel Corporation")
name  dummy_application;
data segment rw publich use32
dontworry db  8 dup  (?)
be happy  db  4ah, 69h,6dh, 20h, 4bh, 26h, 52h
data ends
code32 segment er public use32
```

```
assume                    ds :data, es :data
public                    int0,int1_3,int2,int4,int5,int6,int7,int8,int9
public                    int10,int11,int12,int13,int14,int16
public                    c_startup
                          db '5/3/89', ' Ver 1.00'
                          db ' IntelCorporation '
c_startup : hIt
*************************************************************************
InU    routine
*************************************************************************
int0      proc   far
```

```
        hlt
intO    endp
*********************************************************************
** intl_3 interrupt service routine -- debug register support **
*********************************************************************
intl_3  PROC                    FAR
        hIt
intL3   endp
*********************************************************************
        Int2    routine
*********************************************************************
int2    proc    far
        hIt
int2    endp
*********************************************************************
        Int4    routine
*********************************************************************
int4    proc    far
int4    hIt
        endp
*********************************************************************
        IntS routine
*********************************************************************

intS    proc    far
        hIt
intS    endp
*********************************************************************
   Int6   routine
*********************************************************************
```

```
int6    proc    far
        hIt
int6    endp
********************************************************************************
Int7 routine
********************************************************************************
int7    proc    far
        hIt
int7    endp
********************************************************************************
        Int8    routine
********************************************************************************
int8    proc    far
        hIt
int8    endp
********************************************************************************
        Int9 routine
********************************************************************************
int9    proc    far
        hIt
int9    endp
********************************************************************************
        Int10   routine
********************************************************************************
int10   proc    far
        hlt
intU    endp
********************************************************************************
        Intl11 routine
********************************************************************************
int11   proc    far
int11   hIt
        endp
```

```
********************************************************************
      Int12  routine
********************************************************************
int12  proc    far
       hlt
int12  endp
********************************************************************
   Get    control from  interrupt  13
********************************************************************
   int13  proc    far
          hIt
   int13  endp
********************************************************************
   Int14  routine
********************************************************************
   int14  proc    far
   int14  hIt
          endp
********************************************************************
      Int16  routine
********************************************************************
int16  proc    far
       hIt
int16  endp
code32    ends
       end
```

The following build file illustrates how to link these two pieces of code.

```
FLAT; -- build program id
SEGMENT
*segments (dp1=0), --              Give all user segments a DPL of B.
_phantom_code_ (dpl=0.ra), --      These two segments are created by
_phantom_data_ (dpl=B). --         the builder when the FLAT control is used.
init_code (base=Bffffff8Bh,ra), -- Put startup code at the reset vector code32
(base = BffffefBBh,ra).
data (base = Oh);
TASK
MAIN_TASK                          Dummy initialized task segment
(
```

CODE = c_startup,   Entry point is main, which
DPL = 0, must be a public id.

                                          Task privilege level is 0.
DATA = DATA,   Points to a segment that
                                          indicates initial DS value.

STACKS = (DATA),   Segment id points to stack
                                          segment. Sets the intial SS :ESP.

NO INTENABLED.   Disable interrupts.
PRESENT   Present bit in TSS set to 1.
 );
GATE   Define intial interrupts/faults
i0 (entry=int0, dpl=0, trap),   Divide by zero trap
il (entry=intl_3,dpl=0, trap),   Debug/trap register support
i2 (entry=int2, dpl=0, trap),   NMI interrupt
i3 (entry=intL3, dpl=0, trap),   interrupt 3 debug support
i4 (entry=int4, dpl=0, trap),   Overflow Exception
i5 (entry=int5, dpl=I'J, trap),   Bounds Check Exception
i6 (entry=int6, dpl=I'J, trap),   Invalid Opcode Exception
i7 (entry=int7, dpl=I'J, trap),   Coprocessor not avaiable
i8 (entry=int8,dpl=I'J, trap),   Double fault
i9 (entry=int9, dpl=I'J, trap),   Coprocessor Segment Overrun
ill'J (entry=int1I'J, dpl=0, trap),   invalid TSS exception
ill (entry=intll, dpl=0, trap),   segmentnot present exception
i12 (entry=int12, dpl=0, trap),   --.stack exception
i13 (entry=int13, dpl=I'J, trap),   trap gate disables interrupts
i14 (entry=int14, dpl=l'J, trap),   page fault
i16 (entry=int16, dpl=l'J, trap),   coprocessor error
TABLE GDT
GDT (LOCATION   create GDT
GDLDESC,   In a buffer starting at GDT_DESC[
BLD386   places the GDT base and GDT limit values.
                                          Buffer must be 6 bytes long. The base and limit
                                          values are places in this buffer as two bytes of
                                          limit plus four bytes of base in the format
                                          required for use by the LGDT instruction.

ENTRY
),
(3 :_phantom_ocde_, 4 :_phantom_data_, 5 :main_task
)

Explicitly place segment -- entries into the GDT
IDT
(BASE = 0ffff8000h, ENTRY=(0 :iI'J,
I :il,
2 :i2,
3 :i3,

i4,
i5,
i6,
i7,
i8,
i9, 11'1 ill'J, 11 ill, 12 i12, 13 i13, 14 i14, 16 i16)
) ,

dummyldt
(ENTRY=(1 code32,
data,
inLcode)
) ;
MEMORY

(RANGE (EPROM = ROM(0ffff8000h .. 0ffffffffh), DRAM = RAM(0 .. 0ffffh»,
ALLOCATE = (MAIN_TASK) » ;

END

The commands to assemble and build a boot loadable application named "init" are contained in the following batch file. "Init.asm" is the code to put the 386 CPU in flat mode and "startup.asm" is the dummy application code.

asm386	init.asm debug asm386 startup.asm debug
bnd386	startup.obj,init.obj nolo debug oj (init.bnd) bld386 init.bnd bf (init.bld) bl flat
map386	init

This batch file used version 3.0 of the Intel RLL utilities and Intel 386ASM assembler to assemble and build the code.

5.6 TLB TESTING

The 80386 DX microprocessor provides a mechanism for testing the translation look a side buffer (TLB), the cache used for translating linear addresses to physical addresses. Although failure of the TLB hardware is extremely unlikely, users may wish to include TLB confidence tests among other power-up tests for the 386 DX microprocessor. When testing the TLB, turn off paging to avoid interference with the test data written to the TLB.

5.6.1 Structure of the TLB

The TLB is a four-way set-associative memory. Fig. 5.3 illustrates the structure of the TLB. There are four sets of eight entries each. Each entry consists of a tag and data. Tags are 24 bits wide. They contain the high-order 20 bits of the linear address, the valid bit, and three attribute bits. The data portion of each entry contains the upper 12 bits of the physical address.

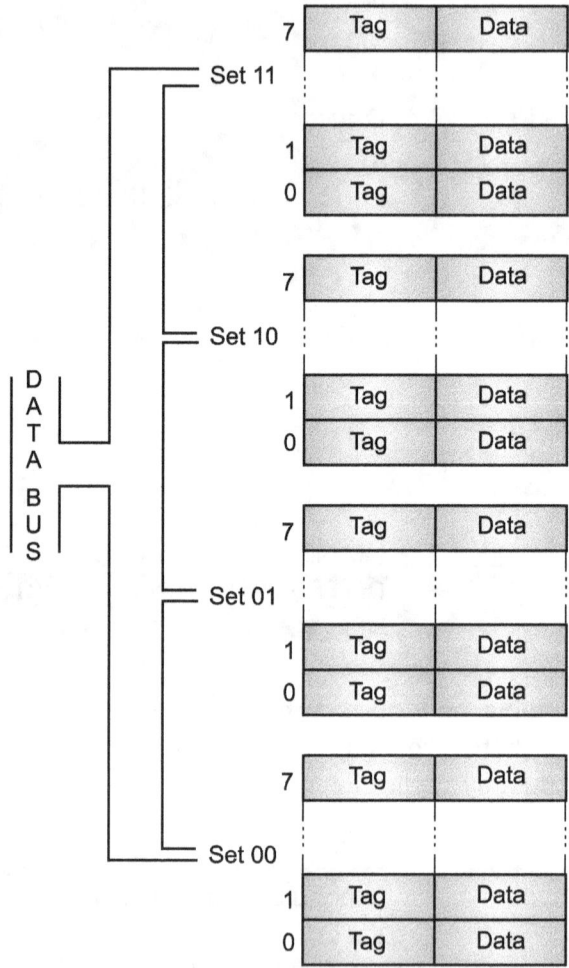

Fig. 5.3 : TLB structure

5.6.2 Test Registers

Two test registers, shown in Fig. 5.4, are provided for the purpose of testing. The TR6 register is the test command register, and the TR7 register is the test data register. These registers are accessed by variants of the MOV instruction. The MOV instructions are defined in both real-address mode and protected mode. The test registers are privileged resources; in protected mode, the MOV instructions which access them can be executed only at privilege level 0. An attempt to read or write the test registers from any other privilege level causes a general-protection exception.

The test command register (TR6) contains a command and an address tag :

C : This is the Command bit. There are two TLB testing commands : write entries into the TLB, and perform TLB lookups. To cause an immediate write into the TLB entry, move a double word into the TR6 register which contains a clear C bit. To cause an immediate TLB lookup (read), move a double word into the TR6 register which contains a set C bit.

Linear Address : On a TLB write, a TLB entry is allocated to this linear address; the rest of that TLB entry is assigned using the value of the TR7 register and the value just written into the TR6 register. On a TLB lookup, the TLB is interrogated per this value; if one and only one TLB entry matches, the rest of the fields of the TR6 and TR7 registers are set from the matching TLB entry.

V : This bit indicates the TLB entry contains valid data. Entries in the TLB which are not loaded with page table entries have a clear V bit. All V bits are cleared by writing to the CR3 register, which has the effect of emptying or "flushing" the cache. The cache must be flushed after modifying the page tables, because otherwise unmodified data might get used for address translation.

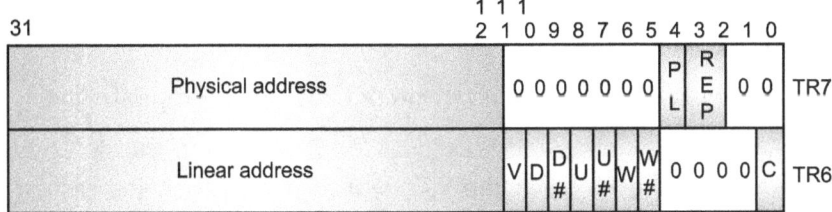

Fig. 5.4 : Test registers

D, $\overline{D}$: The D bit (and its complement).

U, $\overline{U}$: The U/S bit (and its complement).

W, $\overline{W}$: The R/W bit (and its complement).

The meaning of these pairs of bits is given in Table 10-2. The test data register (TR7) holds data read from or data to be written to the TLB.

Physical Address : This is the data field of the TLB. On a write to the TLB, the TLB entry allocated to the linear address in the TR6 register is set to this value. On a TLB lookup (read), the data field (physical address) from the TLB is loaded into this field.

PL : On a TLB write, a set PL bit causes the REP field of the TR7 register to be used for selecting which of four associative blocks of the TLB entry is loaded. If the PL bit is clear, the internal pointer of the paging unit is used to select the block. On a TLB lookup (read), the PL bit indicates whether the read was a hit (the PL bit is set) or a miss (the PL bit is clear).

REP : For a TLB write, selects which of four associative blocks of the TLB is to be written. For a TLB read, if the PL bit is set, REP reports in which of the four associative blocks the tag was found; if the PL bit is clear, the contents of this field are undefined.

5.6.3 Test Operations

To write a TLB entry :

- Move a double word to the TR7 register which contains the desired physical address, PL, and REP values. The PL bit must be set. The REP field must point to the associative block in which to place the entry.

- Move a double word to the TR6 register which contains the appropriate linear address, and values for the V, D, V, and W bits. The C bit must be set.

Do not write duplicate tags; the results of doing so are undefined.

Table 5.2 : Meaning of Bit Pairs in the TR6 Register

Bit	Bit#	Effect during TLB Lookup	Value after TLB Write
0	0	Miss all	Bit is undefined
0	1	Match if the bit is clear	Bit is clear
1	0	Match if the bit is clear	Bit is set
1	1	Match all	Bit is undefined

To lookup (read) a TLB entry :

Move a double word to the TR6 register which contains the appropriate linear address and attributes. The C bit must be set.

Read the TR7 register. If the PL bit in the TR7 register is set, then the rest of the register contents report the TLB contents. If the PL bit is clear, then the other values in the TR7 register are indeterminate.

5.7 DEBUGGING

The debugging support is accessed through the debug registers. They hold the addresses of memory locations, called breakpoints, which invoke debugging software. An exception is generated when a memory operation is made to one of these addresses. A breakpoint is specified for a particular form of memory access, such as an instruction fetch or a double word write operation. The debug registers support both instruction breakpoints and data breakpoints.

With other processors, instruction breakpoints are set by replacing normal instructions with breakpoint instructions. When the breakpoint instruction is executed, the debugger is called. But with the debug registers of the 386 DX microprocessor, this is not necessary. By eliminating the need to write into the code space, the debugging process is simplified (there is no need to set up a data segment mapped to the same memory as the code segment) and breakpoints can be set in ROM-based software. In addition, break-points can be set on reads and writes to data which allows real-time monitoring of variables.

5.7.1 DEBUGGING SUPPORT FEATURES

The features of the Intel 386 architecture which support debugging are as follows

- **Reserved Debug Interrupt Vector**

Specifies a procedure or task to be called when an event for the debugger occurs.

- **Debug Address Registers**

Specifies the addresses of up to four breakpoints.

- **Debug Control Register**

Specifies the forms of memory access for the breakpoints.

- **Debug Status Register**

Reports conditions which were in effect at the time of the exception.

- **Trap Bit of TSS (T-bit)**

Generates a debug exception when an attempt is made to perform a task switch to a task with this bit set in its TSS.

- **Resume Flag (RF)**

Suppresses multiple exceptions to the same instruction.

- **Trap Flag (TF)**

Generates a debug exception after every execution of an instruction.

- **Breakpoint Instruction**

Calls the debugger (generates a debug exception). This instruction is an alternative way to set code breakpoints. It is especially useful when more than four breakpoints are desired, or when breakpoints are being placed in the source code.

- **Reserved Interrupt Vector for Breakpoint Exception**

Calls a procedure or task when a breakpoint instruction is executed.

These features allow a debugger to be called either as a separate task or as a procedure in the context of the current task.

The following conditions can be used to call the debugger :

- Task switch to a specific task.
- Execution of the breakpoint instruction.
- Execution of any instruction.
- Execution of an instruction at a specified address.
- Read or write of a byte, word, or double word at a specified address.
- Write to a byte, word, or double word at a specified address.
- Attempt to change the contents of a debug register.

5.7.2 Debug Registers

There are six registers used to control debugging. These registers are accessed by forms of the MOV instruction. A debug register may be the source or destination operand for one of these instructions. The debug registers are privileged resources; the MOV instructions which access them may be executed only at privilege level 0. An attempt to read or write the debug registers from any other privilege level generates a general-protection exception. Fig. 5.5 shows the format of the debug registers.

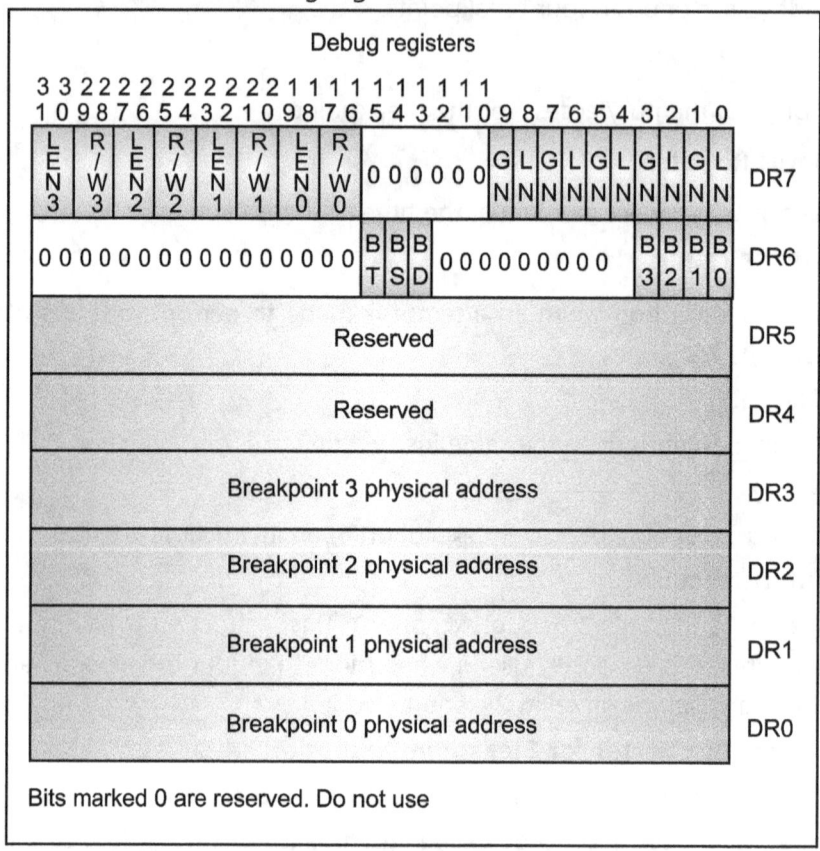

Fig. 5.5 : Debug registers

5.7.2.1 Debug Address Registers (DRO-DR3)

Each of these registers holds the linear address for one of the four breakpoints. If paging is enabled, these addresses are translated to physical addresses by the paging algorithm. Each breakpoint condition is specified further by the contents of the DR7 register.

5.7.2.2 Debug Control Register (DR7)

The debug control register shown in Fig. 5.5 specifies the sort of memory access associated with each breakpoint. Each address in registers DRO to DR3 corresponds to a field R/WO to R/W3 in the DR7 register. The processor interprets these bits as follows :

00 – Break on instruction execution only

01 – Break on data writes only

10 – Undefined

11 – Break on data reads or writes but not instruction fetches

The LEN0 to LEN3 fields in the DR7 register specify the size of the break pointed location in memory. A size of 1, 2, or 4 bytes may be specified. The length fields are interpreted as follows :

00 – one-byte length

01 – two-byte length

10 – Undefined

11 – four-byte length

If RWn is 00 (instruction execution), then LENn should also be 00. The effect of using any other length is undefined.

The low eight bits of the DR7 register (fields L0 to L3 and G0 to G3) individually enable the four address breakpoint conditions. There are two levels of enabling : the local (L0 through L3) and global (G0 through G3) levels. The local enable bits are automatically cleared by the processor on every task switch to avoid unwanted breakpoint conditions in the new task. They are used to breakpoint conditions in a single task. The global enable bits are not cleared by a task switch. They are used to enable breakpoint conditions which apply to all tasks.

The LE and GE bits control the "exact data breakpoint match" mode of the debugging mechanism. If either the LE or GE bit is set, the processor slows execution so that data breakpoints are reported for the instruction which triggered the breakpoint, rather than the next instruction to execute. One of these bits should be set when data breakpoints are used. The processor clears the LE bit at a task switch, but it does not clear the GE bit.

5.7.2.3 Debug Status Register (DR6)

The debug status register shown in Fig. 5.5 reports conditions sampled at the time the debug exception was generated. Among other information, it reports which break-point triggered the exception.

When an enabled breakpoint generates a debug exception, it loads the low four bits of this register (B0 through B3) before entering the debug exception handler. The B bit is set if the condition described by the DR, LEN, and R/W bits is true, even if the break-point is not enabled by the Land G bits. The processor sets the B bits for all breakpoints which match the conditions present at the time the debug exception is generated, whether or not they are enabled.

The BT bit is associated with the T bit (debug trap bit) of the TSS (see Chapter 6 for the format of a TSS). The processor sets the BT bit before entering the debug handler if a task switch has occurred to a task with a set T bit in its TSS. There is no bit in the DR7 register to enable or disable this exception; the T bit of the TSS is the only enabling bit.

The BS bit is associated with the TF flag. The BS bit is set if the debug exception was triggered by the single-step execution mode (TF flag set). The single-step mode is the highest-priority debug exception; when the BS bit is set, any of the other debug status bits also may be set.

The BD bit is set if the next instruction will read or write one of the eight debug registers while they are being used by in-circuit emulation.

5.7.2.4 Breakpoint Field Recognition

The address and LEN bits for each· of the four breakpoint conditions define a range of sequential byte addresses for a data breakpoint. The LEN bits permit specification of a one-, two-, or four-byte range. Two-byte ranges must be aligned on word boundaries (addresses which are multiples of two) and four-byte ranges must be aligned on double-word boundaries (addresses which are multiples of four). These requirements are en-forced by the processor; it uses the LEN bits to mask the lower address bits in the debug registers. Unaligned code or data breakpoint addresses do not yield the expected results.

A data breakpoint for reading or writing is triggered if any of the bytes participating in a memory access is within the range defined by a breakpoint address register and its LEN bits. Table 5-3 gives some examples of combinations of addresses and fields with memory references which do and do not cause traps.

A data breakpoint for an unaligned operand can be made from two sets of entries in the breakpoint registers where each entry is byte-aligned, and the two entries together cover the operand. This breakpoint generates exceptions only for the operand, not for any neighboring bytes.

Instruction breakpoint addresses must have a length specification of one byte (LEN = 00); the behavior of code breakpoints for other operand sizes is undefined. The processor recognizes an instruction breakpoint address only when it points to the first byte of an instruction. If the instruction has any prefixes, the breakpoint address must point to the first prefix.

Table 5.3 : Break Pointing Examples

Comment		Address (hex)	Length (in bytes)
Register Contents	DR0	A0001	1 (LENO = 00)
Register Contents	DR1	A0002	1 (LEND = 00)
Register Contents	DR2	80002	2 (LEND = 01)

...Conti.

Register Contents	DR3	C0000	4 (LEND = 11)
		A0001	1
		A0002	1
		A0001	2
		A0002	2
Memory Operations Which Trap		B0002	2
		B0001	4
		C0000	4
		C0001	2
		C0003	1
		AD000	1
Memory Operations Which Don't Trap		A0003	4
		B0000	2
		C0004	4

5.7.3 Debug Exceptions

Two of the interrupt vectors of the 386 DX microprocessor are reserved for debug exceptions. The debug exception is the usual way to invoke debuggers designed for the 386 DX microprocessor; the breakpoint exception is intended for putting breakpoints in debuggers.

5.7.3.1 Interrupt 1 – Debug Exceptions

The handler for this exception usually is a debugger or part of a debugging system. The processor generates a debug exception for any of several conditions. The debugger can check flags in the DR6 and DR7 registers to determine which condition caused the exception and which other conditions also might apply. Table 5-4 shows the states of these bits for each kind of breakpoint condition.

Table 5.4 : Debug Exception Conditions

Flags Tested	Description
BS = 1	Single-step trap
B0 = 1 and (GE0 = 1 or LE0 = 1)	Breakpoint defined by DR0, LEN0, and R/W0
B1 = 1 and (GE1 =1 or LEi = 1).	Breakpoint defined by DR1, LEN1, and R/W1

...Conti.

B2 = 1 and (GE2 = 1 or LE2 = 1)	. Breakpoint defined by DR2, LEN2, and R/W2
B3 = 1 and (GE3 = 1 or LE3 = 1)	Breakpoint defined by DR3, LEN3, and R/W3
BD = 1	Debug registers in use for in-circuit emulation
BT = 1	Task switch

Instruction breakpoints are faults; other debug exceptions are traps. The debug exception may report either or both at one time. The following sections present details for each class of debug exception.

5.7.3.1.1 Instruction-Breakpoint Fault

The processor reports an instruction breakpoint before it executes the break pointed instruction.

The RF flag permits the debug exception handler to restart instructions which cause faults other than debug faults. When one of these faults occurs, the system software writer must set the RF bit in the copy of the EFLAGS register which is pushed on the stack in the debug exception handler routine. This bit is set in preparation of resuming the program's execution at the breakpoint address without generating another break-point fault on the same instruction.

The processor clears the RF flag at the successful completion of every instruction except after the IRET instruction, the POPF instruction, and JMP, CALL, or INT instructions which cause a task switch. These instructions set the RF flag to the value specified by the saved copy of the EFLAGS register.

The processor sets the RF flag in the copy of the EFLAGS register pushed on the stack before entry into any fault handler. When the fault handler is entered for instruction breakpoints, for example, the RF flag is set in the copy of the EFLAGS register pushed on the stack; therefore, the IRET instruction which returns control from the exception handler will set the RF flag in the EFLAGS register, and execution will resume at the break pointed instruction without generating another breakpoint for the same instruction.

If, after a debug fault, the RF flag is set and the debug handler retries the faulting instruction, it is possible that retrying the instruction will generate other faults. The restart of the instruction after these faults also occurs with the RF flag set, so repeated debug faults continue to be suppressed. The processor clears the RF flag only after successful completion of the instruction.

5.7.3.1.2 Data-Breakpoint Trap

A data-breakpoint exception is a trap; i.e., the processor generates an exception for a data breakpoint after executing the instruction which accesses the break pointed memory location.

When using data breakpoints, it is recommended either the LE or GEbits of the DR7 register also be set. If either the LE or GE bits are set, any data breakpoint trap is reported immediately after completion of the instruction which accessed the break-pointed memory location. This immediate reporting is done by forcing the 386 DX microprocessor execution unit to wait for completion of data operand transfers before beginning execution of the next instruction. If neither bit is set, data breakpoints may not be generated until one instruction after the data is accessed, or they may not be generated at all. This is because instruction execution normally is overlapped with memory transfers. Execution of the next instruction may begin before the memory operations of the previous instruction are completed.

If a debugger needs to save the contents of a write breakpoint location, it should save the original contents before setting the breakpoint. Because data breakpoints are traps, the original data is overwritten before the trap exception is generated. The handler can report the saved value after the breakpoint is triggered. The data in the debug registers can be used to address the new value stored by the instruction which triggered the breakpoint.

5.7.3.1.3 General-Detect Fault

The general-detect fault occurs when an attempt is made to use the debug registers at the same time they are being used by in-circuit emulation. This additional protection feature is provided to guarantee emulators can have full control over the debug registers when required. The exception handler can detect this condition by checking the state of the BD bit of the DR6 register.

5.7.3.1.4 Single-Step Trap

This trap occurs after an instruction is executed if the TF flag was set before the instruction was executed. Note the exception does not occur after an instruction which sets the TF flag. For example, if the POPF instruction is used to set the TF flag, a single-step trap does not occur until after the instruction following the POPF instruction.

The processor clears the TF flag before calling the exception handler. If the TF flag was set in a TSS at the time of a task switch, the exception occurs after the first instruction is executed in the new task.

The single-step flag normally is not cleared by privilege changes inside a task. The INT instructions, however, do clear the TF flag. Therefore, software debuggers which single-step code must recognize and emulate INTn or INTO instructions rather than executing them directly.

To maintain protection, the operating system should check the current execution privilege level after any single-step trap to see if single stepping should continue at the current privilege level.

The interrupt priorities guarantee that if an external interrupt occurs, single stepping stops. When both an external interrupt and a single step interrupt occur together, the single step interrupt is processed first. This clears the TF flag. After saving the return address or switching tasks, the external interrupt input is examined before the first instruction of the single step handler executes. If the external interrupt is still pending, then it is serviced. The external interrupt handler does not run in single-step mode. To single step an interrupt handler, single step an INT instruction which calls the interrupt handler.   .

5.7.3.1.5 Task-Switch Trap

The debug exception also occurs after a task switch if the T bit of the new task's TSS is set. The exception occurs after control has passed to the new task, but before the first instruction of that task is executed. The exception handler can detect this condition by examining the BT bit of the DR6 register.

Note that if the debug exception handler is a task, the T bit of its TSS should not be set. Failure to observe this rule will put the processor in a loop.

5.7.3.2 Interrupt 3 - Breakpoint Instruction

The breakpoint trap is caused by execution of the INT 3 instruction. Typically, a debugger prepares a breakpoint by replacing the first opcode byte of an instruction with the opcode for the breakpoint instruction. When execution of the INT 3 instruction calls the exception handler, the return address points to the first byte of the instruction following the INT 3 instruction.

With older processors, this feature is used extensively for setting instruction breakpoints. With the 386 DX microprocessor, this use is more easily handled using the debug registers. However, the breakpoint exception still is useful for break pointing debuggers, because the breakpoint exception can call an exception handler other than itself. The breakpoint exception also can be useful when it is necessary to set a greater number of breakpoints than permitted by the debug registers, or when breakpoints are being placed in the source code of a program under development.

5.8 VIRTUAL-8086 MODE

The 386 DX microprocessor supports execution of one or more 8086, 8088, 80186, or 80188 programs in a 386 DX microprocessor protected-mode environment. An 8086 program runs in this environment as part of a virtual-8086 task. Virtual-8086 tasks take advantage of the hardware support of multitasking offered by the protected mode. Not only can there be multiple virtual-8086 tasks, each one running an 8086 program, but virtual-8086 tasks can run in multitasking with other 386 DX microprocessor tasks.

The purpose of a virtual-8086 task is to form a "virtual machine" for running programs written for the 8086 processor. A complete virtual machine consists of 386 DX microprocessor hardware and system software. The emulation of an 8086 processor is the result of software using hardware :

The hardware provides a virtual set of registers (through the TSS), a virtual memory space (the first megabyte of the linear address space of the task), and directly exe-cutes all instructions which deal with these registers and with this address space.

The software controls the external interfaces of the virtual machine I/O (interrupts, and exceptions) in' a manner consistent with the larger environment in which it runs. In the case of I/O, software can choose either to emulate I/O instructions or to let the hardware execute them directly without software intervention.

Software which supports virtual 8086 machines is called a virtual-8086 monitor.

5.8.1 Executing 8086 Processor Code

The processor runs in virtual-8086 mode when the VM (virtual machine) bit in the EFLAOS register is set. The processor tests this flag under two general conditions :

*   When loading segment registers, to know whether to use 8086-style address translation.
*   When decoding instructions, to determine which instructions are sensitive to IOPL.

Except for these two modifications to its normal operations, the 386 DX microprocessor in virtual-8086 mode operates similarly to protected mode.

5.8.1.1 Registers and Instructions

The register set available in virtual-8086 mode includes all the registers defined for the 8086 processor, plus the new registers introduced by the 386 DX microprocessor : FS, GS, debug registers, control registers, and test registers. New instructions which explicitly operate on the segment registers FS and GS are available, and the new segment-override prefixes can be used to cause instructions to use the FS and GS registers for address calculations. Instructions can use 32-bit operands through the use of the operand size prefix.

Programs running as virtual-8086 tasks can take advantage of the new application-oriented instructions added to the architecture by the introduction of the 80186, 80188, 80286 and 386 DX microprocessors :

*   New instructions introduced on the 80186, 80188, and 80286 processors.
    PUSH immediate data
    Push all and pop all (PUSHA and POPA)
    Multiply immediate data
    Shift and rotate by immediate count
    String I/O
    ENTER and LEAVE instruction
    BOUND instruction
*   New instructions introduced on the 386 DX microprocessor.
    LSS, LFS, LGS instructions
    Long-displacement conditional jumps
    Single-bit instructions
    Bit scan instructions
    Double-shift instructions
    Byte set on condition instruction
    Move with sign/zero extension
    Generalized multiply instruction

MOV to and from control registers

MOV to and from test registers

MOV to and from debug registers

5.8.1.2 Address Translation

In virtual-8086 mode, the 386 DX microprocessor does not interpret 8086 selectors by referring to descriptors; instead, it forms linear addresses as an 8086 processor would. It shifts the selector left by four bits to form a 20-bit base address. The effective address is extended with four clear bits in the upper bit positions and added to the base address to create a linear address, as shown in Fig. 5.6.

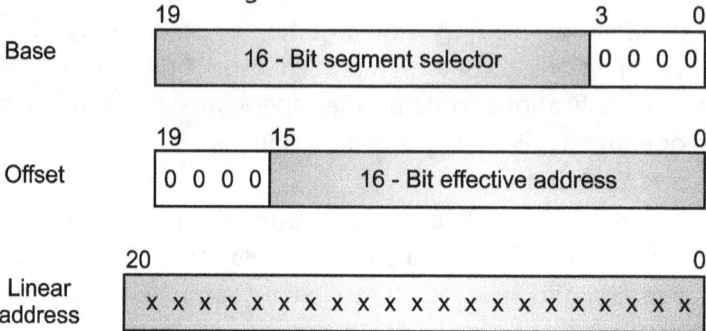

Fig. 5.6 : 8086 address translation

Because of the possibility of a carry, the resulting linear address may have as many as 21 significant bits. An 8086 program may generate linear addresses anywhere in the range 0 to I0FFEFH (1 megabyte plus approximately 64K bytes) of the task's linear address space.

Virtual-8086 tasks generate 32-bit linear addresses. While an 8086 program only can use the lowest 21 bits of a linear address, the linear address can be mapped using paging to any 32-bit physical address.

Virtual-8086 Mode

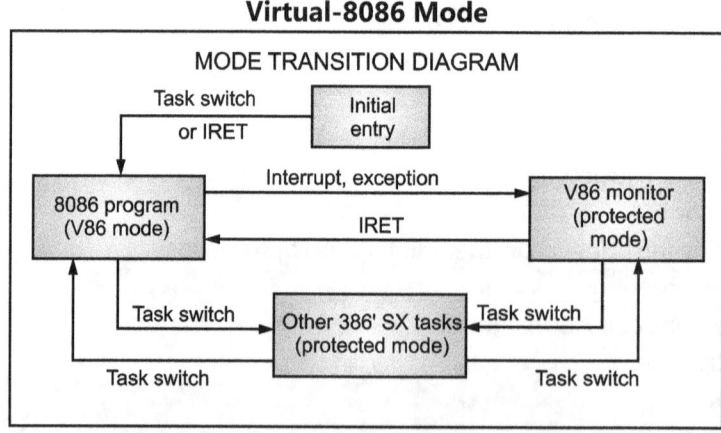

Fig. 5.7 : Entering and leaving virtual 8086 mode

Unlike the 8086 and 80286 processors, the 386 DX microprocessor can generate 32-bit effective addresses using an address override prefix; however, in virtual-8086 mode, the value of a 32-bit address may not exceed 65,535 without causing an exception. For full compatibility with 80286 real-address mode, pseudo-protection faults (interrupt 12 or 13 with no error code) occur if an effective address is generated outside the range 0 through 65,535.

5.8.2 Structure of a Virtual-8086 Task

A virtual-8086 task consists of the 8086 program to be run and the 386 DX microprocessor "native mode" code which serves as the virtual-machine monitor. The task must be represented by a 386 DX microprocessor TSS (not an 80286 TSS). The processor enters virtual-8086 mode to run the 8086 program and returns to protected mode to run the monitor or other 386 DX CPU tasks.

To run in virtual-8086 mode, an existing 8086 processor program needs a virtual-8086 monitor and Operating-system services.

The virtual-8086 monitor is 386 DX microprocessor protected-mode code which runs at privilege-level 0 (most privileged). The monitor mostly consists of initialization and exception-handling procedures. As with any other 386 DX microprocessor program, code-segment descriptors for the monitor must exist in the GDT or in the task's LDT. The linear addresses above 10FFEFH are available for the virtual-8086 monitor, the operating system, and other system software. The monitor also may need data-segment descriptors so it can examine the interrupt vector table or other parts of the 8086 program in the first megabyte of the address space.

In general, there are two options for implementing the 8086 operating system :

The 8086 operating system may run as part of the 8086 program. This approach is desirable for either of the following reasons :

The 8086 application code modifies the operating system.

There is not sufficient development time to re implement the 8086 operating system as a 386 DX microprocessor operating system.

The 8086 operating system may be implemented or emulated in the virtual-8086 monitor. This approach is desirable for any of the following reasons :

Operating system functions can be more easily coordinated among several virtual-8086 tasks.

The functions of the 8086 operating system can be easily emulated by calls to the 386 DX microprocessor operating system.

5.8.2.1 Paging for Virtual-8086 Tasks

Paging is not necessary for a single virtual-8086 task, but paging is useful or necessary for any of the following reasons :

Creating multiple virtual-8086 tasks. Each task must map the lower megabyte of linear addresses to different physical locations.

Emulating the address wraparound which occurs at 1 megabyte. With members of the 8086 family, it is possible to specify addresses larger than 1 megabyte. For example, with a selector value of 0FFFFH and an offset of 0FFFFH, the effective address would be 10FFEFH (1 megabyte plus 65519 bytes). The 8086 processor, which can form addresses only up to 20 bits long, truncates the high-order bit, thereby "wrapping" this address to 0FFEFH. The 386 DX microprocessor, however, does not truncate such an address. If any 8086 processor programs depend on address wrap-around, the same effect can be achieved in a virtual-8086 task by mapping linear addresses between 100000H and 110000H and linear addresses between 0 and 10000H to the same physical addresses.

- Creating a virtual address space larger than the physical address space.

Sharing 8086 operating system or ROM code which is common to several 8086 pro-grams running in multitasking.

Redirecting or trapping references to memory-mapped I/O devices.

5.8.2.2 Protection within a Virtual-8086 Task

Protection is not enforced between the segments of an 8086 program. To protect the system software running in a virtual-8086 task from the 8086 application program, soft-ware designers may follow either of these approaches :

Reserve the first megabyte (plus 64K bytes) of each task's linear address space for the 8086 processor program. An 8086 processor task cannot generate addresses outside this range.

Use the U/S bit of page-table entries to protect the virtual-machine monitor and other system software in each virtual-8086 task's space. When the processor is in virtual-8086 mode, the CPL is 3 (least privileged). Therefore, an 8086 processor pro-gram has only user privileges. If the pages of the virtual-machine monitor have super-visor privilege, they cannot be accessed by the 8086 program.

5.8.3 Entering and Leaving Virtual-8086 Mode

Fig. 5.7 summarizes the ways to enter and leave an 8086 program. Virtual-8086 mode is entered by setting the VM flag. There are two ways to do this :

A task switch to a 386 DX microprocessor task loads the image of the EFLAGS register from the new TSS. The TSS of the new task must be a 386 DX microprocessor TSS, not an 80286 TSS, because the 80286 TSS does not load the high word of the EFLAGS register, which contains the VM flag. A set VM flag in the new contents of the EFLAGS register indicates that the new task is executing 8086 instructions; therefore, while loading the segment registers from the TSS, the 386 DX microprocessor forms base addresses in the 8086 style.

An IRET instruction from a procedure of a 386 DX task loads the EFLAGS register from the stack. A set VM flag indicates the procedure to which control is being returned to be an 8086 procedure. The CPL at the time the IRET instruction is executed must be 0, otherwise the processor does not change the state of the VM flag.

When a task switch is used to enter virtual-8086 mode, the segment registers are loaded from a TSS. But when an IRET instruction is used to set the VM flag, the segment registers keep the contents loaded during protected mode. Software should then reload these registers with segment selectors appropriate for virtual-8086 mode.

The processor leaves virtual-8086 mode when an interrupt or exception occurs. There are two cases :

The interrupt or exception causes a task switch. A task switch from a virtual-8086 task to any other task loads the EFLAGS register from the TSS of the new task. If the new TSS is a 386 DX microprocessor TSS and the VM flag in the new contents of the EFLAGS register is clear or if the new TSS is an 80286 TSS, the processor clears the VM flag of the EFLAGS register, loads the segment registers from the new TSS using 386 DX CPU-style address formation, and begins executing the instructions of the new task in 386 DX microprocessor protected mode.

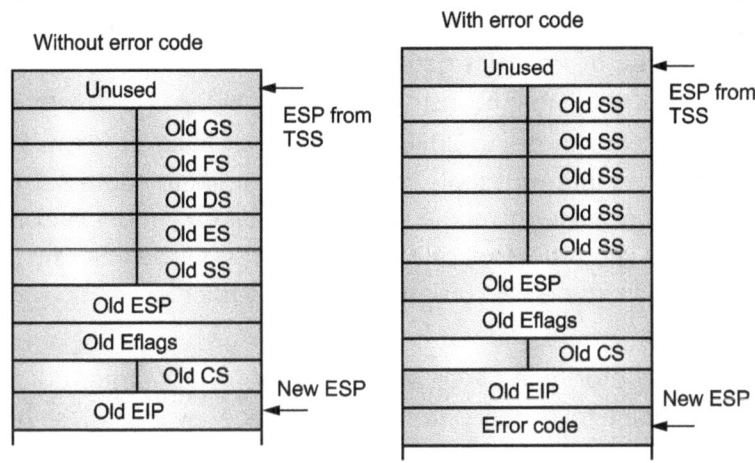

Fig. 5.8 : Privilege level 0 stack after interrupt in virtual 8086 task

The interrupt or exception calls a privilege-level 0 procedure (most privileged). The processor stores the current contents of the EFLAGS register on the stack then clears the VM flag. The interrupt or exception handler, therefore, runs as "native" 386 DX microprocessor protected-mode code. If an interrupt or exception calls a procedure in a conforming segment or in a segment at a privilege level other than 0 (most privileged), the processor generates a general-protection exception; the error code is the selector of the code segment to which a call was attempted.

System software does not change the state of the VM flag directly, but instead changes states in the image of the EFLAGS register stored on the stack or in the TSS. The virtual-8086 monitor sets the VM flag in the EFLAGS image on the stack or in the TSS when first creating a virtual-8086 task. Exception and interrupt handlers can examine the VM flag on the stack. If the interrupted procedure was running in virtual-8086 mode, the handler may need to call the virtual-8086 monitor.

5.8.3.1 Transitions through Task Switches

Task switch to or from a virtual-8086 task may come from any of three causes :

An interrupt which calls a task gate. An action of the scheduler of the 386 DX microprocessor operating system.

Executing an IRET instruction when the NT flag is set.

In any of these cases, the processor changes the VM flag in the EFLAGS register according to the image in the new TSS. If the new TSS is an 80286 TSS, the upper word of the EFLAGS register is not in the TSS; the processor clears the VM flag in this case. The processor updates the VM flag prior to loading the segment registers from their images in the new TSS. The new setting of the VM flag determines whether the processor interprets the new segment-register images as 8086 selectors or 80286 and 386 DX microprocessor selectors.

5.8.3.2 Transitions through Trap Gates and Interrupt Gates

The 386 DX microprocessor leaves virtual-8086 mode as the result of an exception or interrupt which calls a trap or interrupt gate. The exception or interrupt handler returns to the 8086 program by executing an IRET instruction.

Because it was designed to run on an 8086 processor, an 8086 program in a virtual-8086 task will have an 8086-style interrupt table, which starts at linear address. However, the 386 DX microprocessor does not use this table directly. For all exceptions and interrupts which occur virtual-8086 mode, the processor calls handlers through the IDT. The IDT entry for an interrupt or exception in a virtual-8086 task must contain either :

A Task Gate :

A 386 DX trap gate (descriptor type 14) or 386 DX microprocessor interrupt gate (descriptor type 15), which must point to a nonconforming, privilege-level 0 (most privileged), code segment.

Interrupts and exceptions which call 386 DX microprocessor trap or interrupt gates use privilege-level O. The contents of the segment registers are stored on the stack for this privilege level. Fig. 5.8 shows the format of this stack after an exception or interrupt which occurs while a virtual-8086 task is running on 8086 program.

After the processor saves the 8086 segment registers on the stack for privilege level 0, it clears the segment registers before running the handler procedure. This lets the interrupt handler safely save and restore the DS, ES, FS, and GS registers as though they were 386 DX microprocessor selectors. Interrupt handlers, which may be called in the context of either a regular task or a virtual-8086 task, can use the same code sequences for saving and restoring the registers for any task. Clearing these registers before execution of the IRET instruction does not cause a trap in the interrupt handler. Interrupt procedures which expect values in the segment registers or which return values in the segment registers must use the register images saved on the stack for privilege level O. Interrupt handlers which need to know whether the interrupt occurred in virtual-8086 mode can examine the VM flag in the stored contents of the EFLAGS register.

An interrupt handler passes control to the virtual-8086 monitor. If the VM flag is set in the EFLAGS image stored on the stack and the interrupt or exception is one which the monitor needs to handle. The virtual-8086 monitor may either :

Handle the interrupt within the virtual-8086 monitor.

Call the 8086 program's interrupt handler.

Sending an interrupt or exception back to the 8086 program involves the following steps :

Use the 8086 interrupt vector to locate the appropriate handler procedure.

Store the state of the 8086 program on the privilege-level 3 stack (least privileged).

Change the return link on the privilege-level 0 stack (most privileged) to point to the privilege-level 3 handler procedure.

Execute an IRET instruction to pass control to the handler.

When the IRET instruction from the privilege-level 3 handler again calls the virtual-8086 monitor, restore the return link on the privilege-level 0 stack to point to the original, interrupted, privilege-level 3 procedure.

Execute an IRET instruction to pass control back to the interrupted procedure.

5.8.4 Additional Sensitive Instructions

When the 386 DX Microprocessor is running invirtual-8086 mode, the PUSHF, POPF, INT n and IRET instructions are sensitive to IOPL. The IN, INS, OUT, and OUTS instructions, which are sensitive to IOPL in protected mode, are not sensitive in virtual-8086 mode. Following is a complete list of instructions which are sensitive in virtual-8086 mode :

    CLI   -Clear Interrupt-Enable Flag
    STI   -Set Interrupt-Enable Flag
    PUSHF -Push Flags
    POPF   -Pop Flags
    INTn   -Software Interrupt
    IRET   -Interrupt Return

The CPL is always 3 while running in virtual-8086 mode; if the IOPL is less than 3, an attempt to use the instructions listed above will trigger a general-protection exception. These instructions are sensitive to the IOPL to give the virtual-8086 monitor a chance to emulate the facilities they affect.

5.8.4.1 Emulating 8086 Operating System Calls

The INT n instruction is sensitive to IOPL so a virtual-8086 monitor can intercept calls to the 8086 operating system. Many 8086 operating systems are called by pushing parameters onto the stack, then executing an INT n instruction. If the IOPL is less than 3, INT n instructions are intercepted by the virtual-8086 monitor. The virtual-8086 monitor then can emulate the function of the 8086 operating system or send the interrupt back to the 8086 operating system.

5.8.4.2 Emulating the Interrupt-Enable Flag

When the 386 DX Microprocessor is running an 8086 program in a virtual-8086 task, the PUSHF, POPF, and IRET instructions are sensitive to the IOPL. This lets the virtual-8086 monitor protect the interrupt-enable flag (IF). Other instructions which affect the IF flag (such as the STI and CLI instructions) are sensitive to the IOPL in both 8086 and 386 DX microprocessor programs.

Many 8086 programs written for non-multitasking systems set and clear the IF flag to control interrupts. This may cause problems in a multitasking environment. If the IOPL is less than 3, all instructions which change or test the IF flag generate an exception. The virtual-8086 monitor then can control the IF flag in a manner compatible with the 386 DX microprocessor environment and transparent to 8086 programs.

5.8.5 VIRTUAL I/O

Many 8086 programs written for non-multitasking systems directly access I/O ports. This may cause problems in a multitasking environment. If more than one program accesses the same port, they may interfere with each other. Most multitasking systems require application programs to access I/O ports through the operating system. This results in simplified, centralized control.

The 386 DX microprocessor provides I/O protection for creating I/O which is compatible with the 386 DX microprocessor environment and transparent to 8086 programs. Designers may take any of several possible approaches to protecting I/O ports :

Protect the I/O address space and generate exceptions for all attempts to perform I/O directly.

Let the 8086 processor program perform I/O directly.

Generate exceptions on attempts to access specific I/O ports.

Generate exceptions on attempts to access specific memory-mapped I/O ports.

The method of controlling access to I/O ports depends upon whether they are I/O-mapped or memory-mapped.

5.8.5.1 I/O-Mapped I/O

The I/O address space in virtual-8086 mode differs from protected mode only because the IOPL is not checked. Only the I/O permission bit map is checked when virtual-8086 tasks access the I/O address space.

The I/O permission bit map can be used to generate exceptions on attempts to access specific I/O addresses. The I/O permission bit map of each virtual-8086 task determines which I/O addresses generate exceptions for that task. Because each task may have a different I/O permission bit map, the addresses which generate exceptions for one task may be different from the addresses for another task. See Chapter 8 for more information about the I/O permission bit map.

5.8.5.2 Memory-Mapped I/O

In systems which use memory-mapped I/O, the paging facilities of the 386 DX microprocessor can be used to generate exceptions for attempts to access I/O ports. The virtual-8086 monitor may use paging to control memory-mapped I/O in these ways :

Map part of the linear address space of each task which needs to perform I/O to the physical address space where I/O ports are placed. By putting the I/O ports at different addresses (in different pages), the paging mechanism can enforce isolation between tasks.

Map part of the linear address space to pages which are not-present. This generates an exception whenever a task attempts to perform I/O to those pages. System software then can interpret the I/O operation being attempted.

Software emulation of the I/O space may require too much operating system intervention under some conditions. In these cases, it may be possible to generate an exception for only the first attempt to access I/O. The system software then may determine whether a program can be given exclusive control of I/O temporarily, the protection of the I/O space may be lifted, and the program is allowed to run at full speed.

5.8.5.3 Special I/O Buffers

Buffers of intelligent controllers (for example, a bit-mapped frame buffer) also can be emulated using page mapping. The linear space for the buffer can be mapped to a different physical space for each virtual-8086 task. The virtual-8086 monitor then can control which virtual buffer to copy onto the real buffer in the physical address space.

5.8.6 Differences from 8086 Processor

In general, virtual-8086 mode will run software written for the 8086, 8088, 80186, and 80188 processors. The following list shows the minor differences between the 8086 processor and the virtual-8086 mode of the 386 DX microprocessor.

- **Instruction Clock Counts :**

The 386 DX microprocessor takes fewer clocks for most instructions than the 8086 processor. The areas most likely to be affected are :

Delays required by I/O devices between I/O operations.

Assumed delays with 8086 processor operating in parallel with an 8087.

- **Divide Exceptions Point to the DIV Instruction :**

Divide exceptions on the 386 DX microprocessor always leave the saved CS :IP value pointing to the instruction which failed. On the 8086 processor, the CS :IP value points to the next instruction.

- **Undefined 8086 Processor Opcodes :**

Opcodes which were not defined for the 8086 processor generate an invalid opcode or execute as one of the new instructions defined for the 386 DX microprocessor.

- **Value Written by PUSH SP :**

The 386 DX microprocessor pushes a different value on the stack for PUSH SP than the 8086 processor. The 386 DX microprocessor pushes the value in the SP register before it is incremented as part of the push operation; the 8086 processor pushes the value of the SP register after it is incremented. If the pushed value is important, replace PUSH SP instructions with the following three instructions :

PUSH	BP	
MDV	BP,	SP
XCHG	BP,	[BPI

This code functions as the 8086 PUSH SP instruction on the 386 DX microprocessor.

- **Shift or Rotate by more than 31 Bits :**

    The 386 DX microprocessor masks all shift and rotate counts to the lowest five bits. This limits the count to a maximum of 31 bit positions, thereby limiting the time that interrupt response is delayed while the instruction executes.

- **Redundant Prefixes :**

    The 386 DX microprocessor limits instructions to 15 bytes. The only way to violate this limit is with redundant prefixes before an instruction. A general-protection exception is generated if the limit on instruction length is violated. The 8086 processor has no instruction length limit.

- **Operand Crossing Offset 0 or 65,535 :**

    On the 8086 processor, an attempt to access a memory operand which crosses offset 65,535 (e.g., Mov word to offset 65,535) or offset 0 (e.g., PUSH a word when the contents of the SP register are 1) causes the offset to wrap around modulo 65,536. The 386 DX microprocessor generates an exception in these cases, a general-protection exception if the segment is a data segment (i.e., if the CS, DS, ES, FS, or GS register is being used to address the segment), or a stack exception if the segment is a stack segment (i.e., if the SS register is being used).

- **Sequential Execution Across Offset 65,535 :**

    On the 8086 processor, if sequential execution of instructions proceeds past offset 65,535, the processor fetches the next instruction byte from offset 0 of the same segment. On the 386 DX microprocessor, the processor generates a general-protection exception.

- **LOCK is Restricted to Certain Instructions :**

  The LOCK prefix and its output signal should only be used to prevent other bus masters from interrupting a data movement operation. The LOCK prefix only may be used with the following 386 DX microprocessor instructions when they modify memory. An invalid opcode exception results from using LOCK before any other instruction, or with these instructions when no write operation is made to memory.

  Bit test and change : the BTS, BTR, and BTC instructions.

  Exchange : the XCHG instruction.

  One-operand arithmetic and logical : the INC, DEC, NOT, NEG instructions.

  Two-operand arithmetic and logical : the ADD, ADC, SUB, SBB, AND, OR, and XOR instructions.

- **Single-Stepping External Interrupt Handlers :**

  The priority of the 386 DX microprocessor single-step exception is different from that of the 8086 processor. This change prevents an external interrupt handler from being single-stepped. If the interrupt occurs while a program is being single-stepped. The 386 DX microprocessor single-step exception has higher priority than any external interrupt. The 386 DX microprocessor will still single-step through an interrupt handler called by the INT instruction or by an exception.

- **IDIV Exceptions for Quotients of 80H or 8000H :**

  The 386 DX microprocessor can generate the largest negative number as a quotient from the IDIY instruction. The 8086 processor generates a divide-error exception instead.

- **Flags in Stack :**

  The contents of the EFLAGS register stored by the PUSHF instruction, by interrupts, and by exceptions is different from that stored by the 8086 processor in bit positions 12 through 15. On the 8086 processor, these bits are stored as though they were set, but in virtual-8086 mode bit 15 is always clear, and bits 14 through 12 have the last value loaded into them.

- **NMI Interrupting NMI Handlers :**

  After an NMI interrupt is accepted by the 386 DX microprocessor, the NMI interrupt is masked until an IRET instruction is executed.

- **Coprocessor Errors Generate Interrupt 16 :**

  Any 386 DX microprocessor system with a coprocessor must use interrupt 16 for the coprocessor error exception. If an 8086 system uses another vector for the 8087 interrupt, both vectors should point to the coprocessor-error exception handler.

- **Numeric Exception Handlers should allow Prefixes :**

  On the 386 DX microprocessor, the value of CS :IP saved for coprocessor exceptions points at any prefixes before an ESC instruction. On 8086 processor systems, the saved CS :IP points to the ESC instruction itself.

- **Coprocessor does Not Use Interrupt Controller :**

  The coprocessor error signal to the 386 DX microprocessor does not pass through an interrupt controller (an 8087 INT signal does). Some instructions in a coprocessor error handler may need to be deleted if they deal with the interrupt controller.

- **Response to Bus Hold :**

  Unlike the 8086 and 80286 processors, the 386 DX microprocessor responds to requests for control of the bus from other potential bus masters, such as DMA controllers, between transfers of parts of an unaligned operand, such as two words which form a double word.

- **CPL is 3 in Virtual-8086 Mode :**

  The 8086 processor does not support protection, so it has no CPL. Virtual-8086 mode uses a CPL of 3, which prevents the execution of privileged instructions. These are :

  - ➢ LIDT instruction
  - ➢ LGDT instruction
  - ➢ LMSW instruction
  - ➢ special forms of the MOV instruction for loading and storing the control registers
  - ➢ CLTS instruction
  - ➢ HLT instruction

  These instructions may be executed while the processor is in real-address mode following reset initialization. They allow system data structures, such as descriptor tables, to be set up before entering protected mode. Virtual-8086 mode is entered from protected mode, so it has no need for these instructions.

5.8.7 Differences from 80286 Real-Addresses Mode

The 80286 processor implements the bus lock function differently than the 386 DX Microprocessor. This fact may or may not be apparent to 8086 programs, depending on how the virtual-8086 monitor handles the LOCK prefix. Instructions with the LOCK prefix are sensitive to the IOPL; software designers can choose to emulate its function. If, however,

8086 programs are allowed to execute LOCK directly, programs which use forms of memory locking specific to the 8086 processor may not run properly when run on the 386 DX microprocessor.

The LOCK prefix and its bus signal only should be used to prevent other bus masters from interrupting a data movement operation. The LOCK prefix only may be used with the following 386 DX microprocessor instructions when they modify memory. An invalid opcode exception results from using the LOCK prefix before any other instruction, or with these instructions when no write operation is made to memory.

- Bit test and change : the BTS, BTR, and BTC instructions.

- Exchange : the XCHG instruction.

- One-operand arithmetic and logical : the INC, DEC, NOT, NEG instructions.

- Two-operand arithmetic and logical : the ADD, ADC, SUB, SBB, AND, OR, and XOR instructions.

A locked instruction is guaranteed to lock only the area of memory defined by the destination operand, but may lock a larger memory area. For example, typical 8086 and 80286 configurations lock the entire physical memory space.

Unlike the 8086 and 80286 processors, the 386 DX microprocessor responds to requests for control of the bus from other potential bus masters, such as DMA controllers, between transfers of parts of an unaligned operand, such as two words which form a double word.

EXERCISE

1. Draw and explain the contents of the EDX register after reset.

2. Draw and explain the contents of the CR0 register after reset.

3. How does software initialization take place in Real address?

4. Before switching to protected mode, what will happen in system tables, NMI interrupt and PE bit?

5. Explain the software initialization in protected mode in detail.

6. Explain in detail the structure diagram of TLB.

7. Draw and explain two test registers TR6 and TR7.

8. Explain the two steps to write a TLB entry.

9. Write a note on debugging.

10. Explain any 7 features of 80386 architecture which support for debugging.

11. Draw and explain the format of 7 debug registers and also explain the function of each register.

12. Write a note on debug exceptions.

13. Explain in detail interrupt 3 break point instruction.

14. Which new instructions are introduced in 80386 Dx microprocessor?

15. Explain paging for virtual 8086 task.

16. Draw and explain in detail block diagram of entering and living virtual 8086 mode.

17. Explain 3 causes for transition through Task switches.

18. Write and explain additional sensitive instructions in vm86 mode.

19. Differentiate between 8086 processor and vm 86 mode.

CHAPTER 6
80386DX SIGNALS, BUS CYCLES AND 80387 CO-PROCESSOR

6.1 INTRODUCTION

The internal and external bus operations of 80386 have synchronized by the clock signal. The 80386 performs a variety of bus cycles in response to internal requirements and external requirements. The pipeline is the continuous and somewhat overlapped movement of instruction to the processor or in the arithmetic steps taken by the processor to perform an instruction. Without a pipeline, a computer processor gets the first instruction from memory, performs the operation it calls for, and then goes to get the next instruction from memory, and so forth. While fetching (getting) the instruction, the arithmetic part of the processor is idle. It must wait until it gets the next instruction. With pipelining, the computer architecture allows the next instructions to be fetched while the processor is performing arithmetic operations, holding them in a buffer close to the processor until each instruction operation can be performed. The staging of instruction fetching is continuous. The result is an increase in the number of instructions that can be performed during a given time period.

6.2 SIGNAL DIAGRAM AND DESCRIPTION OF SIGNALS OF 80386DX

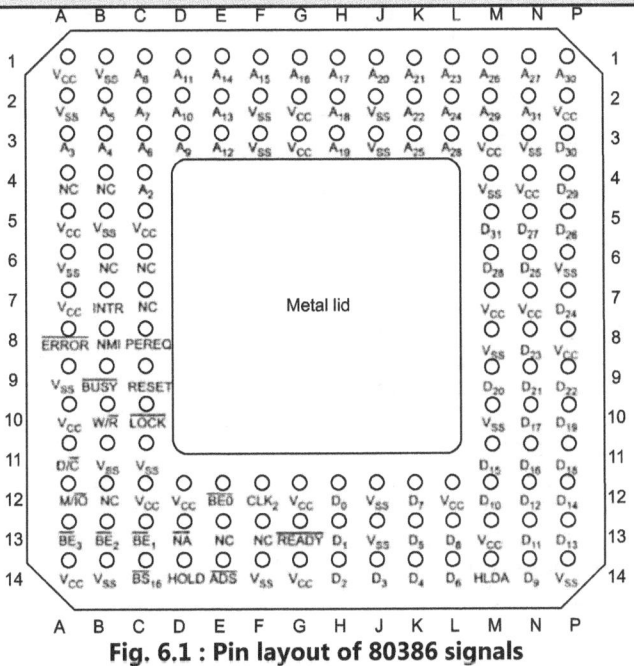

Fig. 6.1 : Pin layout of 80386 signals

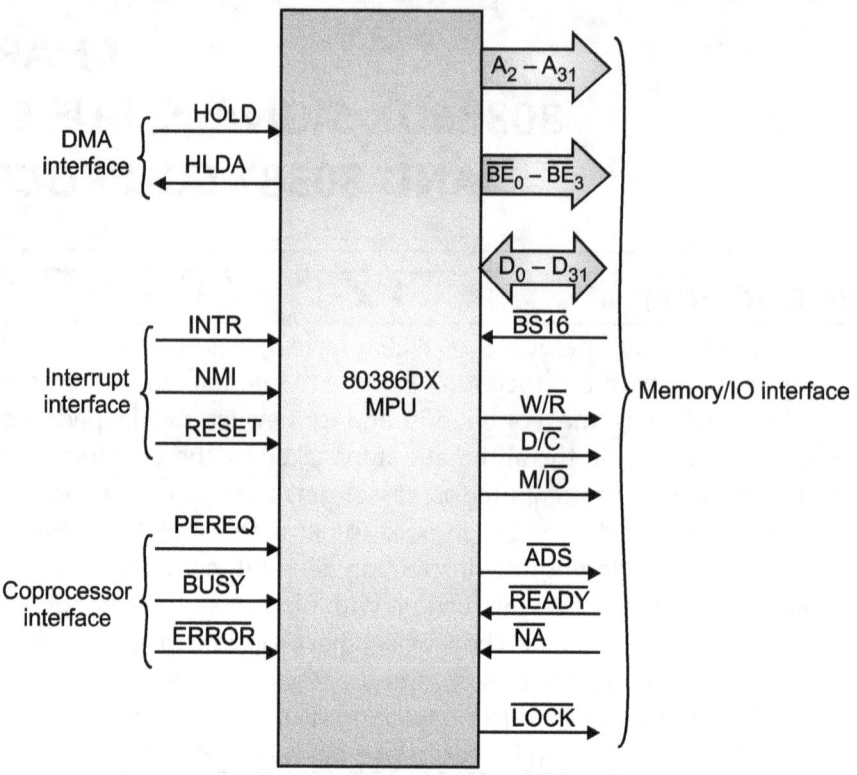

Fig. 6.2 : Signal description of 80386

Table 6.1 : List of 80386 Signals

Name	Function	Type	Level
CLK2	System clock	I	–
$A_{31} - A_2$	Address bus	O	1
$BE_3 - BE_0$	Byte enables	O	0
$D_{31} - D_0$	Data bus	I/O	1
$\overline{BS}_{16}$	Bus size 16	I	0
$W/\overline{R}$	Write/read indication	O	1/0
$D/\overline{C}$	Data/control indication	O	1/0
$M/\overline{IO}$	Memory I/O indication	O	1/0
$\overline{ADS}$	Address status	O	0
$\overline{READY}$	Transfer acknowledge	I	0
$\overline{NA}$	Next address request	I	0

Contd...

LOCK	Bus lock indication	O	0
INTR	Interrupt request	I	1
NMI	Nonmaskable interrupt request	I	1
RESET	System reset	I	1
HOLD	Bus hold request	I	1
HLDA	Bus Hold acknowledge	O	1
PEREQ	Coprocessor request	I	1
BUSY	Coprocessor busy	I	0
ERROR	Coprocessor error	I	0

Signal Description 80386 :

- W/$\overline{R}$: The write / read output distinguishes the write and read cycles from one another.

- D/$\overline{C}$: This data / control output pin distinguishes between a data transfer cycle from a machine control cycle like interrupt acknowledge.

- M/$\overline{IO}$: This output pin differentiates between the memory and I/O cycles.

- $\overline{LOCK}$: The $\overline{LOCK}$ output pin enables the CPU to prevent the other bus masters from gaining the control of the system bus.

- $\overline{NA}$: The next address input pin, if activated, allows address pipelining, during 80386 bus cycles.

- $\overline{ADS}$: The address status output pin indicates that the address bus and bus cycle definition pins(W/$\overline{R}$, D/$\overline{C}$, M/$\overline{IO}$, $\overline{BE}$ 0 to $\overline{BE}$ 3) are carrying the respective valid signals. The 80386 does not have any ALE signals and so this signals may be used for latching the address to external latches.

- $\overline{READY}$: The ready signals indicates to the CPU that the previous bus cycle has been terminated and the bus is ready for the next cycle. The signal is used to insert WAIT states in a bus cycle and is useful for interfacing of slow devices with CPU.

- VCC : These are system power supply lines.

- VSS : These return lines for the power supply.

- $\overline{BS16}$: The bus size – 16 input pin allows the interfacing of 16 bit devices with the 32 bit wide 80386 data bus. Successive 16 bit bus cycles may be executed to read a 32 bit data from a peripheral.

- HOLD : The bus hold input pin enables the other bus masters to gain control of the system bus, if it is asserted.

- HLDA : The bus hold acknowledge output indicates that a valid bus hold request has been received and the bus has been relinquished by the CPU.

- $\overline{\text{BUSY}}$: The busy input signal indicates to the CPU that the coprocessor is busy with the allocated task.
- $\overline{\text{ERROR}}$: The error input pin indicates to the CPU that the coprocessor has encountered an error while executing its instruction.
- PEREQ : The Processor extension request output signal indicates to the CPU to fetch a data word for the coprocessor.
- INTR : This interrupt pin is a maskable interrupt, that can be masked using the IF of the flag register.
- NMI : A valid request signal at the non-maskable interrupt request input pin internally generates a non-maskable interrupt of type2.
- RESET : A high at this input pin suspends the current operation and restart the execution from the starting location.
- N/C : No connection pins are expected to be left open while connecting the 80386 in the circuit.

6.3 80386DX BUS CYCLES

The internal and external bus operations of 80386 have synchronized by the clock signal. The 80386 perform variety of bus cycles in response to internal requirements and external requirements. There are different types of bus cycles / operations are as follows :

- Memory read
- I/O read
- Instruction fetch
- Halt / Shut down
- Memory write
- I/O write
- Interrupt acknowledge

Table 6.2 : Status Signals along with Bus Cycles

M/$\overline{\text{IO}}$	D/$\overline{\text{C}}$	W/$\overline{\text{R}}$	Bus Cycle Type				Locked?
Low	Low	Low	INTERRUPT ACKNOWLEDGE				Yes
Low	Low	High	Does not occur				–
Low	High	Low	I/O DATA READ				No
Low	High	High	I/O DATA WRITE				No
High	Low	Low	MEMORY CODE READ				No
High	Low	High	HALT :		SHUT DOWN :		No
			Address=2		Address=0		
			BE0–	High	BE0	Low	
			BE1	High	BE1	High	
			BE2	Low	BE2	High	
			BE3	High	BE3	High	
			A2-A31	Low	A2-A31	Low	
High	High	Low	MEMORY DATA READ				Some Cycles
High	High	High	MEMORY DATA WRITE				Some Cycles

The above Table 6.2 defined as follows :

- In each bus cycles, corresponding status signals have activated.

- The Table 6.2 shows the status signals along with the bus cycles.

- Table 6.2 shows memory read and memory write bus cycles have locked to prevent another bus master from using the bus. Before going to see bus cycles, it is necessary to know about bus states in 80386DX and system clock.

6.4 SYSTEM CLOCKS

The system clock synchronizes the internal and external bus operations in the 80386DX.

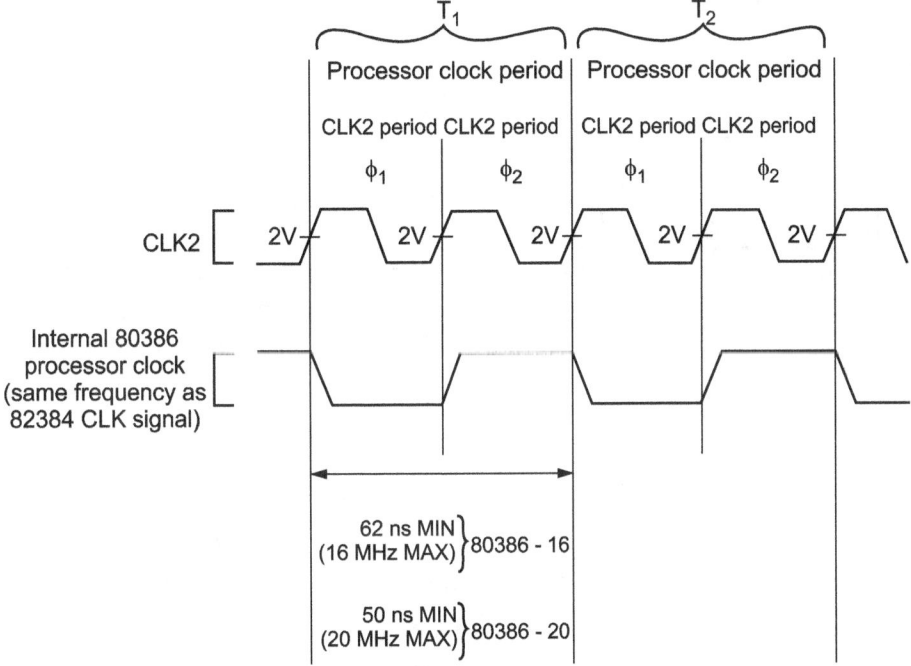

Fig. 6.3 : CLK2 and internal clock signals

The 80386DX can operate on the following different clock speeds :

- 80386DX - 16 (16 MHz)

- 80386DX - 20 (20 MHz)

- 80386DX - 25 (25 MHz) and

- 80386DX - 33(33 MHz)

Operating frequency of the 80386DX is half of the CLK2 frequency. Therefore, CLK2 of an 80386DX - 20 has driven by 40 MHz signal. The Fig. 6.3 defined as follows :

- It has used to synchronize both internal and external operations.

- It has generated by external oscillator.

- Specified in terms of frequency or cycle time.

- Cycle time = 1 / frequency.
- E.g. 20 MHz clock → cycle time = $1 / 20 \times 10^6$ = 50 ns.
- 80386 specifics :
- External pin CLK2 : clock input.
- Internal clock : ½ frequency of CLK2.
- Valid internal frequencies for different 80386 models : 16, 20, 25, 33 MHz.
- One (internal) cycle : 1 "T state".

The Fig. 6.3 shows the CLK2 and internal clock signals.

6.5 BUS STATES

Each bus cycle consists of at least followings types of bus states :
- Bus States T1
- Bus States T2

Each bus state consists of the following types of CLK cycles :
- During the first bus state (T1), address, and bus status pin are active.
- During the second bus state (T2), actual data transfer takes place.

6.6 DYNAMIC BUS SIZING

Dynamic data bus sizing is a feature allowing direct processor connection to 32-bit or16-bit data buses for memory or I/O. A single processor may connect to both size buses. Transfers to or from 32 to 16 bit ports have supported by dynamically determining the bus width during each bus cycle.

- **$\overline{\text{BS 16}}$ Input :**

   The 80386DX microprocessor's bus size 16 ($\overline{\text{BS16}}$) input has used to inform the 80386DX that the currently addressed device is a 16-bit device rather than a 32-bit device. When $\overline{\text{BS 16}}$ signal is activated, the 80386DX performs data transfers with the addressed device using only the lower two data bytes, (D7-D0) and (D15-D8). If the data is more than 16-bit, microprocessor generates additional bus cycle to fulfill the bus transfer request, if $\overline{\text{BS 16}}$ is sampled asserted.

- **Execution of Instruction MOV EAX :**

   Let us consider the actions caused by the execution of the instruction MOV EAX, [4F04] and assume DS = 0000H, the processor is in real mode, and the addressed device is a 16-bit device. The MOV EAX, [4F04] instruction initiates the transfer of a double word (the EAX register is four bytes in size) starting at memory location 00004F04H. At the beginning of the first bus cycle, the 80386DX places address 00004F04H on the address bus (A31-A0) and assert all four byte enable outputs. When the currently addressed device's address decoder detects the address, it asserts $\overline{\text{BS16}}$, informing the 80386DX that the currently addressed device is only capable of communicating over the lower data bytes.

- **Placing Contents of Memory Location on D_7-D_0 :**

  In the first bus cycle the contents of memory location 00004F04H has placed on D_7 - D_0 and the contents of memory location 00004F05H has placed on D_{15} - D_8 by the addressed 16-bit memory device. At the end of the bus cycle, when $\overline{READY}$ has sampled asserted, the 80386DX reads the two data bytes and loads them in the lower bytes of the EAX register.

- **Begins Second Bus Cycle with Same Address :**

  The 80386DX then automatically begins a second bus cycle with the same address (00004F04H) on the address bus and $\overline{BS2}$ and $\overline{BS3}$ asserted. The addressed 16-bit device's address decoder once again asserts $\overline{BS16}$, and the contents of 00004F06H and 00004F07H memory locations have transferred to the 80386DX over the two lower data bytes.

- **Reads the Data :**

  At the end of the bus cycle, the 80386DX reads the two data bytes from the two lower data bytes and loads them into the upper two bytes of the EAX register, completing the overall transfer.

6.7 NON PIPELINED AND PIPELINED BUS CYCLES

The 80386DX provides the following types of the bus cycles are as follows :

1. **Non Pipelined Bus Cycle or Non Pipelined Machine Cycle :**

   The following Fig. 6.4 shows typical no pipelined microprocessor bus cycle, which has, defined as follows :

   - During T1, the 80386DX sends the address bus, status signal and control signals. In case of write cycle, data to be output is also send on the data bus, during T1.
   - As shown in the figure, after address access time read or writes data transfer, it takes place over the data bus. This activity has carried out in T2.

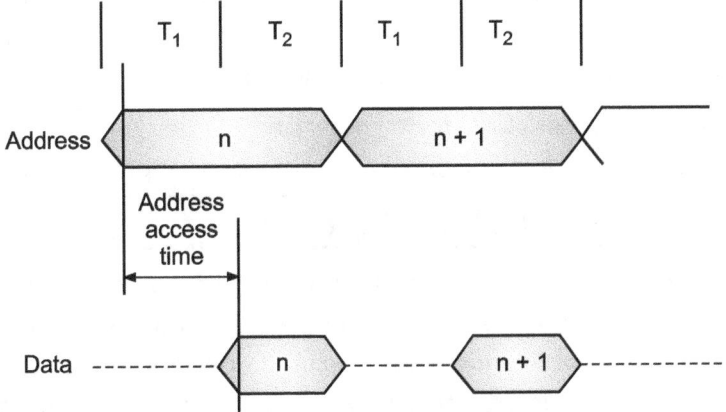

Fig. 6.4 : Typical non pipelined microprocessor bus cycle

2. Pipelined Bus Cycle or Pipelined Machine Cycle :

Pipelining allows bus cycles to be overlapped. The main advantage of pipelining is that it increases the amount of time required for the memory or I/O device to respond. This time has also referred as access time. The 80386DX implements pipelining by overlapping addressing of the next bus cycle with the data transfer of previous bus cycle.

Address-Access Time :

The amount of time that address is stable prior to read/write of data, which contains followings :

- Pipelined mode has longer effective address-access time.
- Given fixed address-access time (equal speed memory design), pipelined bus cycle will have a shorter duration than non pipelined busy cycle.
- I.e. pipelined bus can operate at a higher clock rate than non pipelined bus cycle.

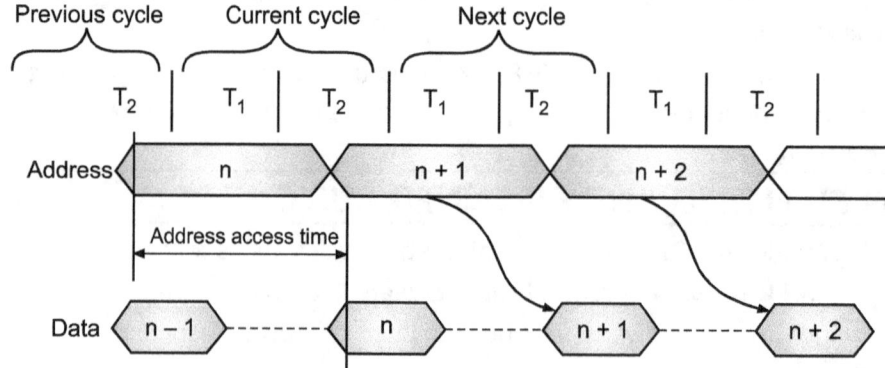

Fig. 6.5 : Typical pipelined bus cycles of 80386DX

The Fig. 6.5 shows that address becomes valid in T2 state of the previous bus cycle, and the data transfer for address takes place in T2-state of the current bus cycle.

It is important to note that the address An + 1 becomes valid during T2 of the current bus cycle and actual data transfer for address An+ 1 takes place in T2 state of the next bus cycle. If the processor is 80386DX-20 then one T-state time is 50 ns.

In pipelined bus cycle, the access time for memory and I/O device is 100 ns whereas access time for memory and I/O device in non-pipelined bus cycle is approximately 50 ns.

6.8 IDLE STATE IN PIPELINED BUS CYCLE

In the pipelined bus cycle, it has defined that addressing of next cycle has overlapped with the data transfer of the current cycle. However, in some situations such as prefetch queue is full and the instruction that is currently being executed does not require to access operands in memory or I/O device, no bus activity will take place. In such situations, bus enters into a state called idle state.

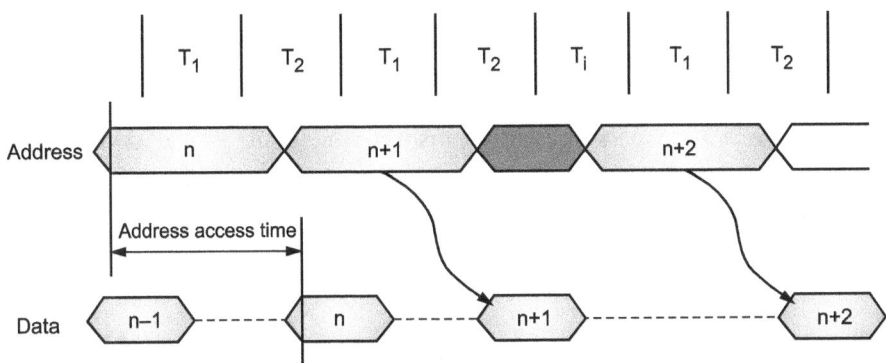

Fig. 6.6 : Bus idle state

6.9 READ AND WRITE BUS CYCLES

The followings are the sequence of events that take place during the 80386DX memory read and write bus cycles.

1. **Non Pipelined Read Cycle :**

    The Fig. 6.7 shows the timings for two non-pipelined read cycles (with and without a wait state). First read cycle is without wait state and second cycle is with wait state.

    The sequence of events for the non-pipelined read cycle is as follows :

a. **Begins Read Operation in T1 State :**

    The read operation starts at the beginning of phase in the T1 state of the bus cycle. In this phase, 80386DX sends the address on the address bus and enables signals (BE0 - BE3) according to data hang type. After sending the address, in the same phase, 80386 DX activates its $\overline{\text{ADS}}$ signal to indicate valid address is place on the address bus.

b. **Activates Bus Cycle Definition Signals :**

    In Phase 1 of T1 - state 80386DX also activates the bus cycle definition signals : M/$\overline{\text{IO}}$, D/$\overline{\text{C}}$, and W/$\overline{\text{R}}$. For read cycle, W/$\overline{\text{R}}$ is low. M/$\overline{\text{IO}}$ is high for memory read and low for an I/$\overline{\text{O}}$ read. D/$\overline{\text{C}}$ signal differentiate between data and instruction code. This signal is high if data is to read and low if an instruction code is to read. At the end of phase 2 of T1 - state, $\overline{\text{ADS}}$ is returned to its inactive logic 1 state. The address bus, byte enable pins, and bus status pins remain active through the end of the read cycle.

c. **Activates $\overline{\text{BS16}}$ Signal :**

    At the beginning of phase, 1 of T2 state external device activates $\overline{\text{BS16}}$ signal. The 80386DX samples this signal in the middle of phase 1 of T2-state. If this signal is high, 80386DX does the 32-bit data transfer; otherwise, 80386 DX performs 16-bit data transfer. The 80386 DX does this data transfer in phase 2 of T2-state.

d. READY Signal :

At the end of the phase 2 of T2-state, the $\overline{\text{READY}}$ signal is sampled by the 80386DX.

The 80386DX, the logic 1 on this signal inserts wait state in the current bus cycle to extend the bus cycle. In wait state (Tw), the signals from T2-state have maintained throughout the wait state period. It is just a repetition of T2-state. Thus, the period of one wait state (Tw = T2) is equal to 50 ns of 20 MHz clock operation. If this signal is low, 80386 DX proceeds with next bus cycle.

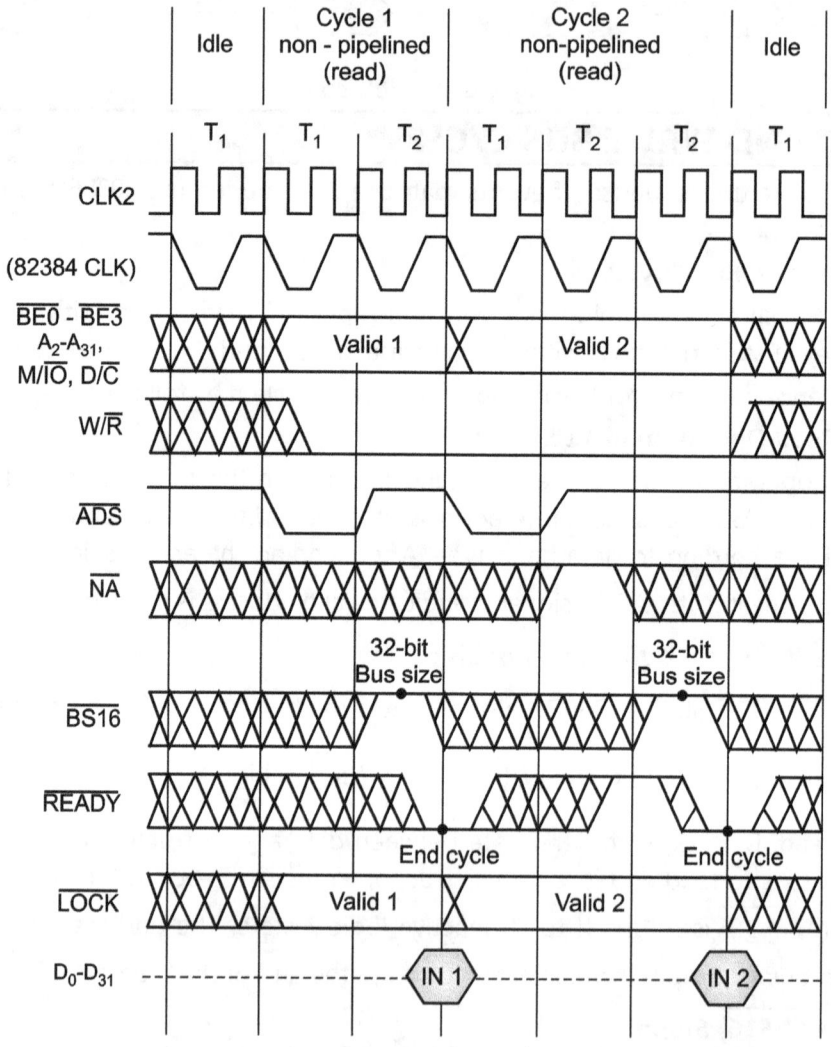

Fig. 6.7 : Non pipelined read cycle

e. Indication of LOCK Signal :

The $\overline{\text{LOCK}}$ signal low indicates it is bus locked cycle. If bus cycles have locked, the other bus masters have not allowed taking control of the bus between two locked bus cycles.

2. Non Pipelined Write Cycle :

The Fig. 6.8 shows the timings for two non-pipelined write cycles (with and without a wait state) first write cycle is without wait state and second cycle is with wait state.

The sequence of events for the non pipelined write cycle is as follows :

a. Begins Write Operations in T1 State :

The non-pipelined write cycle is similar to non-pipelined read cycle. The write operation starts at the beginning of phase 1 in the T1 state of the bus cycle. In this phase, 80386DX sends the address on the address bus and enables signals $\overline{BE}$ 0 - $\overline{BE}$ 3 according to data transfer type. After sending address in the same phase 80386DX activates its $\overline{ADS}$ signal to indicate valid address is placed on the address bus.

b. Activates Bus Cycle Definition Signals :

In phase, 1 of T1-state 80386DX also activates the bus cycle definition signals : M/$\overline{IO}$, D/$\overline{C}$ and W/$\overline{R}$. For write cycle, W/$\overline{R}$ is high. M/$\overline{IO}$ is high for memory and low for I/$\overline{O}$ write. D/$\overline{C}$ signal is high.

c. Sends Data :

At the beginning of phase 2 of T1-state, 80386DX sends data on the data bus. This data remains valid until the start of phase 2 of the T1-state of the next bus cycle.

d. ADS has returned to Inactive Logic States :

At the end of phase 2 of T1 - state, $\overline{ADS}$ is returned to its inactive logic 1 states. The address bus, byte enable pins, and bus status pins remain active through the end of the write cycle.

e. Samples $\overline{BS16}$ Input :

In the middle of phase 1 of T2-State, 80386DX samples $\overline{BS16}$ input. If this signal is high, 80386 DX does the 32-bit data transfer; otherwise 80386DX performs 16-bit data transfer.

f. Samples READY Signal :

At the end of phase 2 of T2-state, the $\overline{READY}$ signal has sampled by the 80386DX. The logic 1 on this signal inserts wait state in the current bus cycle to extend the bus cycle. In wait state (Tw), the signals from T2-state are maintain throughout the wait state period. It is just a repetition of T2-state. Thus, the period of one wait state (Tw-T2) is equal to 50 ns of 20 MHz clock operation. If this signal is low, 80386DX proceeds with next bus cycle.

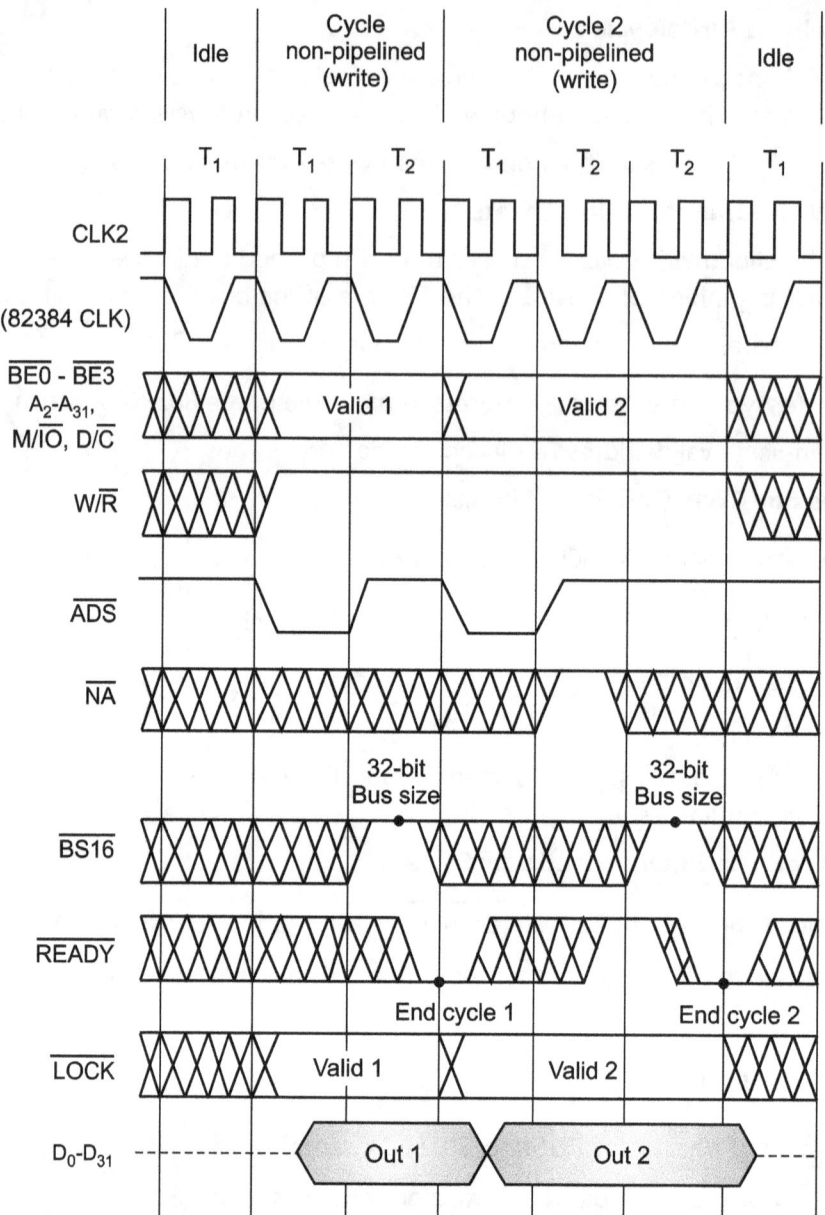

Fig. 6.8 : Non-pipelined write cycle

3. Pipelined Read/Write Cycle

As mentioned earlier, address pipelining allows bus cycles to be overlapped, increasing the amount of time available for the memory or I/O device to respond. The following Fig. 6.9 shows both non-pipelined and pipelined read and write cycles. The cycle 1 and cycle 2 in the diagram show non-pipelined write and read cycles, respectively, whereas cycle 3 and cycle 4 in the diagram show pipelined write and read cycles, respectively. This diagram also shows how wait state can be avoided using pipelined bus cycle.

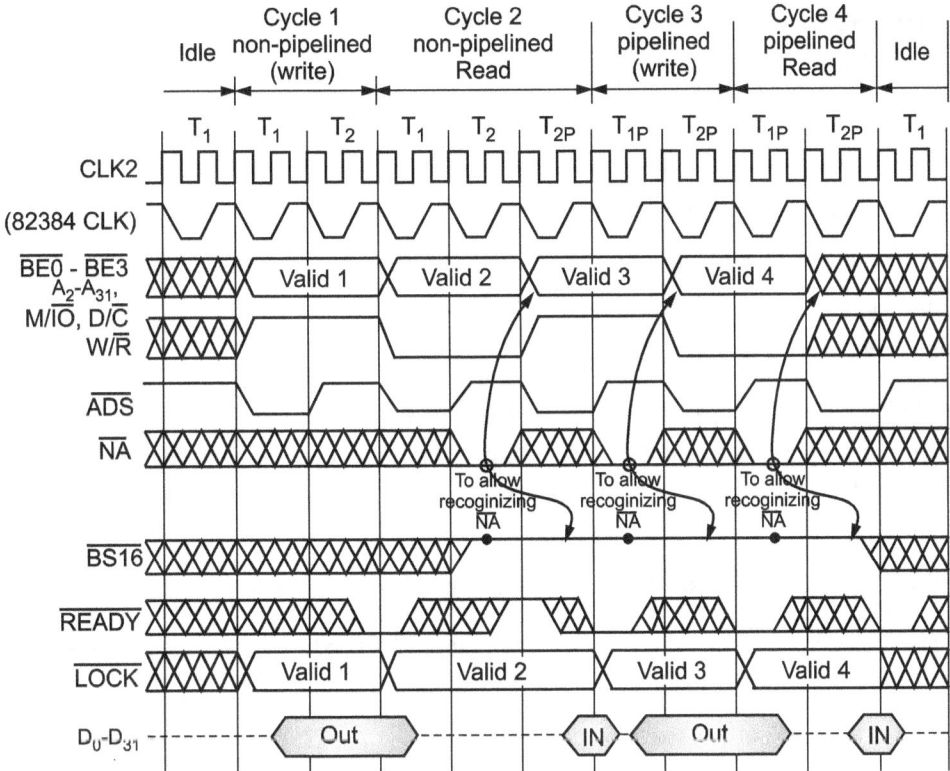

Fig. 6.9 : Non-Pipelined and Pipelined-read/write cycle

(i) Non-Pipelined Read/Write Cycles (i.e. Cycle 1 and Cycle 2) :

a. Cycle 1 (Non-Pipelined Write) :

In the pipelined bus cycle, the address for the next bus cycle has sent during the T2 - state of the current cycle. In 80386DX, $\overline{NA}$ (next address) signal initiates address pipelining. The 80386DX samples $\overline{NA}$ signal at the beginning of phase 2 of any T state in which $\overline{ADS}$ is not active, specifically.

- In the second T-state of a non-pipelined address cycle.
- In the first T-state of a pipelined address cycle.
- In any wait state of a non-pipelined address or pipelined, address cycle unless $\overline{NA}$ has already sampled active.

b. Cycle 2 (Non-Pipelined Read) :

In the Fig. 6.9, $\overline{NA}$ is tested as 0 (active) during T2 of cycle 2 which ensures that 80386DX has to execute next cycle as pipelined bus cycle. The cycle 2 (non pipelined read cycle) is also extended with one wait state because $\overline{READY}$ pin is not active, in wait state, the valid address for the next bus cycle is sent on the address bus as next bus cycle is pipelined bus cycle.

---

ii. Pipelined Read/Write Cycle(i.e. Cycle 3 and Cycle 4) :

a. Cycle 3 (Pipelined Write) :

The next cycle (cycle 3) is pipelined write cycle. In this, data has sent on the data bus in phase 2 of Tip-state and remains valid for the rest of the cycle. The $\overline{READY}$ signal is sample at the end of T2p - state. As it is low, write cycle have completed without wait state. The Fig. 6.9 shows, $\overline{NA}$ is active during T1p of cycle 3, which ensures that 80386DX has to execute next cycle as pipelined bus cycle.

b. Cycle 4 (Pipelined Read) :

The next cycle (cycle 4) is pipelined read cycle. In this, $\overline{READY}$ signal is tested 0 at the end of phase 2 of T2p - state. This means that read cycle has completed without wait state. It is important to note that due to pipelined address cycle access time is extended and one state (T -wait) of read cycle is saved.

6.10 INTERRUPT ACKNOWLEDGE BUS CYCLE

In response to INTR signal, 80386DX executes interrupt acknowledge bus cycle to read an interrupt type from the external device (8259A programmable interrupt controller).

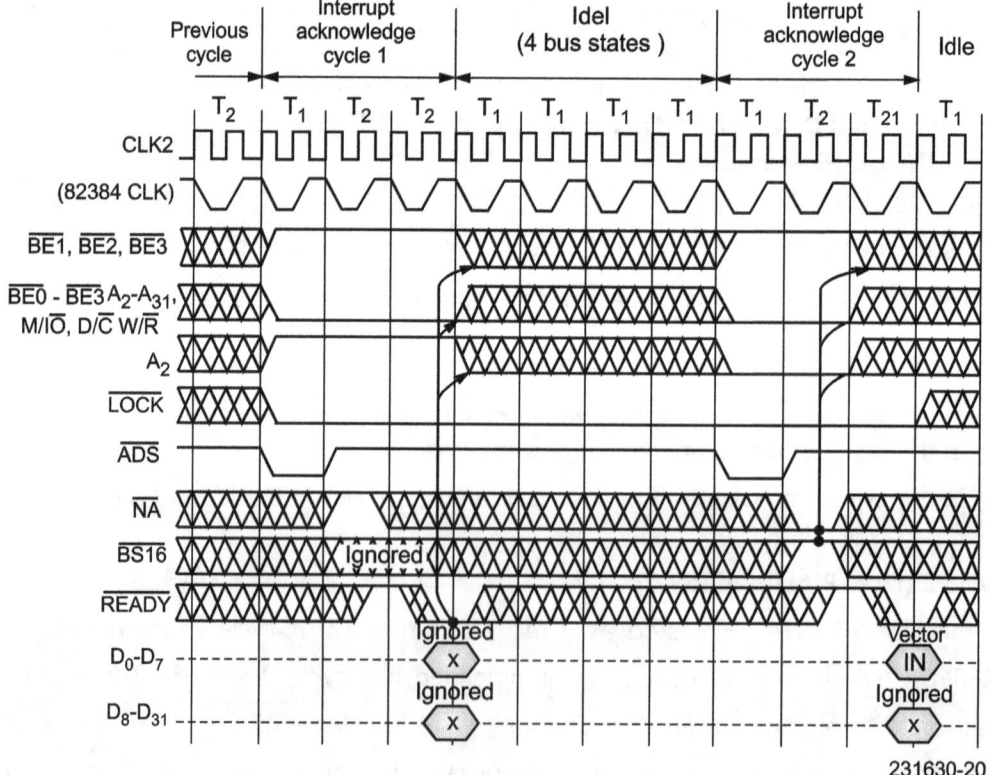

Fig. 6.10 : Interrupt acknowledge cycle

The interrupt acknowledge cycle is a special cycle designed to activate $\overline{\text{INTA}}$ signal for 8259A interrupt controller. Fig. 6.10 shows the interrupt acknowledge bus cycle. Looking at Fig. 6.10, that find there are two extended interrupt acknowledge cycles separated by four idle T-states. The extended cycles and four idle T-states are required to satisfy minimum pulse width requirements of the 8259A.

The Followings steps have occurred in an Interrupt Acknowledge Cycle :

a. Sets Address Lines :

The interrupt acknowledge cycle starts at the beginning of phase 1 in the T1 of the bus cycle. In this phase, 80386DX sets address lines A2 through A31 and $\overline{\text{BE0}}$ to logic 0, A2, and BE1 through BE3 to logic 1.

b. Sets M/$\overline{\text{IO}}$, D/$\overline{\text{C}}$ and W/$\overline{\text{R}}$:

In the same phase, 80386 DX also sets M/$\overline{\text{IO}}$, D/$\overline{\text{C}}$ and W/$\overline{\text{R}}$ signal to logic 0. These signals have latched into external circuitry with using $\overline{\text{ADS}}$ signal. The bus control logic decodes code 000 (M/$\overline{\text{IO}}$ = 0 D/$\overline{\text{C}}$ = 0 and W/$\overline{\text{R}}$ = 0) to generate an signal.

c. Activates the Signals :

In the second interrupt acknowledge cycle same signals are activated, except A2 address is logic 0 instead of logic 1. The 80386DX activates $\overline{\text{LOCK}}$ signal from the beginning of the first cycle to the end of second cycle. This prevents other master to take control of bus before the completion of second interrupt acknowledges cycle.

d. Reads Interrupt Type Number :

The 80386DX floats D31 - D0 for both bus cycles; however in the phase 2 of T2-state of the second interrupt acknowledge cycle, 80386 DX reads the interrupt type number from data bus (D7 - D0), placed by the interrupt controller (8259A).

6.11 HALT/SHUTDOWN

In response to a HLT instruction, 80386 go into halt condition. The shut down condition occurs when the 80386 is processing a double fault and encounters a protection fault.

Similar to other bus cycles, a halt and shutdown cycles are initiated by activating ADS and the bus status pin as given below :

- M/$\overline{\text{IO}}$, W/$\overline{\text{R}}$ are driven high, and D/$\overline{\text{C}}$ is driven low to indicate halt cycle.
- All address lines are set to logic 0.

- For a halt condition, $\overline{BE2}$ is active and for a shutdown condition, $\overline{BE0}$ is active. External devices to identify the halt and shutdown cycles use these signals.

1. EXIT from HALT or Shutdown :

The 80386 will remain in the halt or shutdown condition until the followings :

- NMI goes high
- RESET goes high

This means that when 80386 services NMI interrupt or if 80386 has reinitialized, it is possible to exit from halt or shutdown condition. When 80386 service INTR interrupt, it is possible to exit from halt condition but not from shut down condition.

Note :

The 80386 can service coprocessor request (PEREQ input) and HOLD (Hold input) request in the halt or shutdown condition.

6.12 CONTROL INPUT $\overline{BS16}$ AND $\overline{NA}$

As mentioned, that $\overline{BS16}$ signal specifies bus size for each bus cycle.

- The 80386DX samples this signal at the beginning of phase 2 of T-state in which $\overline{ADS}$ is not active.

- When $\overline{BS16}$ is low the 80386 performs 16-bit data transfers using D15-D0 data lines rather than 32-bit data bus.

- The 80386 automatically performs two or three bus cycles for data transfers more than 16-bits and misaligned (odd-addressed) 16-bit transfers.

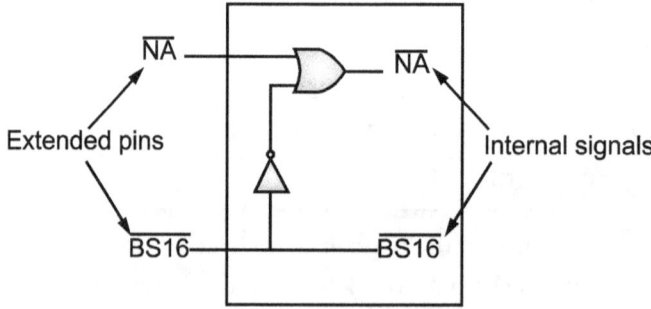

Fig. 6.11 : Internal NA and BS16 logic

- The above Fig. 6.11 shows the internal $\overline{NA}$ and $\overline{BS16}$ logic. Looking at Fig. 6.11, it finds that even though $\overline{NA}$ and $\overline{BS16}$ signals are low on the external pins, internally, these signals cannot be low at the same time.

- To implement address pipelining for 16-bitcycles, $\overline{\text{BS16}}$ must be active at the same time as $\overline{\text{NA}}$, which is impractical. Because 80386 samples $\overline{\text{BS16}}$ and $\overline{\text{NA}}$ simultaneously and as said earlier these signals cannot be active (low) at the same time. The following Fig. 6.12 and 6.13 shows the 16 and 32-bit transfers as follows :

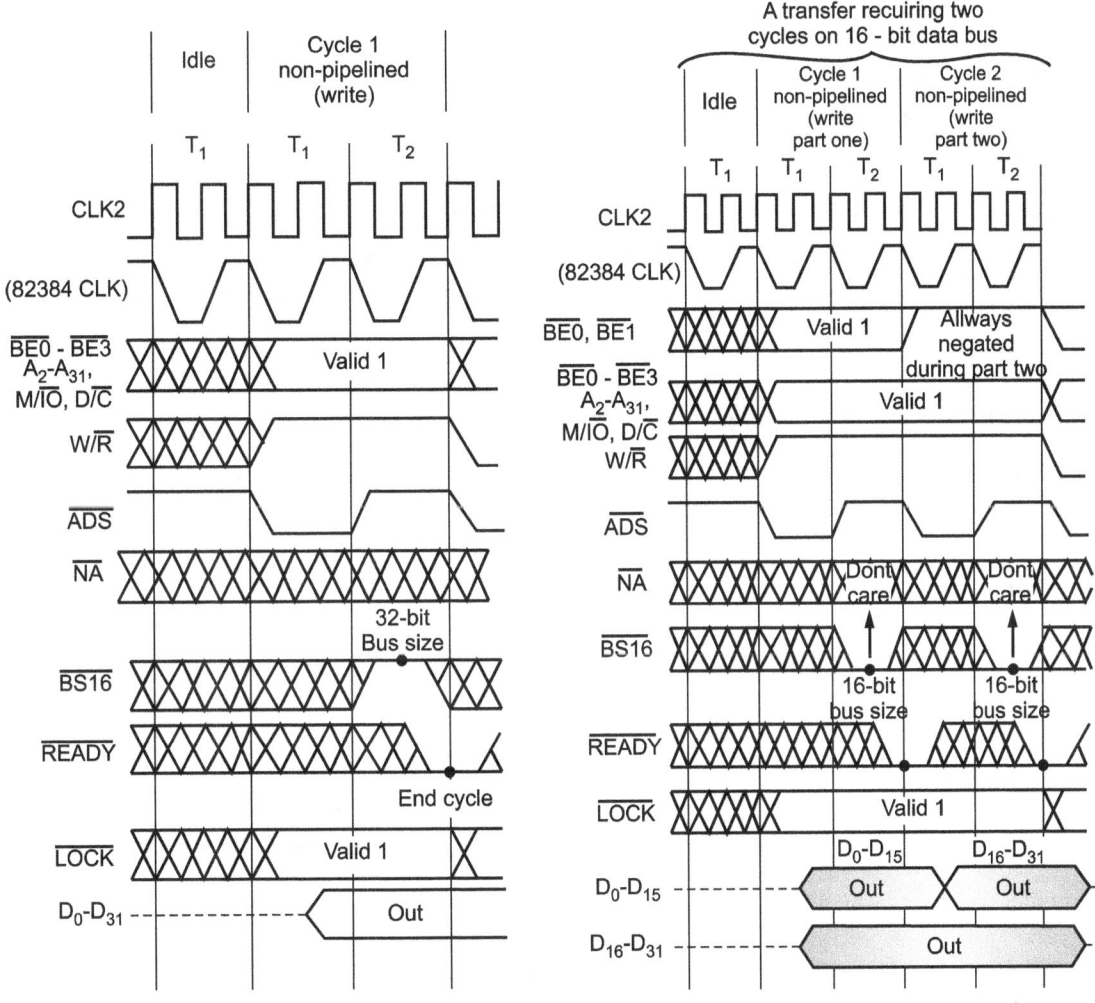

Fig. 6.12 : 16-bit transfer   Fig. 6.13 : 32-bit Transfer

6.13 BUS LOCK CYCLE

There are more than one processor shares the system memory and I/O devices through the common system bus, extra logic must be added to ensure that only one processor has accessed to the system bus at a time.

- **Critical Program Region :**

  When one processor starts executing the program, which uses the common resources, another processor is not allowed to access the used resources. The program region where the common resources are used is called critical program region.

- **Mutual Exclusion :**

  One can restrict another processor from accessing the used resources by using a technique, called Mutual exclusion. In this technique, a binary flag called semaphore is stored in the shared memory to indicate where the shared memory is free (semaphore = 1) to be accessed or busy(semaphore = 0). Testing and setting the semaphore is a critical operation and one processor must perform it at a time. This mutual exclusion technique can be implemented in 8086, 68000 and many other processors which support the multiprocessor environment.

- **Semaphore Implementation in 80386 :**

  In the 80386, the XCHG instruction along with the LOCK prefix can be used to set or reset semaphore.

  Program Sequence :

  ```
                        MOV AL, 0
      LOCK checkagain :  XCHG semaphore, AL
                        TEST AL, AL
                        JZ chaeckagain
                        •│
                        •│ Critical region in which program
                        •│ accesses the shared resources
                        •│
                        MOV semaphore, 1
  ```

The XCHG semaphore, AL instruction exchanges the contents of the AL register with the contents of the memory location in which semaphore is stored.

The XCHG instruction requires following bus cycles :

- During this XCHG instruction, it is necessary to restrict other processor from accessing semaphore. This has achieved by $\overline{\text{LOCK}}$ prefix in the 80386. $\overline{\text{LOCK}}$ prefix activates the $\overline{\text{LOCK}}$ output pin during the execution of the instruction that follows the prefix.

- During the execution of XCHG instruction, the output pin is in the active state, which does not allow other processor to get control of the system bus. After execution of the XCHG instruction, the status of the semaphore is available in the AL register. By checking the contents of the AL register, it is possible to decide whether to enter into critical region of program or to check semaphore again.

6.14 HOLD/HLDA

In multiprocessor systems, more than one processor shares the system resources, which are access through common bus. To gain the control of this common bus and system resources, the requesting processor activates the 80386 HOLD input.

- On receiving HOLD signal, 80386 outputs HLDA signal high as an acknowledgment, after completing its current bus cycle (plus a second locked cycle or a second cycle required by $\overline{BS16}$).

- At the same time, 80386 tri-states all the outputs except HLDA to effectively removes itself from the bus and then requesting processor take the control of system bus.

- A low on HOLD gives the system bus control back to the 80386. During the HOLD state, the 80386 can continue executing instruction in its Prefetch Queue.

- Even though HOLD has higher priority over most bus cycles, but HOLD has not recognized as follows :

  ➢ Between two interrupt acknowledge cycles.

  ➢ Between two repeated cycles of a BS16 cycles.

  ➢ During locked cycles.

  ➢ During Active RESET.

EXERCISE

1. Explain 7 different types of bus cycles / operations in detail.

2. Explain in detail the CLK2 and internal clock signals.

3. Write a note on Dynamic data bus sizing.

4. Explain the idle state in pipelined bus cycle.

5.   Explain the non-pipelined and pipelined machine cycles.

6.   Explain Pipelined Read/Write Cycle in detail.

7.   Explain Non-Pipelined Read/Write Cycles in detail.

8.   Explain interrupt Acknowledge Cycle in detail.

9.   Explain the halt and shut down condition in detail.

10. Draw and explain internal $\overline{NA}$ and $\overline{BS16}$ logic in detail.

11. Write a note HOLD and HLDA.

◈ ◈ ◈

7.1 CONTROL REGISTER BITS FOR COPROCESSOR SUPPORT

Table 7.1 : Control Register bits for Coprocessor support

Bit	Name	Full Name	Description
1	MP	Monitor co-processor	Controls interaction of WAIT/FWAIT instructions with TS flag in CR0.
2	EM	Emulation	If set, no x87 floating point unit present, if clear, x87 FPU present.
3	TS	Task switched	Allows saving x87 task context upon a task switch only after x87 instruction used.
4	ET	Extension type	On the 386, it allowed to specify whether the external math coprocessor was an 80287 or 80387.
5	NE	Numeric error	Enable internal x87 floating point error reporting when set, else enables PC style x87 error detection.

7.2 80387 REGISTER STACK

- The 80387 register stack is shown in Fig. 7.1. Each of the eight numeric registers in the 80387's register stack is 80 bits wide and is divided into fields corresponding to the 80787' extended real data type.

- Numeric instructions address the data registers relative to the register on the top of the stack. At any point in time, this top-of-stack register is indicated by the TOP (stack TOP) field in the 80387 status word.

- Load or push operations decrement TOP by one and load a value into the new top register. A store-and-pop operation stores the value from the current TOP register and then increments TOP by one.

- Like 80386 stacks in memory, the 80387 register stack grows down toward lower-addressed registers. Many numeric instructions have several addressing modes that permit the programmer to implicitly operate on the top of the stack, or to explicitly operate on specific registers relative to the TOP.

- The ASM386 Assembler supports these register addressing modes, using the expression ST(0), or simply ST, to represent the current Stack Top and STU) to specify the ith register from TOP in the stack (0 < : i < : 7).

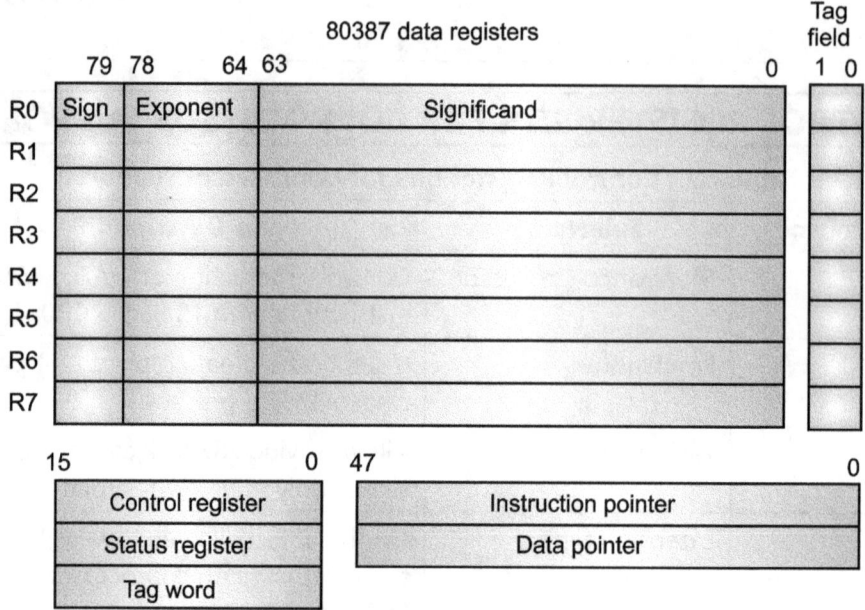

Fig. 7.1 : 80387 register stack

For example, if TOP contains 011 B (register 3 is the top of the stack), the following statement would add the contents of two registers in the stack (registers 3 and 5) :FADD ST, ST(2).

The stack organization and top-relative addressing of the numeric registers simplify subroutine programming by allowing routines to pass parameters on the register stack. By using the stack to pass parameters rather than using "dedicated" registers, calling routines gain more flexibility in how they use the stack. As long as the stack is not full, each routine simply loads the parameters onto the stack before calling a particular subroutine to perform a numeric calculation. The subroutine then addresses its parameters as ST, ST(1), etc., even though TOP may, for example, refer to physical register 3 in one invocation and physical register 5 in another.

7.3 DATA TYPES

Fig. 7.2 lists the seven data types that the Intel387 supports and presents the format for each type. Operands are stored in memory with the least significant digit at the lowest memory address. Programs retrieve these values by generating the lowest address. For maximum system performance, all operands should start at physical-memory addresses evenly divisible by four (double word boundaries); operands may begin at any other addresses, but will require extra memory cycles to access the entire operand. Internally, the Intel387 holds all numbers in the extended-precision real format. Instructions that load operands from memory automatically convert operands represented in memory as 16- bit, 32- bit, or 64-bit integers, 32- bit or 64-bit floating-point numbers, or 18-digit packed BCD numbers into extended-precision real format. Instructions that store operands in memory perform the inverse type conversion.

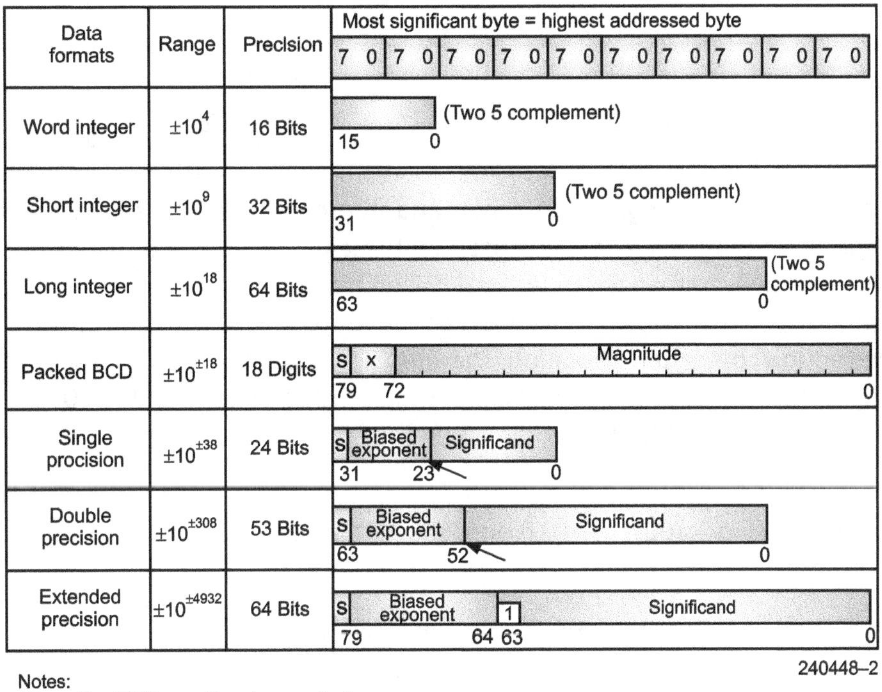

Data formats	Range	Precision	Most significant byte = highest addressed byte
Word integer	$\pm10^4$	16 Bits	(Two's complement) 15 ... 0
Short integer	$\pm10^9$	32 Bits	(Two's complement) 31 ... 0
Long integer	$\pm10^{18}$	64 Bits	(Two's complement) 63 ... 0
Packed BCD	$\pm10^{\pm18}$	18 Digits	S x Magnitude 79 72 ... 0
Single precision	$\pm10^{\pm38}$	24 Bits	S Biased exponent Significand 31 23 ... 0
Double precision	$\pm10^{\pm308}$	53 Bits	S Biased exponent Significand 63 52 ... 0
Extended precision	$\pm10^{\pm4932}$	64 Bits	S Biased exponent 1 Significand 79 64 63 ... 0

240448–2

Notes:
(1) s – Sign bit (0 – positive, 1 – negative)
(2) d_n – Decimal digit (two per byte)
(3) x – Bits have no significance; Intel387™ DX MCP ignores when loading, zeros when storing
(4) Δ – Position of implict binary point
(5) I – Integer bit of significand ; stored in temporary real, implict in single and double precision
(6) Exponent bias (normalized values);
   Single: 127 (7FH)
   Double : 1023 (3FFH)
   Extended real : 16383 (3FFFH)
(7) Packed BCD : $(-1)^S (D_{17}...D_0)$
(8) Real : $(-1)^S (2^{E-Bias}) (F_0 F_1 ...)$

Fig. 7.2 : 80387 data types

7.4 LOAD AND STORE INSTRUCTIONS

7.4.1 Load Instructions

Each of these instructions (Table 7.2 loads (pushes) a commonly used constant onto the stack. ST(7) must be empty to avoid an invalid exception.) The values have full extended real precision (64 bits) and are accurate to approximately 19 decimal digits.

Table 7.2 : Load Instructions

FLDZ	Load + 0.0
FLD1	Load + 1.0
FLDPI	Load π
FLDL2T	Load $\log_2 10$
FLDL2E	Load $\log_2 e$
FLDLG2	Load $\log_{10} 2$
FLDLN2	Load $\log_0 2$

Because an external real constant occupies 10 memory bytes, the constant instructions, which are only two bytes long, save storage and improve execution speed, in addition to simplifying programming. The constants used by these instructions are stored internally in a format more precise even than extended real. When loading the constant, the 80387 rounds the more precise internal constant according the RC (rounding control) bit of the control word. However, in spite of this rounding, the precision exception is not raised (to maintain compatibility). When the rounding control is set to round to nearest on the 80387, the 80387 produces the same constant that is produced by the 80287.

1. **FLDZ**

   FLDZ (load zero) loads (pushes) +0.0 onto the NPX stack.

2. **FLD1**

   FLDI (load one) loads (pushes) + 1.0 onto the NPX stack.

3. **FLDPI**

   FLDPI (load π) loads (pushes) π onto the NPX stack.

4. **FLDL2T**

   FLDL2T (load log base 2 of 10) loads (pushes) the value $\log_2 10$ onto the NPX stack.

5. **FLDL2E**

   FLDL2E (load log base 2 of e) loads (pushes) the value $\log_2 e$ onto the NPX stack.

6. **FLDLG2**

   FLDLG2 (load log base 10 of 2) loads (pushes) the value $\log_{10} 2$ onto the NPX stack.

7. **FLDLN2**

   FLDLN2 (load log base e of 2) loads (pushes) the value $\log_e 2$ onto the NPX stack.

7.4.2 Load Store Instructions

The instruction FSTSW is commonly used for conditional branching. The remaining instructions are not typically used in calculations; they provide control over the 80387 NPX for system-level activities. These activities include initialization, exception handling, and task switching. As shown in Table 7.3, many of the NPX processor control instructions have two forms of assembler mnemonic :

- A wait form, where the mnemonic is prefixed only with an F, such as FSTSW. This form checks for unmasked numeric exceptions.

- A no-wait form, where the mnemonic is prefixed with an FN, such as FNSTSW. This form ignores unmasked numeric exceptions. When the control instruction is coded using the no-wait form of the mnemonic, the ASM386 assembler does not precede the ESC instruction with a wait instruction, and the CPU does not test the ERROR# status line from the NPX before executing the processor control instruction. Only the processor control class of instructions has this alternate no-wait form. All numeric instructions are automatically synchronized by the 80386; the CPU transfers all operands before initiating the next instruction. Because of this automatic synchronization by the 80386, numeric instructions for the 80387 need not be preceded by a CPU wait instruction in order to execute correctly.

Table 7.3 : Load Store

FINIT/FNINI	Initialize processor
FLDCW	Load control word
FSTSW/FNSTSW	Store control word
FSTSW/FNTSW	Store staus word
FSTSW/AX/FNSTSW AX	Store status word to AX
FCLEX/FNCLEX	Clear exceptions
FSTENV/FNSTENV	Store enviornment
FLDENV	Load enviornment
FSAVE/FNSAVE	Save state
FRSTOR	Restore state
FINCSTP	Increment stack pointer
FDECSTP	Decrement stack pointer
FFREE	Free register
FNOP	No operation
FWAIT	CPU Wait

1. FINIT/FNINIT

FINIT/FNINIT (initialize processor) sets the 80387 NPX into a known state, unaffected by any previous activity. It sets the control word to its default value 037FH (round to nearest, all exceptions masked, 64 bits of precision), clears the status word, and empties all floating point stack registers. The no-wait form of this instruction causes the 80387 to abort any previous numeric operations currently executing in the NEU. This instruction performs the functional equivalent of hardware RESET, with one exception :

RESET causes the 1M bit of the control word to be reset and the ES and IE bits of the status word to be set as a means of signaling the presence of an 80387; FINIT puts the opposite values in these bits. FINIT checks for unmasked numeric exceptions, FNINIT does not. Note that if FNINIT is executed while a previous 80387 memory-referencing instruction is running, 80387 bus cycles in progress are aborted. This instruction may be necessary to clear the 80387 if a processor-extension segment-overrun exception (interrupt 9) is detected by the CPU.

2. FLDCW Source

FLDCW (load control word) replaces the current processor control word with the word defined by the source operand. This instruction is typically used to establish or change the 80387's mode of operation. Note that if an exception bit in the status word is set, loading a new control word that unmasks that exception will activate the ERROR# output of the 80387. When changing modes, the recommended procedure is to first clear any exceptions and then load the new control word.

3. FSTCW IFNSTCW Destination

FSTCW /FNSTCW (store control word) writes the processor control word to the memory location defined by the destination. FSTCW checks for unmasked numeric exceptions; FNSTCW does not.

4. FSTSW IFNSTSW Destination

FSTSW, FNSTSW (store status word) writes the current value of the 80387 status word to the destination operand in memory. The instruction is used to implement conditional branching following a comparison, FPREM, or FPREM 1 instruction (FSTSW).

Invoke exception handlers (by polling the exception bits) in environments that do not use interrupts (FSTSW). FSTSW checks for unmasked numeric exceptions, FNSTSW does not.

5. FSTSW AX/FNSTSW AX

FSTSW AX/FNSTSW AX (store status word to AX) is a special 80387 instruction that writes the current value of the 80387 status word directly into the 80386 AX register. This instruction optimizes conditional branching in numeric programs, where the 80386 CPU must test the condition of various NPX status bits. The waited form FSTSW AX checks for unmasked numeric exceptions, the non-waited form FNSTSW AX does not.

When this instruction is executed, the 80386 AX register is updated with the NPX status word before the CPU executes any further instructions. The status stored is that from the completion of the prior ESC instruction.

6. FCLEX/FNCLEX

FCLEX/FNCLEX (clear exceptions) clears all exception flags, the exception status flag and the busy flag in the status word. As a consequence, the 80387's $\overline{\text{ERROR}}$ line goes inactive. FCLEX checks for unmasked numeric exceptions, FNCLEX does not.

7. FSAVE/FNSAVE Destination

FSAVE/FNSAVE (save state) writes the full 80387 state environment plus register stack to the memory location defined by the destination operand. When the 80386 is in virtual-8086 mode, the real-address mode formats are used. Typically, the instruction is coded to save this image on the CPU stack. The values in the tag word in memory are determined during the execution of VE1KNSAVE. If the tag in the status register indicates that the corresponding register is nonempty, the 80387 examines the data in the register and stores the appropriate tag in memory. Thus, the tag that is stored always reflects the actual content of the register.

8. FSTENV IFNSTENV Destination

FSTENV /FNSTENV (store environment) writes the 80387's basic status-control, status and tag words, and exception pointers-to the memory location defined by the destination operand. Typically, the environment is saved on the CPU stack. FSTENV /FNSTENV is often used by exception handlers because it provides access to the exception pointers that identify the offending instruction and operand. After saving the environment, FSTENV / FNSTENV sets all exception masks in the 80387 control word (i.e., masks all exceptions). FSTENV checks for pending exceptions before executing, FNSTENV does not.

When the 80386 is in virtual-8086 mode, the real-address mode formats are used. FNSTENV does not store the environment until all NPX activity has completed.

Thus, the data saved by the instruction reflects the 80387 after any previously decoded instruction has been executed. The values in the tag word in memory are determined during the execution of FNSTENV / FSTENV. If the tag in the status register indicates that the corresponding register is nonempty, the 80387 examines the data in the register and stores the appropriate tag in memory. Thus the tag that is stored always reflects the actual content of the register.

9. FLDENV Source

FLDENV (load environment) reloads the environment from the memory area defined by the source operand. This data should have been written by a previous FSTENV /FNSTENV instruction. CPU instructions (that do not reference the environment image) may immediately follow FLDENV. FLDENV automatically waits for all data transfers to complete before executing the next instruction. Note that loading an environment image that contains an unmasked exception causes a numeric exception when the next WAIT or exception-checking ESC instruction is executed.

10. FINCSTP

FINCSTP (increment NPX stack pointer) adds 1 to the stack top pointer (TOP) in the status word. It does not alter tags or register contents, nor does it transfer data. It is not equivalent to popping the stack, because it does not set the tag of the previous stack top to empty. Incrementing the stack pointer when ST=7 produces ST=0.

11. FDECSTP

FDECSTP (decrement NPX stack pointer) subtracts 1 from ST, the stack top pointer in the status word. No tags or registers are altered, nor is any data transferred. Executing FDECSTP when ST=0 produces ST=7.

12. FFREE Destination

FFREE (free register) changes the destination register's tag to empty; the content of the register is unaffected.

13. FNOP

FNOP (no operation) effectively performs no operation.

14. FWAIT (CPU Instruction)

FWAIT is not actually an 80387 instruction, but an alternate mnemonic for the 80386 WAIT instruction. The FWAIT or WAIT mnemonic should be coded whenever the programmer wants to check for a pending error before modifying a variable used in the previous floating point instruction. Coding an FWAIT instruction after an 80387 instruction ensures that unmasked numeric exceptions occur and exception handlers are invoked before the next instruction has a chance to examine the results of the 80387 instruction.

7.5 TRIGONOMETRIC AND TRANSCENDENTAL INSTRUCTIONS

The instructions in this group (Table 7.4) perform the time-consuming core calculations for all common trigonometric, inverse trigonometric, hyperbolic, inverse hyperbolic, logarithmic, and exponential functions. The transcendental operate on the top one or two stack elements, and they return their results to the stack. The trigonometric operations assume their arguments are expressed in radians. The logarithmic and exponential operations work in base 2. The results of transcendental instructions are highly accurate. The absolute value of the relative error of the transcendental instructions is guaranteed to be less than 2^{-62}. (Relative error is the ratio between the absolute error and the exact value.)

Table 7.4 : Trigonometric and Transcendental Instruction

C3	C2	C1	C0	Value at TOP
0	0	0	0	+Unsupported
0	0	0	1	+NaN
0	0	1	0	–Unsupported
0	0	1	1	–NaN
0	1	0	0	+Normal
0	1	0	1	+Infinity
0	1	1	0	–Normal
0	1	1	1	–Infinity
1	0	0	0	+0
1	0	0	1	+Empty
1	0	1	0	–0
1	0	1	1	–Empty
1	1	0	0	+Denormal
1	1	1	0	–Denormal

FSIN	Sine
FCOS	Cosine
FSINCOS	Sine and cosion
FPTAN	Tangent of ST
FPATAN	Arctangent of ST(1)/ST
F2XM1	2^X-1
FYL2X	$Y \cdot \log_2 X$; Y is ST(1), X is ST
FYL2XP1	$Y \cdot \log_2(X + 1)$; Y is ST(1), X is ST

The trigonometric functions accept a practically unrestricted range of operands, whereas the other transcendental instructions require that arguments be more restricted in range. FPREM or FPREMI may be used to bring the otherwise valid operand of a periodic function into range. Prologue and epilogue software may be used to reduce arguments for other instructions to the expected range and to adjust the result to correspond to the original arguments if necessary. The instruction descriptions in this section document the allowed operand range for each instruction.

7.5.1 FCOS

When complete, this function replaces the contents of ST with COS(ST). ST, expressed in radians, must lie in the range 101 <263 (for most practical purposes unrestricted). If ST is in range, C2 of the status word is cleared and the result of the operation is produced. If the operand is outside of the range, C2 is set to one (function incomplete) and ST remains intact (i.e., no reduction of the operand is performed). It is the programmers' responsibility to reduce the operand to an absolute value smaller than 263. The instructions FPREMI and FPREM are available for this purpose.

7.5.2 FSIN

When complete, this function replaces the contents of ST with SIN(ST). FSIN is equivalent to FCOS in the way it reduces the operand. ST is expressed in radians.

7.5.3 FSINCOS

When complete, this instruction replaces the contents of ST with SIN(ST), then pushes COS(ST) onto the stack. ST(7) must be empty to avoid an invalid exception.) FSINCOS is equivalent to FCOS in the way it reduces the operand. ST is expressed in radians.

7.5.4 FPTAN

When complete, FPTAN (partial tangent) computes the function Y = TAN (ST). ST is expressed in radians. Y replaces ST, then the value 1 is pushed, becoming the new stack top. ST(7) must be empty to avoid an invalid exception.) When the function is complete ST(I) = TAN (arg) and ST = 1. FPTAN is equivalent to FCOS in the way it reduces the operand.

7.5.5 FPATAN

FPATAN (arctangent) computes the function 8 = ARCTAN (Y IX). X is taken from ST(O) and Y from ST(I). The instruction pops the NPX stack and returns 8 to the (new) stack top, overwriting the Y operand. The result is expressed in radians. The range of operands is not restricted; however, the range of the result depends on the relationship between the operands according to Table 7.4. The fact that the argument of FPATAN is a ratio aids calculation of other trigonometric functions, including Arcsin and Arccos. These can be derived from Arctan via standard trigonometric identities. For example, the Arcsin function can be easily calculated using this identity :

$$Arcsin\ x\ =\ Arctan\ (x\ I\ V\ 1\ -\ X2).$$

Thus, to find Arcsin (Y), push Y onto the NPX stack, then calculate X = vi1 - y2, pushing the result X onto the stack. Executing FPAT AN then leaves Arcsin (Y) at the top of the stack.

7.5.6 F2XM1

F2XMI (2 to the X minus 1) calculates the function Y = 2X - 1. X is taken from the stack top and must be in the range -1 < : X < : 1. The result Y replaces the argument X at the stack top. If the argument is out of range, the results are undefined. This instruction is designed to produce a very accurate result even when X is close to O. For values of the argument very close in magnitude to 1, a larger error will be incurred. To obtain Y = 2x, add 1 to the result delivered by F2XM1.

7.5.7 FYL2X

FYL2X (Y log base 2 of X) calculates the function Z = Y - LOG2X. X is taken from the stack top and Y from ST(1). The operands must be in the following ranges :

$$o -< \ <+00$$

$$-00 \ < \ Y <+00$$

The instruction pops the NPX stack and returns Z at the (new) stack top, replacing the Y operand. If the operand is out of range (i.e., in negative) the invalid-operation exception occurs.

7.5.8 FYL2XP 1

FYL2XP 1 (Y log base 2 of (X + 1» calculates the function Z = Y -LOG2 (X + 1). X is taken from the stack top and must be in the range -(1-SQRT(2)j2) <X < I-SQRT(2)j2. Y is taken from ST(l) and is unlimited in range (-00 <Y <+(0). FYL2XP1 pops the stack and returns Z at the (new) stack top, replacing Y. If the argument is out of range, the results are undefined. This instruction provides improved accuracy over FYL2X when computing the logarithm of a number very close to 1, for example 1 + t where E <<1. Providing f rather than 1 + E as the input to the function allows more significant digits to be retained.

7.6 80386DX AND 80387 INTERFACE

As an extension to the Intel386 DX Microprocessor, the Intel387 DX Math Coprocessor can be connected to the CPU as shown by Fig. 7.3. A dedicated communication protocol makes possible high-speed transfer of opcodes and operands between the Intel386 DX CPU and Intel387 DX MCP. The Intel387 DX MCP is designed so that no additional components are required for interface with the Intel386 DX CPU. The Intel387 DX MCP shares the 32-bit wide local bus of the Intel386 DX CPU and most control pins of the Intel387 DX MCP are connected directly to pins of the Intel386 DX Microprocessor.

Table 7.5 : Signal Interface Table

STEN	NPS1	NPS2	CMD0	W/ R	Bus Cycle Type
0	x	x	x	x	MCP not selected and all outputs in floating state
1	1	x	x	x	MCP not selected
1	x	0	x	x	MCP not selected
1	0	1	0	0	CW or SW read from MCP
1	0	1	0	1	Opcode write to MCP
1	0	1	1	0	Data read from MCP
1	0	1	1	1	Data write to MCP

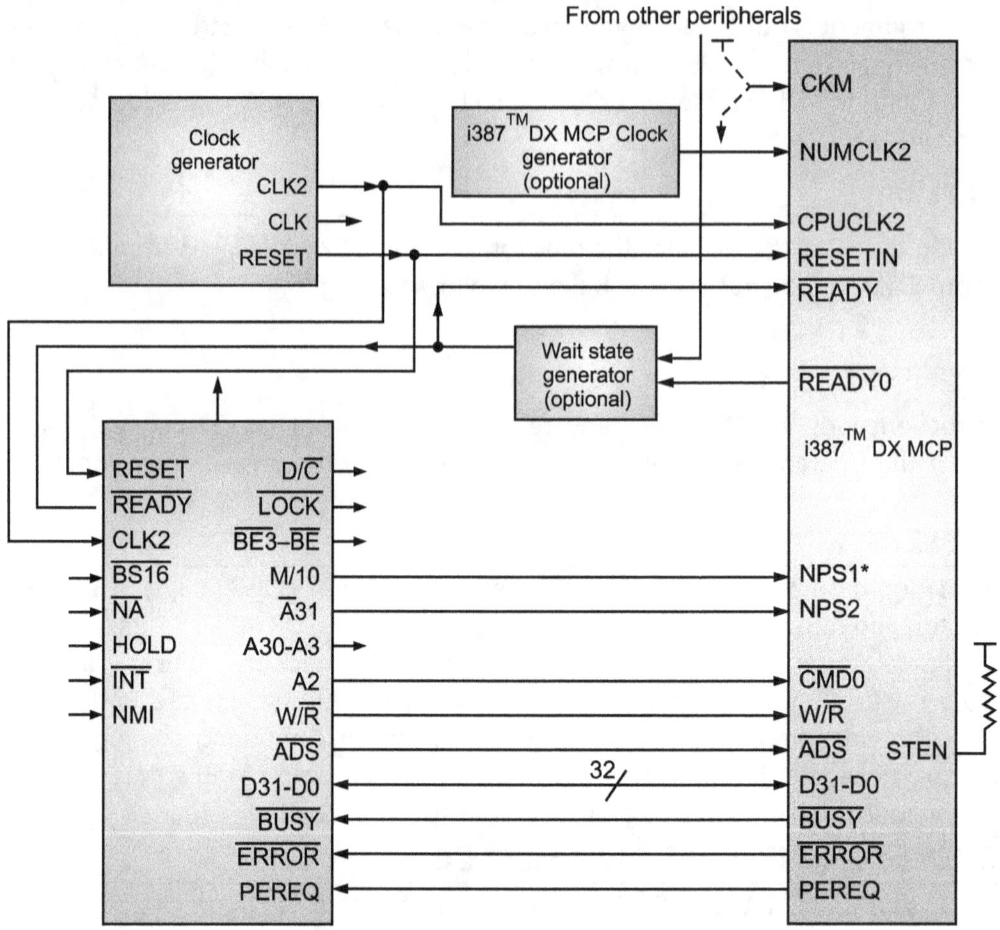

From other peripherals

Clock generator
CLK2
CLK
RESET

i387™DX MCP Clock generator (optional)

Wait state generator (optional)

CKM
NUMCLK2
CPUCLK2
RESETIN
READY

READY0

i387™ DX MCP

RESET
READY
CLK2
BS16
NA
HOLD
INT
NMI

D/C
LOCK
BE3–BE
M/10
A31
A30-A3
A2
W/R
ADS
D31-D0
BUSY
ERROR
PEREQ

NPS1*
NPS2

CMD0
W/R
ADS
D31-D0
BUSY
ERROR
PEREQ

STEN

32

Fig. 7.3 : Signal interface diagram

EXERCISE

1. Draw and explain 80387 Register Stack.

2. What are Trigonometric and Transcendental Instructions?

3. Draw and explain Signal Interface Diagram.

◈ ◈ ◈

ASSIGNMENT 1

Write X86/64 ALP to count number of positive and negative numbers from the array.

```
section .data
        welmsg db 10,'Welcome to count +ve and -ve numbers in an array',10
        welmsg_len equ $-welmsg
        pmsg db 10,'Count of +ve numbers::'
        pmsg_len equ $-pmsg
        nmsg db 10,'Count of -ve numbers::'
        nmsg_len equ $-nmsg
        nwline db 10
        array dw 8505h,90ffh,87h,88h,8a9fh,0adh,02h
        arrcnt equ 7
        pcnt db 0
        ncnt db 0
section .bss
        dispbuff resb 2
%macro print  2
        mov   eax, 4
        mov   ebx, 1
        mov   ecx, %1
        mov   edx, %2
        int   80h
%endmacro
section .text
        global _start
_start:
        print welmsg,welmsg_len
        mov esi,array
```

```
            mov ecx,arrcnt
up1:
            bt word[esi],15
            jnc pnxt
            inc byte[ncnt]
            jmp pskip
pnxt:   inc byte[pcnt]
pskip:  inc esi
            inc esi
            loop up1
            print pmsg,pmsg_len
            mov bl,[pcnt]
            call disp8num
            print nmsg,nmsg_len
            mov bl,[ncnt]
            call disp8num
            print nwline,1              ;New line char
exit:
            mov eax,01
            mov ebx,0
            int 80h
disp8num:
            mov ecx,2                   ;Number digits to display
            mov edi,dispbuff            ;Temp buffer
dup1:
            rol bl,4                    ;Rotate number from bl to get MS digit to LS digit
            mov al,bl                   ;Move rotated number to AL
            and al,0fh                  ;Mask upper digit
            cmp al,09                   ;Compare with 9
            jbe dskip                   ;If number below or equal to 9 go to add only 30h
```

```
        add al,07h              ;Else first add 07h
dskip:  add al,30h              ;Add 30h
        mov [edi],al            ;Store ASCII code in temp buff
        inc edi                 ;Increment pointer to next location in temp buff
        loop dup1               ;repeat till ecx becomes zero
        print dispbuff,2             ;display the value from temp buff
        ret                     ;return to calling program
```

Input/Output/Result:

;[admin@(none) alp]$ nasm -f elf64 msmalb08.asm

;[admin@(none) alp]$ ld -o msmalb08 msmalb08.o

;[admin@(none) alp]$ ./msmalb08

;Welcome to count +ve and -ve numbers in an array

;Count of +ve numbers::04

;Count of -ve numbers::03

;[admin@(none) alp]$

ASSIGNMENT 2

Write X86/64 ALP to perform non-overlapped and overlapped block transfer (with and without string specific instructions). Block containing data can be defined in the data segment.

```
section .data
        nline        db      10,10
        nline_len:   equ     $-nline
        msg          db      10,"MIL assignment 02 : Overlapped Block Transfer"
                     db      10,"-------------------------------------------------"
                     db      10,"    (Without String Instructions)"
        msg_len:     equ     $-msg
        bfrmsg       db      10,10,"1) Block Contents Before Transfer",10
        bfrmsg_len:  equ     $-bfrmsg
        afrmsg       db      10,10,"2) Block Contents After  Transfer",10
        afrmsg_len:  equ     $-afrmsg
        srcmsg       db      10,"Source block          : "
```

```
        srcmsg_len:    equ     $-srcmsg
        dstmsg         db      10,"Destination block :  "
        dstmsg_len:    equ     $-dstmsg
        space          db      " "
        count:         equ     5
        srcblk         db      11h, 22h, 33h, 44h, 55h
        dstblk         times   3 db 0
section .bss
        char_ans       resb    4
;macros as per 64-bit convensions
%macro  print   2
        mov     rax,1           ; Function 1 - write
        mov     rdi,1           ; To stdout
        mov     rsi,%1          ; String address
        mov     rdx,%2          ; String size
        syscall                 ; invoke operating system to WRITE
%endmacro
%macro read  2
        mov     rax,0           ; Function 0 - Read
        mov     rdi,0           ; from stdin
        mov     rsi,%1          ; buffer address
        mov     rdx,%2          ; buffer size
        syscall                 ; invoke operating system to READ
%endmacro
%macro        exit   0
        mov rax, 60             ; system call 60 is exit
        xor rdi, rdi            ; we want return code 0
        syscall                 ; invoke operating system to exit
%endmacro
section .text
```

```
        global  _start
_start:
        print   msg,msg_len   ; "MIL assignment 02 : Block Transfer "
        print   bfrmsg,bfrmsg_len
        call    show_blocks
        call    BT_O
        print   afrmsg,afrmsg_len
        call    show_blocks
        print   nline, nline_len
        exit
BT_O: ; Block Transfer Overlapped
        mov     rsi,srcblk+4
        mov     rdi,dstblk+2
        mov     rcx,count
repeat:
        mov     al,[rsi]
        mov     [rdi],al
        dec     rsi
        dec     rdi
        loop    repeat
        ret
;----------------------------------------------------------------
show_blocks:
        print   srcmsg,srcmsg_len    ; Display Source Block
        mov     rsi,srcblk
        call    display_block
        print   dstmsg,dstmsg_len    ; Display Destination Block
        mov     rsi,dstblk-2
        call    display_block
        ret
```

```
;-------------------------------------------------------------------
display_block:
        mov     rbp,count
back:
        mov     al,[rsi]
        push    rsi
        call    display_8       ; Display number
        print   space,1         ; Display space
        pop     rsi
        inc     rsi             ; Point to next number
        dec     rbp
        jnz     back
        ret
;-------------------------------------------------------------------
display_8:
        mov     rsi,char_ans+1; load last byte address of char_ans in rsi
        mov     rcx,2           ; number of digits
cnt:    mov     rdx,0           ; make rdx=0 (as in div instruction rdx:rax/rbx)
        mov     rbx,16          ; divisor=16 for hex
        div     rbx
        cmp     dl, 09h         ; check for remainder in RDX
        jbe     add30
        add     dl, 07h
add30:
        add     dl,30h          ; calculate ASCII code
        mov     [rsi],dl        ; store it in buffer
        dec     rsi             ; point to one byte back
        dec     rcx             ; decrement count
        jnz     cnt             ; if not zero repeat
        print   char_ans,2      ; display result on screen
```

```
        ret
;------------------------------------------------------------
;Block Transfer : Non-Overlapped with String Instructions
;------------------------------------------------------------
section .data
        nline           db      10,10
        nline_len:      equ     $-nline
        msg             db      10,"MIL assignment 02 : Non-Overlapped Block Transfer"
                        db      10,"-------------------------------------------------"
                        db      10,"        (With String Instructions)"
        msg_len:        equ     $-msg
        bfrmsg          db      10,10,"1) Block Contents Before Transfer",10
        bfrmsg_len:     equ     $-bfrmsg
        afrmsg          db      10,10,"2) Block Contents After  Transfer",10
        afrmsg_len:     equ     $-afrmsg
        srcmsg          db      10,"Source block      : "
        srcmsg_len:     equ     $-srcmsg
        dstmsg          db      10,"Destination block : "
        dstmsg_len:     equ     $-dstmsg
        space           db      " "
        count:          equ     5
        srcblk          db      11h, 22h, 33h, 44h, 55h
        dstblk          times   5 db 0
;------------------------------------------------------------
section .bss
        char_ans        resb    4
;------------------------------------------------------------
;macros as per 64-bit convensions
%macro print  2
        mov     rax,1           ; Function 1 - write
```

```
        mov     rdi,1           ; To stdout
        mov     rsi,%1          ; String address
        mov     rdx,%2          ; String size
        syscall                 ; invoke operating system to WRITE
%endmacro
%macro  read  2
        mov     rax,0           ; Function 0 - Read
        mov     rdi,0           ; from stdin
        mov     rsi,%1          ; buffer address
        mov     rdx,%2          ; buffer size
        syscall                 ; invoke operating system to READ
%endmacro
%macro      exit    0
        mov rax, 60             ; system call 60 is exit
        xor rdi, rdi            ; we want return code 0
        syscall                 ; invoke operating system to exit
%endmacro
;-------------------------------------------------------------

section .text
        global _start
_start:
        print   msg,msg_len         ; "MIL assignment 02 : Block Transfer "
        print   bfrmsg,bfrmsg_len
        call    show_blocks
        call    BT_NOS
        print   afrmsg,afrmsg_len
        call    show_blocks
        print   nline, nline_len
        exit

;-------------------------------------------------------------
```

```
BT_NOS:                          ; Block Transfer Non-Overlapped
        mov    rsi,srcblk
        mov    rdi,dstblk
        mov    rcx,count
        cld                      ; clear direction flag (string in normal order)
rep     movsb                    ; [rdi]=[rsi] counter is rcx
        ret
;-------------------------------------------------------------------
show_blocks:
        print  srcmsg,srcmsg_len    ; Display Source Block
        mov    rsi,srcblk
        call   display_block
        print  dstmsg,dstmsg_len    ; Display Destination Block
        mov    rsi,dstblk
        call   display_block
        ret
;-------------------------------------------------------------------
display_block:
        mov    rbp,count
back:
        mov    al,[rsi]
        push   rsi
        call   display_8        ; Display number
        print  space,1          ; Display space
        pop    rsi
        inc    rsi              ; Point to next number
        dec    rbp
        jnz    back
        ret
;-------------------------------------------------------------------
```

```
display_8:
        mov     rsi,char_ans+1; load last byte address of char_ans in rsi
        mov     rcx,2           ; number of digits
cnt:    mov     rdx,0           ; make rdx=0 (as in div instruction rdx:rax/rbx)
        mov     rbx,16          ; divisor=16 for hex
        div     rbx
        cmp     dl, 09h         ; check for remainder in RDX
        jbe     add30
        add     dl, 07h
add30:
        add     dl,30h          ; calculate ASCII code
        mov     [rsi],dl        ; store it in buffer
        dec     rsi             ; point to one byte back
        dec     rcx             ; decrement count
        jnz     cnt             ; if not zero repeat
        print   char_ans,2      ; display result on screen
        ret

;-------------------------------------------------------------
;Block Transfer : Overlapped without String Instructions
;-------------------------------------------------------------
section .data
        nline           db      10,10
        nline_len:      equ     $-nline
        msg             db      10,"MIL assignment 02 : Overlapped Block Transfer"
                        db      10,"--------------------------------------------------"
                        db      10,"       (Without String Instructions)"
        msg_len:        equ     $-msg
        bfrmsg          db      10,10,"1) Block Contents Before Transfer",10
        bfrmsg_len:     equ     $-bfrmsg
        afrmsg          db      10,10,"2) Block Contents After  Transfer",10
```

```
        afrmsg_len:     equ     $-afrmsg
        srcmsg          db      10,"Source block      : "
        srcmsg_len:     equ     $-srcmsg
        dstmsg          db      10,"Destination block : "
        dstmsg_len:     equ     $-dstmsg
        space           db      " "
        count:          equ     5
        srcblk          db      11h, 22h, 33h, 44h, 55h
        dstblk          times   3 db 0
;----------------------------------------------------------------

section .bss
        char_ans        resb    4
;----------------------------------------------------------------
;macros as per 64-bit convensions
%macro  print   2
        mov     rax,1           ; Function 1 - write
        mov     rdi,1           ; To stdout
        mov     rsi,%1          ; String address
        mov     rdx,%2          ; String size
        syscall                 ; invoke operating system to WRITE
%endmacro
%macro  read    2
        mov     rax,0           ; Function 0 - Read
        mov     rdi,0           ; from stdin
        mov     rsi,%1          ; buffer address
        mov     rdx,%2          ; buffer size
        syscall                 ; invoke operating system to READ
%endmacro
%macro          exit    0
        mov rax, 60             ; system call 60 is exit
```

```
        xor rdi, rdi     ; we want return code 0
        syscall          ; invoke operating system to exit
%endmacro
;----------------------------------------------------------------
section .text
        global _start
_start:
        print   msg,msg_len   ; "MIL assignment 02 : Block Transfer "
        print   bfrmsg,bfrmsg_len
        call    show_blocks
        call    BT_O
        print   afrmsg,afrmsg_len
        call    show_blocks
        print   nline, nline_len
        exit
;----------------------------------------------------------------
BT_O:                          ; Block Transfer Overlapped
        mov     rsi,srcblk+4
        mov     rdi,dstblk+2
        mov     rcx,count
repeat:
        mov     al,[rsi]
        mov     [rdi],al
        dec     rsi
        dec     rdi
        loop    repeat
        ret
;----------------------------------------------------------------
show_blocks:
        print   srcmsg,srcmsg_len     ; Display Source Block
```

```
        mov     rsi,srcblk
        call    display_block
        print   dstmsg,dstmsg_len    ; Display Destination Block
        mov     rsi,dstblk-2
        call    display_block
        ret
;----------------------------------------------------------------

display_block:
        mov     rbp,count
back:
        mov     al,[rsi]
        push    rsi
        call    display_8       ; Display number
        print   space,1         ; Display space
        pop     rsi
        inc     rsi             ; Point to next number
        dec     rbp
        jnz     back
        ret
;----------------------------------------------------------------

display_8:
        mov     rsi,char_ans+1; load last byte address of char_ans in rsi
        mov     rcx,2           ; number of digits
cnt:    mov     rdx,0           ; make rdx=0 (as in div instruction rdx:rax/rbx)
        mov     rbx,16          ; divisor=16 for hex
        div     rbx
        cmp     dl, 09h         ; check for remainder in RDX
        jbe     add30
        add     dl, 07h
add30:
```

```
        add     dl,30h          ; calculate ASCII code
        mov     [rsi],dl        ; store it in buffer
        dec     rsi             ; point to one byte back
        dec     rcx             ; decrement count
        jnz     cnt             ; if not zero repeat
        print   char_ans,2      ; display result on screen
        ret
;------------------------------------------------------------
;Block Transfer : Overlapped with String Instructions
;------------------------------------------------------------
section .data
        nline           db      10,10
        nline_len:      equ     $-nline
        msg             db      10,"MIL assignment 02 : Overlapped Block Transfer"
                        db      10,"-----------------------------------------------"
                        db      10,"          (With String Instructions)"
        msg_len:        equ     $-msg
        bfrmsg          db      10,10,"1) Block Contents Before Transfer",10
        bfrmsg_len:     equ     $-bfrmsg
        afrmsg          db      10,10,"2) Block Contents After  Transfer",10
        afrmsg_len:     equ     $-afrmsg
        srcmsg          db      10,"Source block            : "
        srcmsg_len:     equ     $-srcmsg
        dstmsg          db      10,"Destination block :  "
        dstmsg_len:     equ     $-dstmsg
        space           db      " "
        count:          equ     5
        srcblk          db      11h, 22h, 33h, 44h, 55h
        dstblk          times   3 db 0
;------------------------------------------------------------
```

```
section .bss
        char_ans        resb    4
;-------------------------------------------------------------------
;macros as per 64-bit convensions
%macro  print  2
        mov     rax,1           ; Function 1 - write
        mov     rdi,1           ; To stdout
        mov     rsi,%1          ; String address
        mov     rdx,%2          ; String size
        syscall                 ; invoke operating system to WRITE
%endmacro
%macro  read  2
        mov     rax,0           ; Function 0 - Read
        mov     rdi,0           ; from stdin
        mov     rsi,%1          ; buffer address
        mov     rdx,%2          ; buffer size
        syscall                 ; invoke operating system to READ
%endmacro
%macro exit   0
        mov rax, 60             ; system call 60 is exit
        xor rdi, rdi            ; we want return code 0
        syscall                 ; invoke operating system to exit
%endmacro
;-------------------------------------------------------------
section .text
        global _start
_start:
        print   msg,msg_len   ; "MIL assignment 02 : Block Transfer "
        print   bfrmsg,bfrmsg_len
        call    show_blocks
```

```
        call    BT_OS
        print   afrmsg,afrmsg_len
        call    show_blocks
        print   nline, nline_len
        exit
;-------------------------------------------------------------
BT_OS:                              ; Block Transfer Overlapped
        mov    rsi,srcblk+4
        mov    rdi,dstblk+2
        mov    rcx,count
        std                  ; set direction flag (string in reverse order)
rep     movsb                ; [rdi]=[rsi] counter is rcx
        ret
;-------------------------------------------------------------
show_blocks:
        print   srcmsg,srcmsg_len   ; Display Source Block
        mov    rsi,srcblk
        call    display_block
        print   dstmsg,dstmsg_len   ; Display Destination Block
        mov    rsi,dstblk-2
        call    display_block
        ret
;-------------------------------------------------------------
display_block:
        mov    rbp,count
back:
        mov    al,[rsi]
        push   rsi
        call    display_8    ; Display number
        print   space,1      ; Display space
```

```
        pop     rsi
        inc     rsi             ; Point to next number
        dec     rbp
        jnz     back
        ret
;------------------------------------------------------------
display_8:
        mov     rsi,char_ans+1; load last byte address of char_ans in rsi
        mov     rcx,2           ; number of digits
cnt:    mov     rdx,0           ; make rdx=0 (as in div instruction rdx:rax/rbx)
        mov     rbx,16          ; divisor=16 for hex
        div     rbx
        cmp     dl, 09h         ; check for remainder in RDX
        jbe     add30
        add     dl, 07h
add30:
        add     dl,30h          ; calculate ASCII code
        mov     [rsi],dl        ; store it in buffer
        dec     rsi             ; point to one byte back
        dec     rcx             ; decrement count
        jnz     cnt             ; if not zero repeat
        print   char_ans,2      ; display result on screen
        ret
;------------------------------------------------------------
```

Output:

admin@localhost ~]$ nasm -f elf64 -o A2_BT_O.o A2_BT_O.asm

[admin@localhost ~]$ ld -o A2_BT_O A2_BT_O.o

[admin@localhost ~]$ ./A2_BT_O

(1) Block Contents Before Transfer

Source block   : 11 22 33 44 55

Destination block   : 44 55 00 00 00

(2) Block Contents After Transfer

Source block   : 11 22 33 11 22

Destination block   : 11 22 33 44 55

ASSIGNMENT 3

Write X86/64 ALP to convert 4-digit Hex number into its equivalent BCD number and 5-digit BCD number into its equivalent HEX number. Make your program user friendly to accept the choice from user for: (a) HEX to BCD b) BCD to HEX (c) EXIT. Display proper strings to prompt the user while accepting the input and displaying the result. (wherever necessary, use 64-bit registers)

```
section .data
        menumsg db 10,10,'###### Menu for Code Conversion ######'
                db 10,'1: Hex to BCD'
                db 10,'2: BCD to Hex'
                db 10,'3: Exit'
                db 10,10,'Please Enter Choice::'
        menumsg_len equ $-menumsg
        wrchmsg db 10,10,'Wrong Choice Entered....Please try again!!!',10,10
        wrchmsg_len equ $-wrchmsg
        hexinmsg db 10,10,'Please enter 4 digit hex number::'
        hexinmsg_len equ $-hexinmsg
        bcdopmsg db 10,10,'BCD Equivalent::'
        bcdopmsg_len equ $-bcdopmsg
        bcdinmsg db 10,10,'Please enter 5 digit BCD number::'
        bcdinmsg_len equ $-bcdinmsg
        hexopmsg db 10,10,'Hex Equivalent::'
        hexopmsg_len equ $-hexopmsg
section .bss
        numascii resb 06              ;common buffer for choice, hex and bcd input
        opbuff resb 05
        dnumbuff resb 08
%macro dispmsg 2
```

```asm
        mov rax,01
        mov rdi,01
        mov rsi,%1
        mov rdx,%2
        syscall
%endmacro
%macro accept 2
        mov rax,0
        mov rdi,0
        mov rsi,%1
        mov rdx,%2
        syscall
%endmacro
section .text
        global _start
_start:
        dispmsg menumsg,menumsg_len
        accept numascii,2
        cmp byte [numascii],'1'
        jne case2
        call hex2bcd_proc
        jmp _start
case2:  cmp byte [numascii],'2'
        jne case3
        call bcd2hex_proc
        jmp _start
case3:  cmp byte [numascii],'3'
        je exit
        dispmsg wrchmsg,wrchmsg_len
        jmp _start
```

```
exit:
        mov rax,60
        mov rbx,0
        syscall
hex2bcd_proc:
        dispmsg hexinmsg,hexinmsg_len
        accept numascii,5
        call packnum
        mov rcx,0
        mov al,bl
        mov bl,10                    ;Base of Decimal No. system
h2bup1:        mov dx,0
        div bl
        push rdx
        inc rcx
        cmp al,0
        jne h2bup1
        mov rdi,opbuff
h2bup2:        pop rdx
        add dl,30h
        mov [rdi],dl
        inc rdi
        loop h2bup2
        dispmsg bcdopmsg,bcdopmsg_len
        dispmsg opbuff,5
        ret
bcd2hex_proc:
        dispmsg bcdinmsg,bcdinmsg_len
        accept numascii,6
        dispmsg hexopmsg,hexopmsg_len
```

```
            mov rsi,numascii
            mov rcx,05
            mov rax,0
            mov rbx,0ah
b2hup1:         mov rdx,0
            mul rbx
            mov dl,[rsi]
            sub dl,30h
            add rax,rdx
            inc rsi
            loop b2hup1
            mov rbx,rax
            call disp32_num
            ret
packnum:
            mov bx,0
            mov rcx,04
            mov rsi,numascii
up1:
            shl bx,04
            mov al,[esi]
            cmp al,39h
            jbe  skip1
            sub al,07h
skip1:  sub al,30h
            add bl,al
            inc rsi
            loop up1
            ret
disp32_num:
```

```
        mov rdi,dnumbuff      ;point esi to buffer
        mov rcx,08            ;load number of digits to display
dispup1:
        rol ebx,4             ;rotate number left by four bits
        mov dl,bl             ;move lower byte in dl
        and dl,0fh            ;mask upper digit of byte in dl
        cmp dl,39h            ;compare with 39h
        jbe dispskip1         ;if less than 39h akip adding 07 more
        add dl,07h            ;else add 07
dispskip1:
        add dl,30h            ;add 30h to calculate ASCII code
        mov [rdi],dl          ;store ASCII code in buffer
        inc rdi               ;point to next byte
        loop dispup1          ;decrement the count of digits to display
                              ;if not zero jump to repeat
        dispmsg dnumbuff+3,5 ;Dispays only lower 5 digits as upper three are '0'
        ret
section .data
menumsg db 10,10,'Menu for Conversions ',10
        db 10,' 1.HEX to BCD ..'
        db 10,' 2.BCD to HEX ..'
        db 10,' 3.exit'
        db 10,'Enter your choice : '
menumsglen :equ $-menumsg
msg db 10,'Enter the Hex number : ',10
msglen :equ $-msg
msg2 db 10,'BCD is : '
msg2len :equ $-msg2
section .bss
        option resb 02
```

```
        dispbuff resb 5
        num resb 5
%macro dispmsg 2
        mov rax,01
        mov rdi,01
        mov rsi,%1
        mov rdx,%2
        syscall
%endmacro
%macro accept 2
        mov rax,0
        mov rdi,0
        mov rsi,%1
        mov rdx,%2
        syscall
%endmacro
section .code
global _start
_start:
xxx:dispmsg menumsg,menumsglen
accept option,2
mov al,[option]
cmp al,31h
je d1
cmp al,32h
je d2
cmp al,33h
je d3
d1:
dispmsg msg,msglen
```

```
accept num,5
dispmsg msg2,msg2len
mov ebx,0
mov rsi,num
mov rdi,dispbuff
xor rcx,rcx
mov rcx,04
up1: shl bx,04
 mov al,[rsi]
cmp al,39h
jbe l1
cmp al,46h
jbe l2
cmp al,66h
jbe l3
l1:sub al,30h
jmp l4
l2:sub al,37h
jmp l4
l3:sub al,57h
l4: add bl,al
inc rsi
loop up1
xor ax,ax
mov ax,bx
xor bx,bx
mov bx,10
xor cl,cl
```

```
ab:
xor dx,dx
div bx
push dx
inc cl
cmp ax,0
jne ab
mov rsi,dispbuff
ab1:pop dx
add dl,30h
mov [rsi],dl
inc rsi
dec cl
jnz ab1
dispmsg dispbuff,5
d2:jmp xxx
d3: mov rax,60
mov rdi,0
syscall
```

Output:

[admin@localhost ~]$ nasm -f elf64 -o btoh.o btoh.asm

[admin@localhost ~]$ ld -o btoh btoh.o

[admin@localhost ~]$ ./btoh

Menu for Code Conversion

2: BCD to Hex

3: Exit

Please Enter Choice::2

Please enter 5 digit BCD number::11111

Hex Equivalent::02;67

ASSIGNMENT 4

Write X86/64 ALP to perform multiplication of two 8-bit hexadecimal numbers. Use successive addition and add and shift method. (use of 64-bit registers is expected).

```
section .data
        menu db 10,13,"*****MENU*****"
        db 10,13,"1.Successive Addition Method"
        db 10,13,"2.Shift And Add Method"
        db 10,13,"3.Exit"
        db 10,13,"Enter Your Choice::"
        menulen equ $-menu
        msg db 10,13,"Invalid Choice!Please Re-enter."
        msglen equ $-msg
        msg1 db 10,13,"We are in Successive Addition Method!"
        msg1len equ $-msg1
        msg2 db 10,13,"We are in Shift and Add Method!"
        msg2len equ $-msg2
        msg3 db 10,13,"Enter First Number: "
        msg3len equ $-msg3
        msg4 db 10,13,"Enter Second Number: "
        msg4len equ $-msg4
        msg5 db 10,13,"Multiplication Is: "
        msg5len equ $-msg5
section .bss
        choice:resb 2
        var:resb 1
        num1:resb 3
        result:resb 2
        v1:resb 1
        count: resb 1
        x: resb 1
```

```
        y: resb 1
        n: resb 1
        %macro disp 2
                mov rax,1
                mov rdi,1
                mov rsi,%1,
                mov rdx,%2
                syscall
        %endmacro
        %macro accept 2
                mov rax,0
                mov rdi,0
                mov rsi,%1
                mov rdx,%2
                syscall
        %endmacro
section .text
        global _start
        _start:
        menuent:disp menu,menulen
                accept choice,2
                cmp byte[choice],'1'
                je succadd
                cmp byte[choice],'2'
                je shiftadd
                cmp byte[choice],'3'
                je exit
                disp msg,msglen
                jmp menuent
        succadd:
```

```
            disp msg1,msg1len
            disp msg3,msg3len
            accept num1,3
            call conv_orig
            mov cl,byte[var]
            mov byte[count],cl
            disp msg4,msg4len
            accept num1,3
            call conv_orig
            mov word[result],0000
    up:
            ;disp msg5,msg5len
            mov bl,byte[var]
            mov bh,00
            ;call disp_result
            add word[result],bx
            dec byte[count]
            cmp byte[count],00
            jne up
            disp msg5,msg5len
            call disp_result
            jmp menuent
    shiftadd:
            disp msg2,msg2len
            disp msg3,msg3len
            accept num1,3
            call conv_orig
            mov bl,byte[var]
            mov byte[x],bl
            disp msg4,msg4len
```

```
            accept num1,3
            call conv_orig
            mov bl,byte[var]
            mov byte[y],bl
            mov al,byte[x]
            mov bl,byte[y]
            mov ah,00
            mov byte[n],08
up1:mov dl,al
            and dl,01
            cmp dl,01
            jne l5
            add ah,bl
l5:shr ax,01
            dec byte[n]
            cmp byte[n],00
            jne up1
            mov word[result],ax
            disp msg5,msg5len
            call disp_result
            jmp menuent
    exit:
            mov rax,60
            mov rdi,0
            syscall
conv_orig:
      mov byte[var],00
      mov rsi,num1
   mov bl,[rsi]
      cmp bl,39h
```

```
        jle l1
        sub bl,07h
l1:sub bl,30h
        ;mov bh,00
        shl bl,04
        add [var],bl
        inc rsi
        mov bl,[rsi]
        cmp bl,39h
        jle l2
        sub bl,07h
        l2:sub bl,30h
        ;mov bh,00
        shl bl,00
        add [var],bl
        ret
disp_result:
        mov bx,word[result]
        shr bx,12
        and bx,000fh
        cmp bx,0009h
        jle a1
        add bx,0007h
a1:add bx,0030h
        mov byte[v1],bl
        disp v1,1
        mov bx,word[result]
        shr bx,08
        and bx,000fh
        cmp bx,0009h
```

```
        jle a2
        add bx,0007h
a2:add bx,0030h
        mov byte[v1],bl
        disp v1,1
        mov bx,word[result]
        shr bx,04
        and bx,000fh
        cmp bx,0009h
        jle a3
        add bx,0007h
a3:add bx,0030h
        mov byte[v1],bl
        disp v1,1
        mov bx,word[result]
        and bx,000fh
        cmp bx,0009h
        jle a4
        add bx,0007h
a4:add bx,0030h
        mov byte[v1],bl
        disp v1,1
        ret
```

Output:

admin@localhost ~]$ nasm -f elf64 -o mul1.o mul1.asm

[admin@localhost ~]$ ld -o mul1 mul1.o

[admin@localhost ~]$ ./mul1

*****MENU*****

1.   Successive Addition Method

2.   Shift And Add Method

3.   Exit

Enter Your Choice::1

We are in Successive Addition Method!

Enter First Number: 11

Enter Second Number: 22

Multiplication Is: 0242

*****MENU*****

1.　Successive Addition Method

2.　Shift And Add Method

3.　Exit

Enter Your Choice::2

We are in Shift and Add Menthod!

Enter First Number: 11

Enter Second Number: 22

Multiplication Is: 0242

*****MENU*****

1. Successive Addition Method

2. Shift And Add Method

3. Exit

Enter Your Choice::3

[admin@localhost ~]$

ASSIGNMENT 5

Write X86/64 ALP to switch from real mode to protected mode and display the values of GDTR, LDTR, IDTR, TR and MSW Registers.

```
section .data
        rmodemsg db 10,'Processor is in Real Mode'
        rmsg_len:equ $-rmodemsg
        pmodemsg db 10,'Processor is in Protected Mode'
        pmsg_len:equ $-pmodemsg
        gdtmsg db 10,'GDT Contents are::'
        gmsg_len:equ $-gdtmsg
        ldtmsg db 10,'LDT Contents are::'
```

```
        lmsg_len:equ $-ldtmsg
        idtmsg db 10,'IDT Contents are::'
        imsg_len:equ $-idtmsg
        trmsg db 10,'Task Register Contents are::'
        tmsg_len: equ $-trmsg
        mswmsg db 10,'Machine Status Word:'
        mmsg_len:equ $-mswmsg
        colmsg db ':'
        nwline db 10
section .bss
        gdt resd 1
        resw 1
        ldt resw 1
        idt resd 1
        resw 1
        tr  resw 1
        cr0_data resd 1
        dnum_buff resb 04
%macro disp 2
        mov eax,04
        mov ebx,01
        mov ecx,%1
        mov edx,%2
        int 80h
%endmacro
section .text
        global _start
_start:
        smsw eax                ;Reading CR0
        mov [cr0_data],eax
```

```
        bt eax,0        ;Checking PE bit(LSB), if 1=Protected Mode, else Real Mode
        jc prmode
        disp rmodemsg,rmsg_len
        jmp nxt1
prmode:         disp pmodemsg,pmsg_len
nxt1:   sgdt [gdt]
        sldt [ldt]
        sidt [idt]
        str [tr]
        disp gdtmsg,gmsg_len
        mov bx,[gdt+4]
        call disp_num
        mov bx,[gdt+2]
        call disp_num
        disp colmsg,1
        mov bx,[gdt]
        call disp_num
        disp ldtmsg,lmsg_len
        mov bx,[ldt]
        call disp_num
        disp idtmsg,imsg_len
        mov bx,[idt+4]
        call disp_num
        mov bx,[idt+2]
        call disp_num
        disp colmsg,1
        mov bx,[idt]
        call disp_num
        disp trmsg,tmsg_len
        mov bx,[tr]
```

```
            call disp_num
            disp mswmsg,mmsg_len
            mov bx,[cr0_data+2]
            call disp_num
            mov bx,[cr0_data]
            call disp_num
            disp nwline,1
exit:       mov eax,01
            mov ebx,00
            int 80h
disp_num:
            mov esi,dnum_buff       ;point esi to buffer
            mov ecx,04              ;load number of digits to display
up1:
            rol bx,4                ;rotate number left by four bits
            mov dl,bl               ;move lower byte in dl
            and dl,0fh              ;mask upper digit of byte in dl
            add dl,30h              ;add 30h to calculate ASCII code
            cmp dl,39h              ;compare with 39h
            jbe skip1               ;if less than 39h skip adding 07 more
            add dl,07h              ;else add 07
skip1:
            mov [esi],dl            ;store ASCII code in buffer
            inc esi                 ;point to next byte
            loop up1                ;decrement the count of digits to display
                                    ;if not zero jump to repeat
            disp dnum_buff,4        ;display the number from buffer
            ret
```

Input/Output/Result:

;[admin@(none) alp]$ nasm -f elf64 msmalc03.asm

;[admin@(none) alp]$ ld -o msmalc03 msmalc03.o

;[admin@(none) alp]$ ./msmalc03

;Processor is in Protected Mode

;GDT Contents are::3F604000:007F

;LDT Contents are::0000

;IDT Contents are::81BDD000:0FFF

;Task Register Contents are::0040

;Machine Status Word::8005FFFF

;[admin@(none) alp]$

ASSIGNMENT 6

Write X86 program to sort the list of integers in ascending/descending order. Read the input from the text file and write the sorted data back to the same text file using bubble sort.

```
section .data
i         db 0              ; Value to be incremented
question   db  'Enter a number: '  ; Prompt
questionLen equ $-question
newLine    db 10, 10, 0          ; New blank line
newLineLen  equ $-newLine
section .bss
num resb 5             ; Array of size 5
counter resb 1         ; Value to be incremented
counter2 resb 1        ; Value to be incremented
temp resb 1
temp2 resb 1
section .text
global _start
_start:
mov esi, 0
getInput:
mov eax, 4
mov ebx, 1
mov ecx, question      ; Prints the question
mov edx, questionLen
```

```
int 80h
add byte[i], 30h    ; I'll retain this expression, since the program experienced an error
                    ; when this expression is deleted
sub byte[i], 30h    ; Converts the increment value to integer
mov eax, 3
mov ebx, 0
lea ecx, [num + esi]      ; Element of the array
mov edx, 2
int 80h
inc esi
inc byte[i]
cmp byte[i], 5          ; As long as the array hasn't reached the size of 5,
jl getInput            ; the program continues to ask input from the user
mov esi, 0
mov byte[i], 0
mov edi, 0             ; Index of the array
bubble_sort:
mov byte[counter], 0
mov byte[counter2], 0
begin_for_1:
   mov al, 0
   mov al, [counter]       ; Acts as the outer for loop
   cmp al, 5
   jg printArray           ; Prints the sorted list when the array size has reached 5
begin_for_2:
   mov edi, [counter2] ; Acts as the inner for loop
   cmp edi, 4
   jg end_for_2
   mov bl, 0               ; Acts as the if statement
   mov cl, 0
```

```
    mov bl, [num + edi]
    mov cl, [num + edi + 1]
    mov byte[temp], cl  ; This is the same as if(a[j] > a[j + 1]){...}
    cmp bl, [temp]
    jg bubbleSortSwap
return:
    inc edi             ; Same as j++
    jmp begin_for_2     ; Goes out of the inner for loop
end_for_2:
    inc byte[counter]   ; Same as i++
    jmp begin_for_1     ; Goes out of the outer for loop
bubbleSortSwap:
mov [num + edi + 1], bl
mov [num + edi], cl     ; The set of statements is the same as swap(&a[j], &a[j + 1]);
jmp return
printArray:
mov eax, 4
mov ebx, 1
mov ecx, [num + esi]    ; Prints one element at a time
mov edx, 1
int 80h
inc esi
inc byte[i]
cmp byte[i], 5
jl printArray           ; As long as the array size hasn't reached 5, printing continues
mov eax, 4
mov ebx, 1
mov ecx, newLine        ; Displays a new blank line after the array
mov edx, newLineLen
int 80h
mov eax, 1              ; Exits the program
mov ebx, 0
int 80h
```

Input/Output/Result:

;[admin@(none) alp]$ nasm -f elf64 asc.asm

;[admin@(none) alp]$ ld -o asc asc03.o

;[admin@(none) alp]$ ./asc

; enter the numbers

; 10,56,45,67,43,23

; Sorted List: 10,23,43,45,56,67.

ASSIGNMENT 7

Write X86 menu driven Assembly Language Program (ALP) to implement OS (DOS) commands TYPE, COPY and DELETE using file operations. User is supposed to provide command line arguments in all cases.

```
;CODE
;-------------------------
.MODEL SMALL
.STACK 100
.DATA
PRINTF MACRO MSG
    LEA DX,MSG
    MOV AH,09H
    INT 21H
ENDM
CLOSE MACRO HANDLE
    LEA BX,HANDLE
    MOV AH,3EH
    INT 21H
ENDM
SRC DB 100 DUP(0)
SHANDLE DW 00H
ARR DB 1024 DUP('$')
MSG0 DB 10,13,"INVALID NO OF ARGUMENTS $"
MSG2 DB 10,13,"ERROR OPENING THE SOURCE FILE$"
```

```
MSG4 DB 10,13,"ERROR IN READING THE SOURCE FILE$"
MSG6 DB 10,13,"TOO MANY PARAMETER $"
.CODE
    MOV AX,@DATA
    MOV DS,AX
;--------INT PSP--------------
    MOV AH,62H
    INT 21H
    MOV AH,ES:[80H]
    CMP AH,0
    JE PARAMIS
    MOV BX,82H
    LEA SI,SRC
CONTINUE:
    MOV AH,ES:[BX]
    CMP AH,' '
    JNE ENTER
;SP_CHK:
;    MOV [SI],AH
;    CMP AH,' '
;    INC SI
;    INC BX
;    JE SP_CHK
ENTER:
    CMP AH,0DH
    JE OPEN
;    JNE TOOMANY
    MOV [SI],AH
    INC SI
    INC BX
```

```
        JMP CONTINUE
PARAMIS:
        PRINTF MSG0
        JMP ERROR
TOOMANY:
        PRINTF MSG6
        JMP ERROR
;-------------------------------------
; CODE TO GET THE HANDLE FOR SOURCE FILE
OPEN:
        MOV AH,3DH
        MOV AL,00H
        LEA DX,SRC
        INT 21H
        JNC SKIP4
        PRINTF MSG2
        JMP ERROR
SKIP4:
        MOV SHANDLE,AX
;-----------------------------------
        MOV AH,3FH
        MOV BX,SHANDLE
        MOV CX,1024
        MOV  DX, offset ARR
        INT 21H
        JNC SKIP6
        PRINTF MSG4
        JMP ERROR
SKIP6:
        CLOSE SHANDLE
```

```
        PRINTF ARR
ERROR:
    MOV AH,4CH
    INT 21H
END
.MODEL SMALL
.STACK 100
.DATA
PRINTF MACRO MSG
    PUSH DX
    PUSH AX
    LEA DX,MSG
    MOV AH,09H
    INT 21H
    POP AX
    POP DX
ENDM
CLOSE MACRO HANDLE
PUSH BX
PUSH AX
    LEA BX,HANDLE
    MOV AH,3EH
    INT 21H
POP AX
POP BX
ENDM
SPACE DB 00H
SRC DB 30 DUP(0)
DEST DB 30 DUP(0)
SHANDLE DW 00H
```

```
DHANDLE DW 00H
ARR DB 1024 DUP(0)
COUNT DB 00H
LEN DW 0000
F1 DB 00
MSG0 DB 10,13,"INVALID NO OF ARGUMENTS $"
MSG1 DB 10,13,"ONE FILE COPIED $"
MSG2 DB 10,13,"ERROR OPENING THE SOURCE FILE$"
MSG3 DB 10,13,"ERROR IN CREATING DESTINATION FILE $"
MSG4 DB 10,13,"ERROR IN READING FROM SOURCE FILE $"
MSG5 DB 10,13,"ERROR IN WRITING THE DESTINATION FILE $"
MSG6 DB 10,13,"TOO MANY PARAMETER$"
MSG7 DB 10,13,"SOURCE FILE DOESNT EXIST $"
MSG8 DB 10,13,"DESTINATION FILE ALREADY EXIST $"
MSG9 DB 10,13,"DO YOU WANT TO OVERWRITE [Y/N]$"
.CODE
MOV AX,@DATA
MOV DS,AX
MOV AH,62H
INT 21H
MOV AH,ES:[80H]
CMP AH,0
JE PARAMIS
MOV BX,82H
LEA SI,SRC
CONTINUE:
    MOV AH,ES:[BX]
    CMP AH,0DH
    JE PARAMIS
    CMP AH,' '
```

```
        JE SP_CHK
        MOV [SI],AH
        INC SI
        INC BX
        JMP CONTINUE
SP_CHK:
        MOV [SI],AH
        CMP AH,' '
        JNE DESTI
        INC SI
        INC BX
        JE SP_CHK
DESTI:
        LEA SI,DEST
        MOV F1,0
        INC BX
NEXT:
        MOV AH,ES:[BX]
        CMP AH,' '
        JE TOOMANY
        CMP AH,0DH
        JE CHECK
        MOV F1,1
        MOV [SI],AH
        INC SI
        INC BX
        JMP NEXT
PARAMIS :
        PRINTF MSG0
        JMP ERROR
```

```
TOOMANY:
        PRINTF MSG5
        JMP ERROR
CHECK:
    CMP F1,0
    JE PARAMIS
; CODE TO GET THE HANDLE FOR SOURSE FILESKIP:
SKIP3:
        MOV AH,3DH
        MOV AL,00H
        MOV DX,OFFSET SRC
        INT 21H
        JNC SKIP4
        PRINTF MSG2
        JMP ERROR
SKIP4:
        MOV SHANDLE,AX
        ;CODE TO GET THE HANDLE FOR DESTINATION FILE
        MOV AH,5BH
        MOV CX,0
        MOV DX,OFFSET DEST
        INT 21H
        JC NEXT1
        MOV DHANDLE,AX
        JMP NEXT2
NEXT1:
    MOV DHANDLE,AX
    PRINTF MSG8
    PRINTF MSG9
    MOV AH,01
```

```
        INT 21H
        CMP AL,'Y'
        JZ NEXT2
        JMP ERROR
NEXT2:
        MOV AH,3CH
        MOV CX,00
        MOV DX,OFFSET DEST
        INT 21H
        JNC SKIP5
        PRINTF MSG3
        JMP ERROR
SKIP5:
        MOV DHANDLE,AX
TRANSF:
        MOV AH,3FH
        MOV BX,SHANDLE
        MOV CX,1024
        MOV DX,OFFSET ARR
        INT 21H
        JNC SKIP6
        PRINTF MSG4
        JMP ERROR
SKIP6:
        CMP AX,0
        JE SKIP7
        MOV LEN,AX
        MOV AH,40H
        MOV BX,DHANDLE
        MOV CX,LEN
```

```
        MOV DX,OFFSET ARR
        INT 21H
        JNC TRANSF
        PRINTF MSG5
        JMP ERROR
SKIP7:
        PRINTF MSG1
        CLOSE SHANDLE
        CLOSE DHANDLE
ERROR:
        MOV AH,4CH
        INT 21H
END
```

Input/Output/Result:

;[admin@(none) alp]$ nasm -f elf64 typ.asm

;[admin@(none) alp]$ ld -o typ typ.o

;[admin@(none) alp]$ ./typ

;Menu

;1. TYPE

;2. COPY

;3. DELETE

ASSIGNMENT 8

Write x86 ALP to find the factorial of a given integer number on a command line by using recursion. Explicit stack manipulation is expected in the code.

```
section .text
global factorial
externrpmult
factorial:
pushebp
movebp, esp
subesp, 4 ;creates memory for local variable at ebp-4
```

```
movesi, [ebp+8] ; put n in esi
cmpesi, 1 ; n <= 1
jbe    .done ; if so jump to done
.try:
mov    [ebp-4],esi ;adds n temporarily into ebp-4
decesi ; n - 1
pushesi ; push arugment
call   factorial ;call factorial again stores result in esi
addesp, 4 ;gets rid of the argument
movedi, esi ;copies n - 1 into edi
movesi,[ebp+4] ;gets the original value back (n)
callrpmult ;multiply
jmp    .done ;once it reaches here, finished the function
.done:
movesp, ebp ;restores esp
popebp
ret    ;return the value
```

Input/Output/Result:

;[admin@(none) alp]$ nasm -f elf64 fact.asm

;[admin@(none) alp]$ ld -o fact fact.o

;[admin@(none) alp]$ ./fact

; enter the number

; 8

;2,4,1.

ASSIGNMENT 9

Write 80387 ALP to obtain: (i) Mean (ii) Variance (iii) Standard Deviation Also plot the histogram for the data set. The data elements are available in a text file.

```
section .data
numbers db "The numbers are:102.59,198.21,100.67,230.78,67.93",10
len equ $-numbers
meanmsg db 10,"CALCULATED MEAN IS:-"
```

```
meanmsg_len equ $-meanmsg
sdmsg db 10,"CALCULATED STANDARD DEVIATION IS:-"
sdmsg_len equ $-sdmsg
varmsg db 10,"CALCULATED VARIANCE IS:-"
varmsg_len equ $-varmsg
array dd 102.56,198.21,100.67,230.78,67.93
arraycnt dw 05
dpoint db '.'
hdec dq 100
section .bss
dispbuff resb 1
resbuff rest 1
mean resd 1
variance resd 1
%macro linuxsyscall 4
mov rax,%1
mov rdi,%2
mov rsi,%3
mov rdx,%4
syscall
%endmacro
section .text
global _start
_start:
linuxsyscall 01,01,numbers,len
finit
fldz
mov rbx,array
mov rsi,00
xor rcx,rcx
```

```
mov cx,[arraycnt]
up:
fadd dword[RBX+RSI*4]
inc rsi
loop up
fidiv word[arraycnt]
fst dword[mean]
linuxsyscall 01,01,meanmsg,meanmsg_len
call dispres
mov rcx,00
mov cx,[arraycnt]
mov rbx,array
mov rsi,00
FLDZ
up1:
FLDZ
FLD dword[RBX+RSI*4]
FSUB dword[mean]
FST ST1
FMUL
FADD
inc rsi
loop up1
FIDIV word[arraycnt]
FST dword[variance]
FSQRT
linuxsyscall 01,01,sdmsg,sdmsg_len
CALL dispres
FLD dword[variance]
linuxsyscall 01,01,varmsg,varmsg_len
```

```
CALL dispres
exit:
mov rax,60
mov rdi,0
syscall
disp8_proc:
mov rdi,dispbuff
mov rcx,02
back:
rol bl,04
mov dl,bl
and dl,0FH
cmp dl,09
jbe next1
add dl,07H
next1:
add dl,30H
mov [rdi],dl
inc rdi
loop back
ret
dispres:
fimul dword[hdec]
fbstp tword[resbuff]
xor rcx,rcx
mov rcx,09H
mov rsi,resbuff+9
up2:
push rcx
push rsi
```

```
mov bl,[rsi]
call disp8_proc
linuxsyscall 01,01,dispbuff,2
pop rsi
dec rsi
pop rcx
loop up2
linuxsyscall 01,01,dpoint,1
mov bl,[resbuff]
call disp8_proc
linuxsyscall 01,01,dispbuff,2
ret
```

Output:

amodi@ubuntu:~/MIL/Assign7$ nasm -f elf64 -l asgn7.lst asgn7.asm

amodi@ubuntu:~/MIL/Assign7$ ld -o asgn7 asgn7.o

amodi@ubuntu:~/MIL/Assign7$ ./asgn7

The numbers are: 102.59,198.21,100.67,230.78,67.93

CALCULATED MEAN IS:-00000000000000140.30

CALCULATED STANDARD DEVIATION IS:-00000000000000062.32

CALCULATED VARIANCE IS:-000000000000003954.34

ASSIGNMENT 10

Write a Terminate but Stay Resident (TSR) program for a key-logger. The key-presses during the stipulated time need to be displayed at the center of the screen.

```
code segment para
assume cs:code
org 100h            ;prog seg prefix addrss
jmp initze          ;hex no of 256
savint dd ?         ;for saving address of es:bx
count dw 0000h      ;count of 17 tics
hours db ?
mins db ?
```

```
sec db ?
testnum:
        push ax        ;store all the contents of register
        push bx        ;(not to change original values of register)
        push cx
        push dx
        push cs
        push es
        push si
        push di
        mov ax,0b800h   ;starting address of display
        mov es,ax
        mov cx,count
        inc cx
        mov count,cx
        cmp cx,011h
        jne exit
        mov cx,0000h
        mov count,cx
        call time
exit:
        pop di
        pop si
        pop es
        pop ds
        pop dx
        pop cx
        pop bx
        pop ax
        jmp cs:savint   ;jump to normal isr
```

```
;-----------------convert procedure--------------------
convert proc
      and a1,0f0h
      ror a1,4
      add a1,30h
      call disp
      mov a1,dh
      and a1,0fh
      add a1,30h
      call disp
      ret
endp
;-----------------------time procedure----------------
time proc
      mov ah,02h      ;getting current time system clk
      int 1ah
      mov hours,ch
      mov mins,cl
      mov sec,dh
      mov bx,0f90h    ;location for displaying clk
      mov al,hours
      mov dh,hours
      call convert
      mov al,':'
      call disp
      mov al,mins
      mov dh,mins
      call convert
      mov al,':'
      call disp
      mov al,sec
      mov dh,sec
```

```
        call convert
        ret
endp
;---------------------display procedue----------------
disp proc
        mov ah,0ffh      ;for setting attribute
        mov es:bx,ax   ;write into vedio buffer
        inc bx
        inc bx
        ret
endp
;-----------------initialization----------------------
initze:
        push cs
        pop ds
        cli              ;clear int flag
        mov ah,35h       ;get orignal add
        mov al,08h       ;intrrupt no
        int 21h
        mov word ptr savint,bx
        mov word ptr savint+2,es
        mov ah,25h       ;set int add
        mov al,08h
        mov dx,offset testnum   ;new add for intrrupt
        int 21h
        mov ah,31h            ;make prog resident(request tsr)
        mov dx,offset initze   ;size of program
        sti
        int 21h              ;set intrrupt flag
code ends
end
```

Output:

;[admin@(none) alp]$ nasm -f elf64 fact.asm

;[admin@(none) alp]$ ld -o fact fact.o

;[admin@(none) alp]$ ./fact

ASSIGNMENT 11

Write 80387 ALP to find the roots of the quadratic equation. All the possible cases must be considered in calculating the roots.

```
segment .text
global  _roots
_roots:
    enter  0,0
    xor    EAX,EAX
    fld    qword[EBP+8]          ; a
    fadd   ST0                   ; 2a
    fld    qword[EBP+8]          ; a,2a
    fld    qword[EBP+24]         ; c,a,2a
    fmulp  ST1                   ; ac,2a
    fadd   ST0                   ; 2ac,2a
    fadd   st0                   ; 4ac,2a
    fchs                         ; -4ac,2a
    fld    qword[EBP+16]         ; b,-4ac,2a
    fld    qword[EBP+16]         ; b,b,-4ac,2a
    fmulp  ST1                   ; b*b,-4ac,2a
    faddp  ST1                   ; b*b-4ac,2a
    ftst                         ; cmp (b*b-4ac),0
    fstsw  AX                    ; result of test in AX
    sahf                         ; store AH in flag reg
    jb     no_real_roots         ; jb tests the carry flag
```

```
        fsqrt                          ; sqrt(b*b-4ac),2a

        fld    qword[EBP+16]           ; b,sqrt(b*b-4ac),2a

        fchs                           ; -b,sqrt(b*b-4ac),2a

        fadd   ST1                     ; -b+sqrt(b*b-4ac),sqrt(b*b-4ac),2a

        fdiv   ST2                     ; -b+sqrt(b*b-4ac)/2a,sqrt(b*b-4ac),2a

        mov    EAX,dword[EBP+32]       ; EAX = -b+sqrt(b*b-4ac)/2a

        fstp   qword[EAX]              ; Store and pop

        fld    qword[EBP+16]           ; b,sqrt(b*b-4ac),2a

        fchs                           ; -b,sqrt(b*b-4ac),2a

        fsubp  ST1                     ; -b-sqrt(b*b-4ac),2a

        fdivrp ST1                     ; -b-sqrt(b*b-4ac)/2a

        mov    EAX,dword[EBP+36]       ; EAX = -b-sqrt(b*b-4ac)/2a

        fstp   qword[EAX]              ; Store and pop

        mov    EAX,1                   ; 1 means real roots

        jmp    short done

no_real_roots:

        sub    EAX,EAX                 ; 0 means no real roots

done:

        leave
```

Output:

ret

;[admin@(none) alp]$ nasm -f elf64 Quad.asm

;[admin@(none) alp]$ ld -o quad quad.o

;[admin@(none) alp]$ ./quad

;

Enter coefficients: 1 0 -1   (Should give -1,1)

    Root1 = 1.000000 and root2 = 1.000000

Enter coefficients: 1 0 -1   (Should give -1,1)

02 Root1 = 1.000000 and root2 = 1.000000

ASSIGNMENT 12

Write 80387 ALP to plot Sine Wave, Cosine Wave and Sinc function. Access video memory directly for plotting.

```
ORG 0000H
CLR A
UP : MOV DPTR,#SINE
MOV R0,#24
LABEL: MOVC A,@A+DPTR
MOV P2,A
    CLR A
  INC DPTR
  DJNZ R0,LABEL
  SJMP UP
ORG 050H
SINE :
DB
127,160,191,217,237,250,255,250,237,217,191,160,127,94,63,37,17,4,0,4,17,37,63,94,1
27
END
```

Output:

;[admin@(none) alp]$ nasm -f elf64 Sine.asm

;[admin@(none) alp]$ ld -o sine sine.o

;[admin@(none) alp]$ ./sine

SAMPLE QUESTION PAPER I

End-Sem. Theory Examination

Time : 2 Hour   **Max. Marks : 50**

INSTRUCTIONS :

1. Draw neat diagrams whenever necessary.
2. Assume suitable data, if necessary.
3. Figures to the right indicate full marks.

1. (a) What is significance of MOD R/M and SIB bit in instruction format. Draw and explain frame format of MOD R/M. **[4]**

(b) Write short note on different block structured language instructions. Explain with example. **[4]**

(c) Explain in detail how segment translation takes place with diagram. **[4] OR**

2. (a) Explain following instructions. **[4]**
   (i)   AAM   (ii)   RCL   (iii)   SHRD   (iv)   SBB

(b) Explain following addressing modes with explain. **[4]**
   (a)   Based Index Mode   (b)   Based Scaled Index Mode
   (c)   Based Index Mode with Displacement
   (d)   Based Scaled Index Mode with Displacement

(c) Draw format of segment selector. **[2]**

(d) Draw format of Page Directory Entry. **[2]**

3. (a) What is mean by sensitive and privileged instruction ?Give example. **[4]**

(b) List out the situations where task switching takes place. **[4]**

(c) Draw and explain Error Code Format. **[4] OR**

4. (a) Write short note on how privilege check for control transfer take place without call gate. **[3]**

(b) Explain in detail Task State Segment. **[3]**

(c) What is interrupt 0, interrupt 11, interrupt 13 **[3]**

(d) What is maskable and non-maskable interrupts ? Explain in detail. **[3]**

5. (a) Draw and explain with block diagram of entering and living Virtual 86 mode. **[6]**

(b) Draw and explain two register TR6 and TR7. **[7] OR**

6. (a) Explain three causes for transition through Task switches. **[3]**

(b) Which new instructions are introduced in 80386Dx microprocessor. **[3]**

(c) Draw and explain the format of 7 debug registers and explain the function of each register. **[7]**

7. (a) What is trigonometric and transcendental instructions. Explain with example. **[4]**

(b) Explain non pipelined Read Cycle in detail. **[4]**

(c) Draw and explain internal NA and BS16 logic in detail. **[5] OR**

8. (a) Explain following instructions. **[4]**
   (i)   FLDCW   (ii)   FINIT   (iii)   FLDZ   (iv)   FCLEX/FNCLEX

(b) Explain halt and shut down condition in detail. **[4]**

(c) Draw and explain signal interfacing diagram between 80386 and 80387. **[5]**

SAMPLE QUESTION PAPER II
End-Sem. Theory Examination

Time : 2 Hour   **Max. Marks : 50**

INSTRUCTIONS :
1. Draw neat diagrams whenever necessary.
2. Assume suitable data, if necessary.
3. Figures to the right indicate full marks.

1. (a) Draw and Explain block diagram of Intel80386DX. **[4]**
   (b) What is stack? Explain any 2 addressing modes in detail. **[3]**
   (c) What are system registers? Explain any three categories of them. **[3]**
   (d) Draw and explain control register structure. **[2] OR**
2. (a) Explain the instructions (i) LDS (ii) ADD (iii) TEST (iv) CLD **[4]**
   (b) What is stack ? Explain the use and operation of stack and pointer ? **[3]**
   (c) Write note on different models used by segmentation. **[3]**
   (d) Draw and explain in short format of segment descriptor. **[2]**
3. (a) What are different aspects of protection mechanism in 80386? **[4]**
   (b) How page level protection takes place ? **[3]**
   (c) Explain with the help of diagram Memory-Mapped I/O for 80386. **[2]**
   (d) What is IDT? Explain in detail. **[3]OR**
4. (a) Draw format of TSS Descriptor for 32-bit TSS **[3]**
   (b) Write short note on how privilege check for control transfer take place with call gate. **[3]**
   (c) Classify the exception as a fault, trap, or abort in detail. **[3]**
   (d) Explain CPL and IOLP. **[3]**
5. (a) Explain any 7 features of 80386 architecture which support for debugging. **[7]**
   (b) Differentiate between 8086 processor and VM86 mode. **[6] OR**
6. (a) Explain in detail interrupt 3 break point instruction. **[4]**
   (b) Explain in detail the structure diagram of TLB. **[4]**
   (c) Before switching to protected mode what will happen in system tables? Write comment on NMI interrupt and PE bit. **[5]**
7. (a) Explain in detail CLK2 and internal clock signals. **[4]**
   (b) Write a note on Dynamic data bus sizing. **[4]**
   (c) Draw and explain 80387 Register stack. **[5] OR**
8. (a) Explain Pipelined Read/Write cycle in detail. **[7]**
   (b) Explain interrupt Acknowledge cycle in detail. **[6]**